In the Service of Samurai

His prison's blank, glowing walls glared silently at him as he entered. His sickness washed over him. A dead certainty stole over him then, and though the unearthly cold of the ship was mercilessly flowing into him, he didn't run for his blanket when he was released. Instead, he turned around to face the departing samurai.

"Asaka-sama, please. I beg you!" He sank to his knees, his hands face down against the floor, and his eyes closed in supplication. "Release me. Take me home. I can be of no use to you. Please, I don't belong here!" His voice got caught in his throat. "Please, Lord, I beg you!"

"*Worm.*" He pressed his forehead against the floor's glowing planks, shooting cold passing through it as it was already doing through his knees and hands. He shut his eyes tighter with a prayer, his heart quickening as he heard the sound most dreaded by his people everywhere. His acrid breath hung still in his raw throat as the soft click of a katana being slightly drawn from its sheath reverberated in the room's silence. He waited for the end.

This book is a work of fiction. Names, characters, places, and incidents either are products of the author's imagination or are used fictitiously. Any resemblance to actual events or locales or persons, living or dead, is entirely coincidental.

IN THE SERVICE OF SAMURAI

ISBN: 1-894869-67-2

Cover art by Marlies Bugmann, cover design by Martine Jardin

Published by Zumaya Publications, 2002

Look for us online at: www.zumayapublications.com

In the Service of Samurai

by

Gloria Oliver

Dedication

This is dedicated to John, without whom this book would have never been written.

Acknowledgements

Great thanks to the House of Three Gaijin, especially to Wendy "Dinzumo" Dinsmore, for all their help with the technical details of this book and support. I also want to thank all the great folks at Zumaya for their great patience and efforts. And last, but by no means least, my editor, Cathy, for helping make this manuscript the best it could be.

Chapter 1

The sun dipped beneath the horizon, taking with it the last light of day. Toshi crouched a little lower over his workbench as the light faded, knowing his master wouldn't want the lamps lit while a moment of daylight still remained.

Bought from his family while he was very young, he knew his master's ways well. Just as Master Shun didn't want any money wasted unnecessarily, he also precluded spending it on unneeded frivolities. Toshi ran his hand over his black hair, fingering the old, thin, stretched tie holding it in a ponytail. And though the last few months had seen a growth spurt for him, he knew he would not be receiving a new pair of knee breeches or a loose-fitting tunic for several moons yet.

Still, he was well-fed, and the skills he was learning would earn a better living than some. Aside from his not-so-common profession, he was the same as hundreds of others, a boy with the usual dark hair, brown eyes, slightly tinted skin and almond shaped eyes—characteristics which made it virtually impossible for a foreigner to pass as a native.

With precision gained from long practice, he slid his brush smoothly over the thick rice paper as he diligently copied the curving meridian lines from the yellowing foreign parchment pinned on the desk beside him. As he squinted, he dipped his brush in the small reservoir of ink built into the desk. Gently twirling the brush on the bowl's long lip, he bled off any excess. His steady hand guided the brush in another slow curve, marking the outline of his map. His attention didn't waver from the delicate work, even as he heard the shop's front door slide open.

"If you would please wait a moment, O-*kyaku*-sama, I'll be right with you," he said.

At an unhurried pace, Toshi came toward the end of his curving line. An unusually cool breeze made its way through the long shop, carrying with it the heavy scent of the sea. Like most shops in town, theirs was comprised of two stories, one in which to conduct business, the other for sleeping and eating. Master Shun believed in cleanliness, so a day did not pass during which Toshi didn't have to sweep the entrance or run a wet cloth across the floorboards. On days when it rained and prospective customers tracked in the mud with them, it was all he could do to keep up.

A large counter took up the left side of the front of the shop, while the rear held the working desk and wall-to-wall niches to hold their wares.

He rubbed his suddenly cold feet together, wondering why the customer hadn't bothered to close the door. His gaze snapped up as he realized that the customer had already shut the paper screen door. Yet the scent of salt and seaweed still crowded into his nostrils. It was strange that the smell had come so far and was so strong, since the shop was so far from the port. Dismissing the oddity as he heard the late customer moving about, he set his brush carefully aside.

"O-kyaku-sama, I've finished." He bowed in the general direction of the visitor out of long-ingrained habit though he couldn't see him. "I apologize for the wait. How may I help you?"

He glanced at the shadow-enshrouded figure on the far side of the room, just as the last of the sun's light dwindled away. He quickly left the side of his workbench and its wooden platform. A small, unexplained chill coursed through him as the customer's ever-deepening shadow came to loom over him.

"Sir?"

He didn't receive an answer. Realizing Master Shun wasn't likely to make a sale if his customer remained in the dark, he shifted past the familiar surroundings and reached for the nearest paper lantern.

"I'll have some light for us in a moment, sir. I apologize for it being so dark." He removed the paper covering of the lamp and exposed the candle inside.

"Where's your master, boy?"

The unexpected voice made him jump. Though the customer was

standing less than five arm-lengths from him, the low, monotone voice had sounded as if it issued from far away. He glanced up to answer, but hesitated as he saw a flash of greenish light issue from somewhere around the customer's face. He rubbed his eyes, feeling foolish even as a tinge of unreasonable fear tried to crowd into his mind. Realizing his continued silence could be misunderstood as rudeness, he turned away from the figure and answered the question. At the same time, he reached to light the lamp.

"Master Shun wasn't feeling well today, sir. He retired early. If you wish, you could leave a message for him. I'm sure he'll be feeling better tomorrow."

Warmth tickled his fingers as the wick caught fire. He placed the oval paper covering back over the candle. Its light gently spread over the room. He then carried the lantern to the main counter in the front of the shop and turned to get his first good look at the waiting customer.

The man was facing away from him, so his gaze landed upon well-cared-for armor with its small steel plates hooked on lacquered leather. He wasn't surprised by what he saw, having already figured from the harsh and emotionless tone his customer was samurai—an elite, upper-class warrior. Dressed as if for battle, the samurai wore the commanding rounded helmet with protruding strips of plate to guard the back of the neck. Fitted back plates and metal shoulder pads were attached to the toughened leather that made up the sleeves and the lower skirt. Strapped on leather tubes protected the warrior's legs. No, what made his eyes grow wide and his heart beat faster were the long tufts of wet seaweed hanging from the armor. Droplets of water reflected the lamp's light even as they fell from the armor and the soaked clothes beneath to make a small puddle on the floor. His eyes followed the water trail leading from the samurai's feet back to the front door, his throat growing dry.

He took an unsteady step back, not sure what it all meant. His gaze traveled back to the armor and looked at the family crest painted there. The crest showed three white crescent moons facing each other within a thin circle. He didn't immediately recognize it. It wasn't one belonging to any of the prominent samurai families in town. Perhaps the man was a *ronin*, a masterless samurai; but the good condition of his armor and his kimono suggested otherwise.

Toshi watched with growing curiosity as the samurai slowly turned about to face him. His breath caught in his throat as a demonic scowl stared him in the face. He tried to still his racing heart as he realized the evil, horrifying expression before him was but a mask clipped to the front of the samurai's helmet, hiding the man's true face.

Taking another step back, he forced his eyes to leave the mask. Why would a samurai in full battle regalia come here to see Master Shun? He wondered what time it was and when the city watch would be coming by. Ever since the foreigners, the *gaijin*, had been allowed entry into the ports and even certain regions of the city itself, the curfews and patrols had become more stringent than before. If he ran out to look for them, would they cut him down before he could explain why he had broken curfew? Or worse, would he even make it out of the store if he decided to try?

His eyes fixed on the sheathed swords, the long *katana* and shorter *wakizashi*, hanging from the samurai's side. He wasn't sure he could run past the strange customer to get help before the warrior could draw either blade and make its razor sharpness cut through his hide. Glancing up into the warrior's masked face, he froze. He had seen it again—a flash of greenish light in the eye slits of the mask! Excitement and fear clutched at his breast and a thin sheen of perspiration rose on his brow. He stared hard at the samurai's metal mask, noticing for the first time how dark the area beyond the eye slits were and how the brown eyes that should have been there staring back at him were nowhere in sight.

"Sir, it…it's time for the shop to close. Is there a message you wish me to convey to Master Shun?" He tried not to look at the snarling, demonic mask, though his eyes were drawn toward the unnatural emptiness of its eye slits.

"Can you read gaijin maps, boy?"

Toshi felt surprise rush through him at the totally unexpected question. "Yes, sir. A little. My—my master has had dealings with a number of gaijin to try to learn their ways of making and reading maps. I have studied this with him."

He hadn't meant to say so much. He didn't want to deal with the strange samurai—that was Master Shun's responsibility—but his frightened tongue hadn't known when to stop. With a long, silent shiver, he wished his master would come downstairs right then, even if it meant he would get a flogging.

"Do you have maps for the area with the chain of islands just to the north of here?" The samurai's distant monotone slammed into him even as he tried to figure out what he should do.

When he didn't immediately answer, the seaweed-covered samurai took a long step forward. Toshi took one back.

"Well, boy?" the samurai asked. His impatience was unmistakable even as his voice sounded like it came from a deep well.

Not wanting the samurai to come any closer, he tried to answer his question as quickly as possible. "Yes, sir, we have many maps."

"Show me."

He scurried away to the shop's rear. Against the wall, on the right, racks of small square-shaped shelves were stacked upon each other almost to the ceiling. Ruffling through the carefully rolled parchments in a number of the squares, he grabbed what he was looking for and walked cautiously around the samurai to stand behind the safety of the shop's front counter. He laid the rolled parchment on the end of the counter closest to the unusual customer and then backed away from it.

Without a word, the samurai stepped forward. Toshi watched as the man raised his arm to reach for the map. Filled with a bolt of sudden fear, he jumped back, smashing his head against one of the shop's wooden support beams as the hand he had expected to see reaching for the map never appeared. With spots of color flying before his eyes, he stared in paralyzing horror as fleshless fingers reached instead to claim the waiting map.

"You're *obake*. A monster!" The boy clamped his hands over his mouth as he realized the accusing words were his. He stared at the samurai in cold horror, sure his words would be the end of him.

The samurai ignored him.

As his death didn't immediately manifest itself, Toshi's eyes shrank back to normal. He made no attempt, though, to remove his hands from his mouth.

With dread-filled fascination, he watched the samurai's fleshless hand as it took the rolled map and with another undid the string holding it closed. He observed the skeletal fingers as they spread the map out over the top of the counter.

All the old stories were true. Demons did walk the earth. But why was this demon here? He and Master Shun had done all Shinto prescribed in order to keep out of the reach of evil or mischievous spirits. Shinto—The Way of the Gods—had made them aware of the spirits that inhabited every rock, tree, and mountain, and which spirits were best avoided, and how. The two of them had exorcised the shop and its living quarters above on New Year's like they did every year, driving the evil spirits out and good luck in. They'd gone to the temple and made the prescribed offerings. The prayer strips were all in place. Had the gods decided not to protect them? What had Master Shun done to bring such evil to this place?

"Are all known reefs and other hazards of the area contained within this map?"

The samurai's voice reached out to him. He nodded rapidly, his hands still clamped over his mouth. He suddenly tried crawling back into the beam behind him as the samurai's empty stare turned toward him, a flash of eerie green light momentarily filling the mask's slits. Sweat poured down the side of his face as he realized with a start the samurai hadn't seen his nod and was therefore still waiting for his answer. He forced his hands to move away from his mouth.

"Y—yes, sir." He could barely keep his words from stumbling over each other. "It's...it's all there, as far as I know. Master Shun has spent a lot of money getting the gaijin to help him make accurate maps."

He clamped his hands over his mouth again, knowing he'd just told more than he liked. The samurai's stare shifted away from him back to the map.

"You can read this map? The numbers, the words?"

He hesitated a long moment before nodding as the samurai's eyes turned toward him again.

"Could you guide someone with it if you had the gaijin instruments?" he asked.

Toshi stared at the samurai, caught off-guard by the question. Should he lie? Very few people had the opportunity to meet gaijin, let alone learn their ways. The demon couldn't possibly know the gaijin merchant they'd contracted had taught him a lot more than had been required. Even Master Shun didn't know how much he'd learned. As a demon, he wouldn't sense the lie, would he?

"Well?"

The deep voice didn't sound happy to be kept waiting. Green fire flared in the snarling mask's eyes, and Toshi knew he couldn't take the risk. Though he had a horrible feeling he would regret his truthfulness, he nodded.

"Fetch me paper, ink and brush."

He cringed against the wall, not understanding the reason for the request.

"Move." The samurai's fleshless hand dropped to the hilt of his katana.

Driven by the commanding tone as well as the unspoken threat, Toshi bolted from where he stood to the back of the store.

Searching for the items requested, he hurried back, the skin on the back of his neck prickling as he noticed the samurai standing between him and the door. He almost dropped the wooden inkwell on the counter as he tried to put the requested items down. Laying all the supplies within the samurai's reach, he scurried back to stand against his wooden beam.

The samurai's skeletal hand reached out and expertly took hold of the thin, long-handled brush. Through frightened eyes, Toshi noted as each of the delicate bones in the hand moved with careless grace. Goose bumps covered his arms and back as he saw there was nothing holding the bones together.

With elegant fluidity, the samurai inked the brush and then began to write. Despite himself, Toshi appreciated the evenness of the samurai's strokes. The writing was very clear, and he had no trouble reading it despite it's being upside down to him. With morbid curiosity, he read the message the samurai was writing for Master Shun. Literacy had been one of the few unexpected gifts he had gained since he'd been sold as an apprentice.

His face drained of color as he realized the meaning of what he was reading.

"No! Sir, please don't do this," he pleaded. "Master Shun doesn't want to sell me. I've been his apprentice for too many years. You mustn't do this, sir. You mustn't do this!" Fear overwhelming his sense, he leapt forward to grab the offensive piece of paper. Before his fingers could even brush its surface, the samurai's bony hand lashed out and caught his wrist.

Toshi stared in desperation at the glowing eye slits as an unearthly cold spread into his arm from the samurai's fleshless hand. The cold moved through him like a living thing, paralyzing him where he stood.

Never loosening his hold on the boy's arm, the samurai returned to completing his message.

As the grisly metal face looked elsewhere, Toshi found his eyes and numbed mind free again. He tried to scream so he could wake up Master Shun or attract the watch—anything that might get him away from this demon—but his vocal cords were as frozen as the rest of him.

He read the note again and again, noticing as the samurai finished it that it lacked a signature. Who was this demon? Studying the family crest again, Toshi thought he might have seen it somewhere before. Was it important?

The samurai reached down and brought out a hand-sized silk sack from within the lacquered armor. The jingle of coins echoed through the room as the samurai let the sack drop on the counter. He then reached within a small bag at his side and brought out a long bamboo tube. He carefully rolled up the map and placed it inside. Returning the tube back to the bag, the samurai turned his burning green eyes in Toshi's direction.

"Come," he commanded.

The intense cold that had kept Toshi rooted to the spot lessened. He walked hesitantly around the counter, the samurai pulling on his wrist. His worried eyes swept through the shop, a heavy feeling in the pit of his stomach telling him this would be the last time he'd ever see the place he'd called home since he was six. With a sweeping sense of loss, of leaving all he had ever known, he stopped and planted his feet on the floor, not willing to let it all go so easily.

Without looking back, the samurai yanked his arm, forcing him to pitch forward. Landing hard on his knees, Toshi felt his eyes fill with pain-induced tears as the samurai then pulled him toward the door. The snarling mask, with its glowing eyes, glared at him without the slightest sign of pity or mercy.

With a soft *whoosh*, the samurai slid open the shop's paneled front door and wrenched him to his feet.

"Now walk." The samurai's free hand landed on his sword's hilt once more, reminding the boy of its silent but deadly threat.

Toshi looked away, hating the way he felt as he realized he had no choice. He slipped on his old sandals, sitting just on the outside of the store entrance, and stepped out of his old life forever.

Keeping his eyes on the dirt road, he walked on as the samurai set an easy pace away from the shop. As they walked, a thin fog sprang up around them. He shivered, cold inside and out. In an instant, all that he was being forced to leave behind flashed through his mind: Master Shun, quirky and strange though he was; the Kawa family next door and their gaggle of children; the sweet dumplings he always bought during festival nights from the old woman near the temple; his room and his few possessions; the friends he'd made from the gaijin ship. His heart ached.

Very few lights were on in the bottom floors of the many two-storied buildings surrounding them on either side. A number of the lights in the living quarters on the second floor had already gone dark as well. Only the howling wind and the lonely call of a stray dog disturbed the silence as he was led down the street in the direction of the docks. He shuddered under the warm night breeze as the samurai strolled on as if he were lord of everything around him. Toshi refused to allow himself to look at him, to look at the monster that was ripping him away from all he knew. The scent of the demon's clinging seaweed wrapped about him as they walked.

The buildings changed as they approached the docks. The wood-and-paper homes grew smaller as they crowded in side by side. The wail of a hungry child or a quiet, lonely moan occasionally escaped into the street, the smell of human waste and rotting garbage growing ever thicker. The samurai appeared to be oblivious to it all, yet for Toshi these sounds only too clearly reflected the despair and unfairness welling up inside him.

He slipped a hateful glance at the samurai. Of course, it wouldn't bother a demon if there was suffering and misery in the world or that he was about to add to it. After all, wasn't that what demons were for? He quickly wiped at the tears threatening his eyes, determined not to show any weakness to this demon. Though he hoped for it with every step, the samurai's cold grip never lessened on his wrist. If only he got a chance to try to escape!

With unbelieving eyes, as they crossed the last street intersection before the docks, he spotted two samurai of the watch. Hope sprang into his heart, and he tried to scream for their attention as the demon pulled him on across the street. Though he tried and tried, no sound made it past his lips. The two men continued walking away, even as he felt his last chance for freedom being swept away by fate.

While his soul wailed with despair, his eyes lighted on a rock on the dirt road less than two feet in front of him. He felt an urge to look at the demon beside him, to make sure he hadn't seen the rock. He forced himself to curb the impulse and kept his eyes glued to his one possible means of salvation. Leaving himself no time for thought, he dropped to the ground and swung one of his legs hard, tripping the samurai. The armored figure fell. Toshi lunged for the rock. Gasping, he felt the bitter cold from the fleshless hand that still held him pour greedily into his bones. He couldn't feel the rock as he wrapped his fingers around it. His body slowed as he fought with every ounce of his being to lift his arm so he could throw the stone that might gain the attention of the watch.

Perspiration broke out all over his body from the effort as the flowing cold pierced him to the core. With a silent scream, he watched the two samurai disappear from sight as his arm froze in a throwing stance. Hot pain blossomed on the side of his face.

Unable to move, he couldn't keep from toppling to the dirt, the samurai's blow knocking him off his feet. A whispered hiss fell on his ear, his vision swimming before him.

"Fool."

He would have cringed from the scorn in the samurai's voice, but he couldn't even do that. A hard yank brought him to his knees. He tried his best to ignore the grotesque mask and the glowing eyes before him.

"If you find someone willing to try to stop me from taking you, I'll kill them. Their deaths will be on your head."

The samurai's voice was cold. Toshi looked away. He knew the demon would do as he said.

Another rough yank brought him to his feet. He gasped in pain at the hard pull, the rock he had risked so much to grab falling forgotten from his numb fingers. The samurai's words continued to reverberate in his mind as he was dragged forward once again.

Why would a demon be willing to kill to keep him? Why pay Master Shun instead of just stealing him away? This wasn't the way demons did things.

He offered no more resistance as the samurai pulled him onto the platform for the docks. He kept looking back, however, trying hard to engrave the memory of the home he was being torn from in his mind. He wiped his face with his sleeve, his eyes burning.

The majority of the boats tied close to them were long and flat-bottomed, most of them fishing boats. On the dock's far side were the gaijin ships. Their tall masts and swollen bodies dwarfed all the other boats around them.

The samurai paid him no attention as he pulled him along and strolled down each of the platforms, gazing at all the ships gathered there. After several minutes, they came across a fishing boat with a small skiff tied to its side. He was dragged toward it, even as he wondered what the samurai was planning.

Moving through the fishing ship toward the single-oared boat, the samurai left three coins wrapped artistically in paper next to the ship's tiller. Toshi's eyes strayed to the small bundle, puzzled by the fact that the coins had been prepared as a gift. It then dawned on him what they were being left for. His brow furrowed. Why would a demon have need of a skiff?

With his one free hand, the samurai pulled on the rope tied to the small craft and drew it closer to them.

"Get in." Flashing green eyes turned in Toshi's direction with the barked command.

He tried to do as he'd been told. His legs, though, still filled with the samurai's unearthly cold, were numb and unresponsive. As he tried to get over the edge of the ship's rail, he shifted his weight too quickly and fell. Watching in startled fear as the boat beneath rose to meet his face, he felt his arm wrenched from behind. Pulled upward, he was kept from landing face-first into the boat. His legs continued to go down and smacked onto the side of the craft as he dangled there by his arm, but he barely felt the impact. This bothered him more than the fact he could have been hurt.

The samurai pulled him up further, until he'd gotten his legs into the boat, before suddenly letting go of his wrist. Toshi collapsed to his knees, the thread of cold pouring through his bones replaced by a jolt of warmth from his pumping heart.

The fog that followed them on the streets slithered from the fishing ship down into the skiff as if it hungered for them. He sat still on the bottom of the craft, trying to dispel the memory of the wooden deck rushing toward his face.

The samurai lowered himself into the skiff in a fluid drop, barely rocking the boat. Gazing down at Toshi for a moment, he slid his hand onto the shorter of his two swords before whipping it out of its sheath and slicing through the skiff's mooring line in one smooth motion.

"If you try to leave this craft, I will cut you in half before you can hit the water."

Toshi would have laughed at the irony if he hadn't thought the samurai would cut him down for it. His body felt so numb and slow, he doubted he could even save himself if the boat suddenly tipped over, let alone try to escape. He felt the samurai's green gaze staring at him again. He tried his best not to let his own gaze cross its path.

"Take the oar and row us out toward the middle of the bay." The samurai waved his hand to the back of the boat.

He crawled where he'd been told to and stared at the long, angled oar waiting there. Watching to make sure his hands got around the oar, since he couldn't feel them, he wove it back and forth to get the craft moving.

As the small boat inched away from the docks to deeper water, he glanced back at the city that had for so long been his home. His gaze grew moist as he stared at the dark mass, no hint showing in the darkness of the bustle and life that had made it so dear to him over the years. And now he was being torn from it.

The fog grew in intensity. It cut off his view of the city. In a way, it made it seem as if the city had never existed.

After a time, the skiff picked up speed. Toshi became ever more grateful for the work the demon had given him, as it loosened the numbness from his body. The heat of the work was exhilarating compared to the unearthly coldness that had gripped him before. He stared at the samurai's armored back, seeing nothing but fog and sea beyond. When he was feeling more like himself, he worked up the courage to speak.

"Sir, might I ask where we are going?"

The samurai didn't react to his question, but remained fixed, facing the prow of the boat.

Toshi continued rowing and didn't speak again. He still had no idea as to their destination when his arms began to tire.

"Stop here." The samurai made a chopping motion with his hand.

He stopped rowing, staring at the samurai in surprise, able to see nothing but the swirling fog around them. Keeping his gaze locked on the samurai, he waited to see what he would be asked to do next. An unwanted chill cut through him as he tried his best not to guess at what it might be.

His attention was drawn to the water as bubbles formed on its surface. The bubbles grew to a writhing mass, a soft glow coming from beneath them. The fog slithered away as if afraid of what was happening in the water. Toshi watched the spot of light beneath the bubbles get larger and brighter.

His knuckles turned white as he gripped his oar in apprehension. The knocking of his heart in his chest was the only sound he could hear as an eerily glowing rod broke through the surface of the frothing sea.

The rod rose higher. A crossbeam broke the surface beneath it, long strands of seaweed strung across its length. A tattered square sail followed, a gold-colored replica of the crest he had seen on the samurai's armor on it.

While terror welled within at the sight rising before him, he found his gaze inexorably drawn to the samurai. The warrior slowly turned to face him and stared at him with his burning green eyes.

Toshi shook his head in helpless denial as the samurai stood up and pointed toward the still-rising ship.

"No! This is not my karma," he declared. "I won't go to a cursed ship!"

The samurai stared at him impassively, the green light issuing from the demon-mask's eyes brighter than it had been before. "Row."

He shook his head again, forgetting whom he was denying while in the grip of his welling fear. He let go of the boat's oar as if it had burned him. His gaze darted around, looking for a way to escape, and he saw his only option was to dive into the sea.

He turned, determined to leave the boat. Something solid struck the back of his leg at the knee, folding it under him. As he struggled not to fall over, he saw the samurai's lacquered scabbard flash ahead of him just before it slammed into his stomach. He fell hard onto the deck.

Panic drove him to ignore the flaring pain in his leg and stomach, even as he fought to throw himself overboard. He'd reached the side of the boat when his cotton tunic was wrenched from behind and he was yanked back with it. He tried desperately to pull away, his fists flying; but a shot of unearthly cold wove down his spine, draining his resistance as fleshless fingers wrapped around the back of his neck. He screamed.

His terror and desperation multiplied as the cold spread through him. Still screaming, he tried to pry the bony fingers from his neck, but his hands were slapped away. Soon he could no longer move. With a soundless cry of fear, he shut his eyes, not wanting to see what awaited him.

The flat-bottomed ship had come fully to the surface. Indistinct shapes moving within it silently brought out long poles with hooks and snared the small boat. As the skiff was secured to the side of the larger vessel, a number of fleshless hands reached down into it.

Toshi fought as he felt half a dozen hands attach to his body and pull him upward. The samurai's hand left the back of his neck. In panic, he snapped his eyes open to see why the demon had deserted him. He gazed straight into the face of a grinning skull. Empty eye sockets stared into his eyes, a reddish glow flaring for a moment in their depths. He opened his mouth to scream but no sound ever reached past his lips. The fleshless face came closer. The creature's eyes flared with bright red light. He tried to squirm away, but it was all in vain. His heart threatened to burst from horror before that fleshless grin.

An arm was thrust between them. Sudden hope flared within him even as his frightened gaze shifted to seek the samurai's masked face. He didn't feel the samurai's hand as it latched onto his. His numbed body was turned around, and he glimpsed the rest of those who were on board. His mind wouldn't count them; it didn't want to see them. It shrieked in disbelief as he stared at the white gleaming skeletons before him.

They stood upright and wore clothes he would have seen on men on any common street. Some wore short pants and sleeveless shirts. Others only wore *fudoshi*—a long cloth coiled around the body that covered the genitals like a loincloth—and short vests.

Half-supporting, half-dragging him, the samurai took him toward a door set in the wall of the raised deck housing the tiller. His mind was as numbed by terror as his body was by cold; he didn't resist as he was taken into the small hallway beyond.

Ignoring the ladder going below, the samurai pulled him forward, stopping before the second doorway on the right. Throwing the door open, the samurai thrust him inside. Unable in his paralysis to break his fall, he slammed into the glowing floor. The door was closed and bolted behind him.

The pain of the fall a very faint perception, Toshi gave in to his fear and despair. He scooted to a corner and hugged his knees to his chest, his wide eyes staring at the glow in the room that permeated everything.

Chapter 2

Toshi sat bolt upright, realizing that at some point during the night he'd fallen asleep. He glanced quickly about him, dislodging a thick blanket from his shoulders. He was on a ship—a haunted ship. A chill coursed through him as he recalled all that had gone on before.

He grabbed the fallen blanket, not sure where it had come from, and wrapped it about him. The thought repeated over and over in his mind that normal walls didn't glow like a million fireflies. The cold air in the room made him shiver.

"Would you like some tea?"

He whipped around, entangling himself in the blanket, looking for the source of the voice. He stared in surprise at a well-dressed woman sitting at the far corner of the room, serving tea. The cut and style of her light-green kimono and her lavishly coiffured black-haired wig with its silver bells told him she was geisha, an entertainer. Yet, unlike any geisha he had ever heard tell of, this one wore a Noh mask over her face.

The delicate traditional theater mask of white-painted wood was of a handsome young maiden with large almond-shaped eyes, rounded nose and thin, smiling red lips, but its illusion was dispelled as he noticed the woman's hands and neck were as fleshless as a hundred-year-old corpse.

"Who…who are you? What…what do you want from me?" He inched away from the geisha, his voice cracking as he spoke.

The woman looked up at him, soft blue light showing through the narrow, round eye-slits of the mask. With surprising grace and beauty in spite of her lack of flesh, the geisha bowed to him and introduced herself.

"I am Akiuji Miko. Entertainer for his lordship Asaka Ietsugu."

Feeling awkward at the unexpected show of formality, he made himself return the bow.

"My…my name is Chizuson Toshiro," he said, his mind thinking about how in the rules of the foreigners his surname would have come last, not first. "Though most people just call me Toshi. I was an apprentice mapmaker to Hirojima Shun." He licked his lips, apprehension filling him to the core.

The geisha said, "I'm very pleased to meet you, Chizuson-san."

He glanced away and said nothing, in no way feeling the same. He was also surprised she'd added the honorific to his name. Why would a demon give him such a courtesy?

"Won't you have tea? If you're hungry, I've some rice cakes as well." Her voice was kind.

He stared at the floor and said nothing.

"Won't you do me this small courtesy? It's been a long time since I've had a chance to serve tea." Delicately, Miko lifted a steaming cup and held it out toward him. "Please, Toshi-san?"

His stomach rumbled as the green tea's aroma drifted toward him. His cold hands and feet insisted a little hot tea would do no harm. He wondered why she'd decided to use his given name instead of his surname. That was normally a habit of people who knew each other well.

"Hai."

Keeping his blanket snug about his shoulders, he rose hesitantly to his feet and advanced to the small table set in front of the geisha. Making sure the table stayed between them, he sat down.

Without comment, Miko placed the cup on the table before him.

Waiting until her fleshless hands were well away from it, he took the steaming cup. Thrilled by the warmth flowing from it into his hands, he just held it, his eagerness for the drink itself gone for the moment.

When he finally drank, he closed his eyes, grateful for the warmth spreading inside him. He quickly placed the emptied cup on the table, inwardly hoping for more but not daring to ask.

Miko lifted a plate full of seaweed wrapped rice cakes from a tray beside her and put it before him.

"Won't you have some?" She then proceeded to refill his cup.

Studying the rice cakes and figuring they looked safe enough, he reached out for one of them and took a small, hesitant bite. Finding that it tasted as it should, he gobbled it down and reached for another. Before he realized what he'd done, he'd eaten them all.

"Toshi-san, how old are you?"

He almost smiled, content now that he was full, until he glanced up at his unusual hostess and remembered where he was. "I'm almost sixteen." He wondered why a demon would want to know, but he wasn't about to ask.

Miko held his attention as her head tilted slightly to the side, making the small bells in her hair ring. By the way her shoulders were gently shaking, he got the impression the geisha was laughing behind her white mask.

"All young boys are always in such a hurry to grow up, to go out into the world and meet their destinies." Miko's broad green sleeve rose up to cover the smiling mask's mouth.

He felt his cheeks grow hot. Yes, it was true he was only fifteen, but he would be sixteen—a man—soon enough. What difference did a few months make? Especially to demons!

He stared at his teacup, stung by the geisha's silent laughter. Unhappy about this, he said the first thing that came to mind in an effort to distract her.

"Why do you wear a mask?" He noted with satisfaction that the geisha lowered her sleeve away from her mouth.

"I wear it out of politeness," she said. "You see, I have no wish to make you afraid of me. My features are less handsome than I would desire and don't complement my profession very well at this time."

"Then, you and your lord look just like the crew?" The question had left his lips before he'd given it proper consideration.

"Yes, we do," she answered. "Asaka-sama thought it would be less of a shock to you if we minimized our current states in your presence."

Asaka-sama, or Lord Asaka—the honorific said it all. Asaka was their master, and he looked just like the rest. A small chill crawled down Toshi's back. He tensed as he gathered the courage to ask the only thing he really wanted to know.

"Why am I here?"

Miko's masked face turned away from him, the bells in her hair ringing softly as she moved. "Lord Asaka needs a navigator, one who can read the more detailed maps of the gaijin." She turned to face him again. "It's partially because of the knowledge we lack that we have come to be as we are. It is our hope that with you we'll now be able to complete what we must. To follow the way and regain our honor."

He stared at the geisha. He had no reason to disbelieve her, though who could honestly ever trust a demon. Yet, this couldn't be all they wanted from him. And since when did demons follow Bushido—the samurai code of conduct?

"You mustn't judge Asaka-sama harshly, Toshi-san. I know all of this is a major change for you," she said, "but Asaka-sama wouldn't have done it had our need not been so great. You'll be safe with us. No harm shall come to you."

He turned away to hide his expression of confused suspicion, his hand rising subconsciously to brush back his mussed hair. He never felt the leather band that held his hair in a ponytail loosen and fall on the floor. His long black hair spilled over his shoulders. Only too vividly, his mind recalled the demon mask with its glowing green eyes and the deep voice booming from behind it. He recalled his first view of the crew, and that white skull with the menacing red glowing eyes staring at him. That he would be safe and unharmed here was not something he was in any way willing to believe.

He gazed at nothing, a shiver moving through him, as he remembered the implied threat he thought he'd seen in that one crewman's red eyes.

"Let me fix that for you," Miko said.

He heard the rustle of silk as the geisha stood up and moved behind him. He saw her reach for the fallen leather band. As her skeletal hand rose, it finally dawned on him what she meant to do. With frightened eyes, he jerked away before she could touch his hair.

"No!"

He turned on the geisha in a half-crouch, waiting for her to try to come after him. Instead, he found her sitting perfectly still, her hand half-raised in the air.

"What's wrong?" Miko leaned forward. He scooted away from her. "I was only going to tie your hair. I wasn't going to hurt you."

He watched her suspiciously, even as she harmlessly held out the leather band for him to see.

"No, that's all right, thank you," he said quickly. "I would prefer to do it myself."

Miko turned her head to stare at him at a curious angle. To his amazement, she suddenly bowed before him, her forehead touching the floor.

"Please forgive my thoughtlessness, Chizuson-san. I had forgotten that all you've had from us so far was the paralyzing touch. I had not meant to frighten you."

He felt foolish, seeing her apologizing to him. He was just a peasant boy; she was a geisha and a demon. That wasn't the way things were supposed to happen in the world.

"I just thought..."

Miko's white mask looked up as he hesitated. "Of course. You had no reason to believe otherwise. But it isn't true. When we touch others, it doesn't have to be the paralyzing touch they feel. We can make our touch warm, if we like. Almost as warm as a living human's." Miko sat up. "Won't you let me show you?" With a fleshless hand, she gestured to the floor right before her.

His misgivings showing on his face, he slowly nodded and then inched toward her. Turning his back to her, he knelt on the floor. Despite what she had told him, he bit his bottom lip, waiting for her cold touch to creep into his skin.

He tensed as a comb gently sifted through his hair. He hardly dared breathe as the small comb descended past his shoulder, stopping once to painlessly take care of a tangle. Miko continued to comb his hair, her soft silk kimono occasionally brushing against his arm.

He stiffened more as he felt her gather his hair. The burst of cold he had expected as her hand brushed past his neck, however, never came.

"There, I'm finished. It wasn't that bad, was it?" Her voice was close.

He shook his head as he gingerly turned to face her again.

"Why...why are you being so kind to me?"

Miko stopped in the middle of placing her small comb back into her hair. "Is there a reason why I shouldn't be?"

He stared at his coarse blanket, not knowing what to do with the unexpected rebuttal.

"No. Well, yes," he said. "I'm not a noble or a samurai. I'm a peasant, a lowlife. You shouldn't be wasting your time on someone like me. You are geisha! You are of art, of beauty, of dance, all those things. Why waste your time on one such as me?"

He dared not mention that spirits and demons weren't known for their kindness, either. While his babbling could get him into trouble, he still had no wish to offend Miko, in case her thoughtfulness was, for whatever bizarre reason, genuine.

The geisha laughed out loud. It was a soft and gentle laugh.

"Oh, dear Toshi-san, where do you think geishas come from? While some may like to forget their humble origins once a wealthy lord has bought their contract, their past is still the same. I, like you and countless others, was sold as a child to a merchant who favored me and trained in the arts of the geisha since I was three. I have been lucky compared to those who've ended up in the red lantern districts, and I've never forgotten it. Every evening I send a prayer of thanks to the gods." Her eyes glowed. "You and I have more in common than I do with any of the nobles and samurai I have served during my life, Toshi-san. Do not belittle yourself."

"But, Akiuji-san, you have no idea of what I'm like." He stared at his hands, not sure why he was saying these things to her. "I could be evil or vicious, maybe even a pervert."

Miko's eyes shone a bright blue. "I don't think I have to worry about keeping my virtue intact anymore, do you?"

Realizing he'd yet again made a fool of himself, he nevertheless grinned as Miko's sweet laughter once more filled the room.

"Even if I had to, I wouldn't worry while in your presence." Miko leaned toward him for a moment. "I've always had good instincts for people, and it has rarely failed me. I like you very much already."

He blushed at the flattery and turned away so she wouldn't see. Before he could think of something to say, a bell sounded just outside the door.

"I'm sorry, Toshi-san, but I must go now." Miko's hand rested for a moment on his arm. "Try to get some rest. Asaka-sama will want to test your skills this evening, once it is safe for us to rise above water."

"But—"

"I'll meet with you again before then with your meal. Perhaps you would enjoy some music as well?" Without waiting for his answer, Miko stood and silently slipped past him toward the door.

"Rise above water?" He stared at her, perplexed.

Miko turned back to face him for a moment. "It would be wise if you didn't try to go above during the daytime." With a rustling of silk, she left the room. A cold shiver coursed through him as he forced himself to sit back down.

Alone, with nothing else to do, he examined his room. Other than the small table in the corner with its half-filled teapot, his cup and an empty plate, the glowing room contained nothing else but him, his blanket and two empty buckets sitting against the far wall.

He stared at the closed and possibly unlocked door of his room as the weight of his predicament once more settled down around him. For a moment, he thought of trying to escape again, yet Miko's parting words and his own recollection of the ship as it rose from beneath the water made him realize there was nothing he could do, except maybe die. It was amazing he wasn't dead already. The concept of being underwater, yet still able to breathe, seemed more than he could ponder. And he had other problems besides those. He was to be tested by the samurai that night. He shuddered at the thought. In the unfamiliar silence of his room, he wondered what would happen to him should he fail the test. He doubted Asaka would be gracious enough to return him home. His mind easily pictured his most likely reward.

Now colder than when he had awakened, he curled up in his blanket and returned to his corner.

Chapter 3

"Toshi-san. It's time to get up. Toshi-san."

His heavy eyelids flickered open as he felt himself shaken by the shoulder. A bright silver kimono with glowing gold and red flowers filled his field of vision as Miko knelt at his side. Smiling slightly, glad she was there, he let his eyes close again.

"Toshi-san, it's time to eat. Asaka-sama will be coming for you shortly."

The demon's name brought him fully awake. With a grimace, he opened his eyes and pushed up into a sitting position. Rubbing his face, he gradually became more alert as the scent of freshly brewed tea wove into his nostrils.

"That's much better," Miko said. "Now, come, let me serve you. We haven't much time."

He draped his blanket about himself and rose groggily to his feet before sidling over to the small table in the corner of the room. Serving him tea, Miko also placed in front of him a plate filled with dried fish and rice cakes. To his delight, he also noted she'd brought him a couple of sweet cakes.

As he ate, he watched the geisha as she rose from the table and headed to the door. Sitting beside it, propped against the wall, was a *koto*. He watched with some awakening interest as she picked up the long, gently curving wooden instrument and set it on the floor before her. Miko bowed to him then picked up a small pick after sliding small wooden blocks beneath each of the strings over the main body and setting them up in a specific pattern. Long, lonely notes filled the room as she wove her music for him.

Downing a second cup of hot tea as fast as his throat would tolerate, he listened. With a bit of surprise, he found he was caught up in the music as it turned from sweet melancholy to a brash, more upbeat pace. He became fascinated just watching her play. He slid his plate from the table to set it before him so he wouldn't have to look away to eat. Miko's movements were so fluid, so precise, her fleshless fingers handling the instrument almost as if it were a part of her.

While he sat there, he dared to try and imagine how the geisha might have looked in life. That a spirit could create such beauty dazzled him. He wondered if she were trying to imprison him in some sort of spell. He found that, at the moment, he didn't care if she was.

He continued to eat, lost in the music, until a sudden knock on the door reverberated through the room. Miko stopped playing. The door to the room opened.

Toshi felt his throat go dry as the still-armored samurai stepped into the doorway. He swallowed hard as he bowed.

"Come, boy," the samurai said.

Toshi darted a glance toward Miko and saw her nod. Hiding in his blanket, he stood up and shivered, wondering if he would feel the samurai's cold touch tonight.

"Leave it." A bony hand pointed at his blanket.

Toshi released a heavy sigh. He let the only warmth he'd had fall off behind him and walked to the door as the samurai moved from the doorway.

Asaka walked down the hall, leaving him to follow. The samurai stopped, blocking the way to the exterior door, as splashing sounds rang faintly beyond. They stood there for almost a full minute before the samurai reached to open the door.

A blast of night air smashed into the boy's shivering body as the door was momentarily ripped from Asaka's grasp. As the latter stepped outside, Toshi grabbed for the doorway when the ship abruptly rocked to the left. Nervously, he stared out at the wet, glowing deck. Two columns of skeletal men sat toward the bow of the ship, all holding long oars they were using to move the flat-bottomed vessel. He looked away from them and their fleshless bodies, a shiver crawling up his spine.

Stepping out onto the deck, he noticed the overcast night sky. The blowing wind slapped his face. The ship shifted to the right, and he felt his filled stomach knot up. Doing his best to ignore it, he carefully climbed the ladder next to the doorway, following Asaka. The ship tilted again, but he held on, his stomach knotting up a little more. Reaching the top, he stood uneasily on the glowing deck and waited for the samurai to tell him what to do.

"You'll now determine our present position. Do not attempt to lie, for I already know the answer."

Hating the fear growing inside him at the words, he glanced behind the samurai as a stooped skeleton approached them at Asaka's signal. Stopping before the boy, the retainer offered him the map Asaka had taken from Master Shun's store and a number of gaijin instruments.

Trying to keep his footing as the rocking of the ship grew worse, Toshi took the map, avoiding any contact with the skeleton's hand. His gaze swam for a moment. The map's contents seemed to move with the tilting of the ship.

Attempting to ignore his sudden dizziness, he returned the map and took a heavy coil of measuring rope with a weight at one end and a round cork on the other. Leaning against the rail, he dropped the weighted end into the rolling waves below. He dared not look at the moving water, which strove to make his dizziness worse, as he tried to get a depth measurement as quickly as possible. The choppy water wouldn't allow an accurate assessment, but he was sure the samurai wouldn't care for the excuse. As soon as he thought the bottom had been reached, he noted the marked depth of three fathoms on the rope where the cork bobbed and began to carefully coil the rope up again. He hurried as much as was prudent, his dizziness making his stomach knot up worse than before. Due to the roughness of the water, he decided he wouldn't try for a speed reading.

Returning the coil of rope to the waiting skeleton, he next took a large compass. The small bowl-like contraption had a colorful card face showing all the major directions that was submerged in liquid to keep it still. Quickly looking it over to make sure it was in working order, he stood as still as possible to get a directional reading from the bulky instrument. When he was done, he traded it for a cross-staff. With that, he looked up into the cloud-crowded sky, trying to catch sight of the North Star. Finally spotting it as a bank of clouds broke for a moment, he lifted the cross-staff in its direction. He felt his dizziness worsen as he put the long bar of the cross-staff against his eye, his gaze following the rod upward to the North Star. The ship kept shifting, making the star weave in and out of his sight. He stubbornly fought to keep it in view. He slid the crosspiece over the scale to align it against the star and the horizon to find the angle of their latitude, just as Captain Valéz had taught him.

The North Star wavered again in his vision, and his stomach rumbled. The swirling wind whipped his ponytail up into his face as he handed the cross-staff back. Taking the map again and a few of the other tools, as well as an empty logbook, he sat on the ice-cold deck. He tried to recall all the necessary computations and, though lightheaded, tried to do them as best he could.

He became aware of Asaka's green stare raking over him.

After several minutes, Toshi came up with what might be a close answer. He was about to give it to Asaka when his tortured stomach gave up and heaved with all its might. Clamping his hands over his mouth, he tried to keep in the lumpy, burning mess that suddenly rose from inside him. Forgetting everything but his screaming stomach, he ran for the ship's rail.

Almost falling overboard in his eagerness to get there, he clung to the railing as his stomach heaved again. Not able to hold back anymore, he opened his mouth and let the burning torrent empty to the sea. The acrid smell of vomit filled his nose as his throat burned. His stomach continued to heave long past the point at which it was empty.

Even in his present misery, he couldn't help but notice the quiet, overbearing presence of the samurai who came to stand by his side. It occurred to his tortured mind to wonder if Asaka was considering throwing him overboard. Perhaps it would prove to be a kindness if he did.

"Sir, I mean no disrespect, but I don't think this ignorant boy is going to be of any use to us," the steersman said. "It may take a long time, but I'm sure I can eventually—"

"Silence!" The samurai's voice roared at Toshi's side. He ignored it, still trying to stop his heaving stomach, inwardly grateful the shouting hadn't been directed at him. After another minute, his stomach finally began to settle a little. He closed his eyes, letting the flowing wind cool his face as he tried to disregard the ship's continuing movements.

"I asked you for our location, boy." Asaka's voice bore down on him.

He turned his drawn, pale face away from the rail and stared at the map the samurai held out to him. Leaning against the bar, not trusting his wobbling legs to remain beneath him, he carefully took the map and then the other tools and dropped to the deck, his back against the railing.

He stared at the swaying map and rechecked his calculations. Again getting the same answer, he moved an unsteady finger to point out their position, which lay near the coast.

Refusing to glance at Asaka as the samurai looked over his shoulder, he held his finger in place. Asaka took the map from him, his only acknowledgment of the information being a barely audible *humph.* Not looking back, the samurai strode to the skeleton manning the ship's tiller. Toshi tried hard not to care.

The bent skeleton walked up to him. Though he had no liking for the fleshless grin that approached him, he couldn't find the strength to move from where he was. Never looking directly at him, the retainer took the instruments from his unresisting hands and walked away.

Unable to swallow away the acrid taste still in his mouth, Toshi closed his eyes and sat as unmoving as possible on the rocking deck. He drew his knees up and curled his arms around his legs, the cold seeping into him from the planks. Trying not to moan in his undiminishing misery, he suddenly opened his eyes. He felt someone staring at him. He barely realized it was Asaka before the latter abruptly reached out for his arm. He cringed at the unavoidable touch, a spear of fear shooting through him. Yet, when the fleshless fingers wrapped around his flesh, no trace of the paralyzing touch reached his skin.

"Get up," Asaka said.

Using the rail and the samurai's pull on his arm for support, he scrambled to his feet. He swayed with the ship's tipping movements, but Asaka's firm grip kept him from falling.

Steering him toward the ladder, Asaka held on to his arm until he'd started to descend. Feeling a little steadier when he reached the main deck, the boy didn't wait to be led but quickly stumbled his way to the door. He opened it and tripped inside as his stomach began knotting up on him again. Moaning softly in despair at what might come upon him once more, he shivered, feeling the cold radiating from the walls, assaulting his exposed skin from every angle.

Hurrying to his assigned room, he careened toward the wall as the ship abruptly tilted to the left. A steady hand kept him from smacking into it, making him glance behind him in surprise. It was the samurai. With Asaka's firm grip back on his arm, he was led the rest of the way to his room.

His prison's blank, glowing walls glared silently at him as he entered. His sickness washed over him. A dead certainty arose then; and though the unearthly cold of the ship was mercilessly flowing into him, he didn't run for his blanket when he was released. Instead, he turned around to face the departing samurai.

"Asaka-sama, please. I beg you!" He sank to his knees, his hands palm down against the floor and his eyes closed in supplication. "Release me. Take me home. I can be of no use to you. Please, I don't belong here!" His voice got caught in his throat. "Please, Lord, I beg you!"

"*Worm.*"

He pressed his forehead against the floor's glowing planks, shooting cold passing through it as it was already doing through his knees and hands. He shut his eyes tighter with a prayer, his heart quickening as he heard the sound most dreaded by his people everywhere. His acrid breath hung still in his raw throat as the soft click of a katana being slightly drawn from its sheath reverberated in the room's silence. He waited for the end.

"I will ignore your statement this once. I expect it never to be repeated." Asaka's voice was cold.

He heard the katana click back into place.

"The only release you will find if you do is that of your flesh," the samurai told him. "I will have you, one way or another. If I must kill you and then trap your spirit from rising to its next plane, then so be it. It would mean nothing to me to have you join the ship's crew permanently and find myself one who has the courage to endure what you do not." Asaka left, slamming the door behind him.

Horror and shame poured through him, though he couldn't explain the reason for the latter. Tears ran freely from his closed eyes to fall on the glowing floor as his mind's eye cruelly provided him with a picture of himself as a fleshless, moving corpse.

Chapter 4

Toshi heard a soft knock at the door, but he ignored it. After a moment, he heard the door open behind him and the soft rustling of silk as someone came in. With his back pressed against the corner of the wall, he curled up tighter in his blanket.

"Toshi-san?" It was Miko's voice.

"Go away."

He heard the geisha step farther into the room and set a tray on the table. He hoped with that done she would go. Instead, he heard the gentle rustle of her silk kimono move in his direction.

"I want to be alone," he said. "Please go away, Miko-san."

He knew she had ignored him as he heard her kneel down at his side. He gripped his blanket with both hands in case she tried to pull it from him.

"What's wrong, Toshi-kun? Have I somehow offended you?"

He heard the worry in her voice. Demons weren't supposed to worry over mortals; demons weren't supposed to be kind. He also noticed how the honorific at the end of his name had changed to a slightly more personal one.

"I've brought you more food."

He groaned as his stomach revolted at the mere mention of the word. The swaying of the ship hadn't ceased since Asaka had left him.

"Toshi, what's wrong?" she asked, her worry more apparent. "Talk to me!"

He cringed as he felt her tentatively tug at his blanket. "Nothing is wrong," he insisted. "Please, just go away."

"I won't leave until I find out what's wrong with you. If you persist in keeping me ignorant, you'll find I can be a very stubborn woman when I feel like it." A more forceful tug threatened to remove the blanket from his grasp.

"Please, Miko-san," he said as he struggled to keep hold.

"No." The calm answer told him she was, indeed, serious.

"I'm all right. Really," he said. "I'm just tired and wish to sleep."

"Let me see you."

"Miko-san, I told you—"

"Toshiro, do as I say!"

Embarrassed that she was there, that she'd come when he was like this, yet at the same time grateful she seemed to care, he sat up and pulled his blanket away from his face; but he did so with his back to her.

"Now, turn around so I can see you," she said.

"Please, Miko-san—"

"Do it."

With a sigh, he slowly turned and stared at the floor. He heard Miko gasp as she noticed his puffed eyes, his pale face and, most embarrassing, the grime covering his shirt. He turned away again, too ashamed of his present condition. "It's nothing, just like I said. I've heard of this before," he rushed to explain. "Captain Valéz told me of it. I'm suffering from seasickness."

And, yes, the captain had told him of it, but he had dismissed it. On the gaijin's large ship he had barely felt the waves as they passed beneath. On their ship, there had never been much of a chance for him to feel seasick.

He hoped with all his might that the geisha knew nothing of it. At least, not enough to realize his puffed eyes weren't a part of it, not enough to realize he'd been crying.

"Oh, yes, that," she said in a dawning tone. "I'd forgotten. It was so long ago. It will pass, Toshi-kun."

He tried to keep his stubborn stomach's disbelief from showing on his face.

"It will pass," she insisted. "It did for us. Many of us had never been on a ship before we set out with Lord Asaka. We were ill for many days, but we got better. Asaka-sama was the worst afflicted of us all."

He glanced back at her despite himself, and did so just in time to see her hide her mask's smile behind her sleeve.

"It was a great blow to his manly image," she added. "I teased him about it constantly for days."

He forgot his swirling stomach and puffed eyes for a moment as he stared at Miko in shock. "And he didn't kill you?"

"Oh, my goodness, no." She swept the thought away with her sleeve. "He keeps me around for just this sort of thing. It helps keep him humble. He's told me many a time I'm unlike any woman he has ever known. I like to think he means it as a compliment."

He shook his head and turned away, somehow doubting Asaka would ever be capable of complimenting anyone.

"I'll go find some clothes for you so yours can be washed," Miko said. "Will you try sipping some tea while I'm gone? It might soothe your stomach a little."

He remained where he was until she had gone. He was grateful she would be getting him some clean clothes, but what he craved was a bath. Forcing himself to get up, he made his way to the small table across the room. Ignoring the food waiting there and the faint scent that made his stomach flip, he poured a half-cup of tea. He retreated back to his corner and sipped as he waited for the geisha to return.

His first sip landed like a rock in his stomach. As it cramped, he forced himself to take another. Trying to keep both of them down, he took a third and a fourth. He clamped his mouth shut, expecting the worst, but his stomach quieted. He'd finished off most of his tea by the time Miko returned.

"These will be a little large on you, Toshi-kun." She set the folded clothes down by his side. "If you like, I might be able to prepare some hot water later for you to use to clean yourself."

"I would appreciate that, Miko-san." He hoped she could hear the sincerity in his voice.

Nodding, the geisha sat down. "Aren't you going to get undressed?"

He felt his cheeks grow warm as her blue-lit eyes flashed in his direction. "Well, yes. I mean—"

"Toshi-san, you're modest. What a delight in a boy!" Sweet laughter momentarily filled the air. "Oh, but I've forgotten, haven't I? You're almost a man," she teased. "Which makes this even a rarer find."

Miko's ridicule and light, candid laughter pleased and embarrassed him at the same time. He had never undressed before a woman before, let alone a demon. With Master Shun's long work hours, it was rare for him to have more than a few minutes at the communal baths before it was time for the establishment to close. He'd not had many occasions to be nude before others. Red-faced, he turned his back on her and got out of his soiled clothes. He threw his blue and brown cotton shirt and pants into a small pile and grabbed the clean clothes at his side. He put on the thin undercoat and then reached for the outer garment. The soft silk felt good in his hands as he unfolded the man's kimono and started to put it on. He hesitated for a moment as he noticed the three moon crests emblazoned on the garment's sleeve.

"Miko-san, should I really be wearing this?" He didn't look at her. "I realize Asaka-sama owns me now, but I'm not really a part of his household."

"Do not worry. It's all right. Lord Asaka has approved of this. He has told me he believes you can do what must be done. He gave his permission for you to wear his clothes."

Toshi stopped in the midst of tying the kimono's sash. "*His* clothes?" He heard Miko's silver bells ring as she tried to restrain her amusement at his shock.

"Won't you hurry and finish dressing?" she said, laughter still coloring her voice. "I can't wait to see how you look in them."

As she had warned him, the clothes were too big for him. Though the sleeves were longer than his arms, he found he didn't mind, since it would help him keep warm. The same thought occurred to him regarding his feet.

"Oh, my, how handsome you look." Miko laughed lightly, her soft voice filling the room, as she bade him turn in a full circle before her.

He felt like a child playing dress-up. "Miko-san, can…can Asaka-sama really turn me into one of you?"

The geisha's laughter died. She came closer and asked him to sit down. "Yes, Toshi-kun, I think he could," she confided. "It's my belief that it's only because of him we're all still here, that through his will, and his will alone, he enabled us to return from death so we might complete our journey."

He paid little attention to the last, a fearful shiver running through him as the validity of the samurai's threat was confirmed. "How did you all...die?"

"Would you believe that to this day we are not sure?" she said. "We know it happened late one night as most of us were sleeping. It's thought perhaps we unknowingly drifted into a current and it forced us onto a reef, but no one really knows.

"I awakened to the noise of water seeping into my room. Foolishly, I opened my door to find out why and was swept against a wall by the water that rushed in like a tsunami. I hit my head and went unconscious. It wasn't long after that I drowned."

Miko turned her face from him, making him feel guilty for having asked.

"I'm sorry, Miko-san. I hadn't meant to—"

"It's all right, Toshi-kun. It all happened a very long time ago. It no longer matters." Her tone belied her words. "What matters is that we have you now and, therefore, have a chance to succeed in our mission."

Feeling his stomach knot from something other than seasickness, he curled his blankets more snuggly around him.

"Your illness should dissipate once the sun rises," she said. "The waves of the sea do not affect us as much when we are under water."

He sighed, hoping with any luck it would be soon. "Does the ship travel while underwater?"

"Yes, a little. Though nowhere near as far as when we are above."

"How does it do that?" he asked. "Stay underwater, I mean."

The geisha was silent a moment before responding. "We don't really know. It just does. Many things about our new existence just are. We have no explanation."

He nodded, knowing many things about spirits made little sense. "Why don't you stay above during the daylight, too, then?" he asked. "Wouldn't it get you where you are going sooner?"

Miko picked up his soiled clothes and rose to her feet. "You're a curious one, aren't you?" She started toward the door. "Let me take these from here so they won't smell up the room."

The geisha stood in the doorway and glanced back at him. He

stayed silent, not pointing out her obvious evasion of his question.

"You're in need of other things as well," she said. "Before I return, I'll see what I can find for you."

He then saw her tilt her head toward him; and for some reason he was sure, beneath her mask, she was smiling.

"There are so many things I've forgotten," she said. "You've brought back many memories to me, Toshi-kun."

Not understanding what she meant, he watched her as she silently left and closed the door behind her. Wondering how long she would be gone, he rose from the floor and shuffled over to pour another half-cup of tea.

The geisha was gone for a long time. He'd just begun to doubt she would return when he heard a muffled call from beyond his closed door. Surprised, he got up and rushed to open it.

He stepped back as Miko fell through the doorway. Without thinking, he reached out to steady her. His hands didn't sink through her kimono as he might have expected, but found what felt like a solid body underneath. Trying to hide his amazement, he scurried back as Miko stooped to set her burden down.

"It took a little doing, but I've been able to find a futon and a couple more blankets for you. I did take the liberty of bringing some games and a few other things as well."

His surprise at her solidity was replaced with gratitude as he stared at the thick futons she spread on the floor. Flipping off his sandals, he stepped onto them, eager for the warmth and protection they would grant him. "Thank you, Miko-san. This is wonderful!"

"Well, I only thought if you have to be seasick, you might as well do it while being as comfortable as you can." Miko left the room then, but returned almost immediately with a number of packages.

He paid her little attention, wallowing in the heat he could feel gathering about him as he added the new blankets to the one already about him.

"I must apologize we did nothing about this earlier. While we had thought of some of your other needs, it has been some time since we've had to consider the warmth or coldness of our surroundings."

As she spoke, Miko stepped to sit behind him. Without asking, she began working on his tangled and disheveled hair.

"Miko-san, if I might ask?" he said shyly. "How long have you and the others, well, been as you are now?"

"How long have we been dead, Toshi-kun? You can say it. We've all had a long time to learn to deal with the fact." He felt his dark hair tumble to his shoulders as Miko released it. She combed it as she answered his question. "Our bad fortune befell us over eight years ago."

He tried to glance back at her, his face covered with astonished disbelief. Miko gently turned his head until he was facing forward again.

"So long, Miko-san? And you still haven't completed your journey?"

"We've tried and tried, but fate has not been with us. The same lack of knowledge that impeded us in life still works on us in death—and there have been other things. But it wasn't until recently that a new way opened itself to us, a way to actually find the place we seek." She hesitated for a moment. "You're very important to us, Toshi-kun. With you, we hope to do as we must."

A chill made its way down his spine. It was wrong that they should depend on him, that they might continue to roam the seas for years to come, perhaps eternity, if he couldn't guide them to where they needed to go. He was just a peasant, a slave, a tool for his master. Such responsibility was never meant to fall on someone like him.

He remained silent as Miko finished combing his hair and then tied it up again. After getting him more tea, she suggested they play some games. Wanting a distraction from both his thoughts and his nausea, he agreed.

They played word games. Then, when his nausea proved too distracting, Miko told him stories new and old. He was amazed by some of the ones she chose to tell, for they were quite recent. Though Miko and the others on the ship were all spirits, were they still somehow keeping in touch with those who were living? Even after all this time? He wasn't sure if he would do that if he were undead. He didn't know if he could handle how it would make him feel.

Some time later, he looked up in puzzlement after having added the next two lines to the poem they'd been making for the past half-hour. Something had changed, but he couldn't name what. After a moment, he realized he felt better.

Miko added her verses, which left him with a dead end to produce a new verse. He didn't notice he'd lost, still embroiled in trying to figure out what had changed around him.

"That was a good game, Toshi-san. I think you're taking to it well. If you prove diligent, I might just let you win a game or two."

He totally missed her playful dare. "Is something different, Miko-san?"

"Different?" Miko stared at him, lifting her head as she tried to figure out what he meant. "Oh, dawn is upon us. The ship has gone underwater."

As she said it, he realized it was true. The change he felt was the lack of swaying by the vessel.

"Now that the ship is more steady, perhaps you would consider eating before going to sleep?" Miko asked.

He nodded.

"I must go attend Asaka-sama now," she added. "I will wake you once night is close to falling on us again." Miko rose as Toshi glanced with distaste at the food still waiting for him across the room. "When you've finished with your duties tonight, we can play some more games, if you like."

"I would very much, Miko-san."

She bowed to him, bid him good night and then left.

He looked at the food sitting across the room again and grimaced. After several minutes, he forced himself to get up and head toward it.

Chapter 5

"Toshi-kun. Toshi-kun. Wake up. If you don't hurry, you'll have no free time before Asaka-sama comes for you. Toshi-kun!"

Barely able to open his eyes, he tried to focus his vision as his body was almost violently rocked back and forth. "Mi—Miko-san?"

"Yes, who else?" she said, her voice sounding annoyed and worried at the same time. "I've never had such trouble rousing anyone in my life. Now come on. Asaka-sama will be coming for you soon. You'll want to be ready."

With her help, he managed to sit up, yawning all the way. He tried to rub the sleep out of his eyes, even as his numbed mind tried to come awake.

"Did you always give your master this much trouble? I bet he had to take a stick to you just to get you up." Miko's tone was light.

His eyes felt heavy even as he tried to comprehend what Miko was talking about. "Did I do something wrong?"

"No, you only just about exhausted my patience is all, sleepyhead," she told him, shaking her head. "You have to be presentable and ready by the time Asaka-sama comes for you. He waits for no man, you know, and right now you're a long way from presentable."

He didn't see Miko go to the small table as his eyes closed on their own. He jerked them open, disoriented, as she placed a cup of barely steaming tea in his hands.

"Come on, drink," she said. "It should help wake you. I'll help you undress as soon as you've finished with it. Though it won't be as relaxing as a good tub, I've brought you some water with which you can clean yourself." She began digging him out of his cocoon of blankets.

"Take a stick to me?" He saw Miko snap her head up to stare at him. After a moment, her gentle laugh rose softly to his ears.

"You're not all here this evening, are you?" She laughed as he stared at her blankly. "I had asked you if your old master was in the habit of taking a stick to you to wake you up in the morning. Now, drink your tea."

Staring at her in a half-daze, he brought the teacup to his lips. As the contents trickled down his throat and warmed his stomach, his mind started to clear. "Master Shun never beat me with a stick. Not to wake me up, anyway."

Miko cast him a questioning glance as she dug him out of his blankets.

"I've never had any trouble waking up." He yawned in between some of the words. "I always awoke as soon as Master Shun opened my door. He liked it that way. He didn't believe in wasting time." He drank more of his tea.

As soon as he had finished, Miko took his cup away and bid him to please finish getting undressed. "There's a washcloth for you in one of the buckets. Your towel and clean clothes are by the door."

Feeling more alert, he waited for the geisha to turn away before stripping down to his loincloth. He put his sandals back on to walk across the glowing floor and hurried over to the waiting buckets. His exposed flesh crawled with goose bumps as the eerie cold radiating in the room caressed him wherever he went. Once he'd found the washcloth, he removed his loincloth and began to wash. While definitely not as enjoyable as a long soak in a tub, the feel of the hot water was luscious.

"Do you think you might like to eat something this evening?" Miko said.

Toshi realized he was hungry, his stomach no longer in the aggravated state it had been yesterday. With a sinking feeling, though, he wondered how long that would last once the ship rose back to the surface. "I'm not really sure, Miko-san. Maybe just a little?"

"All right."

He dried off as quickly as he could, the room's iciness sapping the water's warmth and leaving him colder than before. In one hurried move, he grabbed his clean clothes and dived to his futon. He dug into his blankets as deeply as he could and then got dressed.

"You need to hurry, Toshi-san," Miko warned him. "You haven't much time left."

Keeping his covers tightly about him, he got up and sat before the room's small table. He drank the tea Miko served him eagerly. As she proceeded to refill his cup once more, he reached out for one of the rice cakes filling a plate nearby.

Not daring to have more than one, he made it last as long as he could and followed it down with several more cups of tea. Miko was busy for a few minutes fighting to straighten his mussed hair.

Just as his grumbling stomach had almost convinced him perhaps there would be no harm in having a second rice cake, there was a knock at the door. With a trickle of fear, he stood up, knowing there was no way for him to avoid the inevitable. He let his blankets fall down around him as the samurai opened the door.

Holding his breath, he bowed deeply to Asaka. To his surprise, he found the bow returned. Bowing to Miko in farewell, he followed Asaka as he traveled silently up the hall.

As they waited by the outside door, he heard the faint sounds of receding water. Within moments, his stomach sadly reassured him they had, indeed, surfaced once again. Sending a quick prayer of mercy to the water spirits of the area, he followed the samurai out onto the busy deck.

The sky was clearer than the night before, yet the cooler winds still held the scent of threatening rain. With some relief, he noticed the ship was steadier.

He followed Asaka as he climbed up the ladder, glancing at the skeletons rowing in the front half of the ship. One of them stared back, and he felt a small chill course down his back as the skeleton's eyes filled with a red light. Toshi remembered him from his first time on board. He felt uneasy.

He looked away from the cold stare and lipless grin and spotted the bent skeleton already coming toward him carrying his tools. Asaka waved him back. The stooped figure bowed and then retreated.

"Sit," Asaka said. His cruel demon mask stared at Toshi as his armored fleshless arm pointed to the floor next to the rail.

Wondering why Asaka just didn't let him get his job done so he could go back below and escape, Toshi did as he'd been bid.

The glowing cold from the deck seeped through his clothes into his legs and buttocks. He wished for the warmth of his blankets, but knew it wouldn't be forthcoming. His stomach swished and knotted but not as bad as the night before. His one rice cake lay heavily inside him, making him glad he'd only had time to have the one.

Turning his head, he stared past the rail at the dark water. With a mixed sense of despair and sadness, he looked away. He remembered the things he would have seen if he'd been looking out a window at home. As the darkness settled, the city would have been filled with spurts of activity, most of it from fishermen returning home after a long day as they made their way to the inns for some well-deserved drinks. Mothers would be calling for their children as they closed the houses' shutters, preparing for bed. The cries of the oil sellers and food vendors would have filled the air as they tried to make what money they could before curfew forced them off the streets.

The memories lodged a lump in his throat. There was a chance he might never experience those things again. Bitterly, he glanced at the cause of his torment.

Asaka stood on deck, also staring at the dark waters. The glow from the ship reflected off his lacquered armor, making him appear more demonic than usual. Toshi looked away.

He tried for a moment to guess at the samurai's thoughts. But what would such a hateful spirit think about? Horrible plans, tortures for the living, surely. And he would be part of those thoughts as well. With a shiver, he made himself stop, not happy with where his imagination was leading him.

From out of the silence, one of the rowers raised his voice in song. With each line others joined in. Astounded, he listened carefully as they continued. It was a happy song, one about sake and parties going long into the night, an even bigger surprise. And it was one whose rhythm matched that of the rowing and helped make the sea seem less forbidding.

He stared in disbelief as Asaka did nothing to stop them. He had expected the samurai to shout them into silence, but he didn't. It was almost as if he didn't even hear them. Until then, Toshi had thought singing was only something for the living.

"Boy."

Asaka's deep voice made him jump. He scrambled to his feet waiting for the samurai's command. The old retainer walked forward, but Toshi stayed still until Asaka's green lit stare focused on him. He rushed to stand before him.

Asaka stared at him for a long moment. "It is time."

"Hai." Taking the weighted line, he completed a depth reading. He then took a coil of rope with a triangular piece of wood at the end and a small hourglass. Setting the wood upright in the water, he let it go and tipped the hourglass over. When the sands ran out, he took hold of the rope, noting how much of it had played out, and dragged it all back in. He took the compass next and found their bearing before returning it. He entered all the information into the logbook. Feeling nervous, he remembered what had happened the night before, yet his nausea was mild enough for the moment not to distract him too much from his task.

Trying to keep his hands steady, he borrowed the cross-staff. Taking a better look at it than he had the previous night, he felt a cold film of perspiration spread over his face as he realized he'd seen that specific instrument before. With a sense of growing dread, he cast a furtive glance toward Asaka. Seeing the samurai's attention wasn't focused on him at all, he turned the cross-staff over to look at the underside of the crosspiece, hoping not to find the gaijin initials he already knew would be there.

He closed his eyes and struggled to take a deep breath as the initials R.V. glared at him from where he'd known they'd be. Ramon Valéz—it had been difficult to learn to say the name the way the Spaniards did. The captain had been most patient, in this and many other things. He'd not fit the mold painted about foreigners. Unlike many of his counterparts, the captain had even been willing to learn about the ways of the people of Nihon. A storm had damaged his ship, but Master Shun's mapping proposition had helped take the sting out of having to stay in Nihon while they managed repairs.

Though the captain was a foreigner, Toshi thought they understood each other and were friends. And after the many months the foreigners had spent there, the captain had told him the time when they could leave would be arriving soon.

Captain Valéz couldn't possibly afford to lose his instruments. How had the samurai gotten them, anyway? At times the captain had talked of nothing but his strange country and his wish to go back home and perhaps retire. Because Toshi had worked with the foreigner, might this be why it was Valéz's instruments which were taken instead of someone else's? How long had these people been watching him?

"Boy."

His head snapped up as he realized he'd stood still for much too long. Trying to hold his growing anger in check, he brought the stolen cross-staff up to his eye so he could take a reading. Mechanically, he went through all the steps, feeling somehow traitorous to his gaijin friend.

He tried to think of nothing but what he had to do. Returning the cross-staff, he then began his calculations.

"Well, boy?"

Hearing Asaka's impatience, he hurried to him with the open map. Trying not to look at him, lest his stewing anger show, he bowed and showed him their calculated position. They were halfway up the coast of Honshu.

"We are here, sir."

"Very well," Asaka said. "Show this to the steersman."

"Hai." Still not looking at Asaka, he bowed again and walked over to the skeleton holding the ship's tiller. Just as he had done for the samurai, he held open the map and showed the steersman their present position.

Toshi suddenly wished the man before him were still made of flesh so he might have a hope of reading his expression, as the steersman stared at him with the never-ceasing skeletal grin.

"You've gotten lucky twice, boy," the steersman sneered. "You'd better hope you can figure out how to make it last."

He ignored the other's unkind tone and said nothing. He calmly rolled up the map.

"We don't need the help of gaijin-tainted peasants," the steersman continued.

Toshi looked up, more startled than angered by the steersman's attitude. Two points of yellow light flared in his dark, empty eyes as if daring him to contradict him. Though the steersman's opinion was one he had encountered often back home, still, he wondered why this spirit would speak to him like this when, according to Miko, they had true need of him.

"Boy."

He broke away from the steersman's stare to glance back at Asaka. Hurrying toward him with downcast eyes, he waited for whatever he would say.

"Estimate our time of arrival to the Shakute Islands."

He could feel the samurai's cold stare on him as he began to unroll the map.

He found the chain of small islands and, using the distance they'd traveled over the past day as a gauge, he calculated how long it would take for them to get there. He debated whether he should adjust the estimate due to the bad weather they'd traveled in last night, but decided against it. He really had nothing to base the adjustment on.

"Lord, with what I know, it should take at least three more nights." He expected a scathing glare at his slight safeguard, but the samurai never even glanced at him.

"You'll be given the responsibility of caring for the map and the gaijin instruments." Asaka's gaze bore down on him. "Also, from now on, I will expect you to arrive no later than five minutes after the ship has risen. Do you understand?"

"Yes, Lord."

The samurai barely nodded. "You may return to your room."

Bowing at the dismissal, he headed for the stairs. The bent skeleton met him there and handed him a basket containing the gaijin instruments.

"Thank you," Toshi said.

The skeleton bowed to him before returning to his master's side.

Holding tightly onto his new responsibilities, he gratefully returned to the interior of the ship.

Chapter 6

Toshi went back to his room and found Miko waiting there for him. He smiled as she half-bowed to him in greeting, before returning the gesture.

"Did all go well, Toshi-san?" she asked.

He hurried to his blankets. "I—I think so. Though I don't think the steersman is too happy to have me here."

Miko's silver bells tinkled softly as she nodded in understanding. "You should not take it personally. I doubt he really means to seem that way. Though he should know better, Kojiro is bitter, thinking Lord Asaka blames him for our inability to reach our destination." For a moment she appeared as if she would say more, but she didn't.

"Miko-san, do you have any spare paper, ink and brush I could borrow?" He asked with a little trepidation. "I'd like to make a partial copy of the map to track our progress on."

"Of course, but only if you'll let me watch you while you work." Gracefully rising from the floor, Miko left the room to fetch the items in question.

As he huddled in his covers waiting for her to return, his gaze wondered over to the basket with Captain Valéz's instruments. He felt his shoulders tense. Perhaps making a copy of the map would prove a useless gesture. How would he get it into a living being's hand? And if he somehow managed that, how would they help him? He had no ideas on that score. It seemed so futile, to hope he could somehow alert others of where they were going and perhaps get help, but there was nothing else he could try. And he owed the captain at least that much. Didn't he?

Before long, the geisha came back and laid a number of brushes, an ink bowl and a bundle of wrapped paper at his feet. As he sifted through the different brushes, Miko cleared off the small table and brought it over to him.

"Thank you, Miko-san."

Getting the geisha to sit beside him, he spread the map on the table. Hesitantly, he tried to explain to her the gaijin way of mapping—their concepts of longitude and latitude and how they made traveling from place to place easier. Seeing, as she asked a number of pointed questions, that her interest was genuine, he expanded on his explanations even as he copied part of the map. He confined his copy to the area from the point they were at now up to the chain of small islands that was their destination. With delicate care, he copied the section he'd chosen, his experience and technique plainly showing in his work. Time passed quickly, but it was barely noticed. Miko's continued interest coupled with the comforting familiarity of the work drove him long past his normal stopping point.

Sometime during the night, Miko sought her own paper and, stealing only a small part of the table, attempted to emulate his work.

Eyes squinting in order to cut out the glowing deck's glare, he missed the odd sensation signaling the submergence of the ship.

"Toshi-kun." Miko's bells rang softly as she lifted her head to look at him.

He didn't return the glance until he'd finished the delicate stroke he was working on and had placed the brush safely out of harm's way.

"The day began a number of hours ago," she said. "You might want to think about eating and then getting some sleep while you still have time, no?" Her head tilted slightly to the side with the question.

Now that he'd stopped, he felt a satisfied weariness wash over him. He'd missed doing the work. It was hard and something not many of his countrymen knew how to do, but he enjoyed it. He rubbed at his eyes.

"Yes, I guess I'd better. I hadn't realized how late it was." He reached to clear his things from the table but stopped as his right hand cramped.

Forcing his fingers to straighten out with a grimace, he rubbed them with his left hand, trying to soothe his protesting muscles.

"Here, let me take care of that." Miko took his hands in hers.

"It's all right, Miko-san. This happens all the time, I can—" He gasped in surprise as the pain in his hand abruptly stopped and a cool tingling sensation spread from her fingertips to his.

"How?" He stared at the geisha in astonishment, knowing what he'd just felt was different from the deep cold he had felt from her kind before.

Miko's brilliantly burning blue eyes looked away from him, even as her fleshless fingers continued dancing over his own. "I don't know. There are many things we can do now that we could not while we were living."

As she glanced back at him, he noticed her eyes had dimmed back to their normal intensity. Searching for something to say as she retained the light hold on his hand, he thought of their lord. He felt his blood grow cold.

"Miko-san! Lord Asaka." He couldn't quite keep a note of panic from his voice. "Weren't...weren't you supposed to...didn't you need to...hours ago?"

Miko's smiling mask stared at his obvious and sudden worry in tilted curiosity before straightening up as she figured out what he was talking about.

Guilt rose within him at the punishment Miko would surely receive because of him. He watched in alarm as the geisha tilted forward, her hand rising to cover her face.

"This is my fault," he insisted. "I will say so to Lord Asaka. I won't let him hurt you because of me."

He couldn't bear to lose the one person that had been kind to him aboard this cursed ship. His worry grew as he saw her lean even closer to the ground. He reached out for her, sure of the terror now within her, and froze as bubbling laughter suddenly filled the room. He stared at the geisha in incomprehension as she tried hard to stifle her overflowing mirth.

"Oh, Toshi." Laughter overrode what else she might have said for a moment. "I'm so sorry."

Concern flitted across his face as he wondered if he had inadvertently driven her to hysteria. Recently, he had felt close to that himself once or twice. The punishments dealt out by Lord Asaka must be horrible indeed.

"I'll try to fix it somehow, Miko-san. Honest, I will. I won't let him hurt you because of me."

Miko looked up, her fleshless hands still trying to uselessly contain her laughter. She shook her head rapidly, making her bells ring frantically, but couldn't gain enough control to speak.

Sure she was unselfishly trying to stop him from taking the blame, he worked himself up to go and set things right before he might change his mind by thinking of the possible consequences. He started to rise to his feet.

"Miko-san, I will go to him now," he stated. "I'll fix this."

Before he could stand, she reached out and closed her hand on his arm. "Toshi, no, please wait," she said breathlessly. "Give me a moment!"

He hesitated. He was determined not to be swayed from his decision but wasn't sure he could break away from the geisha's hold. Miko's laughter subsided as she stared into his concerned face.

"Toshi-kun, please forgive me," she said. "I hadn't meant to mislead you so. You are such a dear, worrying over me. Who would have thought it? You're so thoroughly delightful."

He stood with his mouth open as it dawned on him he'd made another mistake.

"There is nothing to worry about," she added. "Lord Asaka knows I'm here, Toshi-kun. I asked for his permission earlier. I have been in and out of this room a number of times. I guess you never noticed." Miko gently pulled on his arm trying to get him to sit back down.

He looked away, red-faced, knowing he'd made a fool of himself.

"Please don't misunderstand me, Toshi-san. I'm quite flattered by your concern. There's just no reason for it."

He sat down with a thump. "Yes, no reason." From the corner of his eye, he saw the geisha's hand rise to cover her mask's mouth again. Her renewed amusement made his cheeks burn that much hotter than before.

"I do have to be going, though, and you need your rest for this evening," she said. "From what I understand, you'll be staying above longer tonight than you have before."

A slight chill coursed through him. He heard Miko move as she stood up, but didn't look after her. She set out the food he had missed seeing her bring in earlier to the small table. She then poured him a cup of hot tea.

"I'll come wake you when the time is near," she said.

He barely nodded; still too embarrassed to say much of anything. He was almost afraid to wonder what kind of idiot she must think him to be.

"Toshi-san, I'm grateful for the honor you've shown me by your actions today," she said softly. "I'm not worthy of them."

He yearned to look at her, but forced himself not to. He wasn't sure the sincerity he thought he heard in her voice wouldn't be dispelled if he looked at her and found her hand lightly covering her mouth. He'd rather not do more injury to his already ruined pride.

He almost jumped as a soft, warm hand caressed his cheek. He looked up, but Miko's back was to him as she started back to the door.

"Might I take the copy of the map you made?" she asked. "I'd like to attempt to finish mine while you sleep. I thought I would also show Asaka-sama the excellent job you'd done."

He stared at Miko's back when she didn't turn around for his answer. "Yes, if you like. I'll get it for you." He scrambled to his feet, trying not to trip over his blankets.

Gathering his new copy of the map and her unfinished one, he clumsily handed them to her with a bow. He felt her staring at him, but he wouldn't meet her gaze.

"Toshiro, please try not to misunderstand what I am about to say." She hesitated for a moment. "I realize being here isn't what you want, and that it's been quite difficult for you to accept. But, I am still very glad it was you our Lord chose to come with us on this journey."

Leaving his startled countenance behind, Miko left the room.

Toshi shook his head as he turned away from the door. Not sure what to make of all that had been said, he carefully rolled up the main map and placed it in the basket with his other tools.

Pondering her words, he drank the tea Miko had poured for him and ate.

Chapter 7

"Toshi-kun! You must wake up. You're going to be late."

"Huh?" The word had barely left his mouth before his eyes were closing again. He hardly felt his body shift as Miko grabbed him on the side and shook him hard. Her urgent words meant nothing to him as his mind lay enshrouded in a deep, cold fog.

"Toshi!"

The sound of bells filled the room as Miko leaned down to look into his face and found it wrapped in sleep. Roughly, she pulled away his covers, exposing him to the eerily cold air. Pulling up one of the sleeves of her green-and-gold kimono, she slapped him on the shoulder. His eyes never opened, he just pulled up his legs and made himself into a ball.

"All right, Chizuson Toshiro, you asked for this!"

Kneeling close, Miko undid his sash and opened his shirt. Sneaking her hands over his bare skin, she began to lightly roam the area around his sides.

An odd sensation coursed through him and it poked small holes in the fog about his mind. As the sensation persisted, he became more and more aware of it. The closer he came to awakening, the more annoying the sensation became. He moaned, trying to get away from the bothersome feeling, but couldn't get rid of it.

"Go away," he mumbled.

When it didn't, he curled up tighter. His discomfort grew as the sensation didn't cease, and he also started to feel the cold seeping into his exposed skin. The fog around his mind dissipated. He opened his eyes in surprise, as unwanted laughter bubbled from his lips.

"Stop it!"

Miko didn't stop. No matter what direction he tried to roll to get away from her, he found Miko's hands always following him, mercilessly tickling the sensitive flesh on his sides.

"All bad boys have to pay the price," she chortled. "You should learn to get up sooner."

To his chagrin, the geisha suddenly doubled her efforts. "Please stop. Miko-san. I'm awake now!"

The geisha didn't stop. He felt he might just die. His sides ached horribly, and he could barely breathe. Laughter continued to issue involuntarily from his mouth. "Miko-san, please!"

She stopped. He instantly quit squirming and went thankfully limp. He closed his eyes, concentrating only on taking great lungfulls of air.

"There's no time for that," she snapped. "You must get up, Toshi-kun, and you must hurry. You've only got a few minutes before we surface. Lord Asaka will be waiting for you."

At the mention of the samurai's name, his eyes popped open. His body tensed as he fought to sit up. Without any more prompting, he stood and took off his clothes, rushing toward his waiting bath water.

Shivering as he tried to dry off as fast as possible, he found Miko at his side holding out his clean clothes. He forgot to be embarrassed by her closeness, having at the moment only thoughts for what might happen to him if he were late. He never noticed the garment she held open for him as he slipped into it.

When Miko pressed a cup of hot tea into his hands, he drank it down, cursing himself for having forgotten to put on his sandals before moving over the cold floor to bathe. He rushed back to his futon and the warmth he would find there.

Miko took away his emptied cup as he rubbed his cold numbed feet with one of his blankets. The geisha took over the task after handing him a fresh rice cake.

As soon as he'd gobbled the first one down, Miko gave him another with a new cup of tea. He felt his insides warming up, as well as his abused feet. As he chewed on his new rice cake, Miko uncovered his feet and put warm socks on them. It was only as he watched her that he realized Miko had not given him his normal clothes. Surprised, he stared down at the brown kimono, realizing it fit him perfectly. Miko had just finished putting on his sandals when he thought of trying to protest. He had no business wearing these fine clothes. He was a peasant.

Miko took away his cup and the rest of his rice cake as he opened up his mouth to say just that.

"Hurry, Toshi-kun, get your things. We're out of time!" Miko reached for his arm.

All his protests disappeared as his worries returned. Moving awkwardly in his newly fitted clothes, he rose to his feet while simultaneously trying to fix his mussed hair. He grabbed his basket and rushed for the door. Miko held out a bite of fish to him as he walked past. He stumbled out into the empty hallway.

Cool night air swept over him as he stepped out on deck. The ship's sail was raised high, catching all the wind had to give. In haste, he sent a sweeping glance over the men rowing despite the wind, and headed for the ladder that would take him to his post.

Reaching the higher deck, he bowed to Asaka, who sat regally on a folding stool, his lacquered armor glinting with the ship's permeating glow. The frowning demon mask turned toward him, two green flames filling up its eyes. Asaka said nothing to him, but gave him a slight acknowledging nod.

Toshi set his basket down and took out the coil of measuring rope. His eyes lit guiltily on the stolen cross-staff, and again he wondered if there was any way Captain Valéz might return home without it. He had learned just recently how badly someone could miss a place once he was no longer allowed to return to it. He knew exactly how the Spanish captain and his crew would feel. He hoped never to inflict that on anyone, however long he might have to live.

One by one he took his readings and had already started doing his calculations as he stepped back to the basket to retrieve the map. He stopped in mid-step as he suddenly realized it wasn't there. Frantically, he sifted through his memories of the past few minutes, trying to recall where the map had been the last time he'd seen it.

"Is something wrong, boy?"

His neck prickled with fear as the samurai's deep voice rose up behind him. "I seem to have left the map back in my room, sir." He swallowed hard, his eyes rooted to the glowing floor, dreading the possible reaction to what he had just said. "Might I be allowed to go retrieve it, sir?" He held his breath, not sure of what might come. He felt himself shiver as the samurai spoke again.

"Mitsuo-san, please go to the boy's room and retrieve the map," Asaka commanded.

With a touch of surprise, Toshi watched the bent skeleton as he bowed deeply and then proceeded to the ladder. Asaka remained seated, staring outwards, his demon mask impassive.

That he was being ignored gave him a measure of calm he'd not been able to achieve moments before. If something was to be done to him for so foolishly forgetting the map in his charge, it didn't look like it would be immediate.

Hoping Mitsuo would return quickly, he folded his legs beneath him and sat down. Glancing behind him, he couldn't help but notice the steersman's dim yellow eyes boring into him. His never-changing, fleshless grin seemed to be trying to promise something. With a small shudder, Toshi turned away from the awful stare.

Time trickled along and Mitsuo didn't return. He began to fidget, a feeling of doom tightening his chest. The feeling was only made worse when Mitsuo finally did reappear, and he noticed the obvious hesitation of his pace.

Rising slowly onto the deck, Mitsuo walked to stand before Asaka and bowed almost to the floor. The voice that flowed from the bent frame was slow and soft, tinged with an almost palpable sadness. "Asaka-sama, I searched the entire room, yet there was no map to be found there."

It took Toshi a long stunned moment to realize what had just been said. With large eyes, he stared at the metal demon mask as it turned toward him.

"Boy, explain."

He had no idea where the map was. He had no explanation to give. Forced to say something, he found his tongue lay like lead inside his mouth. "I can't explain it, Lord." He despaired and would have fallen if he weren't already seated, knowing that by his admission he had just damned himself.

"What is there to explain, Asaka-sama? Isn't it obvious the whelp destroyed the map to cover up his actual lack of skill?" The steersman grinned toward him.

"That's a lie," Toshi exclaimed with some heat. "I didn't destroy the map. That would have been stupid!" He closed his mouth, realizing with horror he was the one who had spoken. His heart lurched in his breast. He cursed his loose tongue for making things worse and forced himself to stay still.

"Explain," Asaka demanded.

He didn't realize the command had been aimed at him until he heard no one else answer. Knowing he had nothing to lose, since he was already doomed, he clenched his hands and spoke. "I would have had nothing to gain by destroying the map. I don't want to be here, but doing as you ask is the fastest way to leave. If I had destroyed it, it would have been like committing suicide. I want to go home, not die, especially not here." He had gone too far again. Of that he was sure. He stared at the floor, shaking with despair.

"Likely excuse, Lord Asaka." It was the steersman again. "This boy is nothing but trouble. Now that he has done the deed and realized its foolishness, he's trying his best to find some way to save himself."

A curt gesture from the samurai kept the steersman from saying more.

Silence followed—a silence too deep for Toshi's taste. In it, he could hear the ocean waves as they split whitely against the sides of the ship. He could hear the crewmen's oars as they rose and dipped into the dark water. He waited for his doom to fall, hoping against hope Asaka wouldn't make him into one of them.

Time stretched to agonizing minutes. He stared at the deck, his thoughts turning to the missing map. He hadn't taken the map. Everyone else had been a part of the ship for the past eight years. None of them would do it. None of them would risk being stuck there forever. It made no sense. If only Asaka had brought more than one map. If only there were another copy…

His eyes widened as he realized his stupidity. There was a copy of the map. It hadn't been in his room, so there might be a chance it hadn't been taken. He bowed to the floor on his hands and knees as he tried to get the samurai's attention.

"Asaka-sama, Miko-san has a partial copy of the map. I had about finished it when she took it with her yesterday." Nervously, he risked a glance in Asaka's direction. Despite his fear, he could feel hope welling in his heart.

"Mitsuo-san, would you verify this?" Asaka asked.

Toshi saw the older samurai start on his way. He prayed, hoping fate would decide to be on his side. His hands became numb as he waited, but he didn't dare move. Instead, he tried concentrating on the warm, comfortable feel of the silk lying against his skin.

He glanced to the side as he caught the faint sound of bells. His heart beat faster, hoping for redemption. The sound of bells, however, came no closer.

He glanced to the side again as he heard the ladder creak from someone's weight. Sending another prayer to all the gods and spirits he could think of, he held his breath waiting to hear of his salvation or doom.

"Here's what was found, Lord." The confident edge to Mitsuo's voice brought him much needed hope. He heard paper rustling and then nothing.

For what seemed like forever, he waited for Asaka to speak.

"Boy, get back to work."

Though he had dared to expect those words, his impromptu release from death nevertheless made his vision swim. He swayed from relief. Bowing until his forehead came into contact with the cold floor, he then tried to rise to his feet. His knees protested immediately. The cold had locked them in place. He compelled them to work, ignoring the pain in his legs as he hobbled the rest of the way, having no wish to test Asaka's patience any further.

To his relief, he found that Asaka was paying him no attention, but was instead staring out into the dark sea. He sighed once but then tensed again as he found Mitsuo standing before him. The old, bent figure bowed slightly and offered him the copy of the map. He returned the gesture.

Forcing his numb hands to move, he reached for the map only to find his fingers wouldn't close around it. In embarrassment and shock, he could only watch as the map fell from his unresponsive hand.

He started to bend to pick the map back up, but Mitsuo beat him to it. Not sure of what he might do, Toshi rubbed his hands together, trying to warm them so they would respond. Looking up, he found dark, empty sockets staring at him. A sudden bit of white momentarily flashed within their depths. Looking away, he continued working on his hands until they would finally do as he bid them.

Without a word, he took the map, bowed low and rapidly went on to finish his interrupted task.

After he'd redone his measurements and calculations, he found the ship's approximate location. He stood around nervously as time passed, but Asaka didn't ask to see their position. He looked around, but no gaze met his except the antagonistic one of the steersman.

Working up his courage, he walked aft and bowed to the steersman. The latter didn't return the gesture. Ignoring the obvious insult, he calmly showed him their position on the map.

"You've gotten lucky again, boy," the steersman quipped. "But, sooner or later it's bound to run dry."

After he spoke, Toshi felt himself dismissed. Bowing again, he said nothing and returned to the place where the basket and instruments sat and waited eagerly to be sent back to his cabin.

The order didn't come. He shifted uneasily. He wanted to go back inside to cuddle in his warm blankets, to have tea and to share in Miko's company. There was nothing out here that could bring him that kind of comfort. His brown gaze strayed toward Asaka looking for any signs of a dismissal. After several minutes of no change, he resigned himself to the fact they meant for him to stay.

Sitting down, he stared at the hardworking men rowing the ship through the ocean's watery darkness. A chill made its way up his spine as he watched them rock back and forth with the tireless energy of the undead. Almost against his will, he picked out the one who'd frightened him so much before. His shoulders were hunched over, as if tense; and Toshi soon noticed that a number of others appeared that way, as well.

Time passed and nothing changed. Unlike the night before, the rowers didn't sing but maintained a deathlike silence. A sense of tension permeated the air. He was sure it had something to do with the loss of the original map. If he hadn't destroyed it, that meant it had to have been one of them.

"Boy." He looked up in Asaka's direction. "Take a reading."

Nodding, he was relieved by the excuse for activity.

As soon as he'd calculated their position, he immediately walked over to show it to the steersman. The steersman stared at the map a lot longer than he'd ever done before. When he was through, he ignored the boy as if he didn't exist. Toshi bowed and returned to sit by the basket. He felt the ship's direction change slightly as he sat down.

He was asked to take several more readings during the long night. With only the sounds of the waves and oars to keep him company, he tried to amuse himself by memorizing the map. He ignored his stomach's stubborn grumbling as lunchtime came and went.

A few hours before dawn, he caught himself nodding off from boredom. As he glanced around, trying to stay awake, it looked to him as if Asaka and his retainer hadn't stirred all night through.

"Boy, a reading," Asaka said.

Scrambling to his feet, he did as he'd been bid. After going through the process and showing his calculated position to the steersman, he sighed as he moved to sit down again.

"Boy."

He stopped in mid-squat and glanced up to find the samurai staring in his direction. "Yes, Lord?"

"It is time for you to go below," he said. "Mitsuo-san will accompany you and stand guard at your door. There shall be no more mishaps." The demon mask turned away with a flash of green.

He bowed, surprised but happy he would finally be able to go inside. Scooping up his basket, he rushed for the ladder.

Thoughts of food and warmth hurried his steps along as he reached the lower deck. He fervently hoped Miko would be waiting for him. He didn't think he could stand more of the uncomfortable silence.

Rushing down the small hallway to his door, he took a deep breath before reaching to open it. As it swung forward, he heard the sound of rustling silk coming from within. With a surge of happy relief, he hurried inside.

Smiling, he bowed in Miko's direction before rushing to his waiting blankets. In no time at all, he had built a cocoon of heavenly warmth.

Miko soon knelt before him, offering him a steaming cup of tea. He eagerly took it. He closed his eyes in ecstasy as the hot liquid made its warm way into his innards.

When he opened his eyes again, he saw Miko had already lifted the small table and set it before him. Silently, she traded his empty cup for a full bowl of rice.

With great relish, he scooped the rice into his waiting mouth, now and then using his chopsticks to reach over the table for a sliver of fish from a plate nearby. As soon as he'd finished with the rice, he traded the bowl for more tea. A relieved grin flickered on his face as he recalled how many times he'd thought he would never be doing something as mundane as eating after what had happened that evening, yet there he was.

As Miko handed him a second bowl of rice, his pace began to slow. Little by little, he took notice of Miko's continued silence. He glanced at her off and on, trying to figure out what was wrong. As he did so, he noticed a stiffness to her posture that had never been there before. He suddenly realized he hadn't escaped the silent tension from above after all. A piece of it was there with him.

His appetite dried up inside him. "Miko-san?"

The pale Noh mask turned to face him, its eye slits dark. "Yes, Toshi-kun?"

He hesitated, not sure of how or whether he should ask what he wanted to know. "I'm sorry I was so late. Asaka-sama decided he needed me until just a little while ago."

She barely nodded as she served him more tea.

"There was some trouble early on," he added.

Miko made no response. Her gaze remained averted from his.

"I thought I was going to die today."

Still she said nothing, busying herself with cleaning an already immaculate table.

"Thank you for saving me."

Miko looked up, a soft, blue flash momentarily lighting her eyes. "Toshi." Her gaze shied from his. "You were never in any danger," she said. "Lord Asaka knew of the copy of the map. By your own eagerness to copy it, you had already placed yourself above suspicion."

He didn't realize his mouth had dropped open as he stared at her in surprise. "But, if he knew, why did he wait? He did nothing until I remembered you had it."

Her gaze locked with his. "I don't know. Though I am sure Asaka-sama had his reasons for it."

Miko returned to her previous silence. He felt more confused than before.

"The whole thing doesn't add up, Miko-san," he pressed. "Do you have someone else on board I don't know about? Could he have stolen the map? Anything else just doesn't make sense."

Miko shook her head. "No, there's no one," she answered. "And you're right, it doesn't make sense. Which means the unthinkable must be true." As if she were struggling with a great weight, the geisha rose to her feet.

"Asaka-sama has assigned Mitsuo-san to guard my door." He wasn't sure why he told her this, but he could think of nothing else to say. Inside, he knew she was about to leave him, taking all she knew with her. She was his only source of information, and he wanted to know what could bother all these spirits so.

"He's not doing that to hurt you, Toshi-kun," she said. "He's doing it to protect you. Our problems won't be over now that it's known there's another copy of the map." Miko didn't look at him. After a moment she walked toward the door.

His throat grew dry as he watched her go. If he didn't say or do something immediately, he would lose her.

"Miko-san, please," he pleaded. "You're the only one I can ask about this. There's no one else here who even cares about me!" He saw her hesitate. He knew it would be now or never. "I beg you, Miko-san."

"Toshi." She stopped and turned to face him. "It isn't easy to explain." Her gaze avoided his. Her thin skeletal hands absently worked to straighten the hem of her kimono. "What happened this evening has made certain things very clear—too clear." Her voice dropped to a whisper. "It has told us that at least one of us doesn't want our mission to succeed, even if it strands all of us here forever." Miko lowered her eyes. "It also told us our deaths may not have been the accident we'd thought, but rather an act of sabotage."

He didn't dare breathe, hearing the agony of the awful realization in her voice.

"Can you imagine what this means to the rest of us?" she asked. "Already, through our perhaps not-so-accidental failure, we have reached this wretched state and watched our clan be destroyed. Now, we learn one of us wants to do what we fear most and force us all to stay this way." Her voice rose. "That one of us is willing to lock us all into this mockery of life for the rest of eternity!"

He felt guilty pangs of misery as he listened to her barely restrained horror. He had always assumed, though he knew not why, that it hadn't mattered to them to be as they were. For the first time, he wondered if they were as terrified of what they had become as he was of becoming one of them. "Miko-san, I—"

He never got to finish what he might have said. At the sound of his voice, Miko bolted and left through the door. He was left alone with only the receding sound of ringing bells.

Chapter 8

Fog lay everywhere. Toshi felt as if he'd been swimming through it forever. How he'd gotten here, he couldn't remember, yet he felt no fear. A sound caught his attention, and he turned to look up. It was the sound of ringing bells. He swam upwards toward the sound, up until his eyes fluttered open.

"—progressively worse. While he's been awake, he's been fine, but every time he's slept it's gotten harder and harder to wake him. Something has gone terribly wrong."

Though he heard the words they meant nothing to him. The voice was familiar, though; and it was one that mattered.

"I wouldn't have disturbed you, except I'm not sure what to do now. I've tried everything to wake him, and all has failed. Ietsugu, I am afraid for him."

He turned his head toward the familiar voice. He still couldn't make much sense of the words, but he could hear the worry in them.

"You were right in telling me. This was unforeseen."

A questioning spark lit in his mind at the new voice. He'd heard it before, but at the same time he hadn't. His clouded gaze moved in the direction of the voices. Concentrating, he was able to get his vision to clear just enough to see.

Two figures stood together on the far side of the room. Miko was standing slightly closer to him than the other figure. He was almost sure that it was she—the woman had the wig with its silver bells, the bright yellow kimono. All he needed to make absolutely sure was to see her smiling mask. As if in answer to his wishes, the woman turned partially in his direction. In surprise, he realized it might not be her after all. His gaze hadn't encountered the white mask he knew so well, but rather a fleshless profile. The skull's empty eye sockets glowed softly with blue light. His still-struggling mind eventually realized it was Miko, but without her mask.

"I think what we have become is somehow affecting him," she said. "This cold we cannot feel is trying to claim him for its own."

The male figure became more prominent in his field of view. Neither one was looking toward him. He knew he should recognize the male skeleton with the glowing green eyes. "For him to come to harm was never my intention."

Miko's fleshless hand rose to touch the other's arm. "I know. I've never doubted your intent. But this is not right. If we don't help him in some way, somehow slow down what's happening, we'll lose him. And, with him, perhaps all hope we'll ever be free."

The man turned from her and stared at a blank wall. Toshi's muddled mind continued to try and place him.

"You say he seems unaffected when he is awake?" the man asked.

"Yes, as far as I can tell."

They both stood silent for a moment.

Toshi's eyes started to close. With a small sigh he began sliding back into the foggy depths waiting for him.

"Perhaps—" His eyes flickered back open at the sudden excitement in the geisha's voice. "Perhaps if he slept out in the open air rather than surrounded on all sides by the ship, the effect would be lessened. I know you have need of him at night, but perhaps the fact you would have to disrupt his sleep every once in a while would help as well."

He saw the man nod in acknowledgment. His eyes opened a little more as he realized again there was something familiar about this person, that he should know him. Yet something about him wasn't right.

"I believe you're correct," the man acknowledged. "We'll try this. I will have Mitsuo-san watch him while on deck so we can be certain it's working."

"I'm sure it will, Asaka-sama. It has to," Miko exclaimed. "Too many other things have gone wrong for us. Toshi is our last hope." Her tone was heavy.

It was the samurai! His mind speeded up as it grappled with the concept. Entranced, he watched with some surprise as Miko turned away and the samurai tenderly placed his hands upon her shoulders. "Beloved, I know this has been difficult, but we must persevere," he told her. "We are bound by our duty, and do as we must. There is no longer a question of what might have been for any of us. All that is left are our feelings and striving for the achievement of our task for the honor and peace it will bring us."

Miko withdrew her hands from her face and straightened her shoulders before turning back to face him. "I'm sorry, Ietsugu. I don't mean to be weak. It just hurts so that one of us might be responsible for all our deaths. That one of us cares not for the peace of a higher plane. That one of us would be willing to keep the rest of us from going on."

He stared in fascination as the samurai reached up and caressed a cheek that wasn't there. As he did so again, Toshi's eyes grew in wonder as shimmering light spread from the skeletal hand to her face. Not truly knowing whether what he was seeing was real or not, he watched as the two people before him gained a semi-transparent skin.

Delicate hands reached up to take Asaka's. The geisha's face grew defined, with sculpted cheeks in a beautiful oval-shaped face with full lips. Dark, expressive eyes stared at the samurai with affection.

Rather than the demon face he half-expected, he saw that Asaka had once been as human as any of them. His features were handsome, strong and surprisingly young. His eyes stared into hers, returning the geisha's sentiments softly.

Toshi blinked, a part of him weakly insisting what he was seeing wasn't real. Still fascinated, but with growing disbelief, he looked closely at the young face belonging to his lord. How could that belong to the cruel, silent man who had forced him to enter into this journey? Yet, Miko's features were more beautiful than he could have ever hoped.

Though his fogged mind didn't know why, he felt the sudden need to see her smile. To his delight, a small, delicate smile blossomed on her blushing face. He stared at her so hard the overlay of reality and illusion made his head spin. A small groan inadvertently left his lips as he was forced to shut his eyes to try and stop his growing dizziness. He lay still even as he heard the rustle of silk travel in his direction. He did nothing as he felt his covers pulled away from his face and a warm touch land on his cheek.

"Toshi-san?"

His glazed eyes opened at Miko's soft-voiced query. He stared at her in growing confusion when he didn't see the beautiful face he had expected, but rather saw the familiar Noh mask. "Miko-san?"

"Yes, Toshi-kun, it's me. How do you feel?"

He blinked again, the question not making sense to his mind.

"Do you think you can drink some tea?" she asked.

He blinked again, not knowing how to respond. Asaka walked up behind her and passed her a filled cup.

Seeing that he wasn't about to reply, Miko placed a hand beneath his head and raised it. He did nothing as she pressed the warm cup against his lips.

"Drink, Toshi-kun." Her voice held an edge of command.

He parted his lips and let the warm fluid in. He let his eyes fall closed as its heat flowed through him.

"Toshi?"

His eyes flickered open again as the cup was taken away. Keeping them that way was a struggle as both the seeping warmth of the tea and the ship's cold joined forces to drag him into oblivion.

He felt his grip slipping, but another cup was brought to his lips. As the warmth poured into him again, his mouth held onto the cup more firmly.

"It's time to wake up," Miko said. "Our lord has need of you, and you're already late."

He looked up at her in incomprehension for a moment, before being distracted away by the spreading warmth of the tea. His mind couldn't quite make its way out of the cold-induced fog surrounding it.

"Work with him," Asaka said. "I'll go dress and then come back for him."

"Hai." Miko turned back to Toshi once the samurai had left. "Everything will be all right now, Toshi-kun. You'll see. And, really, it is time for you to get up. You have an important job to do."

His gaze rose to meet hers.

"You'll be all right," she insisted. "You have to be."

He was barely aware of what was happening as Miko sat him up and then held him in her arms. Her softly lit eyes stared into his. He looked at the smiling painted face of the mask and smiled back at it. He sighed as Miko stroked his loosened hair.

Asaka returned not long after, once more dressed in his armored regalia with Mitsuo at his side. "I'll take him now," he stated.

The geisha nodded, keeping her face averted. As Asaka knelt to take her burden, Miko made sure his blankets were firmly wrapped around his body. Toshi barely registered the fact he was being picked up. He lay in Asaka's arms limply and closed his eyes. His mind still struggled to free itself from the cold's power, but it didn't look like it would win.

Startled, he opened his eyes as the night's warm breeze caressed his face. With slightly clearer eyes but little comprehension, he half-watched as Mitsuo rose to the upper deck with his tool basket in hand. He looked up as the older man disappeared and then returned to peer down at him. He didn't protest as Asaka held him up higher and he was given into Mitsuo's care. The latter lifted him and then carefully propped him in a sitting position against the ship's rail.

Crawling, his mind disengaged from the numbing fog that surrounded it. Something hot touched his lips, and he jerked back in shock. Disoriented and suddenly scared, he found he was staring straight into Mitsuo's white-lit eyes. The older skeleton held a cup of steaming tea out to him and, when he didn't respond, took Toshi's hand and wrapped it around the cup before bidding him to drink. As Toshi brought the cup obediantly to his lips, a gust of wind ruffled through his hair; and with abrupt clarity, he realized he wasn't where he should be.

A pang of fear ran through him as he became aware the ship had surfaced and he was on deck. Glancing past Mitsuo, he found the samurai sitting at his usual place.

He didn't remember coming on deck. He didn't even remember waking, let alone eating, or bathing, or any of the other things in his routine. Had he been bewitched in some way? Fear and confusion mixed freely inside him. As if to answer his question, his mind conjured up the image of a young man. Before he could wonder who it might be, he found his gaze moving of its own volition toward

Asaka.

Shaking his head to dispel the mental image, he concentrated on drinking his tea. As its heat rushed through him, he shivered. He closed his eyes, trying to quiet his rising panic.

"More?"

The quiet voice startled him with its gentle request. Opening his eyes, he stared at Mitsuo breathlessly for a moment before returning the cup.

"Yes, please," he said. "I would like that very much."

Mitsuo lifted a steaming teapot at his side and refilled the cup. As Toshi gulped it down, trying not to think, Mitsuo reached within his kimono and brought out four wrapped rice cakes. Toshi gratefully accepted them and wolfed them down.

The food and spreading warmth helped him pull out of his panic. Nothing bad had happened. Asaka sat as immobile as always. He slowly relaxed, though he still had no idea how he'd gotten there. If he'd messed up somehow, perhaps he'd been forgiven. Something had happened, though; otherwise why would he have gotten his breakfast on deck?

"Boy," Asaka said.

He jumped to his feet, his heart racing from the call.

"Yes, lord?" He steeled himself as the samurai's demon-masked stare turned in his direction.

"Your schedule has been changed. From now on you'll remain on deck at night, sleeping in between the time of your readings," the samurai stated. "You're forbidden from sleep while you're below. Is this understood?"

A million questions rose in his mind. He dared voice none of them. Something had gone horribly wrong, and he had no idea what it might be. "Yes, Asaka-sama."

"You will now take a reading."

"Hai." Struggling out of his blankets, he glanced around looking for his instruments. Not seeing them, he looked to Mitsuo, hoping the other knew where they were. He followed the old retainer's pointing hand and spotted his basket sitting beside Asaka's stool. Swallowing hard, he rushed to retrieve it. He hurried back to the railing once he'd fetched it, his feet complaining about the cold seeping in from the planking through his stockings.

Falling into the rhythm of his work, he took his various readings and computed their present position. Once he was done, he walked over to show the results to the steersman. The skeleton's glowing yellow eyes looked more subdued than usual.

Toshi held the map before him, pointed to their calculated position and then made to move away.

"Stop. I'm not finished yet." The steersman reached a hand out for him.

With an apologetic nod, Toshi placed the map back in view, trying to hide his surprise.

The steersman looked at the map for a long time before telling him he was through. With a fear-mixed thrill, Toshi rolled up the map and hurried back to his blankets. They were out of the territory familiar to the steersman. He was being forced to rely on Toshi's calculations whether he liked it or not. It was now Toshi's responsibility, Toshi's burden.

Not sure if he was pleased by this or not, he enfolded himself in his blankets. He checked the instruments and then set them aside before studying the map to become more familiar with the waters ahead. Quietly, Mitsuo sidled up beside him and put the instruments and other tools back in the basket. Without saying anything, he held out his hand, asking for the map.

Not daring to question Mitsuo's actions in front of Asaka, he rolled up the map and gave it to him. Mitsuo bowed slightly before rising to his feet. He walked toward the seated samurai and left the basket next to their lord's stool.

Toshi was slightly surprised as the bent skeleton then returned once more to his side.

"Time to sleep," Mitsuo said.

He didn't need sleep. He'd slept all day and had only been up for a short while. He knew his new orders demanded he sleep while on deck, but somehow he hadn't expected to begin so early. He lay down, not able, despite his confusion, to raise the courage to argue; not when Asaka would be able to hear.

As soon as Mitsuo saw him comply, the old retainer shifted to a position just behind his head. Wondering why he was the object of such scrutiny, he turned on his right side and tried to go to sleep.

It eluded him. His mind wandered, his thoughts lacking cohesion; but still he couldn't make himself fall asleep. Bored after a time, he listened to the sound of the waves slapping against the sides of the ship. In an odd way, they were becoming a reassuringly familiar sound. He wondered what the gaijin captain would make of that.

His eyes had finally started feeling heavy when Mitsuo touched him on the shoulder. Sitting up, wondering what was wrong, he found that Mitsuo had retrieved his tools.

"It is time." The old samurai stared at him.

He nodded and then got up to take his readings. After he'd finished, Mitsuo once more took the basket and the instruments from him and bid him go to sleep. Sighing, he did as he'd been bid, expecting more of the boredom he'd suffered from before. He never noticed when sleep overtook him.

During the night, he was awakened three more times to take readings. After the last of these, he was sure sleep wouldn't come again. He couldn't help but wonder how much longer it would be until the sun would rise.

"Boy." He stiffened at the low voice, not having heard from Asaka since early that evening. "Go below."

Bowing gratefully, he stood up and began folding his blankets. Mitsuo took charge of his basket and, after bowing deeply to Asaka, headed for the ladder. Toshi rushed to follow, the cold coming from the deck into his feet prodding him on. Mitsuo silently waited for him by the door on the deck below and had him go through first. He gave him the basket to take in with him as he opened the door into his room.

Hurrying inside, he placed his basket in one corner and then ran to his futon. He unfolded his blankets and added them to those already there. He snuggled under them as fast as he could.

While wiggling inside his blankets to warm up faster, he noticed he was alone in the room and that his table was empty. He tried to hold back his disappointment, instead concentrating on hunting in his blankets for his leather strip so he could retie his hair into its usual ponytail. He'd just finished tying it on when the door to his room opened. He smiled as he watched Miko come in carrying two buckets of steaming water.

"Good morning, Toshi-kun," she said.

"Good morning, Miko-san."

The geisha carefully set the buckets against the wall and then closed the door. "How are you feeling?" she asked.

He found that to be an odd question. "I'm feeling fine."

"I'm glad to hear it." Blue light flared from her mask's eye slits. "Come and bathe while I go get your supper. You won't want the water to get cold."

"Whatever you say." Gleefully watching the water steam from the buckets against the wall, he stripped. Though bathing was normally done in the evening to take away the cares of the day, his body was too cold to care. In a rush, he dashed across the room and bathed. He was still at it when Miko reentered the room.

Rinsing off the rest of the soap, he made a dash for his covers. He shivered as he tried to wrap the blankets back around him. As he settled in, Miko poured him some tea. "How did it go last night?" she asked lightly.

He reached for the filled cup, his teeth threatening to start chattering. "It went fine, no trouble. Asaka-sama has changed my schedule, though."

"I see."

He stopped in the midst of gulping down his tea as he came to realize from her tone that the geisha already knew this. He stared at her, wondering if perhaps she'd had anything to do with it. "Miko-san, do you know why it was changed?"

"Surely, you don't believe that Lord Asaka confides all of his secrets to me, do you?" Miko's head tilted slightly to one side as she spoke, a teasing tone lacing her words.

"This is important to me." He ended up regretting his hasty words as he saw her amusement turn suddenly serious.

"I asked him to do it, Toshi-san. I was concerned about you."

"I don't understand," he said. "I'm fine, aren't I?" He felt a different kind of cold flow through him.

"Yes, Toshi-kun, you're fine. Now."

A shiver coursed down his spine as he realized what she'd just implied. He recalled how he'd found himself on deck rather than in his room.

"You really should eat," she suggested. "Especially after all the trouble I've gone through—"

He could hear Miko's mood growing lighter. Grateful for it, he reached for the food before him.

While he ate, Miko excused herself and left with the two used buckets of water. She returned within a few minutes carrying her koto. She sat down with it in a corner of the room and began to play a soothing melody.

He slowed his eating and watched the geisha play. As he did so, an image overrode his sight of her—it was one of a real woman, not the false one he could see on the Noh mask. Though it frightened him that he was doing this, since he knew not where the image had come from, he was loath to dismiss it. In a way, it pleased him greatly to believe the beautiful face was really hers.

"Is something wrong?" Miko asked. The image dissipated.

He felt a frown smooth out as she stopped playing. He wasn't sure how to answer her question, especially as she continued studying him with her intense blue stare.

"I was just thinking about how—how beautiful you must have been before—" He stared at the floor, embarrassed by his admission.

"I thought you said you were only fifteen?"

He looked up at her question, not completely understanding it until he realized what kind of thoughts she had assumed had been his. Guiltily, though he'd done no such thing, he looked away, his cheeks growing hot.

Miko's laughter filled the room, the sound of cascading silver bells adding to her ringing merriment. "You have thought of those types of things before, haven't you, Toshi-kun?"

He stared at her, shocked she was asking him this. Swallowing hard, he opened his mouth to reply and found it had turned unusually dry. "I—"

Miko's laughter filled the room again. "That's nothing to be ashamed about. It's only natural for strong, growing boys to have such thoughts. I'm sure you've even been the subject of such thoughts for many developing girls."

"Miko-san!" The geisha's mood had definitely improved from the day before, but he wasn't sure he would survive it. With growing panic, he decided to change the subject. He brought up the first thing that popped into his mind. "Could I see you without the mask, Miko-san?"

Miko's laughter dissipated. She stared at him with subdued amusement. "I would prefer not to do that, if you don't mind," she answered. "Are you finished with your meal?"

"But why not?" he pressed. "I'm used to you now. I know what to expect."

She said nothing for a few moments. She rose from the floor and gathered his dishes. "I'll be honest with you. While it's true at first I wore this mask to ease your fears, I no longer wish to do without it. I realize it's pure vanity, but I just can't bring myself to destroy the illusion I've created for you. You aren't like the rest of us here. You're different. Unless you insist, I'd prefer for things to remain as they have been."

He sighed, disgusted with himself. He would have done better if he'd been born without a tongue.

"I'm sorry, Miko-san. I didn't mean—I just seem to do it all the time." He looked away. "I'm really sorry."

"Don't worry about it," she said brightly. "I don't want you to change. It brings me great pleasure to know you feel comfortable enough with me to say or ask whatever is on your mind."

"I—"

Miko reached over and placed two of her fingers across his lips.

"It's all right!" She stared into his brown eyes until he nodded. "Why don't you get dressed while I get rid of these dishes? You wouldn't want to tempt a woman for too long with all that manly flesh."

Against his will, he felt himself blushing. He knew she couldn't see any part of him through the pile of blankets except for his hands and face. As soon as she left, though, he rushed to get dressed.

When she returned, Miko went back to playing the koto. She played for a time, on occasion adding her clear voice to the plucked tunes. He was more than happy to just sit and listen. His stomach was full, his body warm; and it fascinated his mind to watch her fleshless fingers move over the koto's strings.

"Toshi-kun, have you ever played Go?" Miko asked.

"I've played it a couple of times." He didn't add he'd not been good at it. Master Shun had always taken great delight in trouncing him and then pointing out his lack of skill.

Miko left with the koto and returned carrying a wooden block measuring half an arm in length and height. Thin, black lines crisscrossed its lacquered surface, breaking it up into small squares. The geisha set the block in front of him and sat down on the other side. She pulled open a small drawer on the block's side and removed two silk bags from inside it.

"Would you prefer black or white?" she asked.

"Whichever."

Miko handed him a bag filled with shiny black pebbles. It wasn't long after they'd started to play that he knew he didn't have a chance of beating her. She was even better at the game than Master Shun.

"How long will it be before we reach the islands, Toshi-kun?"

"Huh? Oh, uh, we should get there late tonight or early tomorrow morning, I think." Since she'd brought the topic up, his curiosity egged him on. "Miko-san, why does Asaka-sama want to go there?"

Miko's gaze rose to meet his, the game momentarily forgotten. "Long ago, our lord was given a very sensitive and vital mission. An object thought lost had been found, and it was his task to retrieve it and bring it back to its rightful owner."

"What was it that was lost?"

Miko turned her head away from him. "That I can't tell you."

Ignoring his confused look, she made her next move on the board. Her white pebbles had surrounded a group of his and she took them off the board. He didn't press her, but stared instead at the Asaka family crest painted on the side of the board. Again he had the feeling he'd heard the name and seen their crest somewhere before. "Miko-san, where are the Asaka clan's lands?"

"They're located in a beautiful area in northern Tsuyoi." The light in her eyes flashed.

"Tsuyoi?" He felt his eyes grow wide as vague recollections finally came to light.

"Yes."

He looked away, his heart beating fast as he remembered where he'd seen the crest before. His gaze lingered again on the three moons inside their circle.

"Master Shun came from a fishing village in southern Tsuyoi," he said quietly. "He used to like to remind me how hard life had been when he was a child. How I had it so much better than he had by living in the city and being an apprentice. How I would never have to face the violence and injustice that at times went on in the far provinces."

He sighed. "On days when the sun had been hidden by clouds and rain and he'd drunk too much, he would whisper to me about one of the lords in Tsuyoi. He'd almost be crying as he told me of the great misfortune that had befallen the entire clan and any who'd been closely associated with it, just as fortune had started smiling on them. The whole clan was slaughtered, brutally. They'd been treated as common criminals, not even given the option of committing *seppuku*, ritual suicide. He—he'd sometimes draw something on paper over and over again. It looked just like that." He pointed to the crest on the game. His voice faded to a whisper, as he remembered the fear he had seen in his master's eyes whenever he'd spoken of that particular time.

"Asaka-sama felt the clan pass on, Toshi-kun," Miko said quietly. "I saw it. I think with us already dead, it had forged in him a spiritual connection to his family. The experience almost destroyed him, and with him, our hopes for redemption." Miko stared at her empty hands. "At his command, we returned home. We knew it was too late, but we went anyway."

He held his breath, wanting, yet not wanting her to go on.

"Asaka allowed none of us to go with him to shore. He shut us all from his heart." Her past pain was almost palpable. "We feared for him throughout the night he spent there. We weren't sure what he would do. We weren't sure what would happen to us if he were gone. Ours was a remote clan, and just the fact we'd been given this task had brought us so much honor. But now....

"Our lord returned to us just before dawn. And with a dead voice I pray never to hear again, he told us of the clan's murder, of our loss of honor. He then showed us a copy of the proclamation naming us all traitors of the realm. It told how the Asaka clan had been plotting to assassinate one of the great lords. And such a crime carried the direst of penalties. It meant the death of every man, woman, and child with the name Asaka."

He paled, realizing that all this time, Master Shun had been telling him the truth and not some fabricated tale to pass the time. The penalty for treason was a dishonorable and painful death. Those given the command to carry out the sentence would scour the land until they were sure the traitorous bloodline had been stomped into extinction.

"The proclamation blamed our lord for the plot," she said. "The cited crimes against him were pure lies, yet we could do nothing. We were no longer alive, and the destruction of the clan had already occurred." Miko sighed. "We have lingered this long because of Ietsugu…and *for* him as well. To complete our mission is our only means to try to clear the Asaka family name and restore its stolen honor. Our lord is the only person of his clan still on this plane. Only through him has the family a chance of reclaiming what's been lost."

Silence hung between them. It was thick and filled with emotion. His importance in their quest lay heavily on him, more so than it ever had before. He glanced up at Miko, but averted his gaze when it met hers. He stared at the board again, sure she would leave but knowing of no way to make her stay. Without much hope, he reached up to the board and made a move that captured three of her pieces. He looked up and almost grinned as he saw her hand shift to make a move of her own.

Chapter 9

Each time Toshi was awakened up on deck that evening, it got harder for him to fall back asleep. Every reading showed them to be that much closer to the islands and the samurai's goal. He found a spark of excitement kindling inside him. Soon they would reach the end of the quest. Soon, this would all be over.

"Sir!"

He sat up at the shout, its eager tone undeniable. He spotted one of the crew standing at the front of the ship, pointing out into the darkness. The samurai stood, his gaze riveted in the direction the skeleton was pointing. Toshi's spark of excitement grew, though he himself could see nothing in the darkness that consumed everything beyond the immediate area of the glowing ship.

A low murmur swept through the men rowing below. Their oars came to a stop as all their heads turned to stare at Asaka. A palpable current of excited tension permeated the ship. Asaka finally spoke. "Kenshiro-san, stay as lookout. Kojiro-san, proceed as you will."

Having been given control, the steersman barked out several commands to the men below. As the rowing began anew, Kojiro called for Toshi to bring him the map. After retrieving it from his basket, he unrolled it as he rushed over. His hands shook as he held the map up for the steersman to see.

"Would you like me to take another set of readings?"

The steersman's yellow-lit eyes looked down into his young eager face. "No, that won't be necessary."

Nodding, he continued holding the map up for him. The steersman stared at the paper for a minute and then looked up into the darkness beyond. "You've actually brought us here." There was a strange tone in the steersman's voice. "Perhaps it wasn't all luck after all."

Toshi glanced up into the skeleton's face, surprised. He realized this was as close to an apology as the man would ever give. He bowed, trying to hide the small, pleased smile growing on his lips.

Rolling up the map, he returned to his blankets. Without comment he gave the map to Mitsuo and then sat down. He gazed past the front of the ship, waiting for them to reach the first of the Shakuti Islands.

In less than a half-hour, the steersman called for the rowers to slow down. A deep shadow amidst the night's darkness outlined an island for his expectant gaze.

As the island loomed ever closer, the ship slowed even more. Sand scraped the bottom of the ship as the steersman brought the craft to a halt not far from the beach.

An unusual silence settled over the ship. He hardly dared breathe, waiting to see what would happen next. The splashing of lapping waves on shore sounded loud to his ears.

"We have a few precious hours before dawn," Asaka said. "This is but the first of the Shakuti chain. There is no guarantee what we seek will be here. But we won't be sure unless we are thorough. We have waited a lifetime for this moment. Let us prove we are worthy of our trust!"

As one, the entire crew bowed to their lord. Not sure how he fit into all this, Toshi hurried to do the same. He was startled as he watched Asaka return the crew's bow with one as deep as their own.

The deck then filled with a flurry of activity. Ten men disappeared into the ship. Within moments, some of them returned carrying ropes, which they secured to the left side of the ship. The rest of the men returned soon after with the skiff that had been used to bring him aboard. As they carried it over to the rope-rigged side, he wondered how in the world they'd gotten the thing below and back up again.

The small boat was lowered into the water.

At a nod from the samurai, four of the men climbed over the side of the ship into the skiff. Within moments, they had disengaged it from the ship and rowed toward shore. The rest of the crew, except for three eager souls, lined up against the rail, waiting for their turn to be taken to this island. Those last three jumped overboard and swam to shore instead.

After four trips, the skiff, manned by one of the crew, returned to settle with a soft clunk against the side of the ship. Asaka, who had sat still through all the previous commotion, stood. Toshi found the samurai's green-lit gaze aimed in his direction.

"Boy, Mitsuo will remain here with you. You will stay in your quarters while we're gone," he commanded. "Under no circumstances are you to attempt to go ashore. Is this understood?"

"Hai, Asaka-sama." He bowed, overwhelmed by disappointment. Now that he had been forbidden to go, he found the island calling to him. It told him he should leave this place of strangeness and death and join it—a place of the living.

His gaze jealously following Asaka, he folded his blankets. As he watched the samurai and the others row away, though, it occurred to him his job for Asaka was almost over. As soon as they found what they were looking for, he would navigate them back to the city and he would be free. Suddenly lightheaded, he sent out a long prayer for the quick recovery of the item they'd all come such a long way to find. He then followed Mitsuo below.

The old samurai opened the door to his room for him and, after taking a quick look inside, let him rush in. Mitsuo closed the door behind him. Toshi ran to his waiting futon, dropping the folded blankets on top of it. As he twisted for a moment to put his basket on the floor, he heard something whoosh past his ear and hit the planking not far away from him. A slim, wobbling knife protruded from a glowing board.

He whirled around as he heard something land behind him. He took a step back, stunned by what he found there. A figure dressed in black straightened up before him. A slit in the stranger's mask showed two dark sockets with points of intense red light shining from within.

A bubbling scream rose up in his throat as he recognized the ninja before him. Ninja were hired spies and assassins, people highly skilled at their craft and trained from birth. And this one was the very crewman who had so filled him with fear when he'd first come aboard. Yet, before his scream could cut loose, a black-clad fist appeared from nowhere and sent him sprawling across the room.

Blood filled his mouth—he'd bitten his cheek upon colliding with the wall. Dizzy, battered, he tried hard to recover enough of his breath to try to scream. He attempted to dodge to the side as he saw the black-swathed demon pounce.

He had barely been able to get up on his feet when a steel-like hand clasped his throat. Bolts of numbing cold flooded into him and paralyzed his voice. With horrified eyes, he stared at the ninja's glowing gaze. He struggled to tear the clamped hand from his throat even as he felt the cold mercilessly sap his strength away.

Helpless and full of despair, he reached out to the wall beside him and pounded on it as hard as his waning strength would allow. He was about to strike the wall a third time when the ninja's free hand snapped out and latched onto his wrist. Deep, numbing cold coursed through it, paralyzing it almost instantly.

Toshi struggled to breathe, his insides deadening from the eerie cold still pouring like water into him. He could no longer move, his gaze frozen on the face of his assailant. His vision blurred even as the thought of his impending death got pushed aside for a moment as the ninja's red, glowing eyes were replaced by those of a normal, living man. He could see flesh where moments before there had only been dark emptiness. With an odd clarity, he recalled the visions he'd had of both the geisha and her lord. Filled with wonder, he felt his consciousness falling into a great abyss.

A warrior's yell kept him from going under as the door into the room was kicked open. The ninja shifted, giving Toshi a blurred view of the door. Blinking, he lay amazed as a strong, fierce-looking old man drew a katana from his scabbard.

"*Traitor!*" With another ferocious yell, the bent old man rushed forward, holding his sword in both hands above his head.

The ninja didn't move, his hand still clamped around Toshi's neck. The old man's naked blade rushed down toward the assassin's head. At the last second, the ninja jerked aside and avoided contact with the weapon. Toshi was yanked upwards as the old samurai lunged to strike again.

Without a touch of doubt, he was sure the ninja was about to kill him by using his body to block the warrior's next blow. Looking for the end, he was amazed as he saw the sword enter his field of vision from behind and it abruptly switched directions to cut through the ninja's lower arm. He felt himself falling.

The ninja leapt from him, reaching into his clothing with his remaining hand. As the hand came out, the ninja launched three metallic objects at Toshi's prone form.

The sound of silver bells filled the room as Miko threw herself on top of his body. Mitsuo leapt forward, clanging two of the shuriken out of the air. The third embedded itself into Miko's clothes.

Mitsuo stepped toward the ninja, his sword held threateningly before him. The ninja jumped back and threw something on the floor. The old samurai hesitated as a flash of light, followed by smoke, went up around the assassin. Not waiting for the smoke to dissipate, Mitsuo swung his katana, but the ninja was already gone. Mitsuo rushed out of the room after him.

Toshi swooned as he tried to understand what was happening. Cold surrounded his body, though it no longer issued from the skeletal hand, which was still clamped to his throat. He felt nothing as Miko wrapped him in blankets and then struggled to pick him up.

Chapter 10

"I can't breathe! I can't breathe!" Toshi clawed at his throat, sure the ninja's fingers would continue tightening until they cut into his flesh. He thrashed, fighting for his life, as someone grabbed his wrists and pulled his hands away from his aching throat. "No!"

"Toshi-kun. He's gone! Toshi-kun."

He opened his eyes, confused by the familiar voice, still sure he was dying. He found Miko sitting beside him, fighting to keep hold of his wrists.

"It's all right, Toshi-kun," she said. "It's over. It's all over now."

He frowned at her, his mind a jumble of fear and pain. Only as she continued talking to him, soothing him, did his struggles dwindle to nothing. Gently, Miko moved his hands to his sides and released his wrists. She then reached out to touch his neck, and he flinched at the contact. The burning ache he felt there was numbed.

"Do you think you can sit?" she asked.

He nodded and then tried to sit up. The geisha reached to steady him as he wobbled. As soon as he could sit on his own, she let go and placed a cup of warm tea in his hands. He raised it to his lips but didn't drink as he noticed the circle of skeletons standing around them. Baffled, he looked at Miko, his question plain on his face.

"They're here for your protection," she informed him. "We've been unable to capture the ninja so far."

"Oh." The details of the attack crowded in for his attention.

"Come, drink your tea. Your body needs it," she pressed. "As it is, it's grown a little cool waiting for you."

He stared at his cup, hearing a hint of her past worry in her voice. He drained it dry.

"It'll be dawn very soon," Miko said. "We should try to return you below. Do you feel well enough to try to walk?"

He thought about it for a moment and then nodded. As the night breeze nuzzled his face, it occurred to him to wonder why they had brought him outside while the assassin was still free. He stood up gingerly, not able to come up with an answer. He felt a little woozy, but didn't fall. Out of the corner of his eye, he noticed Mitsuo standing nearby, eyeing him strangely. He turned to study the old skeleton, knowing he had been the one to come to his rescue. What Toshi couldn't understand was why his mind insisted on telling him it had been a man of flesh and blood, not one of bone.

"Toshi?"

He tore his gaze away from Mitsuo and turned to look at Miko's smiling mask.

"Can you manage?" she asked.

He nodded.

Miko and Mitsuo took charge of his blankets and teapot before slowly steering him toward the ladder. The circle of guards walked with them, half-jumping down to the deck below to cover him as he descended.

Toshi felt awkward at all the attention, but a part of him was greatly relieved by it. He watched with detached interest as two of the crew entered the small hallway and inspected it top to bottom. It seemed ludicrous for them to go to such pains for him, a mere peasant. If only Master Shun could have seen this. Only after they'd thoroughly checked the hallway and his room was he allowed to go inside.

Mitsuo and Miko spread his blankets out on his futon and then helped wrap them about him. He huddled inside, feeling colder than normal. Mitsuo bowed to him and then left. Miko lifted the table and set it in front of him before serving him more tea.

"I thought I was dead." His voice was raspy and sounded strange to his ears. "If not for you and Mitsuo-san, I would've been…"

Miko glanced up at him. Her eyes glowed for a moment and then dimmed. "You saved yourself, Toshi-kun. If you hadn't pounded on the wall, none of us would have realized anything was going on until it was too late."

He blushed. "Yes, I know that, but you could have chosen not to come," he argued. "Thank you for saving my life." He bowed to the floor, his throat constricted with pain and emotion. He'd never been important enough to anyone to save before. He wasn't sure if he could deal with it. When he sat back up, he noticed Miko's eyes were sparkling.

"More tea?" she asked.

He nodded and then looked away.

"Your breakfast is very likely ruined, and it will take me a while to make more. I do have some rice cakes left over from yesterday, though," she said. "They might appease your young man's appetite until I can ready something a little more appropriate."

"You don't have to go through all the trouble, Miko-san. Rice cakes alone would be fine." He saw Miko's head tilt in doubt. "Honest, Miko-san."

"Keep warm, then. I'll only be a moment." As she stood, there was a knock at the door. He held his breath as it opened. Asaka walked into the room, and Toshi instantly bowed to the floor. Sitting back up, he saw Mitsuo glance into the room before closing the door again.

"I've been advised an incident occurred here today," Asaka stated. The demon mask's eye slits filled with green as his voice echoed in the room.

"That is so, Lord," Miko answered.

Asaka stared at the geisha for a moment before riveting his attention back in Toshi's direction. "Explain."

"I was attacked by a—a ninja, Asaka-sama." Toshi kept his nervous gaze attached to the floor.

"Why aren't you dead?"

He looked up, caught off-guard by the question. He felt a chill run down his spine as it occurred to him that perhaps Asaka was disappointed.

"Miko-san and Mitsuo-san disturbed him before he was able to..." He stared at the floor again as the samurai grunted in acknowledgment.

Hearing Asaka move, he looked up. To his surprise, the samurai sat down, armor and all, on the room's cold floor. Silence hung heavily in the room as Toshi waited for him to speak.

"A number of things have been revealed by the attack upon your person," he said. "The first and most important of these is the fact we've been under constant surveillance and efforts of sabotage by one of our own. This clears up many things. But, don't concern yourself with it—steps shall be taken to insure your continued safety."

Toshi bit his lip, realizing the samurai believed there might be more attacks. The feeling of a cold, undead hand clutching his throat played in his mind. He could smell his own fear.

"As the search for the proper island continues, four men will be posted to your side whenever you are above," Asaka said. "Furthermore, you will also be given instruction on the proper use of a sword." He paused for a moment. "We can't afford to lose you, so quick proficiency will be expected."

Toshi's gaze rose, his face full of amazement. "But Lord, I'm not—"

"Samurai?" Asaka made a dismissing gesture with his hand. "That is irrelevant. Your safety must be maintained, and the best way to assure that is by making sure you are capable of defending yourself to some degree, at least until help might arrive. In any case, you won't be given a true sword, but a *boken*. However, do not make the mistake of underestimating it solely because it isn't made of steel. When wielded by skilled hands, a boken can prove as deadly as the sharpest katana."

Toshi diverted his worried gaze from the samurai's fierce mask. "Yes, Lord."

"Your lessons are to begin immediately. Take care to learn well all that will be shown to you."

"Hai." He bowed to the floor as Asaka stood. He didn't raise his head until he heard the door close.

"You have been greatly honored, Toshi-kun," Miko said.

He wondered how what she said could possibly be true.

"Our lord is trusting you to learn, trusting you with the responsibility of helping to protect yourself instead of wrapping you up in a blanket of guards like a helpless concubine."

"You truly think so?" He wasn't so sure he should believe her.

Her tone was serious when she answered him. "Well, you would make a rather homely concubine." Her sleeve rose to hide her mask's mouth.

Though he tried to, he could do nothing to stop the hot flush settling lightly on his cheeks.

"Let me go and get your breakfast so you can eat. I'm sure you'll be very busy soon."

Miko was only gone for a few minutes before she returned with the promised rice cakes and a fresh pot of tea. As he forced the last of them down his aching throat, there was a knock. Miko stood up to answer the door. She opened it a crack and looked to see who was there before opening it the rest of the way.

Mitsuo stood framed by the doorway and bowed to them both. A hint of white light flashed in his dark eye sockets.

"I have been asked to begin your lessons now." He stepped inside, and Miko closed the door.

"I had hoped it would be you, Mitsuo-san," Miko said. Bright blue light filled her eyes as she turned toward Toshi. "Though he will never admit it, Mitsuo is a superbly skilled swordsman. Many have come from far away just to try to convince him to teach them his Wind Slicing technique."

Toshi stared at Mitsuo's stooped form and tried to picture him as the great man Miko professed him to be. He remembered, then, the visage of the old man who'd rescued him from the ninja.

Mitsuo bowed slightly in Miko's direction, acknowledging her flattery but making no comment.

Toshi stood up as Miko carried what few objects he had in his room to the far corners of it. Without preamble, Mitsuo approached him and held out a curving piece of carved wood.

"This is now yours," he said. "You will keep it with you at all times, under all circumstances, even while you sleep."

Trying not to hesitate, Toshi took the offered boken.

"Some will tell you this is just a stick, a toy sword, but they're wrong. As of this moment, you'll work at making that boken a part of you, an extension of yourself. You must work at making its use as natural to you as it is for you to use your legs for walking."

From where his katana normally hung, Mitsuo drew a boken of his own. Its scarred surface spoke of years of use, of an uncountable number of battles. Mitsuo's gaze never strayed from Toshi's face, even as he began to whirl the wooden blade. With dazzling speed, the stooped samurai spun it before Toshi's widening eyes. A white flash in Mitsuo's eyes drew his attention even as he felt a soft tap on each of his shoulders. He'd never even seen the blade as it had thrust out to touch him.

Mitsuo said nothing as he stopped what he'd been doing and took a step back. Miko clapped happily from the corner in which she'd chosen to sit. Before long, she was laughing as well at the continued expression of wonder etched on Toshi's face.

"Miko-san, if you would take these?" Mitsuo pointed to Toshi's blankets.

Still too amazed to protest, Toshi didn't stop the geisha as she took all of his blankets and pulled the futon to the side. He scrambled to put on his sandals, already shivering from his lack of protection from the cold. With prickles of excitement, he emulated the position Mitsuo showed him.

The old samurai had him repeat the patterns he taught over and over again. The seemingly simple maneuvers worked muscles in his arms and legs he'd never used before. Each movement demanded his absolute concentration. Mitsuo insisted he mimic him perfectly.

By the time they stopped for lunch a thin sheen of sweat covered Toshi from head to toe. Shivering beneath his returned covers, he tried hard to dispel the cold that had seeped into him despite his exertions. He praised the gods for the warmth of well-made tea.

After lunch, he repeated the maneuvers he'd learned that morning. He followed through each of them, frustrated by his lack of grace and skill. He felt like a monkey trying to pretend he was a crane. Miko encouraged him and sometimes outright embarrassed him. Mitsuo didn't dissuade her from doing so, or ever complain when he fumbled the routines. Instead, he would smack Toshi's arms and legs into their correct positions with his boken. He had him do the routines over and over, smacking him without a word to correct his movements and then changing to another pattern without warning.

By dinnertime, Toshi felt thoroughly achy and sore. Mitsuo left him then, pausing at the door to tell him he had done tolerably well.

The praise barely registered in his brain, though a part of him was pleased by it. Mostly, he wanted nothing more than to give in to his aching weariness.

"Your bath water should be almost ready," Miko said. "I'll go get it for you. I'll only be a moment."

"Hai." He took the subtle hint and began undressing. Once she returned with the water, he felt her gaze on him throughout the entire bath. It made him feel flattered and embarrassed all at the same time.

As he dressed, Miko placed a fresh cup of tea on the table. Gratefully drinking it down, he sat still as she stepped around him to comb out his hair. "Miko-san?"

"We'll be exploring a second island tonight," she said. "What we sought wasn't to be found on the first."

Though he tried to fight against it, his curiosity overcame him. "Does everyone know what we're looking for?"

Miko sighed. "Yes and no. We know what it is, but not why it's important. Our mission was solely to find the object and deliver it, not actually understand what it is for. We heard many rumors of strange things going on when we arrived to receive our mission, but it is hard to say if the two are related. You see, the *Daimyo*, the great lord of the area, had vanished months before. Many said he had been killed, while others thought he had purposely disappeared as a test to see what his three main vassals would do in his absence. We weren't there long enough to learn much more than that, though. And only Asaka-sama was allowed to see the missing Daimyo's main vassal. I believe Asaka-sama was told what purpose the object holds; but even after all this time he has never spoken of it, though it has already resulted in more spilled blood than any item should ever be worth."

He searched for some way to ask what it looked like without seeming to. He'd come no closer to finding a way to do so when he felt the telltale sensation announcing the surfacing of the ship.

"Come. We'll want to get you above before they're ready to leave."

He put on his sandals as Miko took charge of his blankets. Feeling a little awkward, he still made sure to bring his boken along.

Toshi followed Miko out of the room and said nothing as Mitsuo joined them. Toward the end of the small hallway, they were met by three of the crew. They surrounded him as they all exited into the starry darkness outside.

Nervous and a little tense from both the guards' presence and the boken in his hands, he climbed up onto the higher deck. All of them bowed to Asaka, who was seated; and he acknowledged them with a small nod.

The skiff was already being brought up from below even as the rest of the crew readied themselves to go to shore. As he waited for Miko to set out his blankets, Toshi turned to look past two of his guards to try to catch a glimpse of the island before them. He couldn't make out much about it in the darkness, but he doubted it would amount to much in daylight. This brought a suddenly disquieting thought to him. How long had it been since he'd seen the sun? How long had it been since he'd felt its warming rays on his skin? How much longer might it be before he would do so again, if ever?

He slumped down onto his blankets, looking at no one. Surely, he only felt like this because he was so tired. Yet, what he'd give to sit for an hour under an open sunlit sky. He would be free soon; his time would come. He just had to remember that. He told himself this over and over until he started to believe it. At least he'd be able to sleep under an open sky. It would have to do for now.

Lying down, he couldn't help but notice when Miko left him to have some quiet words with Asaka. His ears burned with curiosity, but he couldn't even catch a hint of what was being said. Their conversation didn't last long. She returned to his side, and the samurai stood to go to the deck below.

Chapter 11

Toshi stood up, his muscles protesting, and took a deep lungful of the pre-dawn air. He stared for a moment toward the east, knowing he was about to miss another sunrise. "Miko-san?"

"Yes?"

Her eyes flashed toward him making him wonder if she already sensed this would be one of his uncomfortable questions.

"Why don't you stay up during the day?" He'd asked her this once before but hoped this time she would choose to answer.

Miko didn't reply immediately, but instead busied herself for a few moments with the folding of his blankets.

"That's a little hard to explain. You see, we don't know if it's possible for us to withstand the touch of the sun. None of us has ever tried it. We've always instinctively felt it would be bad for us, somehow. How and why, I do not know. But an inner dread against doing it has been in all of us from the very beginning. We were made in darkness, and it's to darkness we belong."

He felt a chill run down his spine.

"So, since we don't want to test the mercy of the gods," she added. "Let's get you below before we push our luck too far."

How could Miko and the others stand to live that way? He hoped the gods would have mercy on him and not allow him to become one of them.

He, Miko and the guards had just descended to the lower deck when the last of the crew returned from the third island. Asaka was the last to board, his twisted mask scanning the horizon as if looking for something only he would be able to see.

Toshi followed the geisha into the ship's interior. Mitsuo led the way, while the other three guards stayed by the entrance to the hallway.

"Go on ahead without me, Toshi-kun," Miko said. "I'll join you in a few minutes with some breakfast."

"Hai." After watching her disappear into the room next to his, he followed Mitsuo to his own quarters.

Mitsuo double-checked his room and then left him alone. Hurrying to his futon, he piled his blankets about him. He wondered about the type of life that had been forced on all those here, not only by their duty but also by their lord. One was supposed to give his life, if necessary, for his lord, but to be expected to serve him even after death? He wished he could understand all this better.

As he drank the miso soup Miko brought for him, he realized with a chill the number of times he'd come close to joining the ship's crew on a permanent basis. If the ninja had killed him, would he have been trapped here as well? Or did his death have to be by Asaka's hand so that the samurai's strong will would keep him from going on? And which would he prefer?

From these questions rose another, one he'd not yet had a chance to ask. Finishing his soup, he stared at his empty bowl in apprehension as he tried to figure out the answer for himself. Eventually, he gave up, knowing he couldn't.

"Miko-san?"

"You have a question, Toshi-kun?" She looked over at him, a teasing tone lacing her words.

He hesitated. He decided rather than blurt out his question as he usually did he'd try to work gradually up to it.

"There's something I don't quite understand. I've tried to figure it out, but I can't. I was hoping you might be able to help me with it."

"No. You can forget it," she said. "I won't divulge my age to you. I have a reputation to protect."

He stared at the geisha in open-faced confusion. "What?"

Miko began to laugh. "I'm sorry, Toshi-kun. I just couldn't help myself. You looked so serious I just couldn't resist. Though, in reality it doesn't seem like I've brought about much of an improvement—that is, unless you were thinking of going out and catching flies."

He realized his mouth was hanging open. He snapped it closed. He felt his face redden as he sat beneath her amused stare.

"Go ahead, Toshi-chan," she prompted. "You can ask me your serious question now. I promise to behave myself."

It took him several seconds to gather his scattered wits. He didn't miss her use of the personal endearment on his name. He decided to stop trying to work up to what he wanted.

"Miko-san, why would the ninja decide to try to kill me once we'd reached the islands? Why didn't he try before, when I was still sleeping here? He could have done it easily then. He could have done it when he stole the map, but he didn't. Why? There was no reason to wait, was there? Even without me here, I'm sure the steersman could have probably gotten you all back. Why try now?" He held his breath, waiting to see what the geisha would say.

"That's more than one question."

"Miko-san!"

Her laughter filled the room, her soft bells ringing as her body quivered with merriment. Though her laughter eventually subsided, he didn't hold much hope his questions would be answered. He was wrong.

"I have pondered these very questions for some time myself," she said seriously. "To be honest, I had expected you to ask me about them before now." There was a tinge of amusement mixed with mischief in her voice. "Why he didn't try to kill you before is something I can only speculate about. No one ever truly knows the mind of the ninja.

"I had thought at first the ninja believed, as many of us had, that our lord's idea of using the gaijin techniques to help us reach our goal would never work. You ended up proving the assumption wrong. Yet, by destroying the map, he would have stopped us from reaching our goal. He didn't kill you, believing the destruction of the map would be enough. It also left him someone to pin the blame on, and this would keep us from guessing one of the crew had been working against our mission from the start."

He shifted as he listened to her and gathered his blankets closer around him.

"You have to admit, if not for the fact you'd made a copy of the map, we might not have thought of blaming someone else. It would have been extremely difficult for us to believe without proof that one of us was willing to keep himself and the rest of us from going to the next life. It would have been much more comfortable to believe you had done the deed," she said honestly. "But, if the ninja had killed you outright, we would have had no choice but to face the fact one of us was a traitor."

The geisha grew silent for a moment as she took the time to smooth out her kimono. "Now, even after it was obvious his plan had failed, there was still a chance your copy of the map might be destroyed before we reached the islands or that the copy wouldn't be detailed enough to get us here. Mitsuo's presence also made it difficult to get at you, and all the crew were watching each other, trying to figure out who the traitor was.

"When we reached the first island, however, all things fell into place for him. Everyone but the three of us was supposed to go ashore. No one was watching anyone anymore. We'd been trying to get here for so long, we didn't consider that in the confusion that ensued we'd given him the perfect opportunity."

Deftly, the geisha lifted the still-steaming teapot and refilled his cup. He drank it slowly, giving himself time to think.

"But, Miko-san, since we were already here, why try and kill me? Like I said before, the steersman could get you back. And I can't believe he'd kill me out of spite."

"That, Toshi-kun, is easy," she said. "Though we are here, without you we would still be unable to claim our prize."

"*What?*"

The geisha raised her sleeve to cover her mask's lacquered mouth at his outburst. He was too startled to care.

"I don't understand."

"You're not supposed to."

"Miko-san!"

She laughed out loud. He let his shoulders slump forward as he realized he would learn nothing she didn't want him to know.

"Do not despair, Toshi-chan, you will know all there is to know when our lord deems you're ready."

"But, Miko-san—"

She leaned languidly forward, her eyes twinkling with mischievous merriment. "If you do well today, I might just deign to give you a few hints."

Having a feeling those promised hints would tell him a lot of nothing, he gave up and made a face at her. Miko howled with laughter as he stuck out his tongue. She made a grab for it, but he pulled it back before she could catch it. It wasn't long before he was laughing as heartily as she was.

A short while later, Mitsuo knocked on the door and came in. Leaving him to help Miko move the things out of the way, Toshi filched one more cup of tea in an attempt to fortify himself against the cold that would shortly be embracing him. As soon as Mitsuo was ready, he wove through the patterns taught to him the day before.

Miko was even more rambunctious than yesterday and used him as the object of jokes and rather graphic dirty stories. It was all he could do to continue his movements without falling into the trap of listening to her words. His sweeps began to falter as it proved more and more difficult to concentrate on what he was doing. He couldn't help but wonder why Mitsuo allowed her to do it. How was he supposed to learn if she distracted him all day long? Mitsuo always acted as if he heard nothing, though, of course, that didn't keep him from smacking Toshi every time he did something wrong.

Unlike the day before, Mitsuo allowed him to rest often, for which he was very grateful. Miko did her best to keep him full of hot tea.

Toward the end of the day, Mitsuo bid him go through his drills with his eyes closed. With a whisper, he told Toshi to begin, but to pay close attention to what each movement felt like and not to worry so much about whether he was doing them right.

Struggling to feel as he moved, Toshi found he was hesitating here and there, not able to see what he was doing. Mitsuo occasionally sent him directions or corrected his stance. He noticed Miko was silent throughout and was grateful. Even so, he found it difficult to focus on what he was doing.

As one stance shifted to the next, he felt his mind going with the flow of the movements. He could almost feel each muscle as it stretched and shrank at his command. Gradually, he reached the point where he thought he could even visualize his movements in his mind.

Just as he was getting comfortable with the sensations and what they meant, Miko's jokes began again. He began to be distracted despite his efforts. His movements started to falter.

"Do it faster," Mitsuo told him.

The close, unexpected whisper almost made him jump. Cursing at himself, he did as he was told. He tried even harder to shut Miko's voice from his mind.

"Faster."

Concentration bunched his brow as he struggled to comply with Mitsuo's request. Though Miko continued trying to attract his attention, he was working so hard he barely noticed her anymore.

Mitsuo didn't let up even when he tripped more and more during his movements. He even whacked himself with the boken. Each time he faltered, Mitsuo smacked him and forbade him to open his eyes before bidding him to move faster still.

"Stop. You've done enough," Mitsuo said, a note of regret in his voice.

Toshi came to a halt, feeling dizzy. He opened his eyes but found it didn't help at all. Forcing himself to stand up straight, he bowed in Mitsuo's direction and then stood, his muscles shaking, until his teacher had left the room. Only then did he allow himself the luxury of collapsing on the floor.

He lay still, his sweat turning cold on his skin, his breath moving in and out in ragged gasps. Miko appeared beside him and draped his blankets around him. Helping him to sit up, she pressed a cup into his hands.

Without hesitating, he raised the cup to his lips and drank. He gasped as the contents tore at his throat.

"What *is* this?" His throat still burned, though the liquid had already gone on its way. He felt it land heavily in his stomach.

"It's sake, silly-chan," she teased. "Here, have some more of it. It'll warm you right up. And, besides, you deserve it."

Wanting to ask what she meant by that but not quite daring to, he took a more cautious sip of his drink. The rice wine spread inside him, warming him up all over.

"Mitsuo-san is going to be bringing your dinner and bath in a few minutes. Until he returns, I want you to lie down and relax."

Wondering what Miko was up to, he nevertheless did as he'd been bid. The sake spread its warmth to every part of his body. He was wallowing in the sensation when something touched his leg. He jerked away from it.

"Lie still. I'm not going to hurt you," Miko said.

"But what are you—"

"Just be still," she insisted.

He couldn't help himself. Though he tried to relax and stay still, he tensed up every time she touched him. Miko's deft hands worked up and down his legs, massaging his muscles.

After a short while, she had him turn over and began working on his arms and back. Eventually, he relaxed as his muscles welcomed the expertly applied attention. The sensation of her soft hands merged with the sake-induced warmth running through him. His eyes grew heavy, and he never thought to stop them as they began to close. With a slight grin on his face, he headed toward unconscious bliss.

With a yelp, he jumped up to a sitting position, his flesh covered by goose bumps. His sides were still tight from where Miko had applied a tickling caress. "Miko-san!"

The geisha wagged a fleshless finger in his direction. "You're not supposed to go to sleep in here."

He looked away, feeling guilty, knowing he'd ignored Asaka's command. "Sorry, Miko-san."

"Well, I'll forgive you this time, but if it happens again…"

"It won't, Miko-san. It won't."

"All right, I'll believe you—this time. Now, your bath is here, so you'd better take it. And believe me, you need it." The geisha brought up her hand and used it to cover her mask's painted nose. "Yuck."

He got undressed even as Miko set out the food he'd not seen Mitsuo bring in. He was halfway to the buckets when all the geisha had said came back to him. He turned toward her despite the cold already clawing at his skin.

"You can smell?"

Miko turned to look up at him. "I'm only dead, Toshi-kun. Otherwise, I'm still the same."

"I…uh…oh, ah, sorry." He rushed to take his bath before he made any more of a fool of himself.

Chapter 12

Toshi ate with a sense of rising excitement. Soon, Asaka and his men would go looking for the object of their quest, bringing him that much closer to getting home.

When he felt the ship surface he lost no time in getting his things together. Though in his mind he knew it could be several days or even longer before the crew found what they sought, he couldn't quell the feeling that tonight would be the night. He also had the small hope, though he'd never admit it, that he might catch a glimpse of what they'd waited so long to find.

He, Miko and Mitsuo were met by three others on their way out. He gazed out at the newest island as they climbed the ladder to the higher deck.

This one was bigger than those he'd seen so far. He stared at its dark outline even as Miko set out his bedding. He was about to look away when something caught his attention. There, on the far edge of the island, he thought he'd seen a speck of light. Grabbing his basket, he took out the telescope and brought it to his eye.

He scanned back and forth between his guards' shoulders until he was able to catch the light within the glass. He stared at the soft flicker, barely able to distinguish the frame of the house it sat in. He flinched as a figure crossed the light. Taking the telescope from his eye, he stared in the direction of the house, realizing he'd just seen a living being. A living, breathing being….

An almost overwhelming sense of longing cut through him.

"Toshi-chan?" It was Miko.

He jumped at the touch on his arm.

"Toshi-chan, are you all right?" she asked. "You look as if you'd seen a demon."

He grinned. He wondered if she knew how odd the statement sounded coming from her.

"I'm all right, Miko-san," he assured her. "I was just a little surprised to find there are people on this island."

Her gaze ventured in the direction he'd been staring. "That could be a very good sign, Toshi-kun." Her mask turned toward him, the ship's eerie glow brightening the smile. "I'm sure you'll be among them again soon."

He couldn't help but wonder at her thoughts as her gaze returned again to the far-off point of light.

Chapter 13

A warm touch on his cheek brought Toshi's eyes open. A full moon stared down at him from a clear sky. Glancing to his right, he found Miko staring at him. She said nothing.

As she remained silent, a bolt of apprehension shot through him, bringing him entirely awake. He sat up, his gaze riveted to Miko's blue glowing eyes. She still said nothing.

After about a minute, he found he could stand her silence no longer. "Miko-san, what's wrong?"

As his whisper reached her, she turned her face away. Worry growing inside him, he also noticed the stiff backs of the guards around him.

"They've found it."

Though he barely heard what she said, he couldn't miss the excitement coloring her every word.

"They've found the object?" He found his own excitement building.

She slowly shook her head. "No, but they've found the place where it's being kept. It'll be up to you to get it."

A chill of thrilled fear coursed through him at her words. "Why? When?"

"You sound so eager," she accused.

"Miko-san!"

A long sleeve rose up to cover her mouth while the other reached for his hand. "That is not for me to decide. Our lord is there now, but has sent word he will return soon. I'm sure he will explain things to you then."

His gaze traveled past his ring of guards, and he stared out into the darkness. His skin turned cold as he wondered how long it would be before the samurai returned.

Time crawled by. A knot tightened inside him as Asaka continued to be absent. Though Miko had bid him try and go back to sleep, he found he couldn't. His mind wouldn't let him rest; it wouldn't stop trying to guess what was out there waiting for him, what it was an undead samurai couldn't deal with that he must.

After what felt like an eternity, he heard wood hitting the side of the ship. Asaka had returned. He sat up, tense, and watched as the samurai and the last of the crew climbed back on board.

Almost in agony with the rising suspense, he saw Asaka ascend to their deck and calmly move to sit on his stool. Feeling he would soon scream in frustration, Toshi watched as Mitsuo left his side to go confer with Asaka. He felt his mouth go dry as Mitsuo then left the deck.

He didn't know what to make of Mitsuo's departure and tried not to fidget as he waited for his return. The samurai sat still and implacable as always. The waiting threatened to drive Toshi mad.

Trying to divert himself, he glanced at the crew below. He noticed they were milling around, doing nothing. It was as if they felt as restless as he did. He caught them throwing glances in the direction of their lord and, surprisingly, also at him. He swallowed hard.

Mitsuo returned and brought with him some paper, a brush and ink. Saying nothing, Asaka took these things from him and ignored everyone as he began to write.

Toshi felt his nervousness rising, as well as that of the crew.

Asaka called out for one of the crew as he lay the brush and ink aside. The crewman hurried forward and bowed. The samurai held the newly written paper out to him and asked the man to verify it.

Toshi held his breath, watching as the crewman unfolded the paper and scrutinized what he found there. Before long, the crewman refolded the paper and handed it back, declaring it accurate.

Asaka dismissed the man and waited until he'd joined the rest of the crew before turning his green, glowing stare in Toshi's direction.

"Boy," he said.

Toshi's heart leapt into his throat at the call. Though he'd been expecting it, now that it was here he found he was suddenly unprepared. Hesitating despite the need for urgency, he rose to his feet as Miko softly squeezed his arm. He stumbled forward, followed by his guards as they maintained a protective circle around him.

He knelt and bowed to the floor, feeling the deck's unnatural coldness seeping into his hands and knees. He did his best to ignore it as a different sort of coldness grew inside him. "Yes, Lord?"

The green-lit gaze had followed him from where he'd sat and glowed even more brightly as the samurai leaned toward him.

"Prior to dawn, you will accompany me to shore. Until then, you will sleep."

Asaka's gaze left him.

He was caught offguard by the samurai's words. Confused but also knowing he'd just been dismissed, he bowed again before returning to his blankets.

He'd been told nothing! He'd already known he was to go ashore. Why keep him in the dark? Did Asaka not believe he'd do what was required if he knew of it before hand? And why wait until dawn?

His back and shoulders hurt from the tension. Looking at no one, he slipped back into his covers and tried to go to sleep as he'd been told. After much tossing and turning, he was able to fall into a light doze.

Chapter 14

"Toshi-kun."

He sat up in surprise, knowing that, despite what he'd thought, he'd fallen asleep after all. He found Miko sitting beside him. She offered him a cup of tea.

"I've brought some breakfast for you, Toshi-kun, and some lunch for you to take with you. Lord Asaka will be taking you to shore soon," she said.

He nodded, feeling stiff, and took the offered cup. He didn't taste the tea as he realized with a shiver that his new task was almost upon him. Without any real appetite, he reached for the soup and slices of fish Miko placed before him.

While he ate, the geisha slipped to sit behind him and combed his sleep-tousled hair. As she tied the leather thong about a fresh ponytail, he felt her lean close.

"Toshi-kun, we all have the greatest faith in you," she said. "I know you'll come through for us. We'll owe you our everlasting gratitude for what you are about to do." She hesitated. "Promise me you'll be careful."

A large lump formed in his throat. He felt a heavy weight settle on his shoulders as he realized what it was his little trip meant to them. For whatever reasons, they couldn't retrieve the object themselves. If he didn't get it for them they'd be doomed to stay as they were until they found someone who might. He couldn't find his voice to give Miko the promise she'd asked for, his new burden weighing him down. All he could do was nod.

He had just finished his meal when Asaka rose from his stool and beckoned for Toshi to come forward. Gulping down a last swallow of tea, he rose to his feet, his boken held tightly in a sweaty palm.

Trying not to let his fear get out of hand, he took hold of the small bundle Miko handed up to him. She rose and hung a cord around his neck, which was attached to a long bamboo container. He didn't look at her, his gaze glued to the armored figure who waited for him.

Taking a deep breath, he stepped up to join his lord. His ring of guards shifted with him, leaving the geisha behind, like the tide leaving the shore. He followed Asaka down the ladder and across the deck to the side of the ship. The skiff was still attached there, waiting for them.

"Sit there," Asaka said.

He stared at the latter in surprise as the samurai pointed to the bottom of the boat rather than to one of the seats. Doing as he'd been told, he climbed down into the waiting craft. Asaka followed him, taking the seat in front of his post. Two others scrambled in behind them.

Toshi tried hard not to gawk at the armored knees before him as it dawned on him Asaka was using the boat to protect him. He felt bumps cover his arms as he realized the threat of the ninja was still very real. A deadly, almost unstoppable threat when alive, how much more daunting would the assassin be now that he had returned from death. Only the fact they could travel faster than he could might hinder him at all. Toshi tried not to dwell on the danger.

The skiff was unhooked from the glowing ship and aimed toward shore. Toshi stared out over the dark water, trying to spot the house he'd seen the light in earlier that evening. He wondered if the occupants had seen the glowing ship, and, if so, what they'd thought of it. Would he have the chance to meet some living, breathing people again before his task was through?

It wasn't long before the bottom of the boat scraped sand. Mitsuo and the other guard jumped into the salty water and pushed the boat up onto the beach. The samurai bid Toshi to stand only after they'd come to a complete stop.

Three men surrounded him as he got out. Once they'd stood there for several minutes checking out the landscape, Asaka motioned the other two back to the skiff. Without a word, Mitsuo and the other crewman pushed the boat back into the water, got in it and rowed away. Surprised, Toshi watched them for a moment as they headed back toward the ship. He felt cold in the warm night.

"Boy."

"Hai!" He turned to face Asaka, a touch of fear staining his voice. The samurai reached into his armor and withdrew the piece of paper he'd worked up on the ship. He extended it out.

"There isn't much time, so listen well. This paper contains a rough sketch of the route you must take once it has become bright enough for you to travel." Asaka pointed to the trees behind him. "You will enter through here and then move north. The paper will show you what markers you need to look for on the way."

Toshi unfolded the paper but couldn't see much of what it contained in the dark.

"When you reach the temple grounds, you're to search for a black teakettle."

"A teakettle?" He bit his lip, realizing he'd asked the question out loud. He saw the samurai's eyes flare for a moment, but that was the only acknowledgment of his outburst.

"The kettle is emblazoned on one side with a golden sun. When you find it, remain within the confines of the temple grounds until we come to retrieve you at nightfall. Do you understand?"

He could feel the samurai's stare boring into his face. "Yes, Asaka-sama."

The samurai nodded and then walked to the water. "Remember, do not leave the temple grounds until we have arrived and called for you. You will be safe as long as you remain within its walls."

He followed Asaka to the water's edge feeling nervous. He had to look for a kettle? He needed to stay within the grounds? And what was it they couldn't deal with that they thought he could? He didn't understand any of it at all!

The samurai stepped into the water and headed out away from the shore. Toshi lost sight of him as he continued out into the fading darkness. He couldn't help but stare at the lapping waves until long after the samurai had gone beneath them. He jumped as Asaka's voice whispered toward him one last time.

"Tread lightly and stay sharp, Toshiro."

He stared into the darkness, bothered by the samurai's words. Shaking his head to try and dispel the unwelcomed feelings of fear and foreboding, he watched the glowing ship as it sank out of sight. Once it had gone, he proceeded up along the sandy beach and then sat down facing east. His brow was troubled as he awaited the dawn, his breakfast sitting like rocks in his stomach. He tried not to think about what was to come, even as his mind boggled over what he was being sent to retrieve.

The sky lightened, heralding the coming of the sun. The darkness was dispeled by spreading pinks with hints of oranges and reds. It'd been so long since he'd seen the dawn—a sight that had previously been so common he'd taken it for granted. He sent a prayer of thanks to the gods as the sun crested the horizon. His skin tingled in anticipation of its freely given warmth. The scent of the sea mixed with that of the growing vegetation not far up the beach proclaiming he was once again among the living. Despite his worries, he watched a crab as it was swept out onto the beach. The crab ran from the shoreline, moving sideways; its small eyes never wavering from Toshi's form.

He waited until the sun was free of the horizon before he opened the map the samurai had given him. To his amazement, he found that Asaka had gone to a great deal of trouble in making it. Not only had he provided plenty of markers by which Toshi could make his way, but he had approximated the distance between each one of them as well.

After studying the map for a couple of minutes, he folded it and slipped it inside the small bundle containing his lunch. Getting up, he dusted the sand from the back of his pants. He took one long, last look around the beach and then made his way toward the line of trees to the north.

Palm trees flourished next to tall pines and clumps of bamboo, making the deepening forest look like a hodgepodge garden. He stared hard at the palms, not used to seeing them next to these other plants he knew so well.

The day warmed with the humidity, and with it grew the buzzing of insects. He kept his gaze moving from place to place, slapping at the bugs when they drew near. His fear and uncertainty about his task abated somewhat as he was distracted by the unfamiliar sounds and smells surrounding him. He was a city boy, born and raised; and the island forest had a feel of magic to it, like those the heroes encountered in the old tales. Those forests had always been full of spirits and demons. He made sure to tread carefully and with respect.

By the time he found the old road as marked on the map, a thin layer of perspiration stood on his brow. He glanced upward and looked at the clear blue sky showing through the break in the trees. Stepping into a bright ray of sunshine, he let it warm his skin, though he already felt hot. He stood for a short while, enjoying it despite the humidity. He was aware of how not too long ago he had feared he would never feel the sun's touch again.

Moving out of the light into the cooler shadow of a tree, he brought up his bamboo container to his lips. The warm water felt good as it dribbled down his throat. Once he'd finished, he looked up and down the road and wiped his mouth dry. From the weeds growing in the middle of it, he doubted the road was often traveled.

Checking the map again, he turned to the right. After a few steps, he stopped, suddenly tempted to go the other way. If the road was basically straight, as it seemed to be, there was a chance it would lead him to the house he'd seen last night from the ship. Perhaps it was even part of a village. He could join the living again. Perhaps he could even find help there and return home.

His temptation soon melted to nothing. The others would find him. There was nowhere he could hide from them. But, in the end, that realization wasn't all that kept him from trying. Asaka, though he'd not said so directly, had given him a duty, one that was his sole responsibility to complete. He might not be samurai, but he still had honor. He'd been given a task by his present lord, and he would complete it. Surely then they'd send him home. Then he would be free.

Not looking back, he headed east. He made better time on the road than he had in the trees. The next marker on the map was a tree that was split in two. He had no trouble finding it. It stood on the right, dead and bent. Lightning had hit the once-majestic trunk and split it in two. In doing so, it had killed the tree—its path ended forever. He hoped this wasn't an omen of his own future.

The marker following the tree was supposed to be a small roadside shrine. He almost walked past it. Most of the small, ancient structure lay hidden behind a large clump of grass.

The wooden shrine was in bad need of repair. Toshi brought out his wrapped lunch and looked at what lay inside. Tearing off a small piece of his fish and another off one of his rice cakes, he reverently placed both within the shrine as an offering to the island's spirits. Clapping his hands together three times, he bowed his head in prayer and begged them to please tolerate his presence there and, if possible, extend to him their protection while he was there. He hoped they were listening.

Looking again at his map, he pushed his way through the tall grass and got behind the shrine and the large bush growing there. Orienting northwards, he was able to find a dirt path on the other side that was almost completely overgrown. Hoping it was the right way, he started off in the direction indicated by the map.

The path split three ways several lengths ahead, but the map indicated he should remain on the central one. An alteration in how the path was drawn told him to expect it to change, but he wasn't sure how. He'd gone only a short distance before the way became clearer, and he could see parts of a small lane. Its state varied widely as he went on, at times merely covered by short weeds while at others it was so overgrown he was forced to beat his way through.

Gradually, the lane sloped upwards until the grade became rather steep. Wiping away the sweat running down his face, he stopped and took a long swallow of water from the bamboo canteen. He wondered how much longer his climb was going to be—the fact the lane went up so steeply hadn't been a feature Asaka had been able to incorporate on the quick map. He'd already passed a couple of broken statues that had been used as markers for him. With a critical eye, he looked around him but could find no evidence anyone had been through the area in some time. If not for the markers on the map proving they'd been this way, he would have sworn no one had come through there in years. He shivered as he realized he was probably the first living being to travel this way in a long time.

Taking one more large swallow of water, he capped the canteen before going on. With a deep sigh, he held his boken tightly and beat at the vegetation blocking his way. His next marker looked to be a wide set of stone steps. He was beginning to think getting to them and then the temple would take forever when the wall of plants gave way to a clear path. He stopped, breathing heavily, and stared in surprise, as the steps he'd been looking for lay before him.

Smiling with relief, he wiped his forehead with a sweat-stained sleeve and started upwards.

Though he'd hoped to catch a glimpse of where he was going as he ascended the broad stone steps, he found he could see nothing past the drooping limbs of the low-hanging trees that were trying to make the stairs their own. Feeling his exertions catching up to him, he forced himself to hurry that much faster, eager to see the place the samurai had yearned so long to find.

The trees thinned as he climbed higher, giving him a partial view of the sky. The stairs narrowed and eventually stopped before a cobbled walkway. Looking down the walk, he could make out the battered remains of two white walls. Between them were the ruins of a once-formidable pair of doors.

His blood racing with curiosity and excitement, Toshi tread lightly down the walkway. As he came closer, he saw the beaten walls were heavily covered with ivy. Flashes of dark color showed on the walls in the places the ivy hadn't yet grown over. One of the doors lay splintered and rotting on the walk. The other still hung crookedly on its hinges. It gave the impression that the softest of breezes would make it fall.

As he came closer still, he wondered at the almost too-regular spacing of the broken tops of the walls. The door still standing had dents all over its surface and spoke of an occurrence he couldn't quite place.

He slowed, his hand on the hilt of his boken, the hairs on the back of his neck prickling. Something wasn't right. The place was old, that was obvious; but that wasn't it. There was just...something...

As he reached the fallen door, he gave it a wide berth, gaping at it, part of him half-expecting it to move. Dark stains covered the ground around the entrance. He did his best not to step on any of them. He innately knew those stains weren't natural. Whatever had been spilt there shouldn't have been able to withstand the years of rain and wear.

He turned around, sure someone was behind him. There was no one. Still staring the way he had come, he took a step back and tripped. Catching himself before he could fall, he looked down, berating himself for being a fool.

Metal glinted at him from the ground, where an old spear lay partially exposed in the dirt. A broken shaft lay close by, also partially buried. He stared at the broken weapon and then stepped away from it. His palms were moist, making his boken feel slippery. His breathing echoed in his ears, and he could smell his fear as it mixed with the scent of his sweat. He didn't want to think about what it appeared had happened in this place.

He stood beside the still-hinged door and found his gaze involuntarily drawn toward it. Its surface was pitted and rotting and looked to be filled with gouges that had softened over time. Dark words looked to have been hastily scribbled on its surface, but were no longer legible.

A loud squeak made him jump away from the door. Looking for the source of the sound, he found a pair of antagonistic, beady eyes staring at him from a clump of ivy on the wall. The rat hissed at him, coming out into the light. Toshi took a step back as he noticed the white-and-yellow object it held protectively in its paws. He'd been surrounded by skeletons for too long not to recognize the human bone for what it was.

His mouth grew dry, and suddenly it seemed he could see pieces of yellowed bones gleaming all around him. His eyes grew wide as he was overcome by the certainty the bones would soon start reaching toward each other to form a monster who would tear him limb from limb.

He closed his eyes and shook his head from side to side, trying to dispel his building fear. The things he had seen weren't moving. Chances were they weren't even the remains of the dead. It was daytime. He was safe. Demons of bone wouldn't dare to venture out to feel the sun's caress.

Opening his eyes, he forced himself to move. The rat hissed at him again before scurrying out of reach. He ignored it, trying only to think about his need to find the kettle before sunset. The others would come for him then, and he would be safe. He trembled at the thought of having to wait for them after dark in this dead, unknown place.

Avoiding everything but normal ground, he hurried through the entrance into the temple grounds. He stopped just inside and took a long look at the area that would comprise his search.

The courtyard was large with a small, covered well situated in the center . Beyond lay what at one time might have been well-kept gardens. Now, they were wild, overgrown and infested with weeds. Ivy and fungus covered much of the worn and broken statues standing at the garden's edge.

A pebbled path, missing many of its stones, wound through the overgrown garden to a large wooden building. Its once-graceful, arching awnings had been chopped off at three of its four corners. Three smaller buildings sat around the larger one. One of them was an agonized ruin, the ravages of an uncontrolled fire still obvious after all this time. Though Asaka had told him he was going to a temple, he was somewhat surprised to find it really was. The fallen and broken statues of the welcoming spirits looked angry and forlorn. All signs of the temple's name or which of the *kami* it regarded with the greatest esteem had been crossed off or destroyed.

Everywhere he looked, he could see the remains of more of the dark writing he had seen at the gate. He made a word out here or there, but most of it was still illegible. Yellowed paper strips in the shape of lightning bolts hung everywhere to ward off evil spirits. Bumps crawled up his arms as it struck him those were in better condition than they ever should have been.

He tried his best not to think about the violence that had surely occurred here in the past. He kept his guard up as he trekked across the courtyard to the small well. Not sure of who or what might still inhabit the grounds, he wanted to wash his hands and feet in the normal ritual conducted before entering a temple. He wanted to make sure he did absolutely nothing to anger the spirits that surely hung about the forsaken place.

Reaching the well, he found there was no way for him to bring up the water, the line and bucket gone. Knowing spirits didn't normally care for excuses, he used some of his drinking water to wash his hands. He shook them dry, not wanting to soil them again by drying them on his sweatstained clothes.

His gaze rose to center on the large, open entry into the main building. With a small sigh, he started toward it, his sandals occasionally making crunching sounds on the pebbles still remaining on the path. He cringed at the noise as it echoed loudly in the otherwise unbroken silence.

Though the sun was high in the sky, none of its rays shone in through the entry to give him a hint of what lay inside. Hesitating at the first of the steps leading up to the main building, he forced his eyes away from its gaping darkness and made himself pay attention to the aged stairs.

Carefully treading on each step, he hissed every time one of them creaked. Eventually, he reached the top without mishap and stepped onto the temple's wide porch. Glancing around, he noticed a number of jagged holes in its planks and dark telltale stains. Two beady eyes popped up through one of the holes and stared curiously at him. He tried to ignore the insistent prickling on the back of his neck. Disregarding his unwanted visitor, he walked cautiously to the dark entryway.

Toshi moved to the entrance and then stopped. Goose bumps sprung on his shoulders and legs, his eyes still unable to distinguish anything of what lay within. Taking a deep breath, knowing he really had no other choice, he closed his eyes, mumbled a quick prayer and stepped inside.

The temperature dropped as he crossed the threshold. He shivered, his goose bumps multiplying, the prickling on his neck rising to a fever pitch. He opened his eyes, expecting to be enveloped by darkness. He blinked several times as his mind balked at the inconsistency he found around him.

The room was not enshrouded by darkness as he'd expected, but contained only by a few weak shadows. Bright shafts of sunlight poured into the room from holes in the walls and ceiling, as well as from the entry. As he gawked about in disbelief, the goose bumps spread throughout his body. Seeing that the outside looked as he had left it, he decided perhaps it would be best if he didn't think about what had just happened for a while. If he did, he might not have the courage to stay until he'd found what he was looking for.

The room he was in was large and held a broad platform close to the far wall. Though he knew it would normally hold a statue of the main spirit worshipped here or a cabinet with sacred relics, it was empty. All the small statues and paintings honoring the other local kamis were missing as well.

Only a small table sitting before the platform looked untouched. The walls were scarred and so was the floor. The dark writing he had seen outside was here as well. The yellowed, lightning-shaped paper poked out of every possible nook and cranny, accentuating the writing on the walls.

He stepped closer to the wall on his right to get a better look at the writing. The rough, timeworn strokes spoke of demons and evil spirits. They proclaimed the place had been harboring the vilest of horrors. The writings told of how the grounds had been purified and the evil ones destroyed.

He shivered. Skirmishes between religious orders were not unheard-of, but the evidence around him spoke more of persecution than a theological disagreement. How could the priests here have merited such destruction? Could the things those writings said be in any way true? Was this a place of vile horrors? And, if so, why would Asaka be sent here to retrieve a kettle?

He stepped away from the wall, his heart uneasy. Could those writings have anything to do with the reason the samurai couldn't come in here? Or was it perhaps that the spirits of the area were so angry at what had happened they would let no other spirits near?

He glanced nervously about him, knowing he was destined to remain in this place for an unknown period of time. The teakettle he'd been told to find could be hidden anywhere in the compound. His search could take days. He had absolutely no desire to remain in the domain of angry spirits for a few minutes, let alone for that long.

His gaze fell again to the small table before the platform. Impulsively, he walked toward it and placed a small part of his lunch on it as an offering. He bowed his head and clapped his hands together in supplication. Hoping the spirits were listening and willing to help, he asked that his search for the missing kettle be concluded quickly.

"May I help you?"

Toshi twirled around to see who had spoken, his hand instinctively falling to the hilt of his wooden sword. He'd half-pulled it out of his sash when his feet tangled together and he fell to the floor.

His side stung as it smacked the hard floor, but he froze as his gaze landed on the man who had spoken. He wore the black-brown-and-white robes of a priest. A chain of white beads hung from his neck, and he held a tall walking stick with three bronze circlets looped about a ring at its top.

He scanned the firm yet lightly lined face before him. Unlike most priests he had seen in his short life, this one didn't have a shaved head but instead had silver-white hair that flowed halfway down his broad back.

Toshi bowed as he stood back up, nervous as he came to realize the priest was standing between him and the way out. He tried to say something as the priest took a step toward him, but nothing came out.

"Are you all right, son? I hadn't meant to startle you." The voice was kind.

He found his vocal cords still didn't want to cooperate, so he nodded yes.

A hint of a smirk touched the priest's face. Feeling foolish, Toshi slipped his boken back into his sash

"Are you sure you're all right?" the priest asked.

Toshi looked up at him. "Yes, I am. Thank you. I guess I've been a little jumpy today. I'm fine, really."

"You're not from the village, are you?"

From the way he said it, Toshi was sure the priest had no doubt as to the answer.

"No, sir, I'm not. I'm from Toyama." He closed his mouth hard, realizing that, by telling where he came from, he'd opened himself to a number of unwanted questions.

"That's quite a ways from here, isn't it?" the priest said. "You must have grave business to have let it carry you to such a desolate place as this."

Toshi forced himself to stay silent.

The priest's deep-brown eyes pierced him where he stood. "Silence can at times be taken as an indication of admission."

Toshi tore his eyes from that intense stare and looked away.

"You're searching for something."

Toshi's gaze snapped back to him in surprise. He couldn't help but notice the priest's faint smile still clung to his face.

"I am, sir, but please don't ask me about it. You shouldn't get involved. It could be dangerous." He shut his mouth again, realizing he'd been about to say too much once more.

The priest's hard stare seemed to soften. "Might you be looking for a kettle?"

"You know of it?" He instantly cursed himself for a fool. He knew he'd just given himself away.

The priest's smile broadened, but it no longer held a trace of humor. After a moment, he turned and walked away. "Yes, I know of it. Many have come searching for it over the years. None have ever found it."

Toshi waited to see if the priest would say more, but he didn't. He took a step back, his hand falling on the hilt of his boken as a sobering idea occurred to him.

"Are you also looking for it?"

The priest laughed. "There are a number of others that will give better tea than that kettle. I have no need of it, or its mysteries."

"So, you know why it's so important?" he asked.

The priest turned to face him, an odd look in his eyes. "Don't you?"

He started to lie, but changed his mind right before he spoke. "No."

"Then why do you seek it?"

He hesitated, knowing he couldn't give an answer.

The priest suddenly took a menacing step toward him. "Tell me."

He blinked, ignoring the command, startled by the fact he thought he'd seen a flash of light in the priest's eyes. He kept his eyes on the man, trying to see if it would happen again, but it didn't. Had he imagined it?

The priest took another step forward. Toshi took one back.

"Tell me." The priest's tone was more insistent.

"I'm doing it because the others can't," he answered. "Because they've been looking for it for a very long time and deserve to find it.

Because…" He paused. "Because without it, I'll never be allowed to go home."

He didn't know why he'd inserted the last. He felt trapped by the priest's stare and had only meant to say enough to satisfy him and yet give nothing away. He knew he was failing miserably.

The priest released Toshi from his gaze and stepped to the small table containing Toshi's offering. His staff made a jingling noise as he walked, though it had never made a sound before.

The prickling started up again on the back of Toshi's neck. Something wasn't right. He doubted this man was what he seemed.

"Finding the kettle carries a price," the priest said.

Toshi was intrigued by the words despite his fear. "A price? What kind of price?"

The priest glared at him for a moment, not answering. "Are you willing to pay the price?"

Toshi took a step away from him. The prickling on his neck got worse.

"What kind of price?" He held even more tightly to his boken.

The priest stepped toward him.

"Will you pay it?" His voice was soft but very insistent.

Toshi glanced at the entry, and the freedom awaiting him beyond it. Then he looked back at the priest, who seemed to be promising a greater freedom if only he was willing to pay some undisclosed price. He wasn't sure if he should believe him. The longer he hesitated, though, the more convinced he became that, for some reason, this would be his one and only chance to find that which he sought.

He fought to stand straight and took his hand off the boken.

"All right. I'll pay your price." He almost quivered at the cold grin growing on the priest's face.

"So be it." The priest closed in on him.

Toshi tore his eyes from that cold grin even as the room abruptly turned chilly. He felt a wave of dread flow through him. He'd felt that cold before.

He looked up, sure he'd been tricked, just as the priest loomed over him. He gasped as he stared into the priest's eyes and saw two pink lights emanating from within them.

He tried to back away but found he couldn't make his limbs

respond. His eyes grew round as the man before him lost his solidity until Toshi could see through him. With a scream trying to form on his lips, he felt a burning sensation cut into him as the priest's hand disappeared into his chest. The priest stepped forward, merging with Toshi's body. He was swallowed by darkness.

Chapter 15

Toshi worked. There was nothing for him but the work. So much had been left undone for so long. And there was so little time! He had to hurry, hurry. The prize would be his if he could do it all. The past would be erased and everything would be all right again. Balance would be restored. The spirits would be at peace.

He toiled, thinking of nothing but the work, the priest always with him, in him.

The sun hung over him as he swept the paths and cleaned the walls. The statues watched him, giving him strength, bidding him go faster. When the sun disappeared, he worked inside. Old tools found him, and he put them to use. The red words were washed away, driving back the stains that normal eyes couldn't see. The floorboards were pried up and burned, new ones cut to take their place. There was only the price and the prize, the price and the prize. And he had to hurry.

Chapter 16

"Toshi."

A small groan echoed in the room, mingling with the faint remnants of the call. After a small while, he realized he'd been the source of the former.

Someone had called his name.

He blinked his eyes open, but it was several minutes before his mind acknowledged what they were seeing. Something gold and blazing sat before him. He groaned again, this time louder, his brow furrowing with aimless concentration.

Someone called his name again.

He stared at the bright thing before him, and by degrees he tried to make out what it was. Eventually, his fogged mind argued with itself that what was before him was and wasn't the sun. Overwhelmed by the seeming incongruity, he closed his eyes and then opened them again. As he looked once more at the blazing sun, he noticed the deep darkness surrounding it. Something sparked in the back of his mind. He was now sure what was before him wasn't the sun.

The faint voice called his name again.

Allowing his gaze to roam past the object, he realized the field of darkness was finite and curved at the ends. His brow furrowed again as he stared at what he could see, his mind nagging him that what was before him was somehow important to him.

He tried to focus his thoughts to try and remember why the thing was important. Gingerly, he let himself fall back. He discovered he was staring at the ceiling. It occurred to him to wonder where he was. Turning his head, he looked around the room. The place looked familiar, but something about it was different from before.

"Toshi…"

Rolling back onto his side, he struggled to get up onto his hands and knees. Getting there, he then tried to sit. After a long interval he was successful. Yet he'd spent so long on the one task that he had a hard time remembering why he'd done it.

His name was whispered into the room again.

He studied his surroundings more carefully, and noted the new wooden planks lying on part of the floor. Looking up at the walls, he noticed they'd been repaired as well. There were things missing, too, and after a moment he remembered what they were. All the warding paper was gone, and so was all the writing on the walls.

The broken furniture had been taken away, except for the small table by the platform. He sat very still as he stared at the familiar table. His breath quickened in recognition of what he saw there—a long walking staff with bronze rings hanging at one end.

His memories snapped back into clarity as abruptly as a summer typhoon rushing past the coast. Forgetting the staff, he swung his gaze to the object that had been left beside him. The black kettle with its embossed sun stared back.

"Toshi..."

For the first time since he'd awakened, he understood his name was being called from outside. Unable to take his eyes from the beautifully decorated but otherwise common kettle, he waited breathlessly for the call to be repeated. When it was, he listened to it, trying to make sure he wasn't mistaking it for something it wasn't. He violently shook his head from side to side and then waited for the call again. He was sure he had to have heard it wrong. What he'd heard wasn't possible.

The call was an almost unrecognizable shadow of a voice, and it whispered to him again through the bright daylight. He understood what it said, and his mind insisted he knew the caller. But it just wasn't possible.

Could it be some sort of trick? Yet the only person he knew that might be after him would be unable to call him during the day.

He tried to get up but fell back on the floor. Trying once more, but more carefully this time, he was able to stand. He closed his eyes for a moment, feeling a little woozy. After taking a few deep breaths, he was able to get his vision to steady. He glanced outside.

The courtyard seemed very much like he remembered, except it looked cleaner, neater than it had before. No one was there. He scanned as far as he could see, but saw no sign of who was calling to him. He decided to do something about it.

The voice called him again.

With his mind made up, he turned around and checked himself. As far as he could tell, he had no injuries to speak of, though he did feel strangely tired and drained.

Next to the kettle, he found his few possessions lined up in a row. Sitting back down, he checked them. His bamboo canteen was over half-empty and became even more so after he took a long draught from it. A small part of his lunch remained; and he ate ravenously, though he had no memory of ever having eaten any of it.

He felt better after he was through, so he stood up. He bent to pick up his boken and slipped it through his sash. He reached for the kettle's handle, not sure what to expect. There had been no sign of the priest since he'd awakened, other than the staff sitting on the table. Had the priest already exacted his price?

He pushed aside the question as his name rang once more on his ears.

He picked up the kettle. The priest didn't appear. He felt no prickling on the back of his neck. He assumed it was all right for him to take it.

Sending one last glance around the cleaned room, he still saw no trace of the dead priest. He bowed deeply in the direction of the empty platform and thanked the spirits for their help. Turning his back on all of it, he made his way out into the waiting sunlight.

He felt no temperature change as he stepped outside, like he had on his way in. He glanced behind him and found he could easily see into the temple's interior. He was suddenly sure the priest was gone. Whatever had held him there was over.

As he stepped down the new flight of stairs attached to the porch, he found he no longer had any fear of the place. Oddly enough, he felt at peace within it. Grateful for the feeling, he decided not to question it.

Heading toward the broken gates, he was amazed at the amount of work that seemed to have gone on around him. All the leaves had been raked away. The weeds had been pulled from the garden. Rocks had been replaced in the meandering path. The ivy and the dark writing had been cleared away from the inside of the outer walls. Had the priest done all this using his body? Was this what the price had been?

He hesitated at the threshold of the gate. Asaka's final command whispered through his mind. With suddenly wary eyes, he stared at the area surrounding the outside of the compound.

He'd been told to wait within the temple grounds until the samurai came for him. Yet he had no real idea how long he'd been unconscious. If he was responsible for all the work he saw had been done around him, there was no way he could have done it in a day.

He heard his name called again.

The voice was more distinct here than it had been within the temple. Never in his life had he heard such despair. How long had it been calling for him, and why?

If the things Miko had told him before were to be believed, he should be safe from the ninja during the daytime. Though Asaka had told him to wait, he felt a great need to find out who was calling him. If somehow the ninja had found a human accomplice, it would be better to find out now.

With one hand on the hilt of his boken and the other on the prize they'd all come so far to claim, he left the temple grounds.

The sun dipped to the west as he waited for the voice to call again so he might try to follow the sound back to its source. It did so.

He advanced to the right, sure that was the direction the voice was coming from. He kept his gaze sharp as he stared into the shadowed trees. His heart beat a little faster as he followed the right wall of the temple grounds into the forest.

Though he followed the wall, he didn't touch it, for that side still bore the dark writing that had been cleaned away inside. The trees grew thicker the farther away he walked from the compound's entrance.

He held his breath as the call drifted past him again. He tried his best to pick out the direction it had come from. He stared long at the tall pines surrounding him for any sign of ambush. Finding none, he left the certainty of the wall and penetrated deeper into the forest.

He could hear the voice getting louder. He must be getting close. Toshi slowed his pace.

Trying to look everywhere at once as he trekked on, he stopped in mid-stride as he spotted something ahead made of faded multiple colors. Creeping closer, he was able to make out the shape of a woman huddling close against the trunk of a large pine, almost hidden by its shadows. Even from where he was hidden, he could see her shoulders shaking softly as she sat crying.

Though he sneaked to different spots and tried, he couldn't get a look at her face. Not only was she facing the tree but her head was covered by a wide-brimmed hat with a thick veil drooping all around it. He was still trying to decide if he should try to get closer when she half-turned, raised her head and called out his name.

For the few seconds her face had lifted toward the sky, he had seen what looked like a white Noh mask with the painted features of a smiling woman.

"Miko-san?" The question had left his lips before he could think to stop himself. The masked face didn't turn toward him. After a moment, he realized she hadn't heard him. Tears rose to his eyes as he stared at her despairing form.

Sure it was she, though it shouldn't have been possible, he stood up and stepped closer. "Miko-san?"

The sound of bells momentarily filled the air as she spun around to stare at him. The familiar mask smiled coyly at him even as flashes of blue light filled its eyes.

"Toshi!"

Before he could do anything, the geisha had risen to her feet and closed the short distance between them. She half-shimmered as she ran, seeming only partially corporeal. She enclosed him in her arms and held him tight.

"*Toshi*."

A part of him felt a little guilty there was a need for her to be so relieved to see him. He was about to return her embrace to let her know he was happy to see her, too, but hesitated. Though her arms were around him, squeezing him against her, he could barely feel her presence. Though he could see she was holding him with all her might, he felt held by air. He began to feel a different type of guilt, one deeply covered with fear.

Miko's hand felt cold on his neck, but it wasn't the penetrating cold of the ship. It was different. He could feel where her bones pressed against him; the rest of her no longer having the magical feel of flesh she'd had before. Gingerly, he put his arms around her, to make sure she wouldn't vaporize before his very eyes. As he hugged her, the teakettle bumped against her side. With a pain-filled hiss, Miko cringed away from him. Her form wavered as he let her go.

The geisha stepped back to her tree, a low moan escaping from beneath her mask.

"Miko-san, what's wrong? Did I hurt you?" He reached for her as she moved away, but stopped, afraid he might cause her more pain. The geisha collapsed against the tree as she sat down amidst its deep shadows.

"Miko-san?"

"It's all right, Toshi-kun," she said. "I'm too excited. I pushed myself too much, that's all."

He watched in panic as she appeared to fade a little more before his eyes.

"You shouldn't be out here," he said. "Why would Asaka-sama ask you to do this?" He knelt before her, still not daring to touch her as he fanned his sudden anger to forget his fear.

Miko didn't look at him, but brought up her hand to hide her mouth. "Toshi-chan, you're a delight to me, even here."

He shook his head, confused by her amusement. "I don't find this funny. He should have never left you out here in the day."

She reached out her hand to touch his. "Toshi-kun, our lord did not send me here. By now he's figured out what I've done and is probably very angry with me."

"But why be here?" he asked. "You told me yourself the day was dangerous to you. Why did you decide to stay here?"

Miko cradled his hand in hers. He felt a chill of worry flow through him as he noticed a yellowed tint to her bones that had never been there before. Her eyes wouldn't meet his own.

"You've been gone for over three days, Toshi-kun. I was afraid something horrible had happened to you."

"Three days?" It'd been that long?

Her eyes flared and caught his own. "Yes, three days. Asaka-sama came to retrieve you that first night, but you never appeared at the gate. You didn't even answer his call, though he could see a light inside the temple. But he couldn't get into the grounds to find out what was wrong." She looked away. "I came with our lord and his party last night. I saw how the scent of death was shrouding the place. Yet it was Mitsuo who first noticed the courtyard had changed.

"The light was in the temple, just as it had been before. But we still saw no sign of you. We called and called, but you never answered. You had to be there, we knew you were there. If you had left the temple grounds we would have known it."

He opened his mouth to try and explain why he hadn't answered, but held back as she continued on.

"I returned to the ship with the others, but I couldn't stay. I couldn't. I knew Asaka-sama would forbid me to come back, so I didn't ask him. When the boat returned to pick up some of the others, I slipped into the water and returned here on my own. I hoped if I called for you during the day it would make a difference." Her eyes dimmed. "I just didn't know what else to try..." Her voice slipped to silence. With a touch of surprise, he realized she was crying.

Taking great care, he placed his other hand on top of hers. Her hands felt like the bones they were as they scraped softly against his skin. As she tried to take them from him, he could make out some barely audible cracking sounds, making it seem as if her bones were frozen and threatening to break with her every movement.

"Miko-san, I'm so sorry," he whispered. "I had no idea that much time had gone by. But, I found it. I found that which you and Asaka-sama needed me to find."

The white, veiled mask rose to look at him. "You have?"

"Yes. This is it, right here." He reached for the kettle and presented it to her, wanting to do something, anything, to make her feel better. Miko gingerly reached to touch it, as if she weren't quite willing to believe it was really there. As her fingers got close to caressing its black surface, she suddenly pulled her hand away.

"It burns," she said.

"What?"

"It burns." He could hear mystified surprise in her voice. "It must have been what I felt before. I thought I'd pushed myself too far, but—"

"Miko-san, I don't understand. Why would it burn you? You haven't even touched it." What did it mean?

Miko's eyes were rooted to the kettle. "Though we have traveled long, never before had we found a place we could not go to except here. Never was there anything we could not touch except here." She sighed. "People throughout time have practiced ways to keep out evil spirits and to exorcise them from their homes. But never had we thought of ourselves as such. Yet, we found the temple grounds had somehow been prepared against us. We couldn't go in.

"We knew something terrible had happened here. We'd learned of it long ago. Our lord had felt it, just as he had felt the death of the clan—these things are all connected to him. He told me once he might need you to get the kettle for us, but I'd just thought he was being cautious. I never believed until we arrived that the place would be closed to us."

He stared at the kettle in his hands, awed that such a mundane thing could keep one such as she from touching it. With great care, he inspected the kettle from every side, wondering how it could have such power. As he turned it over, he stopped as he noticed writing had been carved on its bottom. It looked like some sort of invocation. "Could this be what burned you?"

Miko stared at the writing, but before long was forced to avert her gaze. "I don't know, Toshi-kun," she admitted. "I have no knowledge of such things. I don't understand their power."

"Do you think they knew of you? That this was done to purposely keep you from your goal?" he asked. "Do you think there are people out there who know you exist?"

Miko sighed. "I can't even attempt to guess. I didn't even believe beings like us could exist until we became them. I suppose, perhaps…the ninja…I just don't know." Her gaze met his as she studied him thoroughly for the first time since he'd come back to her. "Toshi!"

He leapt to his feet, turning around and drawing his boken without falling. His eyes darted everywhere, looking for whatever had startled the geisha so.

"Sit," she said.

Confused, he turned back toward her. "Miko-san, what is it?"

Surely, he'd not hurt her again. He sat down reluctantly, watching her when she didn't answer.

The geisha raised her hand and reached out to touch his mane. "Toshi-kun, what's happened to your hair?"

"My hair?" He reached up and touched it. It felt all right, his ponytail intact. The geisha brought the end forward so he might look at it.

He gasped. That wasn't his hair, and yet it was. While it felt the same and was the same length as before, his hair had completely changed from black to a startling white. He blinked several times, not quite ready to believe what he was seeing. He reached out and touched it, recalling the priest's silver-white mane.

"What does this mean? What happened to you?" Miko asked.

Not able to face her intense gaze, he stared at his hands. "I met a priest in the temple. He told me there was a price to be paid if I was to find the kettle," he said quietly. "I guess this was part of it."

Miko stared at him for a long time before saying anything. "What else was part of this price? What else was been done to you?"

He looked up at the abrupt coldness in her tone. "I think he used me and my body to fix the temple. The priest was trying to restore the balance of *wa* in the compound. He wanted to try and diffuse the lingering violence of the past."

He was surprised by his own statement, but realized it was true. He just had no idea how he knew it.

Miko stared at him in silence. Trying not to fidget under her stare, he looked away.

"It was worth it, though," he explained. "It really wasn't that much to pay in order to allow you and the others to go on and for me to go home."

He found himself suddenly wrapped by her arms. "Toshi, I'm just glad you're all right." She sobbed against him.

He didn't dare move, not wanting to cause the geisha pain in her current condition. He was silent as she cried, happier than he would have ever thought possible that he was no longer alone and that it was

Miko who was with him.

After a while, the geisha quieted and released him. They regarded each other in silence.

"Shouldn't we try and go back to the beach, Miko-san? You really should return to the ship."

The sound of tinkling bells gave him her answer. "No, Toshi-kun, I can't. The sunlight pains me in a way I can't even begin to explain. Under its influence, I can feel myself slowly unraveling to nothingness. I start to lose my sense of self. Even my hat and clothing are no protection against it. Only here in the deep shadows of the trees have I felt a little more like myself." She looked about as if she were suddenly looking for something. "You, however, should return to the safety of the temple grounds. I will be safe here, and I'll call you once our lord has returned. It'll only be for a few hours."

"But, I can't just leave you here," he protested. "You're hurt, and that ninja is still out there. You're in no condition to protect yourself from him. I can't leave you here alone."

"Toshi-kun, it would be best."

He stared at her yellowed bones and frail shape. "I'm sorry, but I don't think it is. I can't leave you here alone. Besides, it doesn't matter—he can't take the kettle. It won't let him. But he can hurt you if he finds you like this. I doubt I could protect you very well, but at least I could try. You've done a lot more than that for me already."

"My very own protector," she said. "I take it your newfound manhood will not allow me to dissuade you?"

He bit his tongue to keep from blushing as Miko's sleeve rose to hide her mouth. He wouldn't falter or show weakness in his resolve—not in this. He clamped down on the surprise that bubbled up as he realized, for good or ill, she'd come to mean a lot to him.

"No, Miko-san, you can't convince me otherwise," he stated. "I will wait here with you until Asaka-sama returns."

She stared at him for a long moment and then nodded.

"Well, then, protector, would you do me the honor of sitting beside me and sharing the shade of this magnificent tree?" She patted the ground next to her.

Not trusting himself to speak, he did as she asked him. As he sat down, he let out a heavy sigh, the unreality of all that had gone on in the last few days washing over him in a weary wave.

"I think I could get to like your hair looking like this," she said.

He thought it looked unnatural but didn't say so. Miko laid her hand lightly on his and hummed a somewhat haunting tune.

His gaze roamed the forest around them, looking for any signs of danger. As time passed, though, he found it harder and harder to keep his eyes open. Miko's tune had soothed away the excitement and strangeness he'd gone through so far, allowing his original weariness to hold sway.

The afternoon wore on, and the sun lowered toward the horizon. He felt his senses become dull though he tried to stay as alert as possible and not leave Miko on her own. Darkness crept up on them, soon cutting his visibility to nothing. A kernel of fear took root as he knew he'd never be able to spot the ninja here if he decided to attack them.

A cracking sound off to the right brought him to his feet, boken in hand.

"Toshi-kun, what's wrong?"

Blind in the shrouded darkness, he stepped back until he felt the bark of the tree press against him. He held his boken before him, still trying to figure out what it was he'd heard in the night.

"Toshi-kun, it's all right," she said. "Our lord has come for us."

As she spoke, he choked as a pair of small green lights swung to stare momentarily at him. At the same time he realized it was Asaka, he also recalled he was pointing a sword in his lord's direction. Overcome by a different kind of fear at the obvious affront, he dropped to his hands and knees and bowed to Asaka.

He stayed in that position, his face close to the ground, waiting to see what would happen. He heard someone move forward and then a strong touch on his arm pulling him upward.

"Report."

"Hai, Asaka-sama." He kept his gaze pointed toward the ground, not really relishing the eerie chills that coursed through him at watching Asaka's green eyes float in the darkness. "I went into the main building of the temple grounds and met a priest there. He gave me the kettle in exchange for remaining with him for a few days."

There was a long pause.

"Where is it?" The samurai's voice was tinged with barely restrained excitement.

Toshi looked up, panic rising in his throat, as he didn't instantly remember where he'd last placed it. He opened his mouth to stumble through some sort of reply when Miko beat him to it.

"Asaka-sama, the object is before you. It is hidden beneath my hat."

Toshi held his breath as he heard the others step closer. Still unable to see anything, he stared in their direction, hoping the kettle would be where it should be.

Fear-laced suspense knotted his stomach as silence reigned around him. His eyes widened as he abruptly saw the kettle light up with a bright flash.

A soft, surprised whisper filled the returning darkness. The shocked emotion made Asaka's cold voice seem more human than it had ever been before. "I can't touch it."

"Chizuson-san found there are incantations engraved into the bottom of the kettle," Miko said.

"This was unforeseen."

A murmur rose among the others but soon fell into silence. Everyone waited for Asaka to speak again.

"Toshiro, you will take the kettle. You and Akiuji-san will stay close to me as we make our way back to the beach."

"Hai." He felt Miko beside him as she placed her hand on his arm. She led him to the kettle. It was only then he realized the samurai had once more called him by name.

With a growing sense of pride, he reached down for the kettle as Miko told him where to reach for it. Holding the wooden handle firmly in one hand, he allowed himself to be led forward. Though he could still see nothing, he sensed the others as they came in close to form a protective cordon around him. He followed Miko's gentle guidance, thrilled by the fact he felt fingers and not just bones holding his arm. Though he'd tried not to think about it, he'd been afraid the damage caused to her by the sun might have been permanent.

He wasn't sure how far they'd traveled when they finally broke through the line of trees. With the light from the stars shining down unimpeded, he was able to see a little of what lay around him. He realized they'd reached the stone pathway leading to the temple complex. Feeling more secure in his footing, he stepped closer to Miko.

"Are you feeling better?" he whispered.

The grip on his arm tightened slightly for a moment. Her lit blue eyes turned to look at him.

"I'm much better. Don't let it worry you."

He was about to press the point when a bright green gaze riveted first on him and then the geisha. He quickly decided to keep the remainder of his questions to himself.

The normal sounds of the night were muted, as if the crickets had been muffled one by one. Miko's sure grip kept him steady as they got off the stairs of stone onto the weed-filled path and then, later, to the road. Eventually, they re-entered the forest. He could clearly hear his footsteps as they crunched on fallen leaves and twigs. He could hear none of the others, though they walked right beside him. If not for Miko's hand on his arm and the occasional flash of light from their eyes, he would have sworn he was alone.

He kept his gaze riveted forward as the scent of fish and salt water filled his lungs. With an eagerness that surprised him, he looked out over the sea as they exited onto the beach, wanting to catch a glimpse of the vessel that had been his home for what seemed like forever. It sat on the dark water like a beacon in the night.

Without delay, Asaka signaled him and Miko to the skiff grounded on the beach, a sentry at its side. Getting in, he sat on the bottom of the boat as he had done before as it was pushed out into the water. Asaka and three others joined them, filling the boat to overflowing. Two more swam at the craft's sides. Keen dead eyes stared out over the water, scrutinizing the starlit darkness.

Toshi held the kettle on his lap. He wrapped his arms around it, making sure it wouldn't touch one of the others. The ride back to the ship proved uneventful.

With a sense of deep relief, he climbed aboard, knowing his part of the quest was done. He looked up, abruptly self-conscious as he found those on board staring at him with lit eyes. Trying to ignore them and the way their hard stares made him feel, he turned around to watch the others board. Mitsuo appeared beside him and helped Miko aboard. Once everyone had disembarked, the small boat returned to shore for the rest.

Toshi followed the geisha and the samurai as they climbed up to the higher deck. Mitsuo disappeared. Asaka ignored everyone and everything as he went to sit at his usual place. Toshi remained standing, surrounded by his ring of guards, the cold already working through his sandals.

Though the men guarding him had never seemed to pay much attention to him before, he now found them occasionally glancing over their shoulders at him when they thought he wasn't looking. Miko stood beside him, still silent. Since he had some light, he tried to study her as indirectly as the guards were studying him. From what he could see, almost all signs of what had happened to her during the day were gone. Her bones appeared as white as ever, and her kimono was once more filled by the illusion of a womanly form. The only thing that hadn't returned to normal were her clothes. Though bright yellows, pinks and greens still filled the red fabric, somehow he suspected they were not as bright as they had been the night before.

Mitsuo returned during Toshi's study of the geisha and brought him a pile of his blankets. Gratefully helping the samurai to set them out, Toshi sat down and placed the kettle beside them. As he wrapped one of the covers around his shoulders, Miko sat down as well.

Soft murmurs filled the lower deck as the skiff returned with the last of the crew. Through it all, Asaka sat as if nothing unusual had happened that night. Toshi didn't understand it. It wasn't the way someone who had gotten something they'd desperately been seeking would act.

As soon as everyone was back on board, the boat was brought on deck. All eyes turned toward Asaka as the skiff was tied down in an unobtrusive place.

With a crawling pace that was maddening, Asaka rose to his feet and faced his people.

"Just as duty decreed, the item has been recovered." The snarling demon mask turned in his direction. "Toshiro."

Hoping he was guessing right, he stood up and held the kettle high. The guards parted before him so the crew could see it.

A loud cheer boomed from the lower deck. He continued holding the kettle aloft even as unexpected joy bubbled up inside him at having helped make this moment possible. Feeling a little giddy, he lowered his arm as the cheers subsided.

"Now, the last part of our journey will begin," Asaka announced.

Toshi sat back down as the crew bolted for their assigned stations. Mitsuo disappeared again, but soon returned carrying the basket of instruments. The ship was prepared to get under way.

Still warmed by the emotion he'd witnessed, Toshi set the kettle on his lap and stared raptly at it. Though it surely was the cause of all his miseries, it was also the means for these people's salvation. As he thought of all he had gone through because of it, he felt the threats pale when compared to what had been achieved. For some crazy reason, fate had chosen him to make a difference, and he had. It felt good.

"Toshiro."

He got to his feet. "Yes, Asaka-sama?"

"Please place the kettle in your room and then come back," the samurai said. "A guard shall be posted there to watch it in your absence."

"Hai." He left to do as he'd been bid, his guards still around him.

Once he returned, the excitement that had been flowing through him started to recede.

"Would you like me to make you some tea, Toshi-kun?"

"I, um, that would be nice, Miko-san," he said.

She sent a small nod in his direction and then headed below. The crew started a song as they put their all into their oars. The steersman turned the ship around and set a course to take them back the way they'd come.

Miko eventually returned and served him tea. "Careful, it's very hot," she said.

"Thank you." He took the offered cup and, while doing so, noticed Asaka looking straight at him. He drank his tea to hide his surprise, trying not to let the fact unnerve him. He wasn't accustomed to getting much attention there—or anywhere, for that matter. The samurai had never before even given him a second thought. Goose bumps crawled up his arms as Asaka continued to stare. He didn't like it, though he had no idea what it meant.

Miko had just refilled his cup when he heard Asaka stand up. To his surprise, the samurai walked over to the ladder. Never before had he seen him leave the deck like this. His heart almost stopped as Asaka turned around to look in his direction.

"Akiuji-san." He stared at Miko.

"Hai, Asaka-sama," she responded.

Asaka turned back around and prepared to go below.

"Toshi-kun, I must go now." Miko rose to her feet as she spoke, "Please try and get some rest."

He stared at her as she left, feeling a sudden surge of dread.

He lay down but couldn't sleep. Time flowed by, and Miko didn't reappear. The longer she was gone, the more he worried over her.

The steersman called for a reading, and he moved through the familiar steps, his mind only partially on his work. The steersman said nothing as Toshi showed him their approximate location. Even distracted as he was, he couldn't help but notice the steersman's gaze as it lingered on his unnaturally white hair.

Miko still hadn't returned, though he had already been called to do three readings. He fought to stay awake in case she did, but he was pulled down by what was left of his previous exhaustion.

Mitsuo awakened him later so he could go below. Once inside the protection of the hallway, he rushed to his room as soon as Mitsuo would allow it. The cold surrounding him couldn't match the cold fear in his heart as he found that Miko wasn't there waiting for him.

Mitsuo placed the blankets on the futon, but Toshi didn't hurry to bury himself in them. He stared at Mitsuo in indecision as the latter headed toward the door.

"Sensei?" he asked.

White points of light flashed in his direction.

"Do you think Miko-san is all right?"

"Why shouldn't she be?" Mitsuo asked.

He was taken aback by the tone of surprise in the bent skeleton's voice. "Ah, uh, no reason. I just hadn't seen her in a while."

The old samurai nodded but said nothing. Toshi felt foolish.

"Perhaps we should see what you remember of your lessons," Mitsuo said.

He almost groaned at the suggestion but made himself nod instead.

Mitsuo had him go through all the routines he had shown him, criticizing his movements now and again.

Toshi felt smug about how much he remembered of what he'd been taught so far, though it'd been a number of days. His congratulations were short-lived, however, as Mitsuo drew his own boken and launched himself at him.

He barely blocked the first attack and was hard-pressed to protect himself from the second and third. The fourth slipped easily past his guard, and Mitsuo slapped him hard on the arm. Without thinking, he moved to block the fifth and was able to do it, only to have the air knocked out of him by the sixth.

Holding onto his stomach with his free arm, he dropped like a sack of grain.

"Your movements didn't entirely crumble when pressed by surprise," Mitsuo said. "That's good, but not good enough. Begin again from the first stance."

Breathing heavily, his abdomen still protesting from the stinging blow, he inched his way back to his feet. He could take this. So far, the two blows he'd received were no worse than those given to him by Master Shun in his beatings. He stood up straight and began from the first stance.

As he worked, his abdomen quieted. His stomach, however, then decided to complain it was empty. He ignored it, but its protest for food had also reminded him of his worry for Miko.

He heard the door open. Hope sprang to his eyes as he half-turned to look. Mitsuo chose that moment to attack.

He saw Miko framed by the half-open door as Mitsuo swung forward, cut through his guard and caught him between the neck and shoulder. With a yelp, he fell hard, his arm numbed. Mitsuo placed the tip of his boken against his heaving chest.

"If the first blow hadn't killed you, you would still be dead," the old samurai pointed out. "You must never allow yourself to be taken by any kind of distraction, but you must also make sure you remain aware of all that is happening around you."

Toshi didn't move from where he lay, just nodded weakly.

Miko came into the room carrying a laden tray. "Mitsuo-san, Asaka-sama asked for you to come and see him when you had the time."

Mitsuo bowed to them and left the room. Toshi sat up, trying his best to minimize the pain shooting from his shoulder. He watched Miko place her tray on the small table. Gingerly, he placed his covers over his shoulders. He was sure the bruise that would soon develop there would remind him of Mitsuo's lesson for a number of days.

"I'm sorry I'm so late," Miko said. "I hope it wasn't too inconvenient."

"No, Miko-san, it's fine. Mitsuo-san kept me entertained." He flinched as he made the mistake of reaching for Miko's offered cup with his right arm. He then reached for it with his left.

"Yes, I saw that," she teased.

He looked away, remembering she'd seen his disgrace.

"Don't worry, Toshi-chan. Mitsuo always tries to teach a degree of humility to all of his students."

He wondered if it could be true—a samurai teaching another samurai about humility?

"You really should eat, Toshi-kun," she suggested, "before it all gets cold."

With his left arm, he reached out to put his empty teacup on the table and grabbed the steaming bowl of rice sitting there. "Miko-san, did anything bad happen?"

"Bad, Toshi-kun?" She tilted her head slightly to the side.

He wanted to ask her about all the time she'd spent with Asaka. He wanted to make sure she was all right. He had no good way of finding out.

"I guess I just wanted to know if you felt okay."

"I returned to normal not long after the sun went down," she said. "I feel all right. Don't I look all right to you?"

He hesitated for a long moment, looking her up and down. "Yes, I guess so."

"You really shouldn't worry about me. I'm already dead, after all."

That had so far never made a difference to him, but he didn't say so. Instead, he let the matter drop. Moving his right arm slowly, he held his rice bowl while awkwardly handling his chopsticks with his left hand.

"I missed your company on deck," he told her. "You were gone so long I started to think maybe something had happened to you."

"Lord Asaka just had a lot of things he wanted to discuss with me." She didn't look in his direction.

He swallowed hard, not sure how he should take what she'd just said. "Was he very angry?"

"Angry, Toshi-kun?" Miko sounded surprised by the question.

His brain told him not to ask, he'd be prying, but his heart just wouldn't leave it alone. "Yes, Miko-san. Did he hurt you?"

She stared at him and then at her lap. He could feel his anger against the samurai kindling again, assuming there was only one possible reason for her silence.

"Oh, Toshi. How can you think such things? Asaka-sama is not like that. Why do you find it so hard to believe?"

He felt his anger drown out with her words.

"Yes, it's true he wasn't overly pleased by my recklessness, but it was overshadowed by his happiness that we were both fine," she said. "He would have been the one calling out to you and taking the risks if we would have ever allowed it. He is our lord, and keeping him safe is our responsibility. He would never hurt me for doing for him that which he wanted but could not do for himself." She reached out and touched his hand.

"I know he's seemed quite harsh to you, Toshi-kun, but it couldn't be helped. The weight he carries on his shoulders was never meant for one man to bear."

He bowed his head, his cheeks coloring with shame. He believed their lord capable of doing horrible things, though in truth he'd never done any of them. Perhaps he had been wrong about him all along.

"Yes, I must admit he's hardened a little, but I think we all have during our ordeal," she added. "The treachery and deceit we've encountered since the beginning of our mission has been greater than anyone would have ever expected." Miko fell silent.

"You know of Bushido, the way of the sword, do you not?" She asked him.

He nodded, not raising his eyes.

"It's the code by which samurai live. It is the essence of what makes them the great warriors they are.

"Yet, though samurai have a code of conduct and philosophy, there are always reports of traitors, assassins, political maneuverings, things that in one way or another go against the very code that forms their existence. The code is abused, misinterpreted and worse. There are even those in the higher aristocracy that don't try to live by it at all."

He looked up involuntarily, stunned by her words. "But that—"

"Think about it, and you'll see the truth of what I say. Ninja are considered the lowest of the low, yet lords, who should be in every way the living embodiment of the code, hire them indiscriminately to spy on their rivals, kidnap their enemies' children, kill people in the most dishonorable of ways."

"But, Miko-san—"

"Samurai are just men," she kept on. "They love, they hate, they have greed and they have morals. They have more responsibilities than you or I, but they're still human. They're not all-knowing, all-seeing, not even indestructible. Yes, most are willing to give their lives at a moment's notice for their lord, but they will also take lives. The more powerful they become, the easier it grows for them to ignore the code or use it to their advantage."

Could all that Miko said be true? It would explain some things that had seemed unexplainable before. If so, a lot of Master Shun's idle gossip about the seedier dealings of those in power might be closer to the truth than he'd ever realized.

"I'm sorry, Toshi-kun, perhaps I've gone too far," she said. "But you need to know these things. Your eyes must be opened to the truth."

Something in her tone made him look up into her face. His food turned into lumps in his stomach.

"Why?" he asked. "Why do I need to know? I have little to do with samurai." Dread covered him as he saw her turn away from his question.

"Asaka-sama wants to speak with you after your training is over today. There is something he wishes to discuss with you."

His dread grew deeper. "What does he want to talk to me about?"

"It is not my place to divulge this to you." Miko wouldn't look at him. There was a resignation in her voice he'd never heard before.

He stared at his hands as it dawned on him that perhaps his part in their quest was far from over. Though he'd never been truly told this, he'd always assumed they would free him once they'd returned to the coast. What else could they want from him? His navigating skills were the only thing they'd told him he'd be needed for, though that had already proved untrue.

"Toshi."

His eyes stung as he figured out what they might want him for. With a clarity all too vivid, he recalled the flash the kettle had made when Asaka had tried to reach for it. He wouldn't be going back. They needed him still. How much longer would they keep him from home and all he knew? He heard Miko shift toward him. He turned away, not wanting her to see his face.

He said nothing as he heard her rise and leave the room. He still said nothing when she returned a short while later. He in no way acknowledged her as she puttered about.

He wanted her to leave, though she obviously wouldn't. So, he said nothing, not wanting to talk to her. Soft music drifted toward him. With unfocused anger, he placed his hands over his ears, not wanting to be soothed. When Miko didn't stop, he lay down on his futon and buried his head under his blankets, trying to muffle the sound. It didn't help much. The music didn't stop.

Not long after, he heard the door to his room open.

"Chizuson-san, it's time for us to continue with your lessons." It was Mitsuo.

Miko continued playing.

Toshi made no move to unbury himself from his covers. He was beginning to think perhaps Mitsuo had gone away when something poked him, landing directly on the sore spot on his right shoulder. Biting his lip in order to keep from uttering a cry of pain, he threw off his covers and glared at his teacher.

"I won't be practicing anymore today!"

Faster than Toshi could react, Mitsuo brought his boken around and poked him on his aching shoulder again.

"Stop it," he growled. He dropped his hand toward his own

weapon and forced himself to stop.

"You will begin practice. You will do so now." Mitsuo hit him again.

"You have no right to do this to me!" His anger grew, the pain in his shoulder making his vision swim.

Miko's sorrow-filled voice filled the room. "No, Chizuson Toshiro, we have no right. But duty forces us to do what we must."

Chapter 17

Sweat poured down Toshi's face as Mitsuo came at him again. He already hurt everywhere, but nowhere as painfully or inconveniently as his right shoulder. Every time he moved his neck or arm, his shoulder complained as if it were being struck anew.

Biting his lip and drawing blood, he tried to keep his attention on the weaving sword before him. At first, he'd been surprised by Miko's words. But as he'd pondered them, he came to realize if he'd been in their place he wouldn't have done anything different. What choice did they really have? It didn't make him like his role any better, but at least he had his practice session to vent his frustrations.

Miko's music wove in his mind. Though he knew she'd left once or twice, her music nevertheless wouldn't leave him. None of her normal bantering had intruded in the lesson so far. It made him worry. He hoped he hadn't pushed her to the point where he'd never hear it again.

He wasn't caught by surprise by Mitsuo's first thrust, but he was too slow to block the second. Trying to twist out of the way, he only ended up putting his injured shoulder directly into the weapon's path. He gasped as pain flared through him, his sight turning dark. With a hiss, he fell hard to his knees.

"Perhaps the two of you have trained long enough for today," Miko suggested. "Don't you think so, Mitsuo-san?"

Toshi wiped some stray strands of damp white hair from his eyes, agreeing silently with the geisha's suggestion.

"Very well," the old samurai conceded. "Tomorrow, however, we will work harder."

Toshi moaned in sad defeat, bowed to Mitsuo and only then let his body sink onto his covers. His perspiration turned cold on his skin, but he made no move to cover himself. He was too tired and aching to care.

He closed his eyes, breathing deeply, and heard Miko and Mitsuo whispering to each other across the room. Not able to make out what they were saying, he decided to concentrate on staying as still as possible. His eyes snapped open a few minutes later as a soft touch caressed his throbbing shoulder.

"It hurts?" Miko's voice sounded close to his ear.

"No, not really." He tried to make his expression neutral.

"Sit up and let me look at it."

Not glancing at her, he struggled to sit up without moving his arm. Miko undid his sash and opened his shirt enough to reveal his injured shoulder. He tried to sit as still as possible as she inspected him.

"You should have asked for your lesson to stop long before this, Toshi-kun," she said. "We don't want you hurt, and it has been a long time since Mitsuo trained a living person."

"I'm all right, Miko-san. It's not bad."

"Isn't it?" Miko squeezed his shoulder.

He had to struggle with all his might to choke back a scream. His eyes watered from the pain, and he tried to turn away from her; but she wouldn't let him.

"I don't want you to ever let it go this far again." Miko's voice was hard.

He looked guiltily away. "Hai, Miko-san."

She said nothing, her fingers probing his arm. He stiffened as a burst of numbing cold shot into his shoulder. He was suddenly free of pain.

"When Mitsuo returns, I'll see if I can find some salve to help it heal."

"Miko-san?"

"Hm?" She sounded distracted.

Shivering from the cold, he turned around to face her and then bowed down to the futon. "I want to ask for your forgiveness. I acted very childishly toward you when all you've ever been is kind to me. I'm sorry. I'll understand if you decide not to forgive me."

He didn't look up, not at all confident she would. He felt his breath catch in his throat as she ruffled his whitened hair.

"There's nothing to forgive, my man-to-be. Your reaction was quite understandable under the circumstances. Only if you had accepted everything I said without question would I have been concerned."

He raised his head and stared at her, his confusion plain. "Then, why?"

"You will have a clearer head when you meet with our lord now," she explained. "You will be prepared for what he has to say. Your aggression and frustration will have already been spent before you ever go in to see him."

He stared at her in wonder. Somehow, she'd planned all of it. What she would have done if he hadn't played into her hands he wasn't sure, but she'd taken it upon herself for his benefit. He felt an aching need to thank her, to let her know he understood what she'd done. If only he could do so without looking like a fool.

"Miko-san—" He hesitated as someone knocked on the door. Mitsuo came into the room with a food-laden tray.

"Go ahead and start without me, Toshi-kun. I'll only be a moment," Miko said.

With a deep sigh, he nodded as Miko got to her feet. He tucked his covers around him and waited for his food.

As soon as Mitsuo had set the table and tray before him, he ate. He caught his teacher studying him as he tried to move as little as possible while eating all he could. Trying to pay him no attention, Toshi reached for the pot of tea and flinched. Mitsuo took it and served him. Thanking him, he drank the tea and returned the cup for more.

Miko returned during his meal with a wrapped bundle and a small earthen jar. She thanked Mitsuo for his help and then took his place by the table. Mitsuo bowed to both of them and then left.

"Your bath water will be ready soon. I'll rub in some of this salve after that." Miko held the small jar between two bony fingers and shook it. "So be good to me, okay?"

"Always, Miko-san." He could feel his shoulder starting to throb again, and he had other aches and pains he'd like to get rid of as well. Miko laughed at his eager response. He found he was smiling, pleased to hear the sound again.

After eating his fill, he watched as Mitsuo brought in his bath water. Undressing, he hurried to the waiting pails and splashed himself with the hot water. To his embarrassment, he noticed both the geisha and his teacher studying him as he washed. With color infusing his cheeks, he turned away from them and tried to hurry.

Once he'd rinsed off, he rushed back to the warmth of his covers. He felt his cheeks reddening again as the two of them whispered to one another, occasionally pointing in his direction.

"Please use this lavishly, won't you, Toshi-kun?" Miko held out the jar of salve to him.

He murmured his thanks as he took it, before totally covering up with his blankets. He gingerly applied the salve on all his aching places.

"Toshi-kun, when you're done, please put these on. Lord Asaka will be expecting to meet with you soon."

A shadow of his earlier dread rose up to haunt him. Trying his best to ignore it, he finished treating his aches before peeking out to find his clothes. As he dragged them in, he couldn't help but notice it wasn't the kimono he'd been allowed to borrow before. Holding it up as best he could, he admired the dark-blue hue of the silk and how it was brightened here and there with light-blue waves cresting with silver thread. It was beautiful.

He felt nervous. As far as he knew he hadn't earned the right to wear such a marvelous thing. Fingering the four crescent moons set in the sleeve, he set the kimono down and started getting dressed.

Once done, he sat up and allowed Miko to fix his hair. As she tied his ponytail with a blue-dyed thong, he felt her lean forward toward his ear.

"Be fair with him, Toshi-kun," she said. "Remember he's only a man, one trying to do what must be done. Please, don't judge him too harshly."

He listened to her soft whisper but said nothing. He had no idea what to say.

"Mitsuo-san, Toshi-kun is ready," she declared. "Would you do me the honor of escorting him to our lord?"

The old skeleton bowed, his white-lit eyes riveting on Toshi's seated form. Feeling self-conscious, Toshi stood, leaving his covers behind. He glanced once at the kettle where it had sat since its arrival on the ship in his room's far corner.

"Turn around and let me see you before you go," Miko said.

Wishing she hadn't asked, he put on his sandals and then turned around for her to see.

"Oh, Toshi-kun. Dressed like this, no mere woman could possibly resist you," she stated with feeling. "If only I were still alive."

He stared at the floor, wishing there were some way he could stop his face from feeling so warm. Not daring to look at her, he turned to the door and glanced at his escort. To his chagrin, he found Mitsuo had turned away to hide his face.

He tried to put the two of them from his mind and headed for the door. Mitsuo sensed his approach and opened it for him.

Miko's voice came after him. "Toshi-chan. Make me proud."

He hesitated at the doorway and nodded once before going on.

Led down the hall to a door on the right, he felt a lump of nervousness moving around inside him. Two guards were stationed, as always, at the door leading out onto the deck. Mitsuo knocked on the door in front of them, waited a moment and opened it. He motioned for him to go on in. Toshi stepped inside before he could think better of it. Mitsuo followed him.

The room was about the same size as his. Four traveling chests crowded the far wall and three wide, painted scrolls decorated the space above them. A large gold replica of the Asaka clan symbol had been painted on the left wall. On the right were eight to ten small black-and-white scrolls. They were beautiful, yet at the same time eerie, when viewed in the ship's unnatural glow. Papers and brushes sat neatly stacked in a corner next to a drawing table.

Though he'd been avoiding it, his eyes were drawn toward the middle of the room. A wide round table occupied that space, a large green cushion sitting on the side facing him. Six small dishes sat on the table around a pot of hot tea. At the table's other end sat Asaka.

The samurai wasn't dressed in his battle regalia, as he had always been before. This time, he wore a soft kimono of a light blue that almost bordered on white. His twisted demon mask, however, was still firmly in place. Toshi got on his knees to bow to the floor before Asaka's green stare lingered too long on him.

"Toshiro, please sit with me." The samurai's voice was soft.

He looked up, surprised by the invitation, almost forgetting what had been said in the process. Scrambling to his feet, he rushed to occupy the cushion, folding his legs beneath him. He was quite grateful for his seat. It would keep his legs warm and off the deck.

Keeping his eyes lowered and placing his hands on his thighs, he waited for the samurai to speak.

Mitsuo walked around the table and set several of the dishes within Toshi's easy reach. He also set a filled cup of tea before him. Mitsuo then bowed and took his leave.

"Please don't hesitate to indulge yourself," Asaka said.

Toshi barely raised his eyes to see what lay on the table before him. Despite the sweets and small appetizers there, what he craved more than anything was the steaming tea. Hesitating, he lifted the cup but didn't drink, letting the heat warm his hands.

As Asaka continued staring at him in silence, he tried to clamp down on his nervousness and forced himself to take a sip of his tea. He realized, with unexpected pleasure, this was a very unusual blend of green tea and not his usual fare. Grateful, he let the liquid slide down his throat to warm up his insides and, with some regret, placed the emptied cup back on the table.

"Would you care for more?" Asaka asked.

He did, but wasn't about to say so. "No, thank you."

The samurai reached across the table. "Please, forgive me, but I insist."

Toshi stared at Asaka as he refilled the cup. The pit of his stomach tightened at the almost personal yet quite formal way in which he was being treated.

"Thank you, Asaka-sama." Still not daring to look at the metal-masked face before him for long, he carefully reached out for his refilled cup.

"I owe you a great debt for what you've done."

He froze, his cup half-raised to his waiting lips.

"You have done more than was expected of you, and you have done all these things well," Asaka said. "For all this, I thank you."

Toshi forced his hand to move and hid his face behind his cup.

"As you must surely realize, we have encountered problems on this voyage beyond those we had foreseen. The attack on the temple by our enemies was known to us. It occurred not long after we returned. Yet, though our enemies were victorious in their attack, they did not discover that which we sought. They tried their best to prepare the place against us, though how they could have known we'd return from death, I can only guess."

Toshi gulped down his tea, still not looking at Asaka, but continued to hold the cup to keep his hands occupied.

"Thanks to your help, we've been able to overcome all that has been placed in our path so far," Asaka said casually. "That is, but for our latest unexpected setback."

He knew the moment he'd been dreading was almost upon him. Against his will, he found his eyes rising to face his doom.

"Your services were only to be required for guiding us here and, if necessary, to retrieve the kettle from the temple if we could not. After you had guided us back to the coast, it had been my intention to return you to your former home."

He tried not to breathe, tense as he waited for what would come next.

"I had always assumed, due to pride, if you will, that once the object was recovered we would continue on our original journey and complete our mission just as it had been given to us so many years ago," Asaka admitted. "The incident on the island, however, has placed these plans at risk."

Toshi swallowed hard.

"You are able to handle the object, but we cannot. Among us, we don't have the knowledge necessary to attempt to undo the spell that's been placed upon it.

"Your service to my family has been invaluable, and I will never forget the price you have already paid in its behalf. Yet, what I would ask of you now will by no means be simple and may ask even more from you than what you've already given. Under the worst of circumstances, it might even cost you your life."

A cold shiver ran down Toshi's back, but he barely noticed it. His attention was completely focused on what Asaka would say next.

"Our journey was to proceed from the islands back to the coast and from there on to Narashi."

"Narashi?" Narashi was one of the largest cities in the land. So large it rivaled the capital in Odan.

"Yes, Narashi. A long, difficult journey, but one that must be made." Asaka fell silent, green light flashing from his eyes. "The burden this would place on you would be considerable. Therefore, the choice of whether or not you will attempt it will be yours to make.

"No repercussions will fall on you if you choose not to try. A debt is already owed you, and time means nothing to us. If you choose not to go, other arrangements will eventually be made."

Toshi found he couldn't breathe for a moment.

"The choice is yours, Toshiro," Asaka stated again. "No honor will be lost if you decide not to go."

The samurai stood and walked to a stand near the door that held his armor. Toshi followed him with his eyes, dead certain he must have misunderstood what he'd been told.

"You will soon be needed above. I suggest you go and retrieve your instruments."

Nodding, he rose and headed to the door, his mind numb.

"I will ask for your answer once we come within sight of the bay," Asaka said from behind him.

Without showing he'd heard, Toshi bowed deeply and then let himself out of the room. Mitsuo was standing in the hallway waiting for him.

He trod back to his room in a daze and retrieved his instruments. He never noticed Miko, who still sat where he'd left her, as she followed him across the room with her eyes. Mitsuo came in after him, staring at him even as he walked over to pick up his blankets.

As he started back toward the door, Mitsuo stopped him and held out to him the boken he'd left behind. He stared at it as if he'd never seen the thing before. After a moment, he blinked and reached for it, still staring at it as he slipped it through his sash. Without a word, he started toward the door again.

He reached the deck and ignored everyone and everything. With a distracted weariness, he went about getting his first readings of the night. Oblivious to all around him, he finished his calculations and showed their present location to the steersman.

Chapter 18

Sitting up at Mitsuo's insistent prodding, Toshi blinked several times before realizing what was expected of him. He got his things together and shook his head, trying to dispel the unbelievable dream he'd been having. A dream about the samurai!

As he got up, his gaze strayed in Asaka's direction. He couldn't help but wonder how his mind could have concocted such strange behavior for the man. That a samurai would give him, a peasant, power over his own fate was preposterous. What could have led him to dream such a thing?

Dismissing it, he brought up his cross-staff. As he did so, the sleeve of his kimono suddenly caught his eye. It was dark blue with light blue waves tipped in silver thread. How could that be? It was the kimono in his dream. With a gasp of dread, he shut his eyes as he swayed slightly. It hadn't been a dream after all. It had been real.

"Toshiro," Asaka said.

He stiffened at the familiar voice. Mustering his will, he forced his eyes open and looked back toward the samurai.

"Is there a problem?" Dots of green light flared from Asaka's mask with an intensity he didn't like.

"No, sir. Everything's fine." Tearing his eyes away from the samurai's questioning gaze, he forced himself to go on and take his readings. When it was over, sleep took him again.

Each time he was awakened, he hoped the dream would be over. Each time, to his chagrin, he found it wasn't a dream but reality, and it looked like it would stay that way.

Feeling exhausted, though he'd had no trouble sleeping through the night, he gladly made his way below after being dismissed. Toshi was barely conscious of Mitsuo's presence as the latter followed him.

Finding Miko waiting for him in his room, he saw his breakfast was already laid out for him. Bowing toward her but saying nothing, he set his basket down in the far corner of the room. He waited patiently for Mitsuo to lay down his covers and then wrapped himself in them. The old samurai shrugged in answer to Miko's questioning look. Mitsuo left, staring strangely at him.

"Toshi-kun, your breakfast is getting cold," Miko said.

"Oh." Glancing at her as if he'd noticed her for the first time, he distractedly reached for the bowl of soup before him.

"How was the sailing tonight?"

"Fine."

"Did you sleep well?" she asked.

"Yes." He could feel Miko's eyes on him, though his never rose to meet them.

"Is something wrong, Toshi-kun?" she asked with a touch of worry.

"No."

"Have I done something to offend you?" She leaned toward him.

"No." He began eating in earnest to cut off any further conversation. He maintained his silence even after he'd finished eating. Miko quietly gathered his empty dishes and headed toward the door. She never saw the look of abject misery that followed her out.

He didn't look up when the geisha returned, but stared instead at the floor. He forced his expression to become blank. He was grateful when Miko didn't try to talk to him. He did glance up, however, as he came to realize she wasn't alone. He saw Mitsuo standing before him even as Miko set up her koto in the corner. Toshi got up slowly, his hand on the boken at his side, knowing what was expected of him.

As Miko tuned her instrument, Mitsuo helped him fold back his long sleeves as he told him what maneuvers he wanted to see. Nodding, but never looking straight at his teacher, he got into position. His bruised shoulder protested as he did the necessary quick sweeping movements with his boken. Making himself concentrate, he tried to ignore the burning question that had come to encompass his every waking thought.

He never noticed as Mitsuo came at him from the side. He dropped in two blows.

"You are not concentrating." Mitsuo's words were more of an accusation than a statement.

Without comment, Toshi forced himself up and started again where he'd left off. He tried his best to keep his attention on the lesson, but his thoughts just wouldn't leave him alone. Every time his concentration lapsed, Mitsuo would deftly step forward and drop him with just one or two blows.

Trying to use his new pains as a reminder, he tried again to push all things from his mind, leaving only his concentration on his movements. He fared a little better after that.

"Time for lunch," Miko said.

Toshi brushed some loose strands of hair from his face, hoping it wasn't a trick of some kind. Glancing toward the door, he saw Miko was, indeed, coming in with food. He bowed toward Mitsuo, hoping to be dismissed, and breathed a sigh of relief as the bow was returned. Moving with a slight limp, he grabbed his blankets and sat down.

His body hurt, yet he felt good. He no longer felt as tired as he had when he'd awakened. He smiled as Miko passed him a cup of tea. Drinking it fast, despite the burns it left on his tongue, he also reached for some fish. He felt unusually hungry.

"You look as if you feel better, Toshi-kun." Miko sounded happy.

He glanced up at her for a moment before returning all of his attention back to his food.

"Perhaps Mitsuo-san ought to be working you harder."

He choked on the piece of fish he was swallowing. He glanced around to see if Mitsuo had heard her comment. It was only then he realized his teacher was gone.

"That really wouldn't be necessary, Miko-san."

"Wouldn't it?" she asked.

He slumped, praying she was just teasing him.

"I have some water heating for you," she said. "Mitsuo-san graciously decided you should have the afternoon free. There are many games I'd like for us to play today."

"If you like, Miko-san."

"Good. You see, you need some loosening up, and I'm just the woman for the job."

Her light tone made him happy, but her words reminded him of his own problem. Trying not to let it show, he hurried through the rest of his meal.

"Sit right there and rest, I won't be long," Miko said.

Left alone, he found it harder and harder to keep his thoughts away from his problem. The same question repeated itself over and over in his mind, with no answer in sight.

By the time Miko returned with his bath water, his mental exhaustion was wearing on him again. He tried to keep his feelings from showing but knew he wasn't being overtly successful.

He washed his body. After that, Miko offered to wash his hair for him. Having no reason to say no, he nodded and watched her sadly as she retrieved the extra bucket. A new question occurred to him—did she know about the choice Asaka had asked him to make?

He leaned forward as Miko asked, and she undid his ponytail. White strands fell past his face and he shivered, his mind wanting to know how much more might be demanded from him if he decided to go. But why should he think of going? He had done enough—more than enough. Asaka had even told him so.

He jumped as Miko poured warm water over his bent head. With experienced fingers, she soaped and cleaned his hair. He shivered, still undressed beneath his blankets. The cold seeped into his wet head and deepened the worry and confusion already moving like a maelstrom inside him. He tried to sit still as she first dried and then combed out his hair.

"Which game do you think you'd like to try first?" she asked.

"I really don't feel like playing any games today."

"Oh?"

He tried not to look at her as her masked face lowered beside him trying to catch a glimpse of his own.

"Toshi-kun, what's troubling you?"

"Nothing—" He clamped his mouth shut, not trusting himself to say more without giving too much away.

"You and I both know that isn't so. Even Mitsuo-san has noticed something is not right."

"There's nothing wrong!" He regretted his outburst as soon as the words left his mouth. He kept his lips shut tight and waited for her to press him again. When she didn't, but only continued combing out his hair, he felt an odd panic flow up inside him. He wanted to ask her questions, but he couldn't bring himself to do it. How was he to tell her of his uncertainty? How could he tell her he might not want to help her gain the freedom she so sought?

He stood, startling the geisha, and walked away, his blankets coiled about his naked form. A need was burning in him, but he didn't know how to get rid of it. He wasn't even sure he wanted to get rid of it. No one of his station had ever been meant to bear so much. He was only a peasant!

He turned around and stared at her. She sat absolutely still, gazing at his tortured face.

"Why, Miko-san, *why*? I don't understand why."

"'Why' what, Toshi-kun?" Her voice was a whisper. Soft blue light shone in her eyes.

He twisted away, feeling his confusion and near despair trying to overwhelm him.

"From what you said before, I had understood my time with you wasn't over, that my services would still be needed. And I had expected what he said. I'd known all along what he would say." His words came out in a rush. "But, Miko-san, he didn't order me to do it. He didn't tell me what he wanted so I would do it, as all servants must. He—he *asked* me! He wants *me* to make the choice. I don't understand it, and I can't. I *can't*!" He doubled over, his own words causing a pain inside him.

"Toshi-kun, don't you realize the honor that's been given to you? The freedom?" she asked him. "According to our ways, you are his, body and soul. He could just have ordered you to go on this journey, and you would have had to comply. Instead, he's given you a choice, a freedom many of us never get, a chance to choose your own path. The freedom to make your own life."

Miko appeared at his side, though he never heard her move.

"I don't see how I'm free. I can't choose!" He felt ill. How could she believe this was freedom?

"You must choose, and you will," she insisted. "Go with what your heart tells you. Don't think of us, think of yourself."

He looked up at her in confused horror, his face puffed and tear-streaked. "How can I think of myself? You're all damned! I would make me go if I were in your place. Why should I have my own way? Don't you want to be free?"

Miko reached out and caressed his flushed face. "What an enigma you are sometimes. Such selfless naiveté," she said. "It just doesn't fit our times."

He could only stare at her. Her words only helped add to his confusion. "Miko-san, I don't understand."

Her hand tenderly traveled past his cheek to his shoulder. She grabbed his blankets and pulled forward. He fell with a small gasp, and before he knew it he was wrapped in her arms. Though he tried hard to pull away, she wouldn't let go of him.

"You must choose what's in your heart, Toshi-kun," she said. "Don't pick one way because you owe someone or another because we're doomed. Don't pick one because you believe you'll succeed or another because you might fail. Rather, choose the one you can live with. Choose from your heart."

He let her cradle him in her arms, knowing what she was doing, knowing it was the same thing Asaka had done. Tears ran down his face, staining her kimono as he cried.

Chapter 19

It was some time later when Toshi got dressed. Night was falling on the world above. Feeling more calm, but still undecided, he ate a little before heading up.

The next few days crawled by. He spent his time practicing under Mitsuo's guidance or amusing himself with Miko's games and stories. He never again brought up the topic of his upcoming choice. Miko did the same. Most of the time, he tried to pretend his problem didn't even exist—though, in the end, he was only too aware it wouldn't make any difference.

When he couldn't set those thoughts aside, however, he could feel a strange tension building inside him as time ran out. No one pressed him. Everyone treated him as they always had before. Even Asaka ignored him as usual. The lack of pressure grated on his nerves. It looked like he'd be making the decision on his own whether he liked it or not.

* * * * *

"It is time to go below, Toshiro-san," Mitsuo said.

He opened his eyes and stared at the old samurai in incomprehension. Had something gone wrong? He'd only been awakened twice so far. "Go below?"

"Yes. It's almost dawn."

He sat up and began gathering his things, even as his mind fought to understand what the discrepancy meant.

He looked out over the dark sea, but couldn't see far. However, he realized he didn't need to see to know there was land out there and that it was very close. He could smell it in the air—the faint scent of fish and grass that hadn't been there before. He hadn't been awakened for a reading because the ship had come to waters the crew were familiar with.

His stomach knotted. Their sea journey was almost at an end. His time of decision would soon be upon him. With a nervous glance, he looked at their lord as he descended to the lower deck. Asaka sat, as unapproachable as ever, in no way acknowledging he knew Toshi was leaving the deck. He hurried to his room.

"Good morning, Toshi-kun."

"Good morning, Miko-san." His voice was muffled as he draped his blankets around him. Settling down, it occurred to him to wonder if she had any idea they were close to the coast. He pulled the map out of his basket and tried to gauge how much farther they had to go.

"Where are we?" she asked.

He hesitated for a moment before pointing to a spot on the map. "I think we're somewhere around here."

"It won't be much longer, will it?" Her tone was neutral.

He had to swallow hard before he could answer. "No."

Time had almost run out on him. With a small shiver, he rolled up the map and put it back. His eyes strayed to the cause of all his woes.

The black kettle sat just as he'd left it, its bright-emblazoned sun sparkling in the ship's eerie light. He tore his gaze away from it, hating it for putting him in this situation. Though he no longer had an appetite, he made himself eat, lest he give Miko the impression something was wrong.

All through the day, his upcoming decision occupied all of his thoughts. It interfered with his practice session, though up to that point he'd been making some progress. He earned a number of new bruises for his lack of concentration.

He lost every game he played with Miko that afternoon as well. Eventually, she gave up on trying to distract him and left him to his thoughts.

Though he'd pondered on it all day, he still hadn't made up his mind as time ran out. He had to make a decision. He had no choice. Asaka would be expecting no hesitation from him once he put forth the question to him again. Yet it made no difference. He had no idea what he wanted to do.

Later, he let himself be led topside. His body was coiled with tension as he made the only computation needed that night. He lay down as expected, but couldn't sleep. He kept his eyes closed, his choices spinning round and round in his head.

If he went, he might never reach Narashi. If he stayed, the crew would remain damned. If he went, they might be freed. If he stayed, he'd doom someone else to do their bidding.

"Asaka-sama, the bay lies around this bend. Should I stop us here?" This came from the steersman.

Toshi's eyes snapped open. He turned on his side and looked at Asaka. The samurai rose from his stool, his gaze locked to their left.

"Do not turn inland, but continue straight ahead." His voice was as impassive as ever. "Bring us to the same position we held on our last visit here."

"Hai."

Toshi held his breath as green, flashing eyes glanced in his direction. The samurai's gaze held his own, telling him the time of choosing was almost at hand. He looked away, knowing he still had no answer. He slowly sat up and stared out past the rail.

A dark mass rose grandly from the sea, obscuring everything beyond it. Though its features were indistinct, he could still see where it curved away not far ahead of them. Unwillingly, his gaze remained there. He knew once they'd crossed it he would be in the waters of the bay of his childhood, the place he'd always called home. He'd made it back.

The large knot in his stomach grew tighter, an unreasoning fear blooming inside him now that he'd returned. His hands shook as he took the telescope from his basket and held it in his moist hands as the ship crossed into the bay.

He held his breath as they cleared the last bit of land. With a soft click, he extended the telescope and brought it to his waiting eye.

Darkness lay like a cloak across the city. Only a few dots of light tried to break past the illusion. These dots sat out over the docks, acting like beacons welcoming late-arriving ships home. Using the power of the telescope and the few lights about, he was able to make out most of the ships at dock. With a pang of guilt and pain, he located the *Corazon*, Captain Valéz's ship. It sat just as he'd seen it last.

"Toshiro, it is time for you to go below," Asaka said.

Memories of the strange gaijin friend crowded into Toshi's mind—his askew mustached grin, his odd foreign views on things, his contagious sense of humor.

With a queer stillness brewing in him, Toshi turned away from the sight. "Hai, Asaka-sama."

After gathering his things, he went below. Mitsuo followed after him.

"We are there, Toshi-kun?" Miko asked as he came into the room.

He found he couldn't look at her. "Yes, Miko-san."

He knew she was aware of what was to come. In minutes, he felt the ship sink into the sea. He buried himself deep in his covers, feeling a chill that had nothing to do with the ever-present cold.

He looked up as Miko caressed his cheek. He thought she was about to say something when the sound of a deep bell rang outside the door.

"I'll be back, Toshi-chan. I shouldn't be gone long." She stared at him for a long moment before going on. "Would you like some tea when I return, or would something stronger be in order?"

She tilted her head playfully toward him as she rose to her feet.

"I would prefer the tea, if you don't mind," he said. "I don't think I could handle sake very well just now."

"As you wish."

He watched her leave and then glanced over at Mitsuo as the latter closed the door. His teacher said nothing. Toshi did nothing to disturb the silence.

With a deep sigh, he attempted once again to push his troubled thoughts aside. He tried to think of some way to distract himself but came up with nothing. His spinning thoughts wouldn't go away.

Miko returned, her eyes bright as she came into the room, bowing formally in his direction. "Lord Asaka requests the honor of your presence in his chambers."

A lump jumped and settled tight into his throat. The moment he'd been dreading was upon him. He stumbled over his words. "I—I would be honored to meet with him."

He stood and headed toward the door, his mind close to panic.

"Toshi-chan, don't you think you should clean up a bit first? After all, you are about to be presented to our lord." Miko's tone was full of mirth.

He stopped and stared at her in confusion, his mind unwilling to understand what she was talking about. As Miko raised her sleeve to hide her lacquered mouth, he recalled his slept-in clothes and mussed hair. His cheeks burned.

"Don't worry, dear one. I'll help you." Laughing as she came to his rescue, Miko straightened out his kimono and redid his hair. "Well, Mitsuo-san, is he ready?"

The old samurai took his time looking him up and down. Toshi tried hard not to fidget, his nervousness increasing.

"It will do," Mitsuo said.

He followed Miko out of the room, and Mitsuo trailed them. Toshi kept having to remind himself to breathe as they walked down the short hallway over to the samurai's door.

Miko knocked and, after a moment, opened the door into the room. He followed her in. Asaka sat at the same place as before.

Toshi gingerly took his seat. He was a little surprised to discover that Miko and Mitsuo weren't leaving. He wasn't sure if it was a good thing or not.

Hot tea and sake were on the table, as well as six small plates of unusual tidbits. Miko knelt down on a cushion placed next to the left side of the table. Gracefully, she served both seated men. Toshi swallowed hard as she placed one of the plates before him and another before their lord.

"Please, Toshiro, have some." Asaka pointed at his plate.

Not sure whether he should consider it a command or request, he reached out for one of the red candies before him. As the sweet taste inundated his mouth, he kept his attention on Miko as she grabbed two empty teacups. Eagerly awaiting the warm tea, he was surprised when she instead poured sake into each of them.

She offered him the filled cup. Desperate for warmth, he took it and sipped. The heat of the alcohol cascaded into his stomach and was soon spreading through his limbs. He had barely set the cup down before Miko was refilling it again.

"I assume you are aware of why I've asked you here."

"Hai, Asaka-sama." His stomach tightened like a fist, the taste of bile rising in his throat. Green flashed at him from the samurai's mask.

"We've gone full circle, yet nothing is as it had been," Asaka said. "I have need of you still, but you have already done much. The time of choosing is upon you, Chizuson Toshiro. Which road do you choose?"

He stared at the samurai's relentless green eyes. He opened his mouth to try and reply, but nothing came out. Miko's words came back to him as he struggled to somehow make up his mind at this late hour. *Choose what is in your heart.*

"I would like...like to continue the journey." He almost felt giddy at finally having made a choice.

Asaka nodded, as if it were the answer he'd expected all along. Toshi took a deep breath, and taking courage from the sake, plunged on.

"But there's a condition—"

Silence filled the room.

"I humbly request Captain Valéz's tools be returned to him."

Impassive eyes stared into his. Toshi's chest tightened to the point where he thought he'd no longer be able to breathe.

"Why is this necessary?" Asaka's voice was low.

He could tell nothing from the samurai's tone. He had already stepped into this; all he could do now was plunge on.

"The captain and his men can't leave Nihon without them. They would be stranded here, far from their home."

Asaka said and did nothing. Though he wanted to, Toshi dared not risk a glance in Miko's direction.

"If their instruments are not returned, you'll be doing to them what was done to you. They'll be stranded here, forever prevented from going where they must."

He held his breath, waiting for the samurai to explode in rage at his impudence. Instead, Asaka slowly nodded.

"Well said. Be assured, their items will be returned."

"Thank you, Asaka-sama." He bowed all the way to the floor. A wave of relief washed through him. He felt his stomach relax now that this part of it was over. He reached for his refilled cup of sake and gulped it down.

"Supplies for your journey will be procured tonight," Asaka informed him. "By tomorrow all you will require will have been readied for you."

"Hai."

"As you know, you aren't able to travel well in darkness, and we can't travel during the day. If you travel with us, we will be unable to offer you any protection while you sleep. But if you travel during the day and sleep at night, the darkness itself will protect you until we can catch up. This will place a great amount of responsibility on you, but you will handle it."

Toshi tried to keep his insecurity from showing on his face.

"You will disguise yourself as a peasant during your travels," Asaka added. "You will avoid all villages and towns until you reach Narashi. A map will be found for you to show the way."

"Hai."

Miko poured him more sake. Though he knew he'd already had more than enough, he reached for it and began to sip the warm liquid.

"Since we must stay out of sight and you can't sleep indoors, you'll be dropped on shore so you may rest. We will retrieve you before sunrise so the final preparations can be attended to. Do you understand?"

"Hai." He nodded while still sipping his sake, a not-unpleasant buzzing in his ears.

"That will be all for now. Go, prepare yourself."

Gulping down the rest of his sake, he rose, bowed and headed toward the door.

"I'll join you in a few moments, Toshi-chan," Miko called out.

He glanced back at the geisha and nodded. Mitsuo opened the door for him and followed him out.

Once back in his room, he retrieved his basket and set out all the instruments on the small table. He checked and cleaned them, and then put them in a neat row. Meanwhile, Mitsuo kept busy folding his blankets. He'd almost finished when Miko entered the room.

"You know, Toshi-chan, I can see how you came to have such a low opinion of our lord," she said. "If he spoke to me with such seriousness and ceremony, I don't think I could find much to like in him either."

He gawked at her in shock.

"I've been telling him for years he needs to learn to relax. He takes everything much too seriously. Though I can't imagine where he could have got it from."

Miko stood with her hands on her hips and stared straight at Mitsuo. The latter said nothing.

Toshi tried to hide a small smile, feeling a little lightheaded as he picked up his boken. The ship tipped slightly, telling him they'd risen to the surface. He felt a dread-laced thrill at the thought he was being allowed to go to shore.

"Hm, it's time. I guess we'd best get you going." Miko turned toward Mitsuo. "Our young adventurer will need all the rest he can get, won't he, Mitsuo-san?"

Toshi followed the geisha sheepishly as she led him out of the room. Halfway up the small hallway, she stopped and turned around to lean very close to him.

"Thank you, Toshi-kun. I know this was very hard on you. I truly appreciate your willingness to try to help us, from the bottom of my heart."

His cheeks reddened at her words. The alcohol in his blood and her close proximity made the hallway feel cramped and stuffy. He swallowed hard, trying to come up with some sort of reply as blue light filled her eyes. Caressing his flushed cheeks, Miko walked away and stepped out into the night. He forced himself to follow after her.

The skiff was waiting for them as they came on deck. Mitsuo climbed down first, taking Toshi's blankets from the geisha once he'd gotten on board. Toshi bowed to her, still having no reply, and made his way into the boat.

Once he was seated, Mitsuo released the ropes holding the skiff to the ship and pushed away from it. The two men on board began rowing toward the dark shore at the lip of the bay.

His alcohol-laden stomach protested as the waves got rougher the closer they got to shore. Wondering how they were going to land without a sloping beach to cling to, he yelped as the two rowers abruptly tumbled overboard. He searched for them but saw nothing in the dark water until a bony hand reached up to attach to the side rail. He sat back, noticing another hand was attached to the other side as well. He kept forgetting that normal dangers didn't apply to Asaka's crew.

The skiff started sliding forward. He glanced back at Mitsuo, but he looked unconcerned.

He held on to the seat before him, sitting down on the bottom of the boat as it rocked up and down while it was being guided. He tried not to moan as his empty stomach made him regret having drunk so much sake.

The heads of the two crewmen rose from the surf as the skiff got closer to shore. They kept the boat steady as the waves crashed against the steep bank before them. They signaled those on board it was time to get off.

Mitsuo clambered past the boy onto the bank and then gave him a hand up. Once he'd helped him onto land and away from the spraying surf, Mitsuo returned to the boat for the blankets.

Toshi then waited for his teacher as the latter scanned the darkened terrain around them for signs of possible danger. Stumbling after him as Mitsuo finally set off, Toshi gratefully stopped as they reached a large, protruding rock formation. Mitsuo carefully laid out his blankets and then bade him lie down.

Before he did so, he looked back toward the water and saw the small boat pulling farther and farther away from shore. With a sigh, he crawled into his blankets and tried to get comfortable even as Mitsuo watched over him. The warmth from the covers and the sake in his blood, plus the cool breeze from the sea, worked together to drag him quickly down to a deep sleep.

An unknown amount of time later, he felt someone shaking his shoulder. Opening his eyes, he found Mitsuo's white, fleshless face close to his own.

"We must go now," Mitsuo said.

He sat up slowly, nodding his understanding, and rubbed the sleep from his eyes. His stomach grumbled unhappily as he looked out toward the water and saw the glowing ship close to shore.

He got up, helped Mitsuo fold his blankets and allowed the old samurai to lead him toward the surf. The small skiff was waiting at the bottom of the steep bank, held by the two rowers.

The tide was ebbing, making the waves seem calmer. As soon as Toshi and Mitsuo were aboard, the two men pushed them away from the bank before climbing on board to row toward the ship. It wasn't long before they had him back. As soon as he could, he made his way below to his room.

"Good morning, Toshi-kun." Miko sat by the small table next to his futon. A plate of mush and fish was waiting for him there as well. "You'll be happy to know all the instruments were returned last night to your gaijin captain."

He smiled as he ate hungrily, nodding with genuine appreciation and relief.

"A visit was also paid to your old home to try and retrieve a few of your possessions for you."

He stopped eating.

"Your Master Shun seems in good health," she said. "He also seems to be a very busy and thorough man. He has already obtained a young apprentice to fill in your vacancy." Her tone was gentle, but he never noticed.

Master Shun had replaced him, and so quickly? Yes, the two of them had never been the closest of people, but Master Shun was still all the family he'd ever really had or known. His appetite deserted him.

"We weren't able to find much, only another change of clothes. Did we miss anything important?"

"I—no, nothing. None of it was important." His voice sounded empty. "It all probably belongs to the new boy now, anyway."

The geisha cocked her heard and stared at him for a long time. "Are you regretting your decision, Toshi-kun?"

"Hm?" He forced himself to eat another bite of fish. "No, Miko-san, it's not that."

"Then what is it? You hadn't really planned to go back to him had you not chosen to come with us, had you?" Her curiosity was obvious. "Lord Asaka had already cleared you of your commitment."

He stared at his teacup as he considered what he should say. Through it all, he'd never contemplated what would happen once he was free. Of course he'd been replaced. That was the type of man Shun was—business always came first. And with the amount of money Asaka had paid for Toshi, he would have easily afforded someone new.

"It's not that. Though I wasn't sure what I would do. It's just—if I don't survive this, it'll be as if I'd never existed. There'll be no trace I ever was."

He half-expected her to laugh at his foolishness, but she didn't.

"Though it may not seem like it to you, Toshi-kun, you've left enough marks in the world for there to never be any doubt you existed," she said. "You've made a difference. You have changed the paths of other peoples' lives. It won't be forgotten."

He looked up at her. "You're too good to me, Miko-san." His tone was serious.

Hers was not. "Yes, and don't you dare forget it."

Chapter 20

After he'd eaten, Toshi sat back as Miko cleared his dishes away. When she returned, she brought a small pail of water. He eyed it with curiosity.

"What's that for?"

Miko looked up at him but didn't answer. Instead, she placed the pail near him and then proceeded to retrieve one of the many packages lining the room. She removed from one of them a large, stoppered jar.

"This, dear one, will transform you back into a normal boy."

"Huh?"

Without answering him, Miko placed the jar next to the pail and then left. She returned carrying drying cloths and a large bowl.

"Miko-san, what did you mean by—"

She held up her hand. "Patience, Toshi-kun. You will see soon enough."

Giving her his total attention, he watched as Miko put the bowl on the table and filled it partway with the water from the pail. His curiosity peaked as she lifted the jar from the floor and took off its top. She tipped it over the bowl, allowing a stream of black liquid to pour inside.

"It's ink." He leaned forward, wondering what she planned to do with it.

"Yes, but it's a special type of ink. And with it, we're going to transform you."

"What?"

Miko looked at his startled expression and laughed. "Can't you guess what this is for, Toshi-kun?"

"Well, uh…" He wracked his brains to find an answer but could come up with none. "No, I can't."

She laughed again. "It's for your hair, silly-chan. We're going to dye your hair."

"Dye my hair?" Without thinking, he reached up to touch his ponytailed hair.

"Yes. For if you're going to go out into the world as a normal young man, it won't do to have you showing off your beautiful white mane."

"Oh." He suddenly felt dense.

Miko hid her mouth behind her wide sleeve. "Come here and sit, Toshi-kun. We'll need to get this on you before the water gets cold."

"Hai." He moved to comply.

"There's enough ink in the jar for three or four full applications," she said. "They're not many, so you'll have to make them last. Unfortunately, water will slowly dilute the ink and make it run. You may be forced to touch it up on occasion. It shouldn't be too difficult if you take care."

He felt the warm water as she scooped it onto his hair and scalp. Miko then ran a comb through it, squeezing out any excess.

"How did you find out about this, Miko-san?"

"All women have their little secrets, Toshi-kun."

He could hear her chuckling softly behind him. After thoroughly dying his hair with the watered ink, Miko removed it from the bowl and patted it dry. Taking an unused cloth, she wound it about his head and with a twist, hid the hair inside and laid it on his head at an odd angle.

"The cloth will absorb any leftover water and help keep your head warm," she told him. "I'll comb it out for you a little later."

"Thank you, Miko-san." Feeling foolish with the twisted cloth on his head, he sat up slowly, trying not to make it fall. Mitsuo took the bowl and pail out of the room as Miko began moving packages.

"Miko-san, what are all those?" he asked.

"These? Different things." Miko opened a number of them, showing him what lay inside. One package held his old clothes, as well as a spare set. Another held clothes fit for a young samurai. A large wicker basket sat in the corner to carry them all, and beside it sat a lined straw hat, a straw coat, foodstuffs and other miscellaneous supplies.

"Oh." He couldn't think of anything else to say.

"What? Is there something we've forgotten?"

"Uh, no. " He saw her give him a disbelieving look. "Actually, Miko-san, I don't know the first thing about preparing for a long journey. I've never been on one before."

She sat down beside him. "Does the thought of going scare you, Toshi-kun?"

He glanced at her for a moment and then looked away. "I'm not sure. I guess so. I haven't really had time to think about it much. I haven't gotten that far yet," he admitted.

"You may not believe it, but I fear for you. My heart aches over your future as if you were my own flesh and blood," she confessed. "I'm afraid of what lies ahead. I'm afraid of what you may have to risk for us."

Her words did for him what his own thoughts hadn't. His throat grew dry and tight as he tried not to let fear overtake him.

"I'm sure everything will be fine, Miko-san. Asaka-sama won't be far behind me." The thought didn't help him feel more secure, but he hoped it would work for her.

"Yes, you're right, we won't be far behind." She didn't sound convinced.

Later, Miko was gently combing through his hair when there was a knock at the door. When Mitsuo opened it, Toshi was surprised to see Asaka waiting beyond. He bowed to the ground, surprised not only by the visit but by the fact Asaka wasn't wearing his armor as usual. Without any ceremony, the samurai strode into the room and sat down not far from him.

"I have brought a number of things you will find necessary for your journey," he said.

Toshi nodded but said nothing. He watched with interest as Asaka reached within his kimono and drew out a small leather bag.

"I am told there should be enough here to obtain anything you might require, should the need arise." The bag jingled loudly as Asaka dropped it onto the small table beside him.

Though he itched to see how much money was there, Toshi restrained himself from reaching for it. Instead, he watched as Asaka reached within his kimono again.

"A map has been found that should help make your trip easier. You're to follow the marked route, deviating only if absolutely necessary. Follow the roads, but avoid contact with others whenever possible. The fewer people that see you, the less of a trail there will be for our enemies to find and follow."

A slow chill coursed up his spine. "Enemies?"

Asaka placed the rolled-up map on the table. "Yes, enemies. How else would you categorize those who engineered our fall from honor? The ninja knows you; he knows your destination and what you carry, though he may not know why. Those who control him will not want us to finish that which they thought stopped so long ago."

Toshi frowned down at the floor, the enormity of what he was taking on dawning on him for the first time.

"Though they'll know your eventual destination, the advantage is still ours, for they don't know how or from where we will come," Asaka added. "This advantage shall remain ours if you take great care in your travels."

"Hai." His gaze strayed to the map, wondering over how great a distance their enemies might have a go at him. Their enemies? Yes, he was one of Asaka's people now, by his own choice. He doubted the enemy would have any more mercy on him than what they'd shown to his lord so long ago. He was grateful for his blankets, for the cover hid his fearful shivering from Asaka.

He glanced up as the samurai removed a thin bamboo cylinder from his sleeve.

"Within this tube rests a parchment given to me by Lord Asano."

Toshi's eyes grew wide, having heard the name before.

"It's a permit, one that allows us to cross into any of his lands and gain help from his subjects without question. It will have to do in lieu of the normal traveling papers." Asaka's voice grew hard. "Don't use it unless absolutely necessary before you reach the castle. It'll be your key to get in. If you use it before then, it might become a beacon to our enemies."

Toshi stared at the tube, not quite daring to believe what was about to be given to him. Free passage through a lord's land? He'd never heard of such a paper being bestowed on anyone.

Asaka set the tube down, then brought out the next item to be presented.

"This I give to you as a symbol of your status as a messenger for myself and Lord Asano. Once you have reached Narashi, wear it proudly, and use it to remind yourself of whom you serve and what needs to be done."

Toshi stared at the samurai in shock as the latter held out a sheathed wakizashi. Its red-colored handle was emblazoned with the Asaka clan's symbol. "I—"

"Take it." Asaka's tone was only momentarily harsh. "You've earned it."

Trying hard to keep his hand from shaking, Toshi took the sheathed blade. Bowing in thanks mostly to keep his red face from being seen, he held on to the short sword. "Thank you, Asaka-sama."

"You must seek out Lord Asano once you've reached his castle in Narashi. I have every reason to believe he's still alive," Asaka continued. "If not, you may deliver the object to his ruling descendant. Under no circumstances are you to give it to anyone else."

"You won't try to see Lord Asano yourself, sir?" He wasn't sure why, but he had a feeling he already knew the answer to his question.

The cold metal mask met his gaze head-on. "Not unless it proves necessary. I'm no longer certain we'll be able to enter the castle grounds. There are too many unknowns at this time to foresee what will eventually occur."

"Hai." He tried hard not to guess at these unknowns.

"At nightfall, you'll be escorted to shore and guided a short way into the mainland. We'll remain with you until dawn. After sunrise, you'll begin your journey. We'll follow the same path at night."

Toshi looked away, the wakizashi gripped in his hand. A dizzy feeling overtook him as things suddenly appeared to be happening too fast. "Hai."

"Do you have any questions? Is there anything you feel you'll need that hasn't been provided for you?" the samurai asked.

He managed to look up and shake his head. "No, Asaka-sama."

"Good. I'll see you again at nightfall."

He bowed as the samurai stood up and stayed that way until he had gone.

"Toshi-kun, are you feeling all right?" Miko touched his arm.

He nodded, not feeling steady enough to speak. His journey would soon be upon him and it made him feverish. "Yes, I'm all right, Miko-san. I—I guess I'm just a little overwhelmed." He tried hard to smile, hoping to disguise his growing uneasiness.

Miko reached out for him and held him close. He was too amazed by the hug to protest.

"You are such a delight. Please, Toshi-chan, don't ever change!"

Chapter 21

"Do the clothes fit all right, Toshi-kun?"

"Yes, Miko-san, they're fine." He considered reminding her there was no reason why they shouldn't, since they were his, but decided against it as he watched her fold his dirty clothes for the third time. "How much longer do I have?"

Miko looked up at the question. She set the folded clothes aside as she realized what she'd been doing. "You've long enough to eat everything on your plates and even let it settle for a little while."

He took the hint and started eating. He watched the geisha out of the corner of his eye as she got up and packed his things into the large basket, including his boken and wakizashi. She placed everything neatly inside except for the kettle and the three things Asaka had given him.

"It might be best, Toshi-kun, if you kept these on your person."

Without comment, he took them from her and slipped them inside his tunic.

"I'll have to leave the packing of the kettle up to you," she said.

Following her stare, he realized he hadn't thought much about the kettle lately. His whole life had been changed because of it, yet he still didn't understand why such a simple item was worth all they had gone through so far. There had to be something about the kettle that wasn't obvious, something he couldn't see. But what?

Leaving the warmth of his blankets, he walked across the room and picked it up. He was somewhat amazed to find the eerie coldness about him ease a little. He wished he'd noticed this before. Opening the basket, he nested the kettle in the packaged foodstuffs and reclosed the lid. With three quick steps he rushed back to his futon and its waiting warmth.

He finished his dinner and fidgeted, knowing the time for his journey would be upon him soon. His muscles tensed as he abruptly felt the ship rise toward the surface. He opened his mouth to say something, only to find Miko staring at him, her eyes ablaze.

"Toshi-kun, it's time," she said.

Nodding as words failed him, he stood as she did. He helped her fold his blankets for the last time. When they were through, he picked up the basket and slipped his arms through its thick straps. He held the wide, almost conical hat, in his right hand.

"I'm ready."

Mitsuo gave him an acknowledging nod and opened the door. Toshi walked out into the hall and tried to ignore the weight resting on his back. Going out on deck, he found all the crew gathered there wearing light infantry armor. Asaka stood before them.

Toshi averted his eyes to the floor and tried to bow. Mitsuo and Miko simultaneously reached out for him as the extra weight on his back tried to pitch him forward. He rebalanced himself with their help, his cheeks flaming. He looked up in surprise as laughter rolled from those standing before him. He was even more astonished to see his lord was standing among them, seemingly unbothered by their amusement or his blundering.

Asaka nodded to him once and then stepped over to the railing of the ship. Mitsuo touched Toshi's arm to urge him forward. Doing as he'd been bid, he followed their lord.

Keeping aware of the load on his back, he swung over the rail to climb down into the skiff. He tensed for a moment as Asaka reached up to steady him. He sat still in the bottom as Mitsuo and Miko came to join them.

He studied the glowing ship as the boat pulled away, knowing his time on it was over. He stared in amazement as the rest of the crew started jumping into the water. He glanced over at Miko, wanting desperately to ask what was going on. He held his tongue as he reminded himself they were in the presence of Asaka.

He kept his eyes on the ship during their trip to shore and continued to do so even as they disembarked onto a small moonlit beach. As the crew appeared from the depths of the sea, he realized every last one of them had left the ship, even the steersman. He couldn't take his eyes away from the ship as the crew gathered together. Something seemed to be wrong with it, but he couldn't quite figure out what. With a gasp, he realized the ship was sinking.

Turning around to tell someone, not sure whether the ship was supposed to be doing that or not, he found he wasn't the only one watching. Every single one of them was looking at the ship, their hands pressed together as if in prayer.

He turned back around, a small chill rising up his back, as the ship continued to sink. It became harder and harder to see; its eerie light was fading. His mind filled with questions, but he couldn't bring himself to disturb the solemn silence around him to ask them.

Abruptly, he found he could no longer stand to look. He'd been a prisoner within the ship for a time, yet it felt as if he were watching it die. Instead, he studied the faces of those around him. He stared at the large variations of color filling each set of empty eyes.

It wasn't long before some of the others turned away as well. Eventually, even Asaka stopped staring out into the sea's darkness and led the way into the mainland.

Trying to watch his footing in the almost total darkness, Toshi made his way to the geisha's side.

"Miko-san?" he whispered.

"Yes, Toshi-kun?"

He hesitated a moment, hoping no one was listening. "What was wrong with the ship?"

Miko's masked face swiveled toward him. "Wrong? Nothing was wrong with it. If anything, everything was right. The ship has been released from its supernatural life. It has become what it should have become some time ago. It has once again become part of the cycle of nature and life."

He stumbled over an unseen rock. Moments passed as he struggled to regain his balance with Miko's help.

"The ship had regained its honor," she said. "It has finished the service it had been meant to perform. Its duty is over. Now, it is free."

"Oh."

He glanced ahead, grass-covered ground spreading before him as far as he could see. Small clumps of bamboo were the only things breaking the monotony. After a short while, the group reached a line of trees. In silence, they all filed into the deeper darkness.

Miko's hand fell on his arm to help guide him, since he'd lost most of what little sight he'd had left. Struggling to be careful with his footing, he was very glad when Asaka called out to them to halt.

"This is where you will remain until daylight, Toshi-kun," Miko said. "Try to get as much rest as you can."

Gratefully removing the heavy basket from his shoulders, he worked hard in the darkness to remove his traveling blankets from inside it. As he laid them out, he realized he couldn't hear the others. Swallowing hard, he tried to fight the feeling he was suddenly alone. A wave of dread coursed through him as he realized this would be how it would feel once he'd started the journey in the morning—alone.

Chapter 22

"We'll be leaving soon, Toshi-kun," the geisha said.

He sat up.

"Dawn is almost upon us, and Asaka-sama wishes to speak to you before we go." Miko was sitting next to him.

"Hai." He straightened his clothes and hair as much as possible, even as Asaka's green eyes floated toward him. Toshi bowed.

"When you feel it is bright enough to travel, head south until you reach the cutter's road. We'll follow behind you as best we can at nightfall. Remember to steer clear of others if you're able." Asaka bowed toward him. "Our trust is with you."

"Thank you, Asaka-sama." He bowed to the ground, swallowing hard. He hoped the samurai's faith wouldn't prove to have been misplaced. He heard the others start to walk away and felt a touch of fear enter his heart. He found Mitsuo and Miko standing before him.

"Young one, remember the lessons I've taught you. Practice them daily. I will know if you do not," Mitsuo said.

He stared at the bent skeleton, caught offguard by the emotion in his voice. "I will, Sensei. I promise."

Mitsuo patted him solidly on the shoulder and then walked away. Toshi stared after him, puzzled by the unusual gesture.

"He will miss you, I think." Miko glanced over at him. "Mitsuo is never as happy as when he has a student to torture into the true way." Her sleeve rose to cover her mouth as she turned to stare fondly at the departing samurai. "I've left breakfast for you over there," she added. "Make sure you eat all of it. Growing boys who will soon be men need to eat all they can."

He nodded gratefully.

"Toshi-kun, please be careful. The world can be a dangerous

place if you don't take care."

"I will, Miko-san, I will." He felt his nervousness rising.

"Keep this with you, for company." She pressed one of her wig's silver bells into his hand and closed it.

He could find nothing to say. He held up the small bell, though he could hardly see it, and made it ring in the darkness.

"We'll see you again. Soon," Miko said.

He felt her hand graze his cheek, and then she was gone. As he was swallowed totally by silence, he knew he was truly alone.

He waited for the dawn, eventually wondering how the others were going to protect themselves from the sun. He knew from experience his companions could survive in the deep shadows of a forest, but would they be able to find such places throughout the course of the journey? Might the group, perhaps, be able to sink into the earth as the ship sank into the sea?

Pondering those questions rather than his abandonment, he fumbled in the dark until he found the breakfast Miko had left for him. With a relish he didn't feel, he ate all he found. His gaze strayed more and more often in the direction the others had gone.

As the sky grew lighter, he sighed and repacked his blankets into the basket. Using the sun to figure out which direction was south, he raised the basket up on his back and shoulders and set off without once looking back.

Chapter 23

It didn't take long for Toshi to find the cutter's road in the cool, misty morning. Following it in a southeasterly direction, he studied his map and wondered how far he'd be able to travel in a day. Though he wasn't well-traveled, he doubted it would take him more than two weeks to reach Narashi.

Or so he hoped. Unlike the foreigners' maps, those of his own country were somewhat less concerned with imparting accurate distances, mostly because they'd yet to find a better way to do it, though they still gave a good representation of what you might expect to encounter on the way. So, it would take about two weeks, unless he ran into trouble. If that happned there'd be no telling how much longer it might take. With effort, he pushed those thoughts away and continued on his way.

The forest was thick on both sides of the road, and the vegetation was trying hard here and there to reclaim it. As the morning wore on, the day began to heat up; and with it came the sapping pull of humidity.

After a time, he stopped next to a small shrine on the side of the road. Grimacing, he removed the heavy basket from his back. He opened up his shirt and then splashed a bit of his water on his shoulders where the basket's straps had begun to rub them raw. With a discontented sigh, he wished he'd thought to bring along some of Miko's healing salve.

Regretting every movement of his arms as he dug out lunch from the basket, he ate but left a small portion of it in the shrine. Kneeling, he sent a quick prayer to the shrine's kami, the guardian of travelers, for protection on the road.

By mid-afternoon, his shoulders felt as if they were on fire.

Periodically, he'd moved the straps to other sections of his shoulders, but by that time there were no spots left untouched. His legs started to complain about carrying the load and walking so long. He doubted he'd ever had to travel so far in his life. In the city, everything you needed was only a few hours away, and that was if traffic was heavy. Out here, there was nothing but beautiful countryside as far as the eye could see.

Though he'd intended to continue traveling until nightfall, he wasn't able to hold out quite that long. With his shoulders screaming in pain, he got off the road a couple of hours before sunset.

He dumped the basket on the ground and then wiped away the sweat covering his face. He fell to the ground and then sat. Carefully, he removed his shirt, being mindful of the tender spots on his shoulders. He stared at the loaded basket with growing annoyance. He had half an urge to kick it for what it had done to him, but felt too tired to get up to do it.

After resting for a while, he was able to work himself up to get some dinner. As he rummaged inside the basket, his gaze happened upon the hilt of his boken. With a groan, he recalled Mitsuo's instructions and his own promise to follow them.

With a louder groan, he took out the boken and placed it in his sash. He got his food and ate, staring off and on at the weapon at his side.

Calling himself a fool over and over for ever having promised to practice without knowing what he was getting into, he finished his meal and stood up. He slipped the boken from his sash and took his first stance, already dreading what the exercise would do to his aching shoulders.

As he warmed up to the routine, a foolish grin grew on his face as he found that, to a small extent, the exercise seemed to be relieving his discomfort. As darkness closed in around him, he stopped and dropped exhausted to the ground. On hands and knees, he made his way to the basket and used his discarded shirt to wipe the sweat from his body. He took out his other set of clothes and changed into them, hanging the other pair to dry. He missed taking baths, but out here he wouldn't even get the choice of hot buckets of water. He wasn't too thrilled at having to live in his own filth, especially as bothersome insects hung around him expecting a sumptious supper.

After that, he took out his blankets and spread them on the leaf-strewn forest floor. Lying down, he dropped instantly to sleep.

The next morning, he opened his eyes to the bright light of a new day. Rubbing gently at his sleep-covered face, he yawned and then stretched. He flinched as his shoulders protested at the movement.

A bit of a morning chill was still hanging about, so he found it hard to get motivated. He gave a long, sad glance toward his basket, knowing what it had planned for his shoulders that day. He sighed.

Making himself sit up, he grew still as he saw his breakfast was already set out for him. He jumped to his feet and looked all around but saw no one. He then stared at what had been left.

A broad grin crossed his face as he spotted a small silver bell on top of the half-wrapped rice cakes. Wondering where Asaka and the others might be, he sat back down and reached for his breakfast. They were still with him. He wasn't really totally alone. In the city, you were never alone; no matter how hard you tried, there was always someone around close by. Out here, in the wilderness, there was no one. And it was eerie. At least knowing someone had been by pleased him more than they would ever know.

After he'd eaten, he placed his new bell with the one Miko had given him the night before. He folded his dried clothes and was about to put them away when his gaze fell on the chafing straps of the basket. His eyes shifted from the straps to his blankets and back. With a small grin, he took out the knife they'd provided for him and carefully cut two long strips from the thickest of his coverings. He put everything away except the strips. Those he wrapped around the higher section of the straps. He put the wrapped bands on his shoulders. Rising to his feet, he painstakingly rearranged them a little, trying to make the weight from the basket sit as comfortably as it could on his shoulders and back. Satisfied with his work, he took a moment to get his bearings and then headed off to the road.

Before stepping out onto the path, he spent a few moments listening to the sounds around him. Hearing nothing out of the ordinary, he peeked out past the line of pines and bamboo and made sure there was no one coming from either direction. He saw nothing. He ventured forward.

The walking was pleasant in the remaining morning hours, but turned hot and humid as the day wore on. His shoulders complained at the long stretches between rests, his legs not too far behind. He ignored them both as best he could.

A small afternoon shower drove him into the shelter of the trees for a half-hour. It eased the heat while coming down, and even heartened the crickets into chirping; but the day became much more oppressive once it was gone.

Toward evening, he came upon a large shrine, the type often used by travelers to rest. He hesitated as he went by, knowing the place would provide a warm and dry place for him to spend the night—a much more pleasant prospect than the forest floor. He looked around the outside of the building and saw no sign of anyone. He drew closer to the open-walled structure.

Finding the inside empty, he decided it might be all right to stay. He made a small offering to the spirits and asked for a safe night.

He ignored the fire pit in the middle of the floor and walked to the back. He set out his bed there, making sure he had a sure way to escape if necessary. He ate a quick meal and then practiced with his boken for a while before going to bed.

Chapter 24

The next few days went much the same. The daily rains increased, and Toshi took shelter in the roadside shrines whenever possible. The rainy season had arrived.

More than once, he was forced to hide as occasional travelers and a samurai or two on horseback passed through. With some regret, he had already been forced to avoid two small mountain villages. As he'd skirted them, he'd watched the simple people as they went about caring for the wide rice patties at the outskirts of clusters of thatched huts. He'd forced his heart to harden at those times. A longing for any kind of company kept trying to sweep over him, but it would have been much too dangerous for him to give in. With stubborn fortitude, he followed the route marked on his map.

He knew his companions were keeping up with him. Every morning he would find breakfast nearby and, on occasion, some extra supplies. He never woke when they came though, his daily exhaustion dragging him under until morning. So, though mentally he knew his companions were keeping up with him, in his heart he still felt alone.

The day grew ominously darker. He eyed the clouds warily as they built up in a dark wall across the sky. The packed-dirt road he was on appeared more traveled than some of the others. Fortunately, he'd yet to spot anyone on it.

Harsh laughter from the other side of an upcoming curve brought him to a startled stop. Realizing someone was coming, he dashed off the road into the safety of the woods. He crouched behind a large clump of bamboo; the plants hid him from view yet still allowed him to keep an eye on the road.

The laughter drew nearer and split into three distinct voices.

Toshi saw three men on horseback round the bend, leading a fourth horse behind them. He ducked down farther behind the bamboo as he noticed the set of swords strapped at the men's sides. Judging from their dirty clothes and ungroomed appearance, he knew those men were ronin, masterless samurai. These were definitely men he didn't want to meet.

He held his breath as the three crossed before him. He swallowed hard as he got a look at the horse following them. It looked to be in better shape than those the three men were riding. An expensive bridle and other gear were strapped onto its back. He could see a set of samurai swords wrapped up in an expensive bag of silk hanging from one of the saddlebags. A bead of perspiration ran down the side of his face. Those men were less than dirt. Not only were they ronin, but thieves and murderers as well. He thanked the gods for having warned him of their coming. If they were willing to prey on samurai, they would have never hesitated killing him where he stood.

He waited a long time before removing himself from his hiding place. Stepping back out onto the road, he noticed the sky looking even more threatening than before.

He walked faster, wanting to put as much distance between himself and the three ronin as possible. He also hoped he might find a shrine before the downpour that had threatened all day came down.

A light sprinkle was falling when he spotted a walled shrine a little ways off the side of the road. With a spurt of speed, he headed for it as the rain increased.

He stopped before the open doorway and peeked inside. Seeing and hearing nothing in the building's dark interior, he took off his worn sandals and went in. He shook off what water he could, and then took off his hat, coat and basket and set them against the corner nearest the door.

Hoping to start a small fire as a chill took the air, he approached the pit in the middle of the room and felt around inside it. To his surprise, he found a stack of wood already prepared for lighting. Not daring to question his good fortune, he dug around in his basket for the flint and steel Miko had provided for him. After a few strikes, he was able to coax his sparks into a warming fire.

"Thank you, stranger. I had been planning on trying to light it in a little while, but now you've saved me the trouble."

He looked up, body tense, trying to penetrate the gloom still covering most of the room. Seeing nothing, he crawled backwards away from the pit, back toward his belongings.

"I'm sorry," the thin voice said. "I hadn't meant to startle you. You have nothing to fear here. I'm only a helpless old man. I can't harm you."

He looked in the direction of the soft male voice where it originated in the back of the shrine. As the fire spread in the pit, he was able to catch a glimpse of the speaker. He was an ancient-looking man who sat in the corner dressed in dark robes. In his hands, he held a large, beaded necklace, which in many ways resembled the man's shaven head. Normally, he would have relaxed in the presence of a priest, but this man was not as expected. He was unusual, just like the priest he'd met on the island not long ago. The ancient old man's eyes were white.

"You're being so quiet," the old man said. "I bet you're looking at my eyes. Go ahead; feel free. I don't mind. They've been like this for a very long time."

"Can you see?" He knew the question was rude, but he just hadn't been able to stop himself from asking.

"I can see, but not in the way you think," the priest replied. "I haven't had sight like other men for almost twenty years. And though the other would make things more convenient, I believe this way is best." The old man smiled, several gaps showing in his yellowing teeth.

Toshi shook his head, not sure he understood the words. Quietly, he began putting on his hat and coat, thinking it might be prudent to seek shelter elsewhere.

"This is going to be a very stormy night. The spirits must surely be angry at someone. This storm has been building up since late last night."

"How could you know—" He stopped, knowing he had no business talking to the old man.

"It is but one of the gifts of my brand of sight," the blind priest said. "As men, there are a lot of things we don't see because we can see. Having your sight taken away, however, can open your inner eye.

And it can make you aware of all sorts of information your eyes had ignored all along."

The old man wiggled for a moment and then brought out a small bag from a pack sitting behind him. "I've already filled the pot hanging over the fire with water. If you wouldn't mind putting some of this in it, I'd be honored to share my tea with you."

The offer was tempting. It'd been almost a week since he'd had some tea. Toshi started thinking perhaps there was no real reason he shouldn't stay. Chances were he wouldn't be able to find shelter before the rain came in earnest. Here, he would be dry and warm. And, truly, there was little the blind man could do to place him in danger. And it'd been so long since he'd spoken to anyone at all.

"Yes, honored sir, I would be happy to."

He put his hat and coat back by his basket and then came over to take the offered tea powder.

"You don't sound like you're from around here. A young man like you really shouldn't be traveling alone. These roads aren't as safe as they once were. A shame, really."

He hesitated, not sure if the priest expected an answer or not.

"You're not a runaway, are you, boy?"

The old man smiled and removed a small jar from his bag. As Toshi stood somewhat uneasily before him, the priest raised the jar. The white eyes rose with the old man's hand. Toshi saw his smile falter but then almost immediately flicker back on.

He took the offered jar, not sure what to make of the priest's odd expression. He distracted himself by preparing the tea.

"You don't talk much, do you, boy?" the old man asked.

Toshi glanced over at him, still waiting for the water to heat up.

"Actually, honored sir, I have a bad tendency to talk too much." He noticed the blind man's eyes were staring right at him, as if he were somehow trying to read Toshi's mind.

Attempting to shrug the odd thought away, he turned his back on the priest and walked over to his basket. Rummaging inside it, he brought out some of his food.

"I have some fish with me, honorable sir. You would honor me if you would have some."

A small, unwanted chill coursed down his back as he found the man still staring at him.

"You are very kind, young man."

He cut and took him some dried fish and a couple of rice cakes before going to check on the tea. He watched the old man put the food away, but wasn't surprised. Buddhist priests didn't eat in the evening.

When the tea was ready, he looked around but found no cups. Before he could ask the old man if he had any, he found the priest already holding two out to him. He took them and ladled out tea for both of them.

"Please, come sit by me," the old priest said. "I want to look at you while you eat."

He stared at the priest, wondering if he was joking. He thought of saying no, but could find no good excuse with which to do so. Grabbing his dinner, he sat meekly down beside the old man.

Dinner passed in silence, with Toshi getting up twice to refill their cups. Small chills continued to occasionally course down his back as the old man's dead eyes never left him.

"Might I touch your face, boy?"

"My face?" He tensed, though he wasn't sure why.

"Yes, I want to see what you look like. It won't take long."

Toshi hesitated, not seeing how letting the old man touch his face would let him see. "Well, I—"

"You don't have to if you don't want to. Though it would be rude," he added. "You already know what I look like."

Feeling guilty over his hesitation, Toshi scooted over to sit before him. He took a deep, steadying breath before reaching out for the old man's frail-looking hand. He placed it on his cheek.

"Ah, thank you. You're most courteous. Don't worry, it will only take a moment."

A smile had returned to the blind man's face, but it seemed somehow detached. Toshi felt the well-callused fingers explore every part of his face. The priest's other hand reached up to touch his hair. Without thinking, he jerked away before the old man could do so.

"Is something wrong?" The priest sounded concerned.

"Uh, no, there's nothing wrong. Please, go on." He forced himself to sit still, even as the man brushed his hands over his hair and ran his fingers through his ponytail. The other hand fell on Toshi's shoulder. He found himself suddenly pinned by an iron grip.

"You've been touched, haven't you?" The priest's voice was hard. The smile had left his face.

Toshi couldn't read his expression. He felt a kernel of fear spring inside him for the first time. "Touched?"

"Yes, touched. Touched by the spirits roaming the land. I had thought I sensed their mark on you. Now, I'm sure."

"No, sir, you must be mistaken," he said, his worry increasing. "I'm only a peasant boy. No spirit would ever touch me."

He tried to break free of the blind man's grip but found he couldn't.

"They've touched you," the priest insisted. "You've been marked by it. You may have hidden that mark from the sight of most men, but there are other ways to see it."

Abruptly, he was free of the priest's grip. Not sure what to think, he backed away.

"You shouldn't be ashamed of it," the old man said. "To be marked is a gift, for it means they've let you live. They could as easily have taken your life as take the time to mark you."

The old man's words disturbed him.

"I'm not ashamed of it! It's just necessary to hide it right now."

"Oh, I see."

He wasn't sure the man saw at all.

The rain was pouring heavily outside, making pattering sounds on the roof of the shrine; but he thought, despite that, it might be time to consider leaving. Staying had been a mistake.

"I'm not saying these things to try and frighten you, boy," the priest said. "It's just so rare to meet someone who's been touched. In all my long life, I've only met two others. One of them was myself." The priest's hand hovered for a moment before his eyes. "Please stay. I know you're thinking of going, but it isn't necessary." His tone softened. "I promise not to ask any more questions if you'd be kind enough to get me more tea."

Toshi wasn't sure if he should believe him. Yet, he had no proof the old man meant him harm. Could it be true, though? Had the spirits touched the priest as he'd been touched? Nodding as he made his decision, he took the blind man's cup and refilled it.

He skipped his usual boken practice for fear it might generate more questions, despite the priest's assurances to the contrary. Taking his blankets out of the basket and staying on his side of the shrine, he let the pattering rain on the wooden roof lull him to sleep.

He awoke to a cool but humid morning. His body begged him to go back to sleep. Fighting its desire, he forced himself to sit up, knowing he had to be on his way.

"Good morning."

He jumped to his feet, startled by the cheerful greeting. His eyes flickered across the room, landing on the old man just as he remembered his presence.

"Good morning, honored sir," he managed to say out loud.

"There's some tea by your side, if you care for it. There's also some fresh rice that should be done by now. Would you be so kind as to check it for me?"

No longer sleepy, he advanced to the fire. A fresh pile of wood was burning in the ashes of the one from the night before. He wondered where the old priest had gotten it. Not daring to ask, he pulled on the rod hanging from the beam in the ceiling that held the pot safely over the fire. With the pot now set safely on the lip of the pit, he took its lid off with the help of a metal hook used for that purpose. He also found a spoon sitting on the edge as well and used it to take a sample of rice.

"It's ready."

"Good, good." The old man sounded pleased. "There are two bowls on the floor near you. Why don't you serve us?"

Getting the bowls, he served up the rice. He gave one of the bowls to the priest and took his own with him back to his side of the room.

"An odd thing happened late last night," the old man said.

Toshi glanced up, forgetting his food for the moment.

"We had some visitors."

"Visitors?" He fidgeted despite himself.

"Yes. An unusual group, really. I've never seen the like before. I wanted a better look at them, so I invited them out of the rain, but they wouldn't come in. Strangely enough, though, they did leave this." The old man lifted a wrapped bundle of food. A silver bell hung from one end. "An odd set of friends for such a young man."

Toshi stared across the room, wondering just how much the man had sensed about his companions with his unusual sight. Had he known them for what they were?

Feeling tense and uncomfortable, he hurried through his breakfast. As soon as he was done, he began packing away his things.

"You're not planning on leaving already, are you?" the priest asked.

A kernel of fear grew in his stomach as he glanced at the blind man's smiling face.

"Yes, honorable sir, I must be going. There are some things I need to do." He bit his tongue as he felt the urge to try and explain further. He grabbed his basket and slipped it onto his shoulders.

"Ah, well, then, thank you for your company, and your help," the priest said. "You'd probably better take this with you, as well, since they went through so much trouble to get it to you." He held the wrapped bundle out in Toshi's direction.

Toshi approached him warily and took the package. He slipped the tinkling bell from it and then laid the package on the man's lap.

"Please, you should have it. I know I must have taxed what little food you had. There are not many travelers on the road, and I wouldn't want you to go hungry. I still have plenty, so, please, keep it. And, if you would, please pray for me and my friends."

Not waiting for a response, he slipped on his sandals and immersed himself in the mugginess outside.

He ran down the muddy, puddle-filled road a long way, desperately needing to put some distance between himself and the old man. As he ran, he paid no heed to the basket as it slapped over and over again against his back.

He had no idea how much the priest knew. He hoped he would tell no one of what he had seen, even as he realized the old man had found out enough to set their enemies after them. He'd been a fool to stay there the night.

The humidity hung on him like a cloak. His feet and legs were thickly covered in mud by the time he was forced to slow down his run to try and catch his breath. He glanced behind him off and on throughout the rest of the day, not entirely sure the blind man wasn't coming after him.

The rain continued to fall sporadically for the next couple of days. When it wasn't heavy, he trudged on, trusting his hat to keep the rain from his hair. During the afternoons, he looked for whatever shelter he could find, always ready to bolt if anyone showed up to share it.

By the third day, all he could think about was how glorious life would be if he could only have a bath. The rain hadn't yet returned to torment him, and sunshine was actually making its way past the clouds. He had no idea how long it would last.

The road he was on had been sloping out of the hills since the day before. The trees were slowly thinning out around him. By midday, the forest had given way to extensive paddies. Staring off into the distance, he saw what appeared to be a large town at the edge of a lake.

Chapter 25

He shouldn't be here. Toshi knew that; but though he'd fully intended to skirt the town, he'd somehow ended up in the middle of it anyway. Luckily, no one seemed to be paying him any attention. After all, he was just a common peasant boy. Surely, his mission wouldn't be threatened when he could so easily hide as one of the crowd.

He knew cities and the many things they offered. How could he turn away from the thought of a hot meal, a bath and even a dry, clean place to sleep? It'd been so long. Surely, he could bend the rules just this once.

He became absorbed by the familiar smells of cooking food, sake, vegetables, that permeated the street, and the normal bustle of people going about their daily business. The calling of vendors assaulted his ears from both sides of the road as they tried to entice him and the other passersby into buying silk cloths, wooden implements, candies, woodblock prints and all other manner of goods. It was a radical change from the silence he'd been subjected to for so many days. It was wonderful to see something other than trees, bushes and lonely, muddy roads.

Entering the first eating establishment he spotted, he stood happily in place as his feet were washed at the entrance before he was shown to a table. He ordered more than he knew he could possibly eat, but didn't care. He enjoyed himself as he ate cold soba and a wide variety of tempura. He ended up surprising himself by eating it all. It was wonderful!

"Has everything been to your satisfaction, young sir?"

"Oh, yes," Toshi said. "It was marvelous. I couldn't have asked for better."

"I'm so very glad you think so." The thin proprietor gave him the wide smile reserved purely for customers.

He knew what was expected as the proprietor stood beaming down at him giving no signs he would leave. So Toshi reached within his shirt to pull out the small bag of money Asaka had given him. As he did so, he realized he'd never taken the time to check what was inside. He held his breath as he opened the bag and glanced in it.

"I—I'm sorry, sir, but could you make change for this? I can't find anything smaller."

He bit his lip as the proprietor's annoyance at his first few words turned into surprise as the man stared at the coin in his hand.

"Will it be all right?"

The proprietor's eyes rose to meet his, his expression unreadable. "Oh, ah, yes, yes, that'll be fine. I can make change for you. Yes, yes, I can."

He watched the proprietor with some trepidation as the latter took the coin and shuffled off toward the back of the shop. Once he'd disappeared, he turned his attention to the bag in his hands. He swallowed hard at the small fortune he found inside it. He pulled it shut as the proprietor returned.

The man forced him to count the change twice before letting him have it. Nervous at the attention, he put the change in the bag and slipped it inside his shirt.

"Sir, could you give me directions to a reputable bath house?" he asked, still worrying about the incident with the money.

"Ah, yes, of course, young sir. There's one just down the street, a couple of blocks down. It will be on your right."

"Thank you." He quickly gathered his things and left.

The bath was ecstasy. He had scrubbed every inch of his body except his head twice before entering the hot pool. Allowing his cares to drift into the water, he listened to the other bathers as they talked about various subjects pertaining to the town—the coming fall festival, gossip about a newly married couple and more. He sighed in contentment. It was almost like being back home.

After lingering for longer than he knew was proper, he regretfully left the pool, dried and redressed. He looked forward to the prospect of finding a pleasant inn to spend the night.

As he left with some directions from one of the attendants, he was suddenly flanked on either side. Looking up in surprise, he saw the two men were samurai. A wave of fear coursed through him as he forced himself to bow.

"You're new in town, aren't you?" This came from the shorter of the two.

"Sir?" How had they known? He'd thought he'd blended in perfectly here.

"We would like to see your traveling papers."

He felt his throat fill with panic. "Papers, sir?"

"Yes, your papers," came the impatient reply. "Come on, let us see them. That is, unless you haven't got any."

The sneer he saw growing on the tall man's face made it pretty obvious he expected him not to.

"I have papers." Reaching inside his shirt, he desperately dug around for the bamboo tube containing the writ Asaka had given him. He cursed himself for a fool, realizing the proprietor of the eatery must have turned him in to the local guards. Someone like him would never be carrying around the high currency he'd used to pay for his meal. He should have realized the man would tell someone he looked suspicious.

He found the writ and pulled it out, breathing out a quick prayer. He opened the tube and handed its contents to the shorter of the two samurai.

Toshi waited anxiously as the man unrolled the yellowing parchment and read it. The boy's brow furrowed as he saw a look of surprise and disbelief flicker across the man's face. The samurai finished reading the paper and then gave him a long, hard look before glancing at his partner.

"Kimura, I think you're right. Take a look at this."

With a cold chill moving through him, Toshi watched the previously sneering samurai read the paper.

"It's perfectly legitimate, sirs," he told them.

"Oh, we don't doubt its authenticity, boy. What we have a hard time believing is that this paper belongs to you." The sneer had returned to the taller samurai's face. His hand clamped down on Toshi's shoulder. "You'll be coming with us."

"But, sirs, the permit is mine," he insisted. "It was entrusted to me with a mission, one I must finish!"

The grip on his shoulder grew painful. "Next you'll be telling me Lord Asano himself gave you this writ, almost nine years ago."

Both men laughed and forcibly led him down the street.

He kept silent, giving them no trouble. There was no way out for him. They'd cut him down if he tried to resist. He had to find a way to make them believe him.

Not far from the center of town, the samurai steered him toward a large wooden building standing on a rock foundation. They took him inside through a side door and dragged him downstairs. Cells covered one wall, all of them having strong, thick gates. As they led him toward them, Toshi felt a swell of panic rush inside him.

"Please, sirs, I'm not lying to you," he pleaded. "That permit was given to me by my lord. I was to be his messenger to Lord Asano. I have to get to Narashi to see him! You must believe me."

The taller samurai held him still as the other liberated him of his possessions.

"And just who might your lord be, boy?" Holding him by the scruff of the neck, the sneering samurai threw him into the nearest open cell. He hit the floor hard.

"I don't think this peasant works for any lord, unless he means the lord of lies."

Both men laughed as they locked the gate to the cell.

Toshi climbed to his feet, infused by a burst of anger. "I do serve a lord! His name is Asaka Ietsugu. He gave me that writ and sent me on a mission for Lord Asano. If you don't release me immediately, you'll have to answer to them."

Both men stared at him, all trace of their previous amusement gone. The taller of the two reached threateningly for his sword.

"You'd better watch your mouth, thief. As it is, your fate will be quite unpleasant upon the magistrate's return tomorrow. If you persist, though, we'll be happy to give you a taste of what you might expect."

Toshi stood defiant, his anger growing with his frustration. They didn't believe him, and he could prove nothing. He had already given away too much.

"Why won't you even try to believe me? You could at least tell me that."

The tall samurai sneered at him and began ruffling through the contents of his basket.

"It's obvious why, thief. Messengers for great lords don't go around passing themselves off as peasants. They also don't go into town in disguise and buy things with coins large enough to rent an entire legion of ronin. You say this writ is from your lord, yet you carry no papers of your own. Need I go on, thief?"

He cringed from the man's sarcastic tone, realizing he had no way to repudiate his logic. His stupidity was going to get him killed.

"Well, well, look at all this."

His gaze snapped to the basket as the tall samurai emptied its contents. A bolt of dread tore through him as the man brought out the kettle he'd gone so far to get. The samurai barely paid it any attention before setting it on the ground.

"A boken. Isn't that interesting, little thief? Is this what you attack your victims with? Do you hit them from behind?"

"I never attacked anyone!" He glared at the man, but the samurai ignored him.

The shorter samurai took the boken as the other continued digging things out. "It looks to have been heavily used."

"Hm, perhaps he belongs to a group," the other speculated. "He may have to be tortured so he'll give us the location of his accomplices."

Toshi felt fear tingling up his spine. He tried not to let it show, but had a hard time of it.

"I tell you, there's no one else. There is no gang. There are no victims! No robbery."

"Save your breath, thief. Everything will come to light in its own time. You can tell all your lies to the magistrate tomorrow."

"But I am innocent!" He rushed to the cell's gate, only to jump back as the shorter of the two men slapped it with his sheathed sword.

"Keep quiet! You're starting to make me regret the fact we didn't just cut you down in the street and have done with it."

He took a step back, horrified by the man's sobering tone.

"Lord Asano will thank the magistrate once we're through with you and have captured those you work with. For your sake, you'd better hope whatever message you intercepted wasn't one of a grave nature. Otherwise, your death could take a very, very long time."

He was about to protest, but a hard look from the taller samurai made him think better of it.

After they'd inspected everything, they repacked it back into the basket. They left without a word, though the taller of the two turned back long enough to spit in his direction.

Toshi shook where he stood, fear and despair overflowing inside him now that he was alone. He had failed. All his trials had been for nothing. In one day, he had destroyed all his lord had worked toward all these years.

He was doomed and he knew it. The magistrate wouldn't believe him any more than his men had. All there was to look forward to were pain-filled days of torture and, eventually, a dishonorable death. He would pay the ultimate price for having craved a few hours of comfort. He'd been such a fool.

He fell to his knees. Even in his worst nightmares, he had never imagined it might end like this.

Chapter 26

The day crawled by. No one came to disturb Toshi's solitude as he sat in the cell's semi-darkness.

His stomach grumbled as the day came to an end, but no food was ever brought to him. Rain started to fall, small trickles of it coming through the partial stone wall to pool on the dirt floor.

Wiping at his swollen eyes, he was forced to move away from where he'd curled up on the far corner of his cell. As the rain kept on, puddles began to form and spread across the floor.

By the time the rain stopped there were only a few spots on the floor of the cell that remained dry. None of them were large enough for him to sit on. Since he didn't want to make himself even more miserable than he already was, there was only one other thing he could think of to do. And if he was lucky, it might even let him forget his problems for a little while.

Stepping out into the middle of the cell and placing his feet in a partially dry area, he took a deep breath as he positioned himself into his beginning stance. Sighing as he brought up an empty hand, he found he missed the weight of his wooden blade. He couldn't see his movements in the darkness, but he could feel them. It amazed him how well he could tell he was doing by just the feel of the movement.

He closed his eyes and pretended he was back on the glowing ship, moving under Mitsuo's critical eye. He latched onto one of Miko's favorite tunes and had it play over and over in his head.

He speeded up his movements as he found his thoughts straying to his lord and his companions. He had to find a way to get out of here. He'd already tested the gate, the stone and the wooden walls. Nothing had given way.

What if he killed himself? He could try and come back, as Asaka had done and perhaps be able to escape this place. Then, he would go find the others and explain what had happened, tell them where the kettle was. But he had no guarantee he could kill himself, let alone come back.

He swiveled on his foot and almost fell as it slipped sideways in a patch of mud. Breathing heavily, he reached down to clean his sandal, cursing at the slippery ground. He was about to resume his practice when a thought brought him up short.

Dropping down on hands and knees, he felt around for one of the small rivulets of water and followed it to the gate. He pushed one finger into the dirt floor and felt it give. With a hopeful heart, he took what water was left in the rivulet and spread it around the immediate area of the gate. He took off one of his sandals and, gripping it tightly, used it to dig at the moist floor.

Scooping up water from other areas of the cell, he softened the packed dirt beneath the gate as much as he could. He focused on the need to be out of there before the sun rose.

Sweat covered his body as he continued working at the wet floor with his sandal, scraping as fast as he could. He had to hurry—he'd missed a good part of the day. Asaka and the others had probably gone past by now. He had to catch up. He wasn't sure how they had been finding him every evening, but he doubted they'd ever think he might have come here. He had to get free.

As he ran out of water, the dirt became more and more stubborn. His sandal fell apart. He took off his other one. Searching blindly in the dark, making sure he'd found every drop of water, he then started digging again.

He felt around in his hole, wondering if it was yet big enough to let him squeeze beneath the cell's gate. He couldn't push away the feeling he was running out of time. Figuring it was probably close enough, he decided to try it. He lay down on his back and squirmed into the hole.

His shoulders and head squeezed through, though he gained a number of scratches doing it. He pulled out one arm at a time and then with both of them pushed against the floor as he tried to get his chest to come on through. With a foolish grin marking his face, he sat up as his hips came even with the gate. In another moment, he was able to pull the rest of his body out of the cell. He was out!

Now all he had to do was find the kettle. Except he had no idea where it was being kept.

Following the dark hallway back the way he'd been initially brought, he searched for the way out of the building. No sound reached his ears, this side of the building seemingly deserted. Crawling the last few feet to the door, he set his ear against it, trying to figure out a way to find out if there was a guard posted on the other side. None had been there when he'd been brought in, but that didn't mean anything. It was too dark, and he had no source of light to risk fumbling around the building trying to find another way out. His only hope was to go through this door. Taking a deep breath, he fumbled for the latch, inched the door open a crack and took a peek outside. The steps rose before him, with no one in sight. He opened the door wider.

Still not seeing or hearing anything untoward, he slipped to the outside, closing the door behind him. He crouched, went up a couple of the steps and looked beyond the sloping stone wall on either side. The street looked deserted in both directions.

He hesitated, not sure what he should do now. He had no money, no writ and no kettle. He had no idea if this town kept patrols at night. He didn't even know where Asaka and the others were. What was he to do?

He stared up and down the street in indecision. A partial moon shone from a clear sky. What was most important? Getting the kettle back. If he didn't, there was no way he'd be able to face Asaka again. Not that he had much chance of finding him, even if he wanted to.

The guards had taken the kettle with them, of that he was sure. But where? He closed his eyes, trying to remember which way the two samurai had gone. He thought they'd gone back this way. If so, then it could be the upper floors of the building couldn't be reached from the cell area or that confiscated materials were kept somewhere else.

If he went around the building, he could look for other ways in and also search for other likely places they might have taken the kettle at the same time. It wasn't much of a plan, but it was more than he'd been able to come up with so far. His course set, he climbed the last two steps and walked out into the street. Keeping low, he followed the rock wall, staying alert for any sign of guards.

Peeking around the southeast corner of the building, he quickly ducked back as he spotted two men standing before a large set of doors. Realizing there was no way he'd get in that way, he headed back the way he'd come and went the other direction.

On the northeast side of the building, a wooden fence extended out more than ten lengths of his arm from the wall. Following the fence, since it was too high for him to attempt to climb over, he reached the end and looked around that corner. He inhaled sharply as he spotted a guard coming his way.

Having little time to lose, he shot across the wide-open street on his side and ducked behind a large empty sake barrel in the alley between two eateries. He peeked around it, waiting for the guard to appear, but he never did. Thinking that perhaps his rounds didn't come all the way to this side of the building, he came out from behind the barrel and rushed back across the street.

Carefully taking a peek once more around the corner, he saw no one. Encouraged by this, he crouched low and headed that direction. A third of the way down, he slowed as he spotted a break in the wooden wall. Slowing even further, he snuck up to it and took a look. Several of the boards had been torn away, revealing a darkened garden. Had the guard gone this way? He saw no sign of him on the other side. Yet, if he'd seen this, he would have raised an alarm. Who had done it?

It didn't matter—it was a way in. And if the guard was even now reporting it to his superiors, it meant Toshi had little time to do what he needed before the way would be blocked. Not sure of what he was getting into, he prepared to go through. As he put his foot into the hole, a hand landed on his shoulder.

He froze, sure the guard had found him after all. His death was but moments away. He grimaced, waiting for the end.

Nothing happened.

Confused by the fact he was still living, he gathered his courage and glanced behind him.

"Toshi-chan, go on through. Asaka-sama would like to have this over with as soon as possible."

"Miko-san?" He stared in disbelief to his left at the familiar voice.

Soft laughter poured toward him as two points of blue light bobbed before him.

He swallowed hard as he realized who had to be standing behind him. Turning around, he prostrated himself on the ground. He felt cold all over; and, though it was the last thing he wanted to do, he forced himself to speak.

"Asaka-sama, I've lost the kettle. It was taken from me when I was brought here. I believe it is somewhere in this building. If—if it can't be found, I swear to do everything in my power to retrieve it. I have no excuse; I did wrong. If you must punish me now, please bring me back so I may hunt it down for you. I—"

"Enough!"

He cringed under Asaka's whispered command, knowing he'd been babbling like a fool.

"The kettle has already been found," Asaka told him in an emotionless tone. "You are needed to remove it. We will leave now."

Dizzy with relief that his life wasn't quite yet over, he hurried to his feet. He heard the rustle of silk in the darkness as Miko took his arm. "This way, Toshi-kun," she said.

He stepped quietly through as she led him into the garden on the other side of the wall. Asaka followed, a long, covered bundle on his shoulder.

Numerous questions bubbled up in Toshi's mind as they followed the garden's cobbled path toward the building. He forced himself to keep silent as they came to an open door.

Stepping into the building, he could see vague shapes of things by the moonlight streaming in from outside. The building was quiet, and he saw no sign of guards. After many turns, Miko pulled on his arm and brought him to a stop as they reached the sliding door of a common-looking room. Asaka knocked on the frame three times. The door opened.

Toshi was taken inside, and instantly he felt the presence of a number of the others there. Bright dual points of light stared at him from a number of places in the small room.

"Toshi-kun, it's over here," Miko said. She laid his hand on top of his strap-rigged basket. He put it on.

As he turned around, he felt something wet and sticky beneath one foot. He jerked away from it, but didn't ask what it was. He didn't want to know.

"We have what we came for," the samurai said. "Let's leave."

Miko grabbed his arm again as the group stepped out of the room. They swiftly made their way back to the garden.

With a touch of unplaced dread, he noticed four of the men before him were carrying something rather large over their shoulders. He forced his gaze away, wanting no clue as to what they were carrying, or why. The size was much the same as the bundle he had seen Asaka carrying with him before.

Upon reaching the back wall enclosing the garden, the skeletons slipped out the hole in the wall one by one. The rest of the group crowded in close, awaiting their turn. Toshi ended up beside one of the men carrying a bundle.

He turned away, still not wanting to know what it was. Instead, he stared into the face of a fresh corpse. He tried to stumble back but was impeded by a hand on his arm. With a pale face, he looked back at who had stopped him and found Miko staring at him.

"Toshi-kun, it's our turn," she said.

Looking at nothing as he followed her lead, he slipped through the hole in the wall out into the street beyond. He stood shivering, trying to ignore everything around him as he waited for the others. He almost jerked away as Miko leaned close.

"Do not worry. They died while carrying out their duty to their lord. There is no greater honor."

He shook his head, knowing she didn't understand. Life was cheap. It was a fact they all grew up knowing. But those men, those samurai, had died because of him, a peasant. It was wrong. It wasn't the way things were supposed to work in the world. He had caused it, but he'd had no right. If not for his stupidity, it would never have happened. He had no one to blame but himself.

He didn't resist as Miko signaled for him to go on. He saw nothing but the dark street beneath him as they quickly made their way through town. His gaze wavered as exhaustion seeped into both his body and soul.

The group kept to the shadows and slowed down as they neared the edge of town. Toshi tripped as they crossed a small bridge over an outlying river, the sounds of his steps loud in his ears. Several pairs of hands reached out to keep him from falling. He never noticed.

Though his exhaustion deepened even more, he kept going, drawn on by Miko's gentle pull at his arm. Pine trees, bamboo and giant ferns began filling up the side of the road, hiding them from view.

They'd run down the intense darkness for some distance when Asaka led them off the road and into the surrounding trees. Toshi was forced to pay attention. The way was uneven and filled with unseen obstacles. The brisk pace made it difficult for him to stay on his feet. Whenever he faltered, those around him would grab and lift him until he was running on his own again.

"Hold on. It shouldn't be much farther." Miko's voice rang close to his ear.

He didn't acknowledge her words, needing all of his concentration just to keep standing. Miko was forced to hold him back as he tried to go on when the others came to an abrupt stop.

He allowed himself to collapse. With aching arms, he removed the straps of the basket from his shoulders. As soon as he'd gotten them off, he lay flat on the ground.

Orders hastily flew around him, but he paid them no attention. Miko knelt down next to him and with a gentle caress began to numb his screaming shoulders. After a short while, she persuaded him to sit up long enough to retrieve his blankets out of the basket. Taking them out, he ignored the food he saw inside, though his stomach grumbled loudly. He set the blankets out and lay down, happy to let exhaustion take him.

"You mustn't leave once you awaken," Miko said. "Remain here for the day and wait for us. Asaka-sama has found a better way for us to get you to our destination. Wait for us. Toshi?"

He nodded as she pressed him, though his mind had barely registered what she'd said. When she said nothing more, he gave in fully to his exhaustion and soon dropped off into a dreamless sleep.

Chapter 27

Toshi's eyes fluttered open. With a start, he sat up as he realized it was full daylight. Berating himself for having overslept, he got up. He groaned as his shoulders and back protested. It didn't look like it was going to be a good day.

He pushed the hair out of his eyes and glanced around. It took a moment to realize he had no idea where he was. With a gasp, he remembered how he had gotten there and why.

His throat burned as he stared at his muddied clothes and body. It had all been such a useless waste. He was worse off in many ways than when he'd first reached the town. It'd been a terrible mistake.

The forest pressed in all around him, no evidence of his rescuers anywhere at hand. Opening the basket, he stared for a moment at his folded set of clean clothes and then ignored them. He scooped out some rice cakes and smoked fish and made himself eat. After that, he cleared a small place before the largest tree he could find and put some food before it. In this makeshift shrine, he prayed for the safe journey of the dead guards' souls to their next life. He also asked their spirits to please not hold a grudge against his lord. He told them their deaths had been all his doing.

As he left the tree, guilt still lay heavily inside him as he made his way back to his blankets. The rising heat and the dried mud on his body made him itch, but he did nothing to alleviate it. He climbed back into his dirty blankets and stared at nothing.

A faint rustling sound brought him awake. He was amazed to be surrounded by darkness, not remembering ever falling asleep. He sat up, wondering if his companions had returned yet.

"Good evening, Toshi-kun."

"Miko-san!" Though he couldn't see her form, there was no

mistaking the twin blue points of light staring his way.

"Are you hungry?" she inquired.

His stomach rumbled at the question. "Yes, I think so."

Miko took his hand and placed a bowl in his palm. In the other hand she placed a pair of chopsticks. Thanking her, he began to eat, hungrier than he could have ever imagined. Miko continued to give him food until he finally declared he'd had enough.

"Thank you, Miko-san. I needed that," he admitted.

"How do you feel?"

"Better," he said quietly.

"That doesn't quite answer my question, Toshi-kun."

He lowered his eyes. "I'm still a little tired, I guess. My arms and shoulders still hurt from all the digging, but only a little. My back feels fine."

"Hm, I guess you'd better let me take a look at them and see what I can do to help."

He sat still as Miko removed his shirt and examined his shoulders and arms. Her light touch numbed all of his immediate pain. He glanced back at her, surprised when she then put a cool substance on his sores. Somewhere she'd found a healing salve for him.

Feeling both glad and guilty for his respite from pain, he stared at the darkness around him and found only a few pairs of glowing eyes. "Miko-san, where is everyone?"

"A few are in the trees and others are keeping watch by the road. Asaka-sama and three others returned to Kyuiji."

"Kyuiji? The town I was in?"

"Yes."

He felt a shiver slither down his spine. "Why did he go back? He's not fighting more samurai, is he?"

Silence hung between them for a long moment.

"No, that's not why he returned. There has been too much death already. Our lord is not that wasteful."

He realized from her tone he'd offended her. He'd known for some time he shouldn't expect the worst from Asaka. Yet, it was a habit he was finding hard to break.

"Please forgive me, Miko-san, I meant no offense. I've been very foolish of late."

She caressed his cheek before she put his shirt back over his shoulders.

"Lord Asaka fears the disappearance of the guards and your escape will come to be connected. He is afraid spies of our enemies will recognize this as a clue if their attention is called to it. Things have now become too uncertain to let you travel alone."

He sighed heavily, feeling guilty.

"While trying to find you," she continued, "we came across the perfect thing to allow you to travel with us. This new idea will also allow us to make better progress, since we do not tire as you do. Lord Asaka has returned to Kyuiji to acquire it."

"Oh." He straightened his shirt, wondering what it was they'd found. "Miko-san?"

"Yes, Toshi-kun?"

"How did you find me last night?"

He heard her get up in the darkness and shift to sit before him.

"Our fates are tied to the kettle you carry. We can feel its presence in a way we can't explain. We followed that presence into Kyuiji. We began searching for you once we'd found the kettle, hoping you'd be nearby."

He shifted uncomfortably. "So, if I'd been taken somewhere else and not been able to escape, you wouldn't have been able to find me?"

"It would have been difficult."

He sat and stared at nothing for a short while. "Miko-san, if you and the others can feel the kettle, wouldn't it mean the ninja can, too? His fate is tied to yours and the kettle's."

He saw her eyes flare.

"I don't know," she said. "It had never occurred to me to think about it before. We are much closer to the kettle than he is likely to be, though. The ship would have brought us to the coast faster than he could have managed to travel in the water on his own. I would doubt he's been able to catch up with us as yet. Perhaps he cannot feel it move from far away."

Toshi didn't think she was convinced by her own answer.

"Well, it'll do no good to worry about it. Whatever the answer is, it's too late to do anything now. What does concern me, however, is how in the world I am going to get you clean."

They'd yet to find an answer to her question after several hours had slipped past. All conversation stopped as the sounds of something moving through the forest filtered into their camp. Toshi felt his tensed muscles relax as he saw a number of familiar floating pairs of small lights approaching.

As the men poured into the camp, he spotted a pair of green-lit dots moving in his direction. He bowed deeply and could feel Miko doing the same.

"There are still close to five hours left before daylight, so we will make use of them. Gather your things," Asaka commanded.

"Hai, Asaka-sama." He hurried to do as he'd been bid and groped in the darkness for his blankets so he could put them back into his basket. With Miko's help, he followed Asaka across the camp once he was through.

"Duck down, Toshi-kun."

He reached out until his hand landed on a smooth wooden surface. Using it as a guide, he ducked and crawled into what seemed to be a box with padding inside. As he got settled, a panel was pulled shut beside him. Still wondering where he was, he saw a small window on the panel open. Within moments, he was lifted off the ground.

"Miko-san, is this a palanquin?" he asked with some surprise.

"Yes, it is. It's a rather nice one, don't you think?" He saw her eyes flash on the other side of the window.

Toshi had never been inside one of the elegant traveling contrivances in his life. Sure, he'd seen them before, the wood box supported by two long poles that extended over the front and back. The passenger would ride in comfort inside it as two to four men lifted the palanquin and carried them to their destination. He would have been more excited if the reason for having to use one wasn't so glum.

"Why don't you try and rest, Toshi-chan? It would be safer if you didn't sleep during the day." The geisha's bells rang in the palanquin's all-encompassing darkness. "I will sing you to sleep if you like."

"That would be wonderful, Miko-san. I have missed your songs very much."

He saw a flash of blue beyond the small window as she broke into song. He let himself be lulled to sleep by her sweet voice and the even movements of the palanquin.

Hours later, a soft touch brought him awake. As he rubbed his eyes, he realized the palanquin had stopped moving. Straightening up as best he could in the small compartment, he grabbed hold of his basket as Miko opened the door the rest of the way.

Darkness reigned outside, but seemed bright when compared to that residing inside the palanquin. He stumbled out and tried to stretch his stiffened muscles.

"Greetings, Mitsuo-san." He looked up at hearing Miko's voice to find two points of white light bobbing toward them.

"Asaka-sama wished you to know this is where we'll be stopping for the day," Mitsuo said. "There is a stream not far from here to the east. There are a number of clefts in the rocks there that can be used as hiding places, if necessary. But, best of all, there's a small clearing by the stream amply suited for sword practice."

Toshi nodded, not in the least bit surprised by the last. "I will remember, Mitsuo-san."

"But, Toshi-kun," Miko added, "remember to bathe as well, especially after practice."

He tried hard not to blush, remembering his less than ideal state. "I will remember that as well, Miko-san."

A hand squeezed his shoulder as soft laughter drifted into his ear. One of these days he would learn not to be so easily embarrassed by her. Somehow, though, he doubted it would be soon.

"Be very careful, Toshi-chan. We'll return as soon as night permits."

He felt something placed in his hands as Mitsuo and Miko took their leave. He bowed in their general direction. When his head rose back up, they were gone. He looked around—everyone else had disappeared as well.

Unable to see in the darkness, he decided to sit. Feeling around the package given to him, he was eventually able to figure out it was food. He hunted in his basket for his water container and ate as he waited for the sunrise.

As soon as it became light enough to see, Toshi got up, grabbed his basket and made his way east. Listening intently, he hadn't gone far before he heard the sound of rushing water. He cautiously made his way toward it, keeping an eye out for the stream.

When he found it, he eagerly put the basket down, stripped and bathed. Once he was done, he turned his attentions to his hair, rubbing at his dirty scalp. Black ink bled from his hair as he kept it submerged in the cold water.

When he'd finished, he grabbed his clothes and blankets and washed them as well. After that, he tried to redye his faded hair.

As the sun rose higher, he spread his clothes and blankets over the rocks to dry. Though not too enthusiasticly, he grabbed his boken and went looking for the small clearing Mitsuo had told him about and then worked through his exercises. He practiced off and on all day, pushing himself as he knew Mitsuo would have had him do if he'd been there. It kept his thoughts from drifting to his deeds over the last few days.

As the day came to a close, he bathed again and then lounged in the cool water for a while. He dressed and put away his things before the light totally disappeared.

Taking out some food from his basket, he climbed up on a large rock and waited for night to fully fall. He realized he was eagerly awaiting the return of the others.

The moon rose early in the summer sky and gleamed brightly off the stream's gurgling water. Though he could hear nothing but the normal sounds of the night, he tensed as he saw a flicker of movement out of the corner of his eye. Ready to run if necessary, he reached down for his boken. He sighed in relief as when he spotted familiar pairs of lights floating toward the stream. Carefully, he descended from his perch to greet them.

Without being asked, he headed to the palanquin they brought into the moonlit clearing. As soon as he'd gotten inside, four of the men lifted it by its poles and followed the others into the night.

Chapter 28

Over the next four days, Toshi stayed awake during the daylight hours and practiced with his boken, sleeping when he traveled in the palanquin at night. Though he was sure they were making faster progress than he would have on his own, it didn't occur to him to wonder what lay at the end of the journey. His days were lonely, but he got by. He wouldn't be foolish enough to make the same mistakes he'd made before. He always looked forward to the time he shared with Miko before he would try to fall asleep.

There'd been no more trouble. As far as he could tell, no one was chasing them. He prayed it would continue to stay that way.

"Toshi-kun." The geisha's voice sounded subdued.

"Yes, Miko-san?" They hadn't been traveling long; but, unlike the days before, she had been unusually silent.

"Asaka-sama believes we will reach the outskirts of Narashi sometime tonight."

"Already?" He sat up too fast and banged his head against the wooden ceiling of the palanquin. "Ow!"

"Are you all right, Toshi-kun?" Miko asked worriedly.

As he reached up to rub his injured head, he noticed the geisha's intense eyes staring at him through the small window of the palanquin.

"I hadn't meant to startle you so," she said.

"No, I should have expected it. We had to reach Narashi sooner or later." A wave of dread swept through him. "I—I don't know if I can do what will be required."

"Why do you say such things, Toshi-chan?" she asked. "You're quite capable."

He looked out, wishing he could see her face, not sure if he should tell her of his misgivings.

"Though I'm close," he said quietly, "I'm not yet a man, Miko-san. I'm a boy, a peasant boy. I won't be taken seriously. No one believed me at Kyuiji. Not when I showed them the writ, not even when I told them who I needed to see or who had sent me. They didn't believe me at all."

He frowned as the geisha's laughter filled his ears.

"Oh, Toshi-kun, you're such a delight. Of course those samurai didn't believe you."

He said nothing, caught off-guard by her words.

"People believe what they see and are swayed in their decisions by it. The samurai who took you saw before them a boy in peasant garb, so, of course, they assumed you could be nothing but that. Why would a real samurai dress like a peasant?"

"But, Miko-san—"

"The writ you have from Lord Asano is very powerful," she continued. "The samurai would assume anyone with it would strut their importance to the world, not hide it. What had they to fear? For us, it isn't that simple, but their preconceptions wouldn't let them see that.

"You had problems in Kyuiji, but you won't in Narashi," she said confidently. "In Narashi, you will be dressed for the part. You will walk right up to the castle gates and demand entry with the power of the writ. You will scoff indignantly if they hesitate, take it as an insult. The writ is your key. They will read it, they will look at you and you will fit their preconceptions. They'll allow you in."

He stared at her with disbelief, but said nothing.

"It really is that simple," she insisted. "If you look right, if you act right, people will assume you are right."

"If you say so, Miko-san." He didn't feel all that sure.

"I do say so, and by tomorrow you'll be finding this out for yourself."

He nodded, his dread of the future not decreasing in the least.

The group traveled through the night.

"Toshi-kun, it's time to make you ready," Miko told him.

"We're there?" He felt his voice rise and clamped his mouth shut.

"We've been here for some time, Toshi-kun," Miko said. "Asaka-sama, however, thought it best to let you sleep as long as possible."

He heard the palanquin door slide open and felt Miko reach for his arm. Grabbing his basket, he scooted over to join her. Staring into the surrounding darkness, he found the others spread out in a large circle around him. His stomach twisted in a knot.

"Toshi-chan, please remove the things from your pack," she bade him gently.

He opened the basket and started to empty it. Once he'd removed the kettle, Miko reached inside to help him.

"Now, take off your clothes so I can dress you. We're about to begin your transformation," she said.

Glad for the darkness, he undressed. He noticed Mitsuo's eyes as the latter came forward and put something down on the ground nearby. He heard the tearing of paper as Miko knelt to retrieve what he'd brought.

The geisha handed Toshi something soft and then helped him put it on. Though he couldn't see it, he assumed it was an inner kimono. Miko then gave him the outer kimono he'd been carrying in his basket all along. The two layers of clothing felt strange to him, but he said nothing. Miko deftly tied a sash on the lower part of his waist and then had him put on a *kami shimo*, a samurai's baggy pants and stiff-shouldered overcoat reserved for formal occasions.

Miko placed both the bamboo tube holding the writ and his moneybag between his inner and outer kimono. She slipped the sheathed wakizashi through the sash close to his left hip.

"Turn around, Toshi-kun."

Doing so, he felt her undo his ponytail. She combed his hair thoroughly and then retied it before asking him to lift his left foot. Miko slipped a tabi sock on it and then an expensive sandal. She did the same to his right foot.

"You do make quite a striking figure when properly dressed, Toshi-kun," she said. "Doesn't he, Mitsuo-san?"

Toshi didn't dare look at her, feeling them all staring at him. His cheeks grew hot.

"Hmph. Just so," Mitsuo replied.

A touch fell on his arm and pulled to lead him to the left. "Come on, Toshi-kun, we don't have much time. We must show you off to

Asaka-sama before the sun forces us to leave."

The thought of both facing his lord dressed like this and the fact he'd soon be left on his own almost made Toshi ill. Miko guided him past the ring of men and a short distance beyond that.

"Our young ward is ready, Asaka-sama," Miko declared. "Does he not strike a handsome figure?"

He held his breath, amazed she would speak so informally to Asaka. The samurai's glowing green stare roamed over him.

"Yes, this is acceptable."

He dared breathe again.

"On this day, perhaps the hardest of tasks shall begin for you," Asaka stated. "From the moment you enter the city, your every word, your every action shall prove to be a reflection upon the Asaka family. Its very honor will rest in your hands."

Toshi swallowed hard, never having expected the additional and heavy responsibility.

"You've done well in all that's been placed in your way. But you must remain on guard, for, while you'll be going into our lord's castle, you will not necessarily be safe there. Though I have no proof, it has been my belief for some time our betrayal originated from within those walls. You must take great care and trust no one. Is this understood?"

"Hai, Asaka-sama." A trickle of fear crawled up Toshi's spine as he thought perhaps he understood too well.

"You will give the kettle to Lord Asano," the samurai said. "Under no circumstances is it to be given to anyone but him."

Toshi swallowed hard. "Hai."

"You must request a private audience with Lord Asano. This may prove difficult. You will have to be persistent."

He nodded, though he didn't quite understand.

"Never let the writ out of your sight. You must keep it with you at all times. The writ will give you some immunity from those who might be scheming within the castle. And, as long as you have it, they can't make you leave. Finally, the writ will help you prove to our lord you were truly sent by me."

He shifted uneasily, the scope of what lay ahead of him growing to even larger proportions than he had imagined before.

"Do you understand all this, Toshiro?"

"Y—yes, Asaka-sama."

"Good. Then we'll move on. You shall be dropped off within the city proper. If you follow the road there, you will soon see where Lord Asano's castle lies."

"Hai." He bowed before allowing himself to be led back to the palanquin. Before getting in, Miko had him pick up the kettle, leaving the backpack and his other unnecessary possessions behind. He climbed inside the palanquin.

As soon as he had settled, the palanquin rose and began moving forward.

"I wonder if I'll ever get him to relax in front of others," Miko mused out loud. "He takes things much too seriously. It makes him come across so stiffly."

Toshi made no comment.

"You'll be able to do what's necessary, Toshi-kun. I have faith in you. I know you can do it. Just make sure to always maintain the proper frame of mind," she said. "Remember you're an important messenger for a great lord. Act like one. Get into the role. Think of yourself as playing the great Musashi in a large play. Look at your wakizashi as a reminder. It is a symbol of your new status. Let it guide you. Always remember, samurai are men and have the same passions as others."

His grip on the kettle turned his knuckles white. "I will try, Miko-san."

"I know you will, Toshi-kun. That's why I have such confidence in you. Many would have given up long before now," she said. "You will succeed."

He sighed deeply. "Yes, Miko-san."

Not much time had gone by before the palanquin stopped and settled on the ground. Miko opened the door, and he got out. He turned to look upon the city holding his destiny, but couldn't see much through the all-encompassing darkness.

"Toshi-kun, take these," Miko said.

He looked toward her as she placed what felt like silk in his hands. "What are they?"

"*Furoshiki.* One is for the kettle, so you can wrap it and keep it hidden from prying eyes. The other is a bundle of spare clothing."

Thinking both a good idea, he quickly wrapped the kettle with the cloth after tucking his other bundle under his arm. When he was through, he discovered he was closely surrounded by his companions.

"There is one more thing, Toshi-kun," Miko said. "Since you are now to be samurai, we must give you a different name to carry. Chizuson would give away too easily that you're not of samurai rank, since it states your occupation."

He nodded, not having thought of that.

"So, for the duration of this part of your mission, let yourself be known as Kazete Toshiro. Don't you think it will do?"

"I guess so, Miko-san." He had no idea how to tell.

"It is here we must leave you, Toshi-kun. Remember the things I told you. Remember who you are now," Miko said.

"I will, Miko-san."

He tensed as a strong hand abruptly fell on his shoulder from behind.

"Though the first part you must do alone, we'll try our best to join with you again."

He shivered in odd delight and fear, having recognized Asaka's voice.

"Keep your wits about you and always remember you're representing the Asaka clan in every deed."

"Hai, Asaka-sama."

"Good luck, Chizuson-san."

Surprised at the samurai's remark, Toshi took a deep breath, wondering what he should say, only to realize they were already gone. He was alone.

Reminding himself they'd promised to join him when they could, he faced the city that would either bring salvation to his companions or an end to his own life.

Chapter 29

Toshi strolled down the wide street as the city of Narashi awakened around him. People ignored him as he walked past, too busy with the rituals of opening their shops and restaurants. The strong scent of cooking rice and fish began to permeate the air, reminding him he'd yet to have breakfast.

Disregarding his awakening hunger, he stared only straight ahead, not letting himself be distracted by all the activity around him, and tried to look fierce as he'd seen samurai do. The kettle felt heavy in his hand.

He passed a couple of samurai, and it took all his will not to cringe and shy away from them as they passed each other. They paid him no attention as they strolled by.

A steep hill soon rose before him, the way paved with worn, flat stones split into long tiers. Merchants along the road shouted at him from their colorful stores, trying hard to draw his attention to their wares, making it sound like his life couldn't be complete without some new cups, melons or wine. He felt a pang inside him as the activity reminded him of home.

Lord Asano's castle grew like a mountain before him. Its white, multi-storied towers reached grandly toward the sky. Its dark, angled roof beckoned him ever closer.

As he reached the top of the long hill, he noticed the huge stone wall surrounding the castle grounds. He stared at what he could see of the buildings beyond it, their white, magnificent walls gleaming in the sun.

Excitement mixed with nervousness as he forced himself to go on and try to find the castle's main gate. Moving along the slow curving wall, he eventually came upon it.

The wooden gates stood open. They were as tall and thick as a man and reinforced with studded iron bands. It was obvious they would be able to withstand all forms of attack. Beyond them, he could see a broad, paved road leading into the interior. Three samurai stood on either side of the entrance, and they stared at him as he approached.

Trying hard to remember what Miko had told him about whom he was supposed to be, Toshi strode purposefully toward them and ignored their stares. As he started to enter through the gate, the samurai moved to block his path.

"Move out of my way. I have urgent business with Lord Asano," he commanded. He hoped his voice didn't reflect the fear he felt. A shiver shot through him when the men didn't stir.

"We had not heard anyone was expected to visit our lord today," one of the guards said.

"I am not expected." He tried to put a touch of impatience in his voice as he saw the guards tense before him. "This will explain everything."

He reached inside his kimono and removed the bamboo tube. He carefully removed the writ from its container and handed it to the nearest samurai. He tried his best to look indignant, trying to imitate Master Shun's favorite expression as the man read through it.

"I see. Sorry, sir, for the delay," the samurai said quickly. "I'll escort you to the next duty station immediately."

Toshi tried to hide his relief and retrieved the writ from the guard. Following him, he attempted not to stare at the steep walls on either side of the road as it wound into the castle grounds. They hadn't gone far before the road began to narrow and then took a ninety-degree turn. Four guards waited around the corner and questioned him on his business. As soon as he'd shown them the writ, the samurai that had walked up with him turned back around and returned to the main gate. One of the four guards volunteered to escort him to the next duty station.

Though he could catch glimpses of the castle proper as they continued up the winding road, the high walls kept all else from view and also kept him disoriented. He was about to despair of ever reaching the end when a large, closed gate came into view around a bend. A brawny samurai stood before a door cut into the gate. His guide led him right to the man.

"This man has business with our lord, Kitaro-san."

"Is that so?" Kitaro said. Toshi tried not to flinch at the guard's haughty tone. "Well, there may be a problem, then. Orders are no one is to be allowed within unless it is under the express orders of Tsuyu-sama or Asano-sama."

Automatically, Toshi presented the writ with a crisp twist of his arm. The samurai's left eyebrow arched high as he read the parchment. His gaze rose to meet Toshi's. Toshi kept his face expressionless, telling himself over and over he had every right to be there, and this man wouldn't be able to stop him.

The samurai's hard gaze rested on him for a few moments more and then broke away. Toshi held out his hand for the writ. Reluctantly, the guard returned it to him.

"What are the contents of the bundles you carry?" the guard asked.

He opened his mouth to give some sort of lie, then clamped it shut. He stared the samurai in the face and didn't answer. He nervously waited for something to happen, not willing to give anything away so early in the game.

With a slight nod, the samurai turned away and pounded on the door.

"Rin, open up. Our lord has a visitor." His words were followed by a coded knock.

The door built into the gate swung inwards. The brawny samurai stepped out of the way.

"Thank you." Toshi slightly bowed toward both samurai and then, with curiosity welling inside him, he stepped through the doorway.

Eight guards stepped aside as he entered. As he walked forward, two of the samurai fell in with him, one in front and one behind. Following their lead, he crossed an immaculate courtyard to an open entrance leading into one of the castle's white, tall buildings.

He tried to quell a sharp spear of excitement as he readied the writ to hand to one of the two samurai standing at the entrance. Once it'd been verified things were in order, his escorts returned to the gate. The two guards at the door stepped aside to let him pass.

Trying to seem confident, he strolled on in. There, he found a small foyer with a place for him to remove his shoes. Slipping off his sandals, he turned to face away from the door and allowed his gaze to sweep across the simple room. As he began to wonder what he should do next, a young woman, probably three to four years older than he with a bright smile appeared from a side room he hadn't noticed before.

"Welcome to Shiroyama Castle, young sir." The woman bowed low, and he did the same.

"I am here to see Lord Asano," he told her.

"I understand. Please, if you would follow me?"

Holding the handle of the wrapped kettle a little tighter, he followed the woman down a broad, wood-paneled hall. Unable to help himself, he stared into every open room they passed on the way. He admired the dark, thick columns and roof beams and the thick scent of oiled wood. The beams looked as solid as mountains. Everything around him was immaculate and perfect.

The young, dark-blue-dressed woman reached a huge wooden staircase and bade him follow her upstairs. The stairs narrowed and continued past the third floor. He watched servants and guards as they went about their daily business, none of them paying him any attention.

He followed the woman down a small corridor to the left of the landing. They'd gone about halfway down when she stopped before a sliding door and gracefully opened it for him.

"Please, go right in. Kirin-san schedules Asano-sama's appointments with all visitors," she said.

"Thank you." After they'd exchange bows, he peered after her as she strode back the way she'd come. Once she'd disappeared, he took a deep breath and entered the room.

The place was small and sparsely furnished. All it contained were a low table and a niche at the back displaying a colorful scroll that brightened up the otherwise drab room. Sitting behind the table was a thin, gnarled man who was hunched over, writing.

He slid the door closed behind him. The old man didn't look up. Toshi bowed toward him. "My name is Kazete Toshiro, and I desire an appointment to see Lord Asano."

The thin face turned up to him. "Lord Asano is not seeing any visitors."

Toshi stared at him in surprise as the man looked back down to continue his writing as if nothing else needed to be said.

"It is urgent I see him," he said. "I've a very important package to deliver to him."

"I'm sorry, but our lord doesn't have time to see every messenger that requests an appointment. If you have something for him, please leave it here and I'll see that it eventually reaches him."

He heard a touch of impatience sift into the old man's tone.

"This must be delivered in person," he insisted.

"That is impossible."

He felt a tendril of anger growing in him at the man's indifference.

"This should make it possible." He removed the bamboo container from his kimono and laid it on Kirin's table.

With a touch of curiosity showing on his face, the gnarled man reached for the cylinder and carefully extracted the writ from inside. He brought it close to his narrowed eyes and raked over its contents. There was an intensity in his gaze when he looked up at Toshi that the boy hadn't seen in him before.

"This document is quite old. How did you come by it?" Kirin asked.

"My lord entrusted it to me so I might finally finish the task for which it had been originally issued. Lord Asano has waited for what I carry for a long time, and it is my task to deliver it only to him."

"Hm, yes, I see. Well, young sir, getting in to see him may not be easy. Things are not as they once were."

Wondering what the old man meant, Toshi retrieved the writ as Kirin handed it back to him.

"I make the appointments for visitors, but I need to confer with the man responsible for his internal appointments, and then with the secretary of Lord Asano's affairs. Only then will I be able to request for a time to be allotted for your appointment." Kirin rose to his feet.

"I would appreciate anything you could do."

The old man nodded, his gaze not meeting Toshi's.

"I'll send someone to show you to the waiting room. I'll notify you as soon as an appointment has been arranged."

"Thank you." He sat down on the tatami floor and wondered at the odd things Kirin had said once he had gone. After only a short while, the same young woman who had brought him here showed up at the door.

"Kazete-sama, my name is Yuko," she said. "I've been assigned to care for you while you wait for your appointment. If it's convenient, I'll show you to the waiting room."

He nodded and then rose to his feet to follow her out into the corridor. They walked back to the landing and, crossing it, turned down another hall. Yuko led him to a lively decorated room on the left.

"Refreshments will arrive shortly," she said. "If you have need of anything, please call, I won't be far."

"Thank you." He watched Yuko close the door, leaving him alone. Sitting down in the middle of the six-mat room, he took his time studying the diversified paintings on the panels forming the walls. Gold leaf around their rims increased what small amount of light poured through the small, strategic windows set high on the wall. He hadn't been looking at them for long before Yuko returned.

He felt his mouth water as she set a tray of sweet cakes and tea before him. With practiced ease, Yuko served him.

"Thank you."

"If I might ask, sir, you're not from around here, are you?" she asked as she gazed at him curiously.

He took a long sip of tea, wondering why it always seemed so obvious to everyone he was a stranger.

"No, I'm new to these parts. This is my first time in Narashi. Why do you ask?"

Yuko smiled. "Just curious, sir. You see, this room has lain empty for a long time. No one has come asking for an audience with our lord, not since—"

He saw her eyes suddenly narrow suspiciously, and she didn't finish what she had been about to say.

"Yes?" he prompted.

"I'm sorry, sir, I guess I was getting a little carried away. Please forgive me." She stood up to leave. "If you're still here during lunch, I'll make sure something is brought to you."

He watched as she bowed and left, confused by her abrupt change in attitude. First Kirin had mentioned some rather disturbing things, and now Yuko had done so as well. What was going on here?

He puzzled over what he had heard for a while. As time crept by, he realized he hadn't seen or heard anyone since Yuko had brought him his tea. It somehow didn't seem natural.

Bored, he stood up and walked about the large room to look more closely at the paintings. He ignored his stomach as it clamored for more food. He turned around as he heard the door slide open.

"Sir, would you like me to serve you?" Yuko bowed from where she sat before the door, a filled tray beside her.

"Please, if you would."

Not totally displeased his visitor was Yuko rather than Kirin, he sat and waited as she served him a healthy portion of soup, rice and steamed vegetables. He was eager to start in on his meal, but held back as she got up to go.

"Yuko-san, would you please tell me what you meant by what you told me earlier?"

The young woman stopped in the midst of gathering his morning tray.

"I spoke out of turn, sir." She wouldn't meet his eyes. "It was wrong of me to have brought it up. Please, forget about it."

"No, you must tell me," he insisted. "I'm new here. I need to know what's going on. Please, Yuko-san."

The young woman stared at him for a long time before she replied.

"It is my duty to care for the needs of those waiting for an audience with our lord. Normally, it kept me very busy, but that isn't so anymore. For some time, I've had more free time on my hands than I might have ever wished for."

"So, no one comes to see Lord Asano? Do you know why?"

He studied Yuko's almond-shaped face as she hesitated. He saw her take a quick glance toward the door before answering him in a whisper.

"Asano-sama is not the man he once was. Tsuyu-sama runs everything now. I don't know if our lord is even aware of the fact." She hesitated. "Asano-sama isn't allowed visitors without Tsuyu-sama's consent. No one is allowed into the castle without his invitation." She stared at him oddly at the last. "I really must be going, sir. I'll return later."

He sighed once she'd gone. He couldn't help but wonder how these developments would affect his mission. He ate his lunch with less enthusiasm than he would have before.

Chapter 30

Toshi saw no one all afternoon except for Yuko—and she never tarried long. From utter boredom, he got up and paced through his exercises. He did so empty-handed, only too aware of what might happen if he dared bare a weapon within the lord's castle.

As the room darkened toward evening, he glanced at the door as it smoothly slid open. Yuko bowed toward him, holding a lit paper lantern in one hand.

"Kazete-sama? Kirin-san wanted me to inform you he was regrettably unable to schedule your appointment today, but he will try again tomorrow. Until then, he asked for your indulgence and begged that you accept our hospitality and spend the night. A room has already been prepared for you."

Trying hard not to let his disappointment show, he rose to his feet. He should have known it wouldn't happen soon. From what little he had heard today, it sounded like it might take him a while before he could gain an appointment. If Asano was no longer interested in the affairs of the castle, he might even try to delegate Toshi's appointment to someone else.

Yet, Asaka's instructions had been most specific. If he ended up having to talk to Tsuyu, how could he insist on delivering the kettle to Asano personally without insulting the man? Surely, Asano had given Tsuyu power because he trusted him. Did Asano not have children? It did seem a little strange to give the running of the place to someone not of the same clan.

Toshi followed Yuko out of the room and down the stairs to the first level. A large number of candles and lanterns lighted the way, but he noticed once they'd walked down a large hallway the number of lights decreased. He thought it very strange.

"This wing of the castle is filled with rooms to house Lord Asano's guests. There are three guests here at this end to work on some of Tsuyu-sama's business. Your room is farther on."

For reasons he couldn't name, Toshi felt a shiver course down his spine at her words. Other than the light coming from Yuko's lantern, this end of the castle was dark. Yuko gave no indication this was in the least bit unusual as she led him down the hall. She opened the partition into a brightly lit chamber.

Looking inside, he noticed six lanterns strategically placed around the room. A neat stack of bedding lay waiting in the center. Beside it sat a tray laden with covered dishes with wisps of steam escaping from the sides. A light breeze wound through the room from an open doorway at the far end. The light in the chamber shone outwards, revealing the edge of a large garden. The scent of flowers floated gently on the breeze.

Yuko walked into the room, setting her lantern down by the door. Without waiting for him, she served his dinner. Unlike before, she lingered while he ate. She gathered the dishes once he was through.

"Would you like a bath before retiring for the evening?" she asked.

His heart jumped at the idea, but he hesitated before answering. "That would be most welcomed, Yuko-san."

Yuko led him to the baths and then back to his quarters. She set out his bedding for him.

"Would you be wanting someone to warm your evening, sir?" she asked reasonably.

He choked, and was incredibly grateful she hadn't been looking in his direction when she'd asked. He felt his cheeks grow hot, though he shouldn't have been surprised by the question.

"There seem to be enough covers. I should sleep quite warmly." He didn't dare look at her.

"Should I come wake you in the morning, then?" She didn't sound offended. "And would you prefer your breakfast here or in the waiting room?"

"Yes, please wake me, and the waiting room would be fine."

Yuko took the dishes left from his dinner and bid him goodnight.

He lay down after she'd gone, realizing nothing so far had gone as he'd expected.

Chapter 31

The next morning, Toshi gathered his things and made his way to the waiting room. As time passed, he began feeling unnaturally nervous. It bothered him he could feel so lonely in such a large place. The activity he knew should have been there—the bustling of servants, magistrates, and other visitors—was nonexistent on this side of the castle. It was eerie.

The day went much like the one before, and so did the two after that. No one spoke to him or came to see him except Yuko; and he was sure he made her uneasy, though he didn't know why. He'd seen no sign of Kirin since the first day.

When Yuko came in with his afternoon tea, he decided he'd had enough. "I wish to see Kirin-san."

Yuko looked up at him, surprise etched on her face. "Sir?"

"I wish to talk to Kirin-san, and I'd like to do it today. I want you to arrange this for me."

"But, sir, he's already doing all he can for you."

"I realize that. But I want to talk to him anyway!" He saw her eyes widen as he snapped at her. He struggled to hold back his anger and frustration before he made more of a fool of himself.

Yuko prostrated herself before him, her face very close to the floor. "I'm sorry, sir, I meant no offense," she said. "I'll see immediately if Kirin-san can come and meet with you." She scrambled to her feet and was gone.

He sighed. He should have never lost his temper. He was supposed to be behaving like a samurai, not some spoiled child off the street. As a samurai, he had the right to take her life without explanation. It horrified him to have been responsible for the fear he'd seen in her eyes, since she actually believed that power was his.

Yuko didn't return for the rest of the afternoon; evening was falling before he heard the door open again. His apology was already rising to his lips when he abruptly realized his visitor was not the maid.

"Good evening. I apologize I was not able to come any sooner." Kirin bowed and then came in, shutting the door behind him.

Toshi bowed in return and watched the old man as he approached to sit very close. He thought it rather odd, considering they were alone, but made no comment. He was distracted by the fact that, now he had the man here, he wasn't at all sure what he should say. He wracked his brain trying to find a way to start off the conversation, even as Kirin sat expectantly and silently before him.

"I have been somewhat surprised not to have met anyone in the last few days," he began.

Kirin nodded approvingly. "Shiroyama Castle has not been the center of activity it once was for a number of seasons. Our ways of life have been changing."

This told Toshi nothing he didn't already know. He decided to probe a little deeper. "Yes, so I've heard. Yet, these changes don't seem to be for the better."

Kirin nodded. "Just so, Kazete-san. Such is the way of all things here. Though time flows like a great river, there is no wind with which to fill our sails to try and travel against it. So, we end up being dragged along by the current."

Toshi said nothing right away, trying to decipher all Kirin might have just inferred. "Will the writ not prove strong enough to summon the wind, in my case? It is from Lord Asano himself. Surely, it's worth something." He couldn't read the old man's expression.

"I have been serving our lord for a very long time, Kazete-san. I have held many posts, seen many things." Kirin's voice dropped to an almost-inaudible whisper. "I know whose paper you hold, for Lord Asano has only issued such a writ once in his lifetime. It would prove most inopportune if your document was seen too often, and the truth came to light."

Toshi felt his pulse quicken as he realized Kirin might really know all he implied he did. This also told him that Tsuyu might very well be one of the enemies Asaka had feared might already be within Asano's walls.

"I will try my best to gain you the meeting you seek, if you will only indulge me with your patience," Kirin continued. "The gods have smiled upon you, that is certain; or you would have never made it this far. Let us hope they'll continue to do so and give aid to me to grant you what you seek."

"But, Kirin-san, what about—" He forced himself to stop as Kirin bowed before him, ending their conversation. As he watched the older man leave, he realized his waiting was far from over.

Not long after Kirin left, Yuko appeared. Meekly, he let her lead the way back to his room.

Chapter 32

Toshi met the dawn sitting in his spacious room. The sliding panels facing the garden had been pushed back, letting in the cool morning air and the pleasant scents springing from beyond.

He hadn't slept well. His mind had been too preoccupied with his dilemma and his inability to solve it. No real choices were left to him, and he knew it. Though he didn't like it, he would have to trust in Kirin's ability to arrange a meeting for him with Asano. Making a fuss would only draw attention to himself, and that was the last thing he wanted—especially if his growing suspicions about Tsuyu were true.

So, in the meantime, he would just have to be content with waiting.

On the verge of desperation, he fervently wished he could talk to Miko. He wished he could share his troubles with her and bask for a while in her company.

With those thoughts in mind, he started wondering where she and all the others were. Were they hiding in the city, or were they still out in the lands surrounding it? Perhaps they were waiting just beyond the castle walls. Would they know something had gone wrong? Or would Asaka believe him to have reneged on his task?

He shook his head, trying to drive such thoughts away. He sent a prayer to Buddha that the Enlightened One might lend him the patience of the sun. It never hurried or grew impatient. The sun traveled the path of the sky every day without fail. He needed to do the same.

Having nothing better to do, he stripped to his underwear and began practicing his exercises. A thin layer of perspiration covered his body when a soft rap at his door brought him to a stop. He sat down next to his folded clothes.

The door slid open and Yuko bowed to him from the hallway. *"Ohayo gozaimasu."*

"Good morning," he replied.

Yuko smiled and came inside with his breakfast. "Kazete-sama, will you be taking lunch in the waiting room?"

He hesitated a moment before replying. "No, here will be fine. I won't be going to the waiting room today."

Yuko nodded, making no comment at the change in his routine.

He ate his breakfast in silence as she sat nearby, ready to serve any need. Though he longed for company, her presence made him uncomfortable. Yuko treated him as a samurai, which he wasn't. She even treated him as if he were older than she, which he also wasn't. On top of that, he was a little afraid to trust anyone here—he had too much to lose.

After breakfast, the rest of the morning wore on slowly. It didn't help him to know this was but the first of an indefinite number of long days to follow.

As he had sat, stared and fidgeted in the waiting room before, he now did the same on the small porch outside his room. He had his lunch there, staring out into the immense garden. Lunch consisted of grilled eel, rice, crisp seaweed, sake and tea; yet it all tasted like gruel to him. He wondered dejectedly how long Asano's people would let him stay there eating the lord's food, sleeping in the lord's rooms, using up the servants, before they would get tired of it and kick him out, his quest unfulfilled.

Yuko moved quietly around him, serving, pouring, even cleaning; but he barely noticed her presence. He never let the wrapped kettle out of his sight for any reason, though. The crux of his duty lay always at his side.

Why had so many people died for that kettle? What was so important about it that people were willing to kill for it? Did the rumors Miko heard when Asaka first came here have anything to do with it or not? He doubted daimyos disappeared every day. But, despite that, why was it proving so difficult to give the kettle to the man who'd supposedly wanted it all along? Had something happened because he hadn't gotten it when he'd first sent Asaka on his mission?

Could that be why things here had changed so much? But what could a kettle have to do with something that important?

He sighed, not knowing the answer to any of his questions. It looked like he might never find the answers. He would never meet Lord Asano. Asaka-sama and the others would spend eternity wandering the earth because of him, their duty unfulfilled because they dared entrust this task to a foolish peasant boy.

"Stop it!" He slapped his thigh hard, trying to snap himself out of the cascading despair he was falling into.

"Sir?" Yuko looked up from behind him, a teapot in one hand.

"I'm sorry. I didn't mean you, Yuko-san," he quickly explained. "I think I'm going for a long walk in the garden."

Not waiting for a response, he grabbed the wrapped kettle, slipped on some sandals and stepped off the porch. Stoking the anger he felt and using it to keep back the despair, he stiffly took the first stone path he came on.

The sounds of birds gaily flitting through the trees drifted all around him. A small waterfall poured into a pond full of brightly colored giant carp. The echoing sound of bamboo striking stone came at regular intervals as a miniature stream filled a hollow rod that would tip down, once full, to spill its contents and then start the process all over again.

Though the beauty and solitude around him should have helped to calm him, he could find no comfort in his surroundings. Privacy was something everyone coveted, but not like this. Not when there was no end in sight.

Feeling alone, though he was in a city of thousands, he stopped as he strolled amidst a clump of bamboo and tall pines, deciding he should turn back. A frightening hunger for human company had grown inside him. He decided he should satisfy it even if it was only with watching Yuko work.

Turning to go back, he arrived at an intersection. He stared at it, unable to remember from which of the two paths he'd come. He looked around but couldn't spot his room. He realized he had no idea how long he'd been walking. He'd never thought the garden would be as extensive as it was.

Just as he was about to pick one of the paths at random, he

stopped as he heard a rapid rustling sound somewhere behind him. He turned, wondering who or what might be there, and let his hand fall to the hilt of his wakizashi.

Seeing nothing untoward, he stepped deeper into the trees.

The shadows on the path were long and deep. He kept his eyes moving, looking for anything that might be hiding in them. A small part of him screamed he'd been discovered, that his enemies had found him. He paid the small voice no heed. As he went on, he heard a muffled sound off to his right. Tensed and ready, he noticed the path branched off into the deeper shadows. Taking a deep breath, he took the new path.

The bamboo thickened on either side, crowding out the trees. He couldn't see what lay ahead on the curving path. His heart beat faster. The muffled sound came again as he rounded the turn. He stopped, surprised by what he found there.

A large bench sat nestled in the shadows of bamboo at the end of the small path. Draped over part of it was a young woman. Her voluminous cherry-blossom-colored kimono spread out grandly about her with its many layers. Long, glistening black hair flowed almost to the ground, hiding some of the blood-red flowers stitched onto the pinkish fabric of her clothes. The woman's face lay hidden from him.

He realized the muffled sounds he heard were the sounds of weeping. Not wanting to interfere, or to let the woman know he had witnessed her pain, he stepped back to get out of the grove. His gaze stuck to her, though, as her shoulders shook with misery. He backed up onto a broken piece of bamboo and stumbled.

He fell hard on the path and cried out before he realized what he was doing.

"Who's there?"

The fierceness in the voice caught him off-guard. He tried to scramble backward out of the grove but ended up smacking into a clump of bamboo. He struggled to his feet as he gazed upon one of the most beautiful and stoic faces he had ever seen.

For a moment, it occurred to him that maybe he hadn't stumbled on a woman at all but rather some kind of spirit in disguise. What else would explain the delicate oval features, the rounded lips, the soft, tearstained cheeks and the flaming brown eyes that pinned him where he stood?

"Please, forgive me. I hadn't meant to intrude." He felt his tongue trying to trip him. "I'd come into the garden for a walk and ended up losing my way. I heard a noise and came to investigate. I never meant any offense. Truly, I—"

He forced his mouth shut, hearing himself starting to babble like a child. With some misgivings, he stared at the small, sheathed blade he saw the beauty holding in her hands.

"Who are you?" she demanded.

"Oh, yes, that. Please, forgive me. My name is Kazete Toshiro. I'm a visitor here." He bowed low, realizing from the diminutive painted brows on her face she was an aristocrat and a samurai. He noticed she barely returned his bow as she began dusting off her kimono.

"Hm, I've never heard the name, and I am pretty familiar with most prominent samurai families." She turned her steely gaze on him. "Have you any idea who I am?"

"No, my lady, I'm sorry, but I don't." He stumbled the words out even as he pondered if telling her the truth might have been a mistake.

She stared at him long and hard, almost as if she didn't believe him. "My name is Himiko." She turned away from him, extracting a handkerchief from the long sleeve of her kimono.

"Again, I wish to tell you how sorry I am for my rudeness. I will leave you to your privacy." He bowed again, ready to make his exit.

"You will not leave," she commanded.

He stopped. Her tone left no doubt this was not a request. He wondered if he'd somehow offended her again.

"I wish to speak with you, if it would not prove too inconvenient." Her voice softened.

"I would be honored to, Lady, if it is what you wish."

"Good, I'm glad to hear it."

He was shocked by her bluntness but didn't dare let it show on his face. With a calculated swirl of silk, Himiko moved to sit on the bench she'd moments ago been leaning against. Seeing her sit down, he immediately sank to the ground, keeping his head lower than hers, hoping to cause no further offense.

"You say you are a visitor, yet real visitors haven't been allowed entry to the castle for some time. How do you account for this?"

He glanced at her and had his gaze met by one of steel. Somehow, it seemed out of place in her delicate features.

"I have a writ from Lord Asano. It was able to get me in past the guards."

"From my father?" He saw a wispy look of surprise cross her face, but in no way did it equal his own. Himiko was Asano's daughter?

"Do you still have this writ?" Her tone made it quite clear she hadn't believed a word he'd said.

"Yes, Asano-sama, I still have it."

"Show it to me." Her tone was hard.

Nodding, he reached into his kimono and extracted the bamboo case holding the writ. He was forced to move forward on his knees before he was close enough to hand it to her.

Himiko snatched the case from his hand and opened the container, taking out the paper safeguarded within. Ignoring his presence, she read the writ twice before carefully studying the stamped signature at the bottom. He saw a second look of surprise cross her features, but it was quickly replaced by enmity and distrust.

"How did you come by this? I suppose my father gave it to you himself!"

He cringed as she threw the writ at him. "No, Lady, Lord Asano didn't give this to me. It was my lord, the original recipient of the writ, who passed it onto me."

She eyed him warily. "Why would a lord give such a valuable document to you?"

He bristled at the implied insult but at the same time realized the reason for her question. "My lord has fallen on hard times. As unworthy as I am, I was still the only one left with any chance of accomplishing that which Lord Asano had bidden my lord to do."

Her small brow arced high, though the rest of her remained impassive. "And just what was it my father had supposedly bidden your lord to do?"

He hesitated, but after a moment realized he really had no choice. If she was truly Lord Asano's daughter, she might prove his only way to reach his goal. "Your father had asked my lord to find and deliver this to him."

He brought his wrapped bundle before him.

"Let me see it."

He stared hard at the ground. "No."

"I believe I just told you to show it to me."

He hung his head low. "I'm sorry, Lady Himiko, but I can't." He forced himself to go on. "I won't. This package is meant for Lord Asano's eyes alone."

He heard her scoff, but refused to react to it.

"I could have you killed for your impudence and see the contents anyway," she said.

He bowed, his blood turning cold at the seriousness in her tone. He lowered his head all the way to the warm earth but never let his hand stray from the kettle. "If that is your wish."

He waited in silence to see what she would do next.

"You're not Tsuyu's man, are you," she said.

Her odd statement made him look up. He saw a strange expression cross her face as she looked away to stare at the bamboo around them. Abruptly, her gaze returned to him, pinning him where he knelt.

"You're obviously not from Narashi. Would you tell me where you come from then, Kazete-san?"

He hesitated, not sure what to make of her new conversational tone. "I come from the north, from the port city of Shinsha. It is in the Toyama Bay."

"How long have you been in Narashi?"

He glanced up at her again. "Five days."

"Have you seen much of it?" she asked eagerly.

He sat up, seeing true curiosity in her face. "Only what could be seen on the streets on the way up to the castle."

She sighed, her eyes drifting from him. "That's a pity, for Narashi is a marvelous city, what with its grand, paved streets, its eateries, its most excellent shopping districts and, best of all, its plays and art." Himiko looked up, as if seeing what she spoke of in her mind's eye. "You really should have availed yourself of them before coming here."

Toshi once again became the object of her stare. He saw her eyes soften before she turned to look away.

"Please forgive me for my previous rudeness," she said. "Things just haven't been as they once were, and I'm forced to be careful."

He bowed to the ground again, accepting her apology but also wanting to hide his confusion.

"My father hasn't granted an audience to anyone for some time. My father hasn't been my father for some time." Her words were all matter-of-fact. It was the way. "Please stop groveling in my presence. We're both samurai. We're alone, and, in truth, I hold no position of importance."

Hesitant to break decorum, he sat up slowly. Himiko scooted over to one end of the bench.

"Come, sit here with me." She patted the empty seat beside her. "You're getting your clothes dirty."

With some relief he noticed her sheathed blade was gone. He stood up, retrieving the thrown writ, and dusted off his clothes.

"Sit here, next to me. It's been a long time since I've had anyone new to talk to."

"I mean no offense, Lady Himiko, but I don't really think it would be proper that I—" She slapped her hand against the stone bench, cutting him off. He could see a touch of anger growing in her eyes.

"I don't care about what's proper. You will sit here!"

Bowing in apology, he hurried to the bench and sat on it as far away from her as he could.

"That's much better. Thank you." Himiko stared at him without saying anything else for several minutes. He tried hard not to squirm under her intense gaze. "How long has it been since your lord met with my father?"

She offered him the bamboo tube; and he shyly took it back, putting the writ inside it.

"It's been a number of years. Eight or more," he said.

"How old are you?"

He didn't dare look at her as he answered. "I'm fifteen."

"Fifteen?"

He felt his cheeks growing hot.

"You say your lord had no one else he could send but a boy of fifteen? Surely, he's in desperate times. Either that, or you are an unusually remarkable boy."

Though he tried, he couldn't make sense of her light tone. Was she making fun of him, as she probably should; or did her words imply something else?

"Kazete-san, please, tell me about yourself," Himiko said. "I'm terribly interested in hearing about your trip here. Please, give me every detail."

He stared uneasily into her face and was surprised by the genuine eagerness he saw there. "Himiko-sama, I—I haven't really done much. None of it is really all that interesting."

"Yes, yes, but tell me anyway." Her eyes were bright.

He couldn't tell her the truth, of that he was sure. He somehow had to come up with a convincing tale for her. Luckily, he never got a chance to try.

"Himiko-sama! Himiko-sama!"

He turned in the direction of the distant call.

"Damn them."

He looked back as he heard Himiko curse under her breath. He stared at her, astonished at the anger on her face. She noticed his stare and smoothed the feelings out of her features.

"My retinue is looking for me," she explained. "I'm going to have to leave you so they may find me. The wretched creatures never leave me a moment to myself." There was a flicker of her hidden anger in her eyes as she looked in the direction of the calls. "It would be best if you remained here after I leave, at least for a short while. It would be inconvenient if word got out you and I had spent time together, alone. I will send for you by the proper channels so you may visit me later. Please, take care until then."

Moving faster than he would have thought possible in her layers of silk, Himiko left the grove. He stared after her, wondering at her strangeness, and waited for a long while before he left as well.

Chapter 33

After some searching, Toshi was eventually able to find his room again. Not sure if Asano's daughter would really call for him, he sat down on his porch to wait. As time slipped by, he grew excited at the prospect of getting to see her again.

The sun was lowering on the horizon when a soft knock came at his door. He stepped into the room as Yuko slid it open and bowed toward him.

"Kazete-sama, I've brought a request from the Lady Himiko. She asked if you would honor her by joining her for some tea."

He couldn't help but hear the wonder coloring the woman's voice. "The honor would be mine," he replied. "Please tell Lady Himiko I would be greatly pleased to join her."

He was puzzled as Yuko bowed very deeply and hid her face from him as she spoke. "The lady anticipated your reply and asked I take you straight to her."

Trying not to seem eager, he waited for her to stand up. He brought the kettle with him as he followed Yuko out of the room. "Yuko-san, would you tell me about her?"

Yuko slowed her pace as she lit their way. "Lady Himiko is our lord's only daughter. He has four strong sons, but over the last few seasons they've been assigned to far-off provinces, despite their wishes. Of all his children, she is the youngest. Her father had always adored her, granting her every whim. Yet, even with her he has become as distant as with everything else."

He had to strain to hear her. She fell silent as they entered the lighted area of the castle. The farther they went in that direction the more people they encountered. Through their buzzing activity, Yuko led him to a flight of stairs. He followed her as she led him two floors up.

Four guards glared at them from the landing. He was surprised to see two of them wearing a different crest than Lord Asano's. The new crest was made of a large triangle with a smaller one at each tip. Yuko led him past without interference, though he could feel their eyes on his back.

Two doors stood open not far from the landing, revealing a large room. Yuko stopped before the opening, bowed and indicated for him to go inside. He took a deep breath and did so. Once there, he knelt on the floor and bowed deeply.

A number of stockinged feet shuffled past him, followed by partially muffled giggles. As he sat up, he heard the doors slide shut behind him.

Looking around, he saw a giant paneled painting in the back of the room that colorfully depicted the goings-on of a busy city street. On the rest of the walls were less colorful but still magnificent paintings depicting nature's sweet serenity.

"I'm glad you accepted my invitation, Toshiro-san." Himiko sat across the room from him, a soft blue-green kimono immaculately arranged around her. A low table sat at her side and two well-dressed women sat a foot or so behind her. "Please come forward. Share some tea with me."

She gracefully used a folded fan to point to a place not far from her.

A little nervous now that he was with her, he rose to do as he'd been bid. As he sat, one of the two women shuffled forward and served him tea as the other presented him with a dish full of delicate tidbits. He felt Himiko's gaze lingering on him as he took a sip of his drink.

"Have you seen any good Noh plays lately?" she asked.

He looked up at her as she delivered her evenly paced question.

"No, I'm afraid I haven't. I haven't seen a play in some time."

"A pity," she said. "Normally, I go see every new Noh play or group that comes into the city. Noh, Bunraku, even the rising Kabuki—I love them all. Unfortunately it's been beyond my power to get away to enjoy any of late."

He looked at his cup, wondering at the words she'd chosen. Were the troubles in this castle even worse than he'd thought?

"I've never been outside Narashi," she added. "This city is Nihon to me. It always fascinates me when someone from the outside comes here. It's almost like being visited by gaijin."

He saw an undercurrent of excitement fill Himiko's face. He knew the look; he'd had it himself when he'd first met Captain Valéz and his crew. It had been a very frightening and wondrous thing to meet gaijin.

"Have you ever been outside Nihon, Toshiro-san?" she asked.

He felt all their eyes glued to him. "Well, ah, no, I haven't. Though I have made copies of maps and charts of other countries brought to us by gaijin."

Himiko leaned forward, her eyes alight. "Do you think you could draw one for me?"

"It wouldn't be exact—" Her gaze held his. "But I guess I could try."

"Excellent! Akiko, please fetch paper and ink for Toshiro-san."

Within moments, the servant returned with what he required. After arranging it all on the small table that had been brought for him, he blocked out everything but the empty paper before him. He planned in his mind what would go where—the compass points, the equator—and then carefully rolled his brush in the ink and started to draw. As the countries took shape, he wrote down what names he could remember. He purposely left Nihon for last.

"That's us?" Himiko asked in amazement.

He jerked his head up, not having realized she had risen to sit beside him.

"Uh, yes, that's Nihon." He licked his lips, nervous to have Lord Asano's daughter so close. The sweet fragrance of her long black hair coiled around him as she leaned past him to point at the map.

"It seems so small. I had always thought it would be larger."

Not sure if he should say something or not, he found the decision torn from him as the doors slid open with a bang. Everyone in the room turned to stare in surprise.

Dominating the open doorway was a hefty man with fists set on his hips and an arrogant look plastered on his face. His clothes bore the new crest Toshi had seen on two of the four guards at the landing.

Toshi glanced at Himiko as she rose to her feet. Her expression was as hard as stone.

"Lord Tsuyu." She did not say the name kindly.

"Ah, good evening, Himiko-chan." He used the endearment as if she were trivial rather than a close friend. "I hope you don't mind my impromptu visit."

Tsuyu barely bowed in her direction as he came into the room. Himiko didn't return it.

"It's always so pleasant to see you." Himiko's voice was cold.

"Yes, so nice of you to say so." The hefty man's penetrating gaze left her and stabbed at the two servants. They instantly rushed to serve him where he stood. Tsuyu sipped his tea as the tension palpably grew in the room. "I see you have a guest, Himiko-chan. Aren't you going to introduce us?"

With a slight nod, she turned in Toshi's direction. He saw a look of worry momentarily flash across her eyes. "This is Kazete Toshiro. Kazete-san, this is my father's current main vassal, Lord Tsuyu."

Toshi bowed low. "I am honored to meet you, sir." As he sat back up, he heard Himiko move away to return to her original seat. She didn't invite Tsuyu to sit.

"So, Kazete-san, how long have you been here in the castle?"

"Only a few days, sir," he answered.

"Are you on urgent business?" The question was asked pleasantly enough but at the same time seemed forced.

Toshi stared into the lord's antagonistic face and didn't like what he saw there. "No, sir, nothing urgent."

"Kazete-san and I were introduced at a Noh play a year or so ago," Himiko said. "We spoke at some length during the intermission. He happened to mention he was about to go on a long journey in which he would get to meet gaijin. Since I've never been outside Narashi, I invited him to visit me upon his return. Father had been well enough then to sign a permit allowing Kazete-san to visit me once he did so."

He dared not move lest it be taken as a sign she might be lying.

"How unusual. I'd heard nothing of this." Tsuyu's eyes were dark. "How long had you been planning to stay?"

Toshi looked away, not liking the question. "It shouldn't be long."

"I would think not," Tsuyu responded haughtily. "Asano-sama has not been well, and we can't have his guests abusing his hospitality."

"My father has not minded your long stay or that of your associates. I doubt he would care about one more, especially since he'd previously approved it," Himiko told him without emotion. "If you wish, though, we could bring the matter to his attention and let him decide how long Kazete-san may stay."

Tsuyu paled with anger. Toshi didn't understand the game they were playing. Were there things Asano had not given Tsuyu the authority to deal with?

"I doubt that will be necessary," Tsuyu said quickly through gritted teeth. "Your father is a very busy man and should not be bothered by such petty concerns." His dark gaze raked Toshi from head to foot before he abruptly changed the subject. "He's met gaijin, you say?"

"Yes, just so." Himiko's gaze turned toward Toshi. "Kazete-san, why don't you show Lord Tsuyu the picture you drew for us?"

He took his drawn map from the table and offered it to Tsuyu.

"That is what the world looks like outside of Nihon. A humbling sight, wouldn't you say, Tsuyu-san?" Himiko's eyes were hard.

Toshi watched the large man stare carefully at the map before his eyes rose to stare neutrally toward Himiko. "Perhaps I've come at a bad time. I think it would do you good, however, if you could learn as much about traveling as you can from your friend. For, though, you've never traveled before, you'll soon be leaving Narashi forever."

Tsuyu nodded curtly to both of them then departed as abruptly as he had come in. As Toshi glanced away from the doorway, he saw Himiko sag forward.

"Himiko-sama!"

He and her two attendants rushed to her side even as she forcefully straightened up and waved them away. Her face looked pale. "Akiko, Suyako, we have been very negligent. Surely, our guest is very hungry after all that work. Please fetch our dinner, and close the doors on your way out."

The two women looked at each other, making no move toward the door.

"Should we not send in some of the others while we're gone,

Himiko-sama?"

"No, you will not. Now, get out!" With fire flashing in her eyes, Himiko grabbed an empty teacup and threw it at them. The two women jumped out of the way of the missile, bowed and rushed from the room.

As soon as the doors had closed, Himiko sagged again, hiding her face behind her hands. Having no idea what he should do, Toshi turned away so as not to shame her and stared at the doors as she cried softly behind him.

He was surprised a few minutes later when Himiko whispered to him, sounding calm, "You must take care, Toshiro-san. I have been careless in my selfishness and now have placed you in great danger. Tsuyu is a cold and ruthless man. He has taken over as my father's spirit has waned. It is he who controls who comes and goes from the castle. It is he who has imprisoned me here."

Toshi glanced over his shoulder to look at her. Her profile was toward him, her gaze far away.

"Not long ago, I loved it here," she said. "Often, my father and I would stay awake late into the night talking. It was a time when he took an interest in things. It was a time when he valued my opinion. It was a time when Shiroyama was a happy place, infused with a life all its own. It was a time before Tsuyu."

Her voice grew hard.

"Then he arrived, a visiting lord from some far-off province. No one paid him much attention when he came. He was but one of many others, the son of an old rival. Only, something happened, something between him and my father. Everything began to fall apart.

"My father distanced himself from everyone and everything. He handed Tsuyu the reins of power piece by piece, though he had sons and though there were many more capable and deserving than he." She grew quiet. "Things have continued to slowly degrade ever since." She faced him, her gaze locking with his. "You must be careful. Though I've no idea what you carry, my father wouldn't have issued such a writ unless he wanted it badly. Anything he wanted so much might seem like a threat to Tsuyu. And if he perceives you as a threat, he will even bargain with demons to be rid of you."

The servants returned with their dinner, disturbing the shocked silence. As the women served them, Himiko smiled and gave no hint anything had happened to interrupt her evening at all.

Toshi quietly ate his dinner, a thousand questions piling up inside him. He made light conversation and followed Himiko's lead, trying to appear as unworried as she.

"Toshiro-san, I'm feeling a little unwell, I think I ate too much. Would it offend you greatly if we cut the evening short?"

Himiko's servants were busily collecting their dinner dishes.

"Not at all, Himiko-sama. I hope you will feel better soon." He bowed deeply and picked up the wrapped kettle as he prepared to leave.

"I would like to make it up to you," she called after him. "Could I impose on your time tomorrow?"

"I would be honored if you would, Himiko-sama."

"Thank you. It means a lot to me. I have very little with which to distract myself of late."

Bowing again, he took his leave, the image of Himiko's delicate face haunting him. To his surprise, he found Yuko waiting for him in the hallway. She bowed before silently leading him back to his room.

As they entered the dark wing filled with empty guestrooms, he couldn't help but notice the oppressive silence of the place. Anything could happen to him in that silence. Himiko's warning replayed over and over in his mind.

He tried to shake off his growing dread as Yuko set out his bedding. With a brief glance out into the garden and its own forbidding silence, he slowly closed the panels leading onto the porch. He bade Yuko goodnight when she had finished with his bed and listened to her footsteps as she left. With goose bumps playing over his arms and legs, he disrobed before getting beneath his covers. He tucked the wrapped kettle in with him and made sure to keep his wakizashi at his side. Wide-eyed, he watched the candles burn down in their lanterns as he vainly sought the courage to try to sleep.

Chapter 34

Around mid-morning the next day Himiko and her entourage appeared in the garden outside his room.

"Good morning, Toshiro-san," she said.

"Good morning." He bowed, glad to see her smiling.

"Isn't it a beautiful morning? An excellent time for a friendly stroll, don't you think?"

He grabbed the wrapped kettle and walked outside. The women surrounding Himiko parted as he joined her. He noticed her servants stuck very close to them as they walked, until Himiko curtly gestured at them with a closed fan. The women hesitantly dropped back a small distance.

They walked in silence for a while, until they entered a flowering path almost as bright as Himiko's flower-studded kimono.

"After our two meetings yesterday, you must surely think ill of me." Her tone was pleasant, but her eyes stared only straight ahead, making no move to look at him.

"No, Himiko-sama, I don't," he responded. "We don't always act the way we would normally when pressed by stressful circumstances."

She glanced coyly in his direction for a moment. "You talk as if from experience, Toshiro-san."

He was silent, not having realized until she'd said it that it was true. "I guess we have something in common, then," he said. He didn't add being prisoners within the castle was another thing they shared. She was forcibly kept here by an enemy; he was kept here by his need to see his mission through.

Himiko raised her voluminous sleeve to hide her mouth as she laughed for a moment. He liked the sound and was pleased he'd somehow been responsible for it.

"Yet, I'm not really sure that's such a good thing to have in common." She stared at him, her face becoming serious. "I was not exaggerating about what I told you last night. Tsuyu is an extremely dangerous man. He has plans, and he will do whatever is necessary to see them succeed. I, among others, tried to warn my father of what we saw in him, but by then it was too late. My father would listen to no one but Tsuyu."

Toshi frowned. "But his power is only temporary, isn't it? Your father is the true lord, and his sons will inherit his lands after he's gone."

Himiko gave him a humorless smile. "Oh, Tsuyu knows this and has already taken steps to rectify it. Somehow, he's convinced my father to offer him my hand."

He stared at her in surprise, Tsuyu's comment of her upcoming travel echoing in his mind. "I'm sorry."

"That's not necessary. It is my fate. So be it. But Tsuyu will rue the day he marries me." Her smile was filled with malice. He could see a streak of stubbornness and strength inside her greater than his own.

"He is very well aware of my feelings for him and of the fact I tried to dissuade my father from listening to him. He demands respect, but shows none. So, I give him none. In his pettiness, he ordered that I was to no longer be allowed to leave the castle. Since my father did not contest his command, I have been stuck here ever since. Yet, make no mistake, his hold is not complete. There are those who are not cowed easily by Tsuyu's wishes; and, occasionally, my father thwarts him, though I think this is more for amusement than spite. And he's not married to me yet, so at least for now he has no choice but to at least appear to be doing things in my father's best interest."

Her face lightened. "But enough of that. Come, let me show you the beauty that lies in our garden. And perhaps, in return, you will dazzle me with tales of gaijin."

He smiled in answer and spurred her on. He knew the great trust she'd just placed in him by telling him what she had. Perhaps, in time, he might be able to return the honor.

Chapter 35

The day went by much too quickly, as Himiko showed him the major sights of the castle. Though they were never alone, they pretended they were as they roamed all around. They spoke of anything and everything, though never straying close to those topics bothering them most.

The next two days passed just as rapidly. Toshi awoke each morning yearning to see her, and felt almost mournful when they had to part at night. He wished now and again that Miko were with him. He craved her opinion of Himiko, and perhaps she could even explain to him the odd feelings moving inside him of late. Waiting to see Lord Asano no longer seemed to be such a terrible burden.

Yet, at the same time, he knew he was only fooling himself. At some point in the near future Himiko would be forced to marry Tsuyu and then be carried off to some far province for safekeeping. He would still be here, waiting for a meeting that might never come.

He glanced up at the sky and realized the sun was much higher than it should have been. Himiko had never been this late before. Had Tsuyu called on her again or had something else gone wrong?

He turned around at a soft tap at the door. Rising to his feet, he hurried toward it even as the panel slid open. He slowed to a stop as he realized it was just Yuko with some tea. Sighing, he sat down as she stepped inside.

"I appreciate the gesture, Yuko-san, but I'm really not thirsty," he said.

"It's no trouble, sir. And, really, it would be best if you had some."

Not wanting to argue, he said nothing as she went ahead and served him. As she leaned forward to set the filled cup before him, she angled her head enough to whisper in his ear.

"Lady Himiko regrets she will be late today. She begs your forgiveness and promises to come for you as soon as possible. She hoped you would enjoy this special tea while you wait."

He tried to read Yuko's expression but couldn't. Why had she whispered? Why hadn't she just said so? He reached for his cup and remained silent. With practiced care, he raised the cup to his lips and took a taste while trying to keep his confusion from showing on his face. The vibrant flavor of the expensive tea was shadowed by the worry gnawing at him.

Was he being watched without his knowledge? Could that be why Yuko had whispered her message? Something had happened between last night and today. Had Tsuyu somehow found out more about him?

With great care, he studied the garden outside, trying to spot anything out of the ordinary. He saw nothing. He wasn't sure if he should be reassured or not. Closing his eyes, he tried to center himself by thinking and feeling nothing except for the taste and warmth of his tea.

Yuko returned to bring lunch, but he ate little. The longer Himiko remained missing, the more difficult he found it to push his worry away.

Restless, but knowing he had no choice but to wait, he left the porch, reentered his room and achingly went through his exercises as precisely as he could. He forced his thoughts to stick only to his lessons, driving all else out. Time, in a sense, stopped for him. There was only the flow of his movements, the careful shifting of muscles, the end of one pattern weaving into the beginning of the next.

Perspiration sprang on his brow, though by his slow pace it would have appeared he wasn't exerting himself. He pushed on through every step and position Mitsuo had taught him. As he came to the last of them, he discovered he felt oddly relaxed and satisfied.

He turned to pick up the wrapped kettle so he could return to the porch and realized for the first time that the door to his room was open and a number of people were gathered there looking inside.

"Himiko-sama." He quickly bowed, his face warming with embarrassment. Just how long had she and her maids been sitting there? He stared at them self-consciously, even as Himiko lowered her gaze. A splash of color lit up her cheeks.

"I hope I didn't disturb you, Toshiro-san," she said.

"No, no. I was just passing the time." He felt an excited shiver run through him as she looked up at him with a shy, pleased smirk on her lips.

"Will you walk with me, Toshiro-san?" she said.

"Hai." He nodded, thrilled she'd come. He was eager for the walk and the privacy it would give them for his questions.

Once they'd gotten underway, he glanced at her, intending to speak. He held back as he caught her studying him shyly from the corner of her eye. As soon as she noticed him looking at her, she turned her eyes away. He wasn't sure what to make of it.

"I was afraid I wouldn't be seeing you today," he said timidly.

"There are things happening, Toshiro-san. Odd things. Perhaps unpleasant things."

He stared at her, almost bursting with his questions. Her neutral tone held him back.

"There are people loyal to my father, loyal to me, who see Tsuyu's influence on us to be as evil as I do. I've been informed by them that Tsuyu had an unusual visitor last night," she said. Her voice was oddly subdued. "One no one but he ever saw. The visitor was never seen entering or leaving the castle. I haven't been able to find out if he or she is even still within the castle grounds."

Beneath Himiko's neutral tone, he thought he caught an undercurrent of confusion and excitement. How could someone enter the castle yet never be seen?

"I've spent all this time finding out what little I could, but no one knows anything. I thought perhaps it was a trick of some sort or even an illusion, until Tsuyu came and called on me late this morning. He was more uncouth than usual, which is always a dangerous sign. Most of the time it means something major has gone his way. He mentioned our upcoming marriage in such a way as to imply it no longer held much importance in his life."

Himiko stopped and turned toward him, her face taut. Her hands were clasped tightly before her. "I have no proof, but I know from the bottom of my soul something has gone terribly wrong for all of us. There is danger here, horrible danger." Her eyes sought his. "I gave up on my life long ago, for it shall come to an end by my own hand; but, Toshiro, I fear for you. You should leave this place while you still can. I'm certain you're in terrible danger."

"But—" He felt his throat go dry as she reached for his arm, forbidding him to speak. She gave him a hard look that softened as he watched.

"Do not concern yourself about me. My fate was decided long ago. I won't allow that dog to taint my family. But you, you must leave today!" She resumed walking before the servants got much closer.

"Himiko-sama, I—I appreciate your concern, but I can't leave. Too high a price has already been paid to get me here. I can't leave now." He heard her sigh. With a gentle squeeze, she released his arm. A sad smile met his questioning gaze. He had to strain to hear what she said next.

"Sometimes, the road can be difficult. I'm glad you'll be here to share mine, even if only for a little while longer."

Chapter 36

Most of the afternoon was spent in silence. What conversation arose was light and fleeting. Their dinner that evening was lavish; and, to his surprise, he found Himiko had even been able to arrange for them some humorous entertainment.

Though he laughed at all the right places, he didn't really find any of it funny. Himiko's concern for his safety both flattered him and made him fear. How could he be a threat to Tsuyu? What was so important about a kettle?

Toshi thought of Kirin. He'd not seen the man since the night the latter had warned him of the delicacy of things, so many days ago. Was Kirin taking a risk in trying to gain him an audience? He didn't understand any of it. He felt totally lost in matters as they stood, having no true idea of the stakes being waged around him and sure there was no way for him to find out.

He found his gaze straying in Himiko's direction. He watched her smiling profile as she brought up her sleeve to hide a building bubble of laughter. He found it hard to imagine her fierce spirit quenched forever, to picture her as her life's blood soaked into the tatami floor as the thick red liquid flowed from her throat where a sharp blade would have helped her end her life. Ritual suicide—the ultimate form of protest. But would her father even heed the warning her death would be trying to give him? He shook his head, chilled by the thought.

She was stubborn, very stubborn. All she had been through and endured told him so. Himiko had the will of a battle-tested samurai. In death, would she keep her soul from going on to its next life so she might reap vengeance here? If he were faced with death, could he be as brave as she?

It was late when he finally excused himself and bid Himiko goodnight. Yuko was waiting for him out in the hall, as always, to lead him to the baths and then to his room. For the first time, it occurred to him to wonder if there was more to Yuko's attentiveness than just her standard duty. He shook his head, not comfortable with such thoughts.

He felt his brow furrow as Tsuyu's guards didn't give him their usual scowl as he walked past. They looked through him as if he weren't there. It chilled his blood. He turned his face away so they wouldn't see his discomfort. He followed Yuko in silence the rest of the way back.

* * * * *

Toshi's eyes fluttered open, a chill coursing down his spine. A tendril of swirling wind caressed his face as it made the low, burning lanterns flicker for a moment.

He sat up, realizing with growing panic the panels leading out into the garden were open. Three quick, soft *thunks* sounded just behind him. Glancing back, he saw three small needles embedded in his futon and wooden pillow.

With a surge of fear-inspired energy, he threw his blanket in the direction the needles had come from. As the blanket flew across the room, he picked up his wakizashi and the kettle and rolled away from the center of the room.

His skin prickled at the unnatural cold permeating the air. He backed into a corner even as he saw his blanket efficiently cut to tatters. He let the sheath of the wakizashi fall to the ground. His blood turned to ice in his veins as he saw the black figure standing confidently across the room from him. The intruder's mask's eye slits were glowing with an eerie red light.

Himiko's rumors about Tsuyu's unseen visitor now made perfect sense. The undead ninja had caught up to him at last. This also meant Tsuyu knew everything, and his own fate lay sealed.

Toshi crouched into a fighting stance. The ninja's eyes flashed, and he dove at him. Toshi prepared to block his thrust as the ninja switched his blade's direction and drove it under his protective arc.

Without thinking, Toshi brought up his left arm. The ninja's sword clanged against the kettle, splitting the cloth around it in two. The sound of the impact rang in his ears as the force of the blow tipped him to the right. He hit one of the paper panels and it collapsed under his weight, spilling him out into the hallway.

Struggling to regain his feet, he hesitated a moment as he saw Yuko staring wide-eyed at him from bedding set next to his door. "Yuko, get out of here!"

The girl didn't react to his command, her gaze moving dazedly between him and the broken end of the ninja's sword that had fallen point-first into the floor, inches from her foot.

"Yuko, go!"

He didn't get a chance to see if she went as bright pain flared in his right shoulder. Falling to the floor, he bit back a scream as the pain unexpectedly intensified. He tried to sit up as the smell of freshly spilt blood wove into his nostrils. By the light falling into the hall from his room, he saw the other half of the ninja's sword lying beside him, its broken end covered with his blood. He looked up to find the ninja's red eyes staring at him. The ninja leaped.

He felt a rush of cold seep into him as the ninja tumbled with him to the floor, the creature's sole hand clamped around his neck. No one would save him. No one could possibly reach him in time. The cold spread through him, trying to freeze him in place. The ninja's eyes burned before him, multiplying as Toshi ran out of air.

Desperate, he ignored the pain in his right shoulder and tried to attack with his wakizashi. The blade cut easily into the ninja's clothing, but the ninja himself didn't react in pain. Toshi was forced to release his blade as the ninja used his handless arm to beat at his wrist.

Having no choice, Toshi made his left arm move and smashed the kettle into the ninja's side. Instantly, the light in the ninja's eyes went dark and the flow of cold into Toshi's body momentarily decreased. With rising hope, he brought the kettle back and pressed it against the ninja's side again. He felt the skeleton's body shiver, the grip on his throat lessening ever so slightly.

He raised his free hand, his shoulder screaming in pain. He grabbed hold of the ninja's tunic and pulled. The hand around his neck was yanked loose as the fleshless body fell over. It didn't try to rise.

Heaving in great gasps of warm air, Toshi attempted to sit up. His vision spinning, he used his right arm for support so he wouldn't fall. With some difficulty, he removed the cut cloth from the kettle and used it to try and staunch the flow of blood still oozing from his right shoulder. His brain felt slow, his body numb.

He was beginning to warm up, his body shivering in reaction, when the ninja's eyes flashed as the latter sat up in one fluid motion. Toshi crouched as the skeleton reached for his wakizashi on the floor. Without hesitation, he brought up the kettle and shoved it bottom first at the ninja's exposed breastbone.

The ninja had been about to plunge the wakizashi into Toshi's side as he and the kettle connected. The skeleton's head reared back, his unnatural scream filling Toshi's mind to bursting. The kettle was covered in frost as he let go of it, instinctively trying to cover his ears as they protested in pain at the sound. The moment he released the kettle, the scream died.

Toshi forced himself to look and found the kettle on its side, the ninja a collapsed heap behind it. The skeleton's breastbone was charred, an imprint of the kettle's bottom now embossed on it. Breathing heavily, he reached for the kettle, still staring at the ninja, trying to catch any signs of movement. Seeing none, he raised the kettle above his head and brought it down with all the might he could muster. The kettle landed directly on the ninja's breastbone and shattered it like brittle wood.

Ignoring the damage he had caused, he raised the kettle again and brought it down hard. Over and over he repeated the maneuver, smashing the kettle against every part of the ninja's body. His shoulder started bleeding again, burning, but he ignored it. This time he would make sure the ninja never got up.

Toshi let his head hang, sweat dripping off his brow as he felt dizzy and faint. He was safe. The ninja would be unable to hurt him anymore. His stomach heaved.

"Kazete-san?" It was Kirin.

He glanced up, noticing for the first time the bright light that had for some moments flooded the hallway. Yuko stood by its source, her arms wrapped tightly about herself. Beside her stood Kirin, and two guards holding lanterns. He saw Kirin take a hesitant step forward as he once more called Toshi's name.

Not sure of what would happen to him now, he struggled to stand, the kettle gripped tightly in his left hand. The small group came forward. He felt his knees quiver just before they gave out on him. One of the guards was able to grab him before he hit the floor.

"Kazete-sama, you're wounded!"

He flinched as Yuko pressed the kettle's bloodied cloth back against his shoulder.

"You cannot remain here," Kirin said. "Yuko will get your things. You must be moved."

He ignored the words, instead staring dazedly at the ninja's remains. Kirin helped him up and tried to lead him away. He resisted. "Get...get it out into the sunlight—full sunlight...no shadows. I don't know if it can come back, but I—we—" He swallowed hard, his throat sore.

"I understand, Kazete-san," Kirin said. "It shall be done just as you ask. But, please, we must get you away from here. You are not safe."

He nodded and let Kirin pull him away. He stumbled as they walked along, not really aware of where he was being taken. He didn't even realize they'd reached their destination until they made him sit down and a warm cup of sake was pressed to his lips. A blanket was thrown over his shoulders.

As the sake wove its way down, warming his throat, he put the kettle in his lap and reached to hold the cup still being held for him. After he'd finished it all, he extended the empty cup and it was refilled. Finishing that one, he felt his gaze clear a little.

"Kazete-san, I will be gone but a moment to get someone to tend to your wound," Kirin said. "These men will remain here to guard you. I won't be long."

He nodded, not quite able to focus on Kirin's face. Time meant nothing after the old man left, so he wasn't sure how long Kirin had been gone before a keen-eyed old woman was brought in to see him.

The old woman bowed as Kirin introduced them. He barely nodded as she pulled his blanket aside to get a look at his wound. He placed his hand protectively over the kettle as she noticed it in his lap. The old woman nodded at him and then concentrated solely on his shoulder. Pain rushed through him as she prodded the area around the wound.

The woman turned away from him for a long moment and then handed him a cup of darkened sake. "Drink, boy. It will help the pain and make you rest."

He stared dubiously at the cup.

"Come now, do as O-baa-san tells you." She prodded his hands to bring the cup closer to his face.

He gulped the cup's contents down and soon felt his mind losing coherence. Darkness gathered around him, and he gratefully let it take him away.

Chapter 37

"Will he be all right? Are you sure? You should have had someone send for me sooner!"

Toshi frowned at the familiar voice and the concern that lay within it.

"I'm sorry, my lady, but it wasn't possible to do so," Kirin said. "Yuko tried to gain entry to your rooms several times last night, but Tsuyu's men wouldn't allow her. She could not insist, for this might have brought her to the interest of others. I thought such would not have been your wish."

Toshi allowed his eyes to crack open.

"I'm sorry, old friend," Himiko said. "You did what was right, as always. I should have known better."

Wondering what Kirin and Himiko were both doing in his room, he tried to sit up. He hissed as pain stabbed in his shoulder and fell back down. Immediately, he was the center of everyone's attention.

"Toshiro-san!"

He ignored Himiko's excited whisper as he recalled all that had happened to him the night before. He whipped his gaze around, looking for the object of his mission. Spotting the kettle sitting innocently beside him, he brought it closer and sighed with heartfelt relief.

"Toshiro-san, how do you feel?" Himiko asked.

He looked up into her worried face and felt himself blushing at her concern. "I'm all right, I think. Kirin-san and Yuko-san have been taking good care of me."

Her smile made him tingle all over. He stared at her delicate face, drinking in the sight of her. If things had gone just a little differently, he would have never been able to see her again. His heart shrank from the thought, and he bade his mind to dwell on other matters.

"Kirin-san, what was done with the ninja's remains?" he asked. "Were they placed in full sunlight?"

Himiko stared from one to the other of them, obviously lost. He waited expectantly for Kirin's answer.

"Yes, Kazete-san." Kirin's voice had fallen to a mere whisper. "Fortunately, we were able to remove what remained before it could be discovered by others. The clothing was burned and the bones were set out in a private spot, which is fully open to the sun's purifying gaze. I personally made an offering to Amaterasu as her sphere rose into the sky. I was informed that as soon as the sun's rays fell fully upon the bones they began to disappear. Nothing remains of them."

Toshi sighed as if a weight had been lifted from him and briefly touched his bandaged shoulder.

"All traces of the previous evening have been disposed of as well," Kirin said. "Your room and the hallway are once again as they have always been."

He stared in admiration at the older gentleman. It seemed he'd somehow made an ally.

"Disappearing bones?" Himiko's confused and disbelieving tone pulled at his attention.

"Himiko-sama, I know this will be hard to believe, but my attacker last night was a restless spirit, one I had met before." He waited for a look of incredulity to cross her face but instead she looked at him in awe and wonder.

"You have met a spirit? Like in the Noh plays? Truly? How did you do it? Are you a priest in disguise?"

He looked away, taken aback by her eager questions. "No, Himiko-sama, I'm not a priest, but I've met spirits. Fate brought me into contact with a group of them, and it's for their sake I'm here."

He almost missed the slight widening of Kirin's eyes, as if the thin man had just realized something. Toshi waited to see if he would speak of it, but Kirin said nothing. Toshi glanced back at Himiko and could tell there were things she wanted to ask. He looked away, hoping she wouldn't. There were questions he wasn't yet ready to answer.

As if on cue, Yuko appeared beside him with a tray holding bowls of rice and soup. "Breakfast, Kazete-sama?"

"Thank you."

With Kirin's help, he sat up, and Yuko placed the tray on his lap. Silence hung over them as he tried to master the art of eating one-handed. During his reprieve, he couldn't help but notice Himiko's gaze lingering on him. Kirin, on the other hand, seemed far away.

While he ate, he studied his surroundings and realized he'd been brought to Kirin's office. With a touch of misgiving, he also noticed the four guards stationed at the corners of the room. Himiko noticed what he was doing.

"These men are here to protect you, Kazete-san," she said. "They are loyal only to the Asano clan and have seen the danger posed to it by Tsuyu, as we do." He felt bumps rise up his arm as she touched his hand with her own."I've already begun preparations to get you safely out of the castle," she added.

"Please, Himiko-sama, don't."

"But an attempt has been made on your life," she argued. "There are bound to be others if you remain here."

He stared at the floor, a number of emotions flowing through him. "I can't, Himiko-sama, I must stay. Leaving would serve no purpose. I'm sure Tsuyu knows who I am now and why I'm here. He won't let me live with what I know and carry."

"My lady, he is right."

Toshi stared at Kirin in surprise.

"Lord Tsuyu can't afford to let him live. What he's involved in is too important."

Now it was Himiko who stared at Kirin. The surprise on her face was promptly subdued, turning her expression into a blank mask.

"You seem to know more than I, Kirin-san. Would you care to enlighten me?" The question was toned more as a command than a request.

Kirin glanced at Toshi, who nodded, also curious as to the enlightenment he might give them.

"Many years ago, when the great Daimyo Shura disappeared, his lands were split into equal shares and given to his most loyal vassals. It was part of a provision contrived by the Daimyo, since he'd yet to succeed in begetting an heir," Kirin began.

"The provision was unusual, and many wondered at it. The Daimyo could have easily adopted any one of the three men and had them continue his line. Such things were not unheard of. Rumor had it he'd been actually preparing to do just that when he mysteriously disappeared.

"When the Daimyo could not be found, his written wishes were followed and the lands were divided. Lord Asano was honored in that he'd been given the general's most prized lands. Our lord had expected trouble to come from this, for one of the others was an old rival and had coveted these lands. Yet, trouble never came."

Toshi fidgeted as Kirin paused to drink some tea.

"Everything proceeded as it should until a servant uncovered a hidden letter addressed to our lord," Kirin said. "What the letter contained, I do not know, for after reading it, Asano-sama destroyed it. An immediate inventory was ordered of all that was to be found in the castle. There was no need for it, but our lord never gave any explanation for the order.

"Once the list had been compiled, Asano-sama went over it with excruciating care. He would roam the castle at odd times of day and night to look for something he'd found on the list. After a time he stopped.

"Yet, it was around this time he sent for the son of one of his most remote vassals. Rumors ran rampant. What possible need could our lord have from such a removed clan when here he had vassals waiting on his every command? Asano-sama met with the young man alone. Never had his lordship been so secretive. No one but he knew what was being planned." Kirin sipped his tea.

"The young samurai stayed with us for only a few days. We knew he was about to undertake a journey on behalf of our lord, but no one knew where. He left here with Asano's blessing and a number of sealed papers. The only thing we were ever able to learn was the young samurai's name. Asaka."

Toshi waited for Kirin to continue, his excitement growing.

"The young samurai never returned. Within a year, his family was accused and convicted of crimes whose details were never made totally clear. It was the Tsuyu clan who found the evidence against them, and they who carried out the sentence. The Tsuyu clan assumed the lands once occupied by the Asaka clan and made them their own."

"Tsuyu. That clan seems to exist only to perpetuate misery." Himiko's hard gaze locked with Toshi's. "So, somehow you come from this man, Asaka, and with what my father sent him out for. Tell me, what did you bring for my father? What is so important as to drive the Tsuyu clan to do as they have done even after all this time?"

Hesitantly, still pinned by her blazing gaze, he brought the kettle before him. Saying nothing, he studied the growing look of disbelief taking hold on her face.

"A kettle? All this over a kettle? I don't understand!"

He stared down at the object of their scrutiny. "I can't enlighten you, though I'd like nothing better, Himiko-sama. But I was told nothing other than that getting this kettle into your father's hands was the most vital of tasks."

Kirin pensively stared at the kettle. "It doesn't appear to have ever been used. There are no marks of a fire's touch around its base."

"It doesn't make any sense," Himiko insisted.

"I know, but I'm sure there's got to be a reason; and, even if there isn't, I've got no choice but to try to deliver it."

The three sat in silence.

"Himiko-sama, I hadn't dared ask before because you hadn't offered it, but things are getting desperate. Is there not some way you could help me to get in to see your father?"

She didn't look at him. "Oh, if I could have done so for you, Toshiro-san, I would have days ago. But, just as he has cut me off from going into the city, Tsuyu has also kept me from my father. That's how I discovered I was being watched. It was on my last visit to him I could stand it no more and spoke violently against the dog invading our home. The very next day Tsuyu's men stopped me from entering my father's rooms. When I confronted Tsuyu about it he was only too delighted to tell me my father had agreed not to see me until after our marriage."

Though she stated all this in a neutral tone, he couldn't help but wonder at the depths of pain she must be hiding inside.

"Kirin-san, is there any hope you can get me in to see Lord

Asano?" He already knew the answer, but felt obliged to ask.

"Before, when Tsuyu had been ignorant of your mission, there'd been a small chance, but now..."

He nodded, accepting the inevitable.

"Toshiro-san, since it's hopeless, I beg you to consider leaving before it is too late. Tsuyu does not control everything, no matter how much he'd like to think so. He has to watch what he does or all will discover his evil. We can make sure you leave here alive." Himiko's face was calm, her tone level; but her eyes pleaded with him to say yes.

He looked away, more tempted by the offer than he wanted her to know. He was saved from giving an answer by a soft rap at the door. Kirin stood to answer it, using his body to block the view into the room. He spoke to whoever was there for a moment and then closed the door.

"Lady, your retinue has become most concerned over your absence. Word has come they are preparing to inform Lord Tsuyu of it."

"I'm sorry, Toshiro-san," Himiko said quietly, "but it seems I've run out of time. If you would return to your room in an hour, I shall meet with you there for our daily walk."

"I will be there, Himiko-sama." He bowed where he sat as she graced him with a smile. She rose to her feet and in one fluid motion dropped out of her outer kimono. Kirin returned from a small hidden closet in the room and held out a servant's kimono for her. After putting it on, she swept up her long hair and slipped it under an unimpressive wig. She then wiped away what little make-up she wore to look as bland as possible, working especially hard to remove the aristocratic dots that looked like a second set of eyebrows on her forehead.

Toshi watched in rapt amazement. With a grin, Himiko turned toward him so he could fully view her transformation. Though she was still herself, if he hadn't known her so well he would have thought her a servant, especially when she cast down her eyes and acted demure. He realized Miko had been right all along—people did see what they expected.

Kirin folded Himiko's outer kimono and handed it to her waiting arms. "Thank you, Kirin-san. Until we meet again, Toshiro-san." She bowed very low in their direction and then left the room.

"Does she do that often?" Toshi asked.

Kirin gave him a knowing grin. "Only when necessary. Though it has been a game of hers for a number of years."

Chapter 38

With Yuko's and Kirin's help, Toshi got dressed but left his bandaged shoulder exposed. The old lady from the night before showed up to check on him and then allowed them to help him stand. Kirin assigned one of the four men in the room to guard him and Yuko when they were ready to return to his room.

Though he'd been told the room and hallway were put back in order, he was still amazed to find no sign of the struggle. If his shoulder hadn't been there to constantly remind him, he would have doubted the reality of the battle he'd survived.

With a small sigh, he sat down by the open doors to the garden. He stared out at the green lushness, feeling a little tired. He cradled his arm, trying to ease the growing discomfort in his shoulder. He also pulled the rewrapped kettle beside him where he could keep it in sight.

There was no hope—he knew that now. If he stayed, he wouldn't receive an audience with Lord Asano and would most likely die waiting. Yet, if he left, it would be unlikely Tsuyu would just let him walk away. Lord Asaka might protect him if he asked, but he would never be able to bring himself to do it. Just facing his lord to tell him he'd failed would require more courage than he had. It would be better to die trying than live his life with the shame of failure. Though his own fate seemed certain, still, he wished he could find some way to help Himiko out of hers.

"Toshiro-san."

He looked up and found the object of his thoughts gaily waving to him. Making sure to grab the kettle, he stood, a sad smile on his lips. If only there were a way out for both of them.

He walked out onto the porch only to find himself the center of attention.

"Toshiro-san, your shoulder! Have you been injured?" Himiko's voice was aghast.

He stared wide-eyed into her shocked face. Her retinue stood around her, whispering as they stared at him. With a start, he suddenly realized what she was doing. The only problem was how was he going to explain it. Trying to buy himself a few seconds, he stared at the ground as he joined her.

"Actually, Himiko-sama, this is nothing but proof of my own foolishness," he said. "I heard strange sounds in my room last night and had laid out my blade so I might be ready if anything untoward happened." He turned away from them, knowing the embarrassment that would soon be his at the lie. "I fell asleep while waiting and accidentally rolled over onto the exposed blade."

Ill-concealed laughter bubbled up behind him. He smiled as he heard Himiko's unforced laugh join the others.

"Oh, please forgive me, Toshiro-san! It is so rude of us to laugh, but it was such an unexpected reason," she explained. "We've never heard of a samurai attacking himself before."

A fresh wave of giggles erupted. He let his shoulders slump, trying to appear ashamed and embarrassed. As it was, he didn't have to pretend much. His cheeks colored, though he knew quite well nothing he'd said was true.

"We're so sorry, Toshiro-san. Come, let us take our walk before our rudeness scares you away." Himiko appeared at his side and hooked her arm in his. She turned him toward the path, always keeping his back to her servants. Soon, they'd left their giggles behind.

"That was masterful," she exclaimed in a low voice. "Not only did you come up with a plausible explanation, but now, due to your horrible embarrassment, they will let us be for a while."

He turned his face away, knowing his "masterful stroke" had only been sheer luck and desperation.

"Have you thought about my offer though, Toshiro-san?" she asked him. "I know there would be danger outside the castle as well as in it, but your chances for survival would be better out there. I can make sure you're supplied with everything you'd need."

He sighed. "I appreciate what you're offering me, but I can't accept it. I can't face my lord with the fact I've failed." He tried to look at her to see if she understood, but Himiko had turned her face away.

"There must be something I can do to help you," she insisted. "I don't wish to see you sent to your next life before your time."

He stared at his feet, troubled by the blooming joy he felt at her obvious concern for him. "You shouldn't give up on me so easily. I'm sure between the two of us we can come up with something."

His words were filled with a confidence he didn't feel, but he hoped she would believe them.

"Himiko-sama, does your father ever leave his rooms? Is there a place where I might intercept him? Or some place where I might gain his notice in some way?"

Himiko walked in silence for so long he thought she might never answer.

"Tsuyu has his men constantly guarding my father and watching his guards. All the servants who serve Tsuyu and my father are known to the guards in that section of the castle as well," she finally answered. "Every room is checked before he is allowed to enter. It might not be possible to see him without an approved appointment."

"I see." He looked away, realizing this wouldn't be easy, if even possible. Still, it did seem like something he might try. He just couldn't bring himself to tell her. He had already involved her too much in his troubles when she had so many of her own. "Maybe we might still come up with something later."

Himiko didn't look at him. "I will do all I can to think of a way."

They followed their usual routine for the next few hours. Toshi discovered he tired easily and decided it might be an excuse he could use to leave Himiko for a time and try out his own plan.

"Himiko-sama, would it offend you greatly if I returned to my own room for a while? I must admit, I am not feeling quite myself today."

She looked at him, a hint of alarm in her eyes. "I'm sorry. I had not meant to impose on you so much. Yes, please, go rest. I'll check on you later this afternoon."

"I'd like that, Himiko-sama." He felt a little guilty at the subterfuge.

Once he returned to his room, he found Yuko. He rested for a short while and then decided to move on with his idea. He tried not to think about how little chance it might actually have of working.

"Yuko-san, would you take me to Asano-sama's audience chamber—or, at least, tell me how to get there?"

She stared at him, a look of confusion on her face. "They will not let us through. You do not have an appointment."

"Can we at least go by there?" he asked.

Yuko nodded, her confusion still obvious. "If that is what you wish, sir."

He followed her out of the room, bringing the wrapped kettle. They left the guests' area to go to a broad main hall. After a long walk, the hall intercepted another even wider. The walls he could see beyond it were heavily embroidered and covered with gold flakes. In the middle was a large set of thick wooden sliding doors. Every three feet, a guard stood, gazing outwards. They wore the Asano crest—except for every fourth man, who wore Tsuyu's. Asano's men stood rigid, staring about them, one eye on the hallway and another on Tsuyu's men. Tsuyu's men were doing the same with Asano's. The tension about them was almost palpable. He wondered how they could stand it day after day.

As he watched, a woman walked by carrying a tray. She shuffled rapidly to the wooden doors and was stopped by the guards. Asano's men as well as Tsuyu's carefully scrutinized the woman and even checked the covered dishes on her tray. His heart sank. Though he'd not yet thought too deeply on this score, one of the ideas in the back of his mind had been to try and pass himself off as one of the servants. Himiko seemed to be quite adept at the skill; and, with Yuko's help, he'd thought he'd have a chance to get away with it. But not only did it look like he couldn't approach the room without being challenged—it looked like it would do no good to try using a disguise as well.

Slightly disheartened, he hurried on with Yuko, already noticing he'd inadvertently attracted the attention of a couple of the guards for lingering too long at the intersection.

"Can you take me by the lord's living quarters now?" He asked this once they were well away from the audience chamber.

"As you wish."

Asano's private chambers were located on the second floor of the east side of the castle.

"Yuko-san, are these the stairs Asano-sama would use to go to his rooms?" he asked hopefully. There'd be little the guards could say if he hung around a common stairwell then, as Asano came by, somehow attempted to get his attention.

"No, Kazete-sama, they are not," Yuko informed him with a slight shake of the head. "Beyond the audience chamber Asano-sama has his own private set of stairs that lead to a small hallway that will take him to his rooms. The way is heavily guarded and no one but those authorized may go through there."

He nodded. Yet another possibility proved worthless. Still, he wasn't done. "And his rooms are in this direction?"

"Yes."

"I'll go on alone from here, then," he said. "Thank you for your help."

Yuko hesitated. "Are you sure you should be doing this? It is not my place to point out such things, but this may not be a wise course."

"Thank you for telling me. I promise I'll be careful." He had to try, whether it was a wise thing or not.

He left Yuko behind, staring uncertainly after him.

Toshi walked quietly in the direction of Asano's rooms, not entirely sure what he planned. Himiko had told him each room was searched before Asano was allowed inside. Still, if he could find one Asano was sure to try to enter and he could remain undiscovered until Asano came, surely, he could make enough of a fuss that Asano would overhear. And then, if he said enough of the right things, the lord might grant him an audience right then and there.

Even as he thought of it, the plan seemed risky, at best; but, at the moment, it was all he had.

He knew he was getting close to his goal when the quality of the walls improved, the amount of decorations multiplied in their intricacy and incense scented the air. He slowed down, looking about for any prospective places to hide, hoping he could find what he needed before anyone caught him walking about.

A strange birdcall suddenly whispered from the floor. He thought it almost sounded like a nightingale. Confused, he looked down and realized it came from his own feet where he stepped on the boards. He stopped in shock. He'd heard of this, though at the time he hadn't put much stock in it. These were nightingale floorboards, created with a strange ingenious contraption that made a sound resembling a nightingale when they were stepped on. It was supposed to deter ninja trying to sneak in to assassinate lords in the night.

If a ninja couldn't cross this strange flooring quietly, what chance had he? He wouldn't be able to sneak anywhere in this area. As if to prove his conclusion right, a guard rushed into the hallway from around the corner.

"Stand right there, do not move!"

He did as he was told, relieved only a little that the guard wore Asano's symbol rather than Tsuyu's. Still, all his plans had one by one crumbled to nothing. What was he supposed to do now? Toshi tried not to think about it, this problem being more pressing at the moment.

"What are you doing here?" the guard asked, his hand on the hilt of his sword.

"I'm—I'm sorry. I think I am lost. I was trying to find the appointment office."

The man studied him up and down, weighing his response. "It's not here. Go back the way you came and go to the next floor. Someone there will show you the way. You should not be wondering the halls alone."

He bowed deeply. "My sincerest apologies. I will do as you say." He turned to go.

"Wait!"

Toshi glanced over his shoulder, as a new man turned into the corridor. This one wore Tsuyu's symbol at his shoulder.

"Who is this boy?" the new guard demanded.

The other gave him an irritated look. "I've taken care of this. It's none of your concern."

"Anything that affects Asano-sama affects Tsuyu-sama, so this is my concern."

The two men glared at each other with mutual dislike. It was becoming ever more obvious to Toshi that Tsuyu had a lot less control than he made it seem. Though he was good at manipulating what power he had obtained, all obviously did not go easy for him.

"I'm sorry, sirs. Again, this was all my fault. I did not realize I was not where I meant to be."

"What is your name?" Tsuyu's guard demanded.

The question made him pause. He considered lying but then discarded the idea. How many wounded people were there about the castle? If he lied, it would be found out; and the deceit might give Tsuyu an excuse to hold him for deeper questioning and put him somewhere where he could be dispatched quietly before anyone was the wiser.

"My name is Kazete Toshiro. I am a guest of Asano-sama's."

He saw Tsuyu's guard's eyes narrow, as if the man were irked he hadn't bothered to lie. It seemed Tsuyu had briefed his men about him.

"Do you see now? I'd taken care of this like I said." Asano's man said.

"He still looks suspicious to me." Tsuyu's man eyed Toshi, as if looking for anything he could use to back up his claim. "Perhaps we should detain him."

Toshi felt a bead of perspiration roll down his neck. He forced himself to keep his mouth shut.

"A boy with a wound? What about that do you find threatening, Ishi? The others will laugh you right out of here if you try it." The guard's barking laugh echoed down the hallway.

Tsuyu's man's face reddened, and he sent a look of death in Toshi's direction.

"I will gladly cooperate in anything you wish me to do." He bowed as he spoke, though falling into Tsuyu's hands was the last thing he wanted.

"That won't be necessary," Asano's man said. "Please, be on your way—and be more careful next time."

"I will. Thank you very much." He bowed to them again. Without looking back, he went the way he'd come.

"Kazete-sama!"

He was a little surprised to find Yuko at the head of the stairs once he'd made his way back. It looked like she'd been waiting for him. "You didn't have to wait for me, Yuko-san."

The young woman actually blushed. "I—I was concerned. I'm glad to see you are all right." Her eyes met his for a moment. "May I guide you back to your room?"

He nodded, knowing there was nothing more he could accomplish here. "Yes, please."

Once back in his room, he sat outside, considering his options. All his plans had come to nothing. Himiko was right—there seemed no way to get to her father. Before, he'd been stumped by the layers of bureaucracy Tsuyu had helped establish between Asano and everyone else in order to have control as to who did or did not have access to the lord. This had been compounded by Toshi's need to keep his business a secret. Now that Tsuyu knew who he was, the official ways would be blocked for him permanently. What few alternatives he'd come up with on his own had now proved to be blocked as well. His only hope was that Himiko had somehow seen a possibility he hadn't; otherwise, he'd have no chance to ever complete his mission.

He rubbed his shoulder as he tried not to get depressed. Yet, when Himiko arrived a while later the unreadable expression on her face told him she'd not had much success on his behalf either.

"Toshiro-san, were you able to rest?" she asked him lightly.

He bowed and then go up. "Yes, I am feeling much better."

"Shall we go, then?" She waited for him to join her.

They walked a short way without either of them saying anything. Though he knew the answer already, he decided he had to ask.

"Himiko-sama, were you able to come up with anything?"

She didn't look at him as she answered. "I'm afraid not. I've done nothing but ponder on this since you left and…"

Despair colored her words. He decided he wanted to make it go away. "Is there anything that motivates your father anymore? Does he at any time vary from his routine?"

Himiko slowly shook her head. "The only thing, the only weakness, I've ever seen in him is his love of a good mystery. How that could help you, I just—" She stopped walking and turned to look at him. A touch of excitement filled her voice. "There might be a way. I don't know if it will work, and it will make you very vulnerable;

but it might have a chance."

"I'm willing to take the risk. What's your idea?" He felt his own excitement rising. Could there still be some hope?

She nodded and resumed walking. It was several minutes before she answered him.

"In the early morning and late evening, my father takes the same route from his rooms to his audience chamber and back again," she said. "Part of the route goes through a hallway that has five or six small windows on the second floor, which look out upon a raised stage we use for special ceremonies.

"If my father saw you sitting there for a few days, it might just intrigue him enough to start asking questions. If he does, I can make sure he's informed you've been waiting to meet with him. He might just start wondering what could be so important you'd go to such lengths just to get him to notice you. And, if you're so desperate, why it is that an audience was never granted you in the first place."

"You think it could work?" It seemed like such a slim hope.

Her walnut-brown eyes wouldn't meet his. "I truly don't know. I haven't recognized the man who sits as my father for a long time. I'm not really sure how he'll react. I don't know if Tsuyu's hold is so strong he'll ignore everything," she admitted. "I just don't know."

He didn't press her further but walked on in silence. He jostled his mind for any other alternatives, in case inspiration struck him, and found none. Though her plan might prove ineffective, it was the only option he had.

"Himiko-sama, would you show me the courtyard?"

"You're going to do it, then?" Her face was serious. "Are you sure you realize the danger of this course? You'll be highly vulnerable in the courtyard if you stay there both day and night, as you must. If my father asks, he will be told of your constant vigil and only if you've never left will he be intrigued by your commitment, and wonder at it as well. We will have witnesses who'll be able testify to the fact. For, only something truly unusual will catch his eye.

"Tsuyu will try to get rid of you once he realizes what you're doing. Yet the game he has been playing is dangerous, and he has much to lose if he is ever exposed. He has power only at my father's sufferance, so if anything tipped my father's favor against him…

"But Tsuyu is also very impetuous and will surely try something by indirect means, where no blame will stick on him."

Toshi shook his head, not ready to be discouraged. He was amazed, however, at the politics going on all around. Peasants weren't made for such games.

"I have nothing to lose by trying, Himiko-sama. My life is forfeit whether I do this or not. I'd rather have some hope than none." He felt his throat dry up, knowing only too well what he was committing himself to. Though death was never longed for, he oddly discovered he had no regrets. Asaka had allowed him to choose his road, and he would remain on it until the end.

Glancing at Himiko, he realized she, too, had made a choice and wouldn't shy away from it. It brought him a slight sense of satisfaction that if things went wrong at least he wouldn't be around to hear of her death on her wedding day.

Chapter 39

In the course of their wanderings, Himiko led Toshi to the courtyard she'd talked about that afternoon. Feeling tired but resolved, he studied the area where he would play his hand.

The castle walls rose grandly about fifty yards from him. Six long, narrow windows were cut into the wall directly facing the small stage. The back of the courtyard was surrounded by a curtain of trees cutting it from view of the castle's main thoroughfares. The area was quiet and serene.

"Those windows are part of the hallway my father will be walking through. If he looks out, he can't help but see you. Unfortunately, if my father notices you, so will Tsuyu," Himiko pointed out. "Out of what he thinly disguises as respect, Tsuyu escorts my father back and forth each day. That he'll do something once he sees you is without question."

She grabbed his arm. Her hands were cold. "I'll try to do what I can to protect you," she said, with some emotion. "I will speak to Kirin-san, and he will get a message to our guards. They will make sure Tsuyu doesn't have his men block the windows. I'll also have him post guards here so they can protect you and act as your witnesses. I will do my utmost to give you as much of a chance to gain my father's attention as I can." She glanced away. "I want you to live a long and happy life for the both of us."

He found her face unreadable, but her eyes were sparkling. He looked away, feeling strange inside.

"Come, Toshiro-san, it is yet too early for you to begin your vigil. We don't want the dogs to pick up your scent before we've even begun."

Though he was tired and his shoulder was becoming more

insistent in its aches, he went along with her as she showed him a number of other courtyards. Himiko's retinue followed, never far behind.

"Toshiro-san, I will speak with Kirin-san about the guards as soon as we part today. I'll have him send them over as soon as I can. After I leave you, explain to Yuko what you're going to do. Then, make your way to the courtyard. You must be there before my father's had a chance to return to his rooms."

"Thank you, Himiko-sama."

Their eyes met for a moment; and, to his amazement, she blushed before looking away. "You look tired again. I've been inconsiderate of your injury. We could sit here together and rest for a while. I could even have some of the maids get us some tea."

He nodded eagerly at the idea. He knew the time for her to leave would be coming upon them soon. Any delay seemed worthwhile.

Himiko's retinue gathered around as they settled under a tree close to a running brook. No longer free to discuss their troubles, the two of them passed the time discussing trivialities, acting for the moment as if their lives were free of complications.

Time passed much too swiftly; and, before he knew it, Toshi had emptily promised to join Himiko later for dinner as she dropped him off at his room. As soon as she and her retinue were gone, he found Yuko and quickly explained what he was about to do. After he was through, he went back out into the garden and made his way to the courtyard that could very well determine his ultimate fate.

* * * * *

He found the courtyard empty. A bolt of nervousness cut through him as he realized this was the point of no return. Trying not to let his worry overpower him, he crossed the courtyard and climbed onto the stage. He sat down, making sure he faced the six small windows on which so much depended. With a nervous hand, he set the kettle before him and unwrapped it. He turned it until its sun-emblazoned side was toward the windows as well.

He tried to look at what lay beyond the high windows but could see nothing. He realized with a sense of irony he would never be aware if anyone saw him or not.

As the sun descended gradually to the horizon, two men, both bearing Asano's crest, appeared. Without a sound, they lit ten lanterns and hung them around the open space. When they were finished, they went to stand guard at the only path leading into the courtyard.

Sadly, Toshi watched what little he could see of the sunset before it was cut off by the castle's tall outer walls. He realized in chagrin he had missed dinner. He hoped Yuko would pity him in the morning and bring him something to eat.

The sound of far-off crickets eventually filled the night. His shoulder itched, but he tried to ignore it. Though he attempted to sleep sitting up, the best he could manage was to doze for a few moments a time or two. Time seemed to crawl. When morning arrived, he felt even more tired than he had the day before.

As he waited for dawn, he heard the tinkle of bells. Glancing rapidly about him, he saw the two guards were still in place. He then scanned the lines of trees behind him. The sun rose, and he spotted something shiny hanging from a branch. The more he stared at it, the surer he became it had to be a small silver bell. Miko had been there! She had seen him! How had she entered the castle grounds? He wished desperately the lights had somehow burned out during the night. He needed to talk to her, to hear her welcome voice. He wanted to tell her and Asaka all that had happened so far. He wanted their advice on what he should do next.

Toshi rubbed his shoulder, excited the others had somehow made it there. He got to his feet and stretched his tired muscles. Taking great care, he worked through a few of his exercises, trying not to push his shoulder too hard but wanting to get his blood pumping. His shoulder complained about what he was doing; but, despite that, he felt better. After he was through, he took one long look around him and then sat to stare again at the windows holding all of his hopes.

He was startled by harsh whispers coming from the entrance into the courtyard. He glanced in that direction and noticed the guards who had been with him last night had been replaced by two others. There were also two more, but these wore the triangle crest belonging to Tsuyu. He frowned as he noticed the four arguing with Yuko, who was standing in the middle. The remains of what may have been breakfast lay where it had fallen on the cobbled path.

As soon as Yuko saw him staring in their direction, she started toward him. One of Tsuyu's men grabbed her roughly by the arm. Asano's men tensed and reached for their swords. Tsuyu's men followed suit.

"*Stop!*"

All five of them turned to stare in his direction.

"Yuko-san, it's all right," he said. "It's not worth it."

The young woman ceased trying to pull away from the guard. Toshi smiled, trying to reassure her, then forced his gaze back to the windows. At least Tsuyu hadn't gained an excuse for direct interference—not yet. He told himself this over and over as his stomach grumbled about the missed meal.

The day wore on very slowly, even more so than had the night before. The sky darkened threateningly in late morning, thankfully reducing the heat of the day. Having nothing better to do, he dozed. Now and again he was awakened by harsh voices. He stopped paying attention to them, even though the number of Tsuyu's men had risen to six. He couldn't help but smile when he realized they had purposely stationed themselves where they couldn't be seen from the windows. Himiko had been right—Tsuyu's hold wasn't as strong or encompassing as he would like them to believe.

Himiko arrived with her retinue sometime in the early afternoon. She sneaked into the courtyard by cutting through the curtain of trees. Tsuyu's men spotted her as she walked toward the stage and rushed to block her path. Toshi's blood raced through his veins as he saw the iron expression on her face. Would she win through? His empty stomach hoped so as he spotted Yuko walking behind her with a laden tray.

From where he sat, he couldn't hear Himiko's words as she spoke to the guards. By the tension he saw in their backs, he was sure they were tipped with steel. One of the men removed a parchment from his sleeve and showed it to her, keeping it well out of reach. Her maids called to her as they started back the way they'd come. He saw Himiko smile coldly and then turn away. In an instant, she'd spun back around with Yuko's tray in her hands. Before the guards could stop her, she'd thrown its contents on them.

Without comment, she turned her back to them and left. The two guards bearing Asano's crest rushed forward to protect her. Her retinue scurried after her with shock-filled faces.

Toshi returned his attention to the windows as the soiled guards turned to stare at him in anger. He tried hard not to think about the naked blades that might then be heading for his back. After a few minutes, he finally dared to look and saw the men had gone back to their posts. A grin plucked at the edge of his mouth as it occurred to him that Himiko's actions held a certain amount of justice. The food, after all, hadn't gone totally to waste.

The sky darkened even more, the air reaching a dead calm, the scent of threatening rain tainting the day. The lamps set about the courtyard were lit early. Glancing about him, Toshi counted ten of Tsuyu's men, but still only two of Asano's. He shifted uneasily, wondering how long Tsuyu would play the game. He hoped Asano wouldn't wait too long much longer.

A misting rain settled on him as the sun disappeared from view. He shivered, though the drizzle wasn't cold. He could tell this might well be a very long night. He sighed, knowing there was no alternative.

The wind began to blow, and the rain intensified. He looked about as he became soaked, trying to see how the guards were coping. He wondered if they, like he would have not long ago, had given up this madness and decided to escape to the warmth indoors. He spotted both of Asano's men trying to take shelter beneath a large tree next to the entrance. Without much surprise, however, he found no sign of any of Tsuyu's men. He wondered if they would get caught and punished. He hoped so.

The paper lanterns went out one by one as they were overwhelmed by the rain. Darkness swallowed him whole. He groped at the area before him until he grabbed the kettle. He placed it on his lap.

If there were a time to try to strike him down, this would be it. He tensed as he tried uselessly to peer into the darkness, the wind driving the rain into his eyes. He drew the wakizashi at his waist.

As the minutes crawled by, nothing changed. Even so, he couldn't get rid of the feeling enemies were waiting for him out there, and they would eventually come for him that night.

The sky violently lit up for a moment, which was followed seconds later by a booming clap. Toshi turned, startled, though not by the thunder. He could have sworn he'd just heard a strangled scream mixed in with the sounds from the sky.

A second crack of lightning flashed above, showing him a crumpled form on the paving stones, while another fought several dark opponents for its life. He leapt to his feet as the thunder boomed, ignoring the added weight of his soaked clothes, intending to go to the man's aid.

"Toshi-kun, wait!"

"Miko-san?" He spun around, trying to pinpoint the source of the familiar voice. "Miko-san, where are you?"

"Toshi-kun, you must sit and remain very still," she cautioned. "There are a large number of ninja in the castle grounds, and for some reason they seem to have a strong dislike for you."

He realized he was grinning foolishly even as he did as he'd been bid.

"You have nothing to worry about," Miko added. "We are with you now."

Three lightning bolts lit the sky in succession as armored skeletons surrounded the stage from every side. His grin grew wider.

He felt a warm hand on his bandaged shoulder. Turning his head, he found Miko's blue-lit eyes staring at him.

"You're hurt," she said.

Euphoria gurgled through him. "It's nothing. An old woman took care of it for me. Lord Asaka need never worry about the traitor ninja again."

The sounds of steel on steel echoed through the rain-stained night.

"So, he was here." Her voice was close. "We'd suspected as much over a day ago but weren't sure and couldn't get in to warn you—that is, until the other ninja came. It was from them we learned how to get past the walls and into the castle grounds without being seen. They can be so crafty."

The silly grin just wouldn't leave his lips. It was insane—he was sitting on a stage, soaked to the bone, surrounded by a pack of assassins, but he was still terribly happy. He might die at any second, but his companions were with him once again.

Lightning tore through the sky, with thunder following immediately after. The courtyard was filled with black-shrouded shapes darting back and forth in dizzying patterns as they tried to break through the armored forms before them. The undead men parried their attacks. Flying pieces of star-shaped metal struck at them from afar. The guards ignored them, having no flesh for the shuriken to harm.

Another flash of lightning showed him that Miko was sitting very close to him, her arm and long sleeve raised behind his back to block him from view. With wide eyes, he noticed the glinting points of a number of the shuriken stuck in its other side.

He saw two ninja bring out long pieces of paper, which they slapped to the sides of one of the fighters. Steam rose in the air as the skeleton fell to his knees. The two assassins rushed past him before the gap could be closed. Toshi realized the ninja had brought sacred wards to use against them. The tide might be turned.

Asaka's men struggled harder to cut the other ninja down as the latter strove to place wards on them as well. Blinded again by impenetrable darkness, Toshi tensed as he heard something fall not far ahead of him. Miko touched his arm reassuringly.

A rapid volley of lightning showed him Mitsuo's bowed form to his right. He stared breathlessly as the stooped form swooped like a hawk to cut down one of the two ninja that had leapt onto the stage. To his left, another sword slashed just as fast. That one belonged to Asaka.

The rain fell in ever-greater sheets. The lightning accentuated pieces of time. Water ran in rivers off him, but Toshi no longer noticed. With a calm he'd never known he possessed, he watched the deadly battle rage around him.

A grunt rang out somewhere behind him; and, all at once, Miko screamed. He twisted around and spotted one of the wards stuck on her shoulder as a man in black loomed over them both. Not pausing to think, Toshi struck upwards, his wakizashi sinking it into the man's flesh. Hot blood splattered on his face before he yanked the sword out and propelled the wounded ninja backwards off the stage.

"Miko-san!" A grimace on his face and panic in his heart, he tore away the ward from the geisha's shoulder, her pained scream still ringing in his ears. "Are you all right?"

A raging anger was building inside him. How much more were they going to be asked to pay?

"Thank you, Toshi-kun." Miko leaned heavily against him. "I am fine. I only need a moment."

He held onto her and, looking up, saw a pair of green lights stare at them for a moment and then look away.

More ninjas broke through the line.

Miko pulled him closer to the center of the stage. He kept his wakizashi ready to defend them in one hand and the kettle in an iron grip with his other. Asaka and Mitsuo dominated the stage and brought down anyone coming too close. Toshi guarded their rear, though he could see very little.

"Toshi, to the right!"

He didn't hesitate, just swung out where the geisha had directed, his blade slicing through flesh. A flash of lightning showed a ninja stepping back, blood flowing thickly down his leg. Mitsuo pivoted from the man falling before him and backslashed the bleeding ninja, cutting his breast in two. The man dropped without a sound onto the ground.

The rain continued, the lightning, thunder and wind waxing and waning in the raging storm. Though he had half-expected it, no alarm ever rang through the castle to announce the battle going on within it. By the end of the night, the courtyard was littered with black-clothed bodies, though occasionally one or two of them would disappear.

As the rain trickled to a stop, dead silence fell. The air felt cold, and shivers wracked Toshi's body. His shoulder throbbed, not appreciating his efforts in the night. Though the attacks looked to be over, no one moved or attempted to relax. Still blind, and more so as the storm receded, he tried to remain as alert as his companions.

It was some time before he realized dawn was creeping up on him. Vague shapes grew in his vision, and not much later something warm touched his face. Still feeling the warm sensation on his cheek, he looked up and to the side to find the sun just rising over the top of the walls. With rapt attention, he watched it. As it came fully into view, he allowed himself to accept the fact he was still alive.

Realizing he'd won the night, he looked around for the others. His lord and all his people were gone. He'd never heard them leave. He comforted himself that they were still somewhere on the grounds, then heavily berated himself for not having taken the time to talk to Asaka. It was essential he talk to his lord, that he explain what it was he was doing on this stage. Asaka had to be told how things had degenerated since his last visit.

All but two of the ninja bodies were gone. The two that remained were on the stage with him. No sign of those killed elsewhere in the courtyard remained. His eyes turned toward the windows. Would these two bodies be enough to gain Asano's attention? Would the mystery prove strong enough now?

His grip on the kettle tightened, turning his knuckles white. If this sight didn't succeed, nothing would. What he'd do then he had no idea.

A shrill scream snapped his attention to the courtyard's entrance. Yuko stood there with two samurai, staring at Asano's murdered guards. What would have been his breakfast lay splattered on the ground. Toshi groaned.

A shiver ran down his spine as the three looked up in his direction. His brow furrowed in confusion as he saw Yuko raise her hands to cover her mouth in fear. The guards' faces were unreadable but looked strained. One of them spoke some quick words to her, but Toshi couldn't understand what was being said. Yuko made no response, so the man spun her around and pushed her roughly from the courtyard. Toshi heard the echo of her wooden shoes as she ran toward the castle proper.

Their hands coiled about the hilt of their swords, the two guards trotted toward the stage. Their eyes constantly roamed about the courtyard, avoiding him as they looked for any signs of danger. Neither looked directly at him as they reached the stage and bowed. He returned the bow as best he could and watched as they positioned themselves on either side of the stage. One went so far as to draw his blade and stab at both of the bodies lying on it to make sure the ninja were really dead.

Toshi's vision swam momentarily as the sound of many running feet intruded into the courtyard. Both guards tensed, their hands still on their weapons. He grimaced as he noticed the new arrivals all wore Tsuyu's crest. Both of Asano's men shifted to stand between them and the stage.

A rather stocky man stepped out from the others. "That man is to come with us. Move out of the way," he ordered.

"Kazete-san is to go nowhere," Asano's man barked back. "Murder has been committed here, a guest has been attacked and our security has been breached. Nothing shall be moved until our superiors have had a chance to examine what has befallen here!"

Asano's men put their hands on the hilts of their swords.

"We have our orders. We will take this man," the captain insisted. Tsuyu's group took a step forward.

"Is this what we've come to? That guests of our lord need fear aggression from his men as well as ninja?"

All eyes turned to look back toward the courtyard's entrance. Toshi strained and glimpsed Himiko. Tsuyu's men reluctantly parted as she stepped forward. With some surprise, he noticed Kirin was with her, as well as a large number of armored men.

He tried to hide a smile as Himiko glanced toward him. He sobered, however, as her eyes grew wide. She pried her gaze away from him and then turned to deal with Tsuyu's men. What had she and Yuko seen that he hadn't? He shivered.

"Where is your honor? How dare you demand *anything*?" Her voice was cold. "Until his death, this is my father's house, and this man is my father's guest! And so shall he be treated." She pointed toward Toshi with her closed fan. "Instead of trying to order him around, you should be spending your time assuring our lord is safe from the scum that have obviously penetrated the castle!" Her small form shook with rage as she confronted the leader of Tsuyu's men. "Ninja have invaded our household!" She slapped his breastplate with her fan. "Assassins!" She did it again. "Yet you dare stand around and threaten someone who has valiantly already done some of your work for you?"

Several of the men near the front took a step back at Himiko's vehemence. Most of them were staring at the ground. "Lady Himiko, I'm sorry, but we have orders to take this man."

She crisply turned her back on him and joined the two guards at the stage. "If you decide to do so, you'll have to go through me to take him." Though her back was to him, Toshi still heard the sound of a small blade being removed from its sheath.

"Himiko-sama!" His protest went unheeded. He knew she wouldn't back down even if they attacked.

"Make your decision, Captain," she said. Her voice was laced with ice.

"Captain, if you make a move toward her, you will force us to attack you." Kirin's voice was as cold as Himiko's.

With bated breath, Toshi waited for the captain's decision. His own hand had already taken hold of the hilt of his wakizashi. He was therefore shocked when Himiko turned her back on the captain and the danger he represented to smile up at him. "Kazete-san, would you like to accompany me inside for some tea?" she asked pleasantly. Her face showed no trace of the tension brewing behind her.

If Asano had felt nothing upon looking in the courtyard that morning, it would never happen. It would serve no purpose for him to remain there any longer. "I would be honored, Asano-san."

Ignoring his exhaustion, he forced his legs to move so he might rise. He could feel Himiko's eyes glued to his every movement. He tried to ignore the way his damp clothes stuck to him. His gaze wavered as he stood, a long shudder coursing through his body. Perspiration beaded on his forehead. He tried hard not to sway.

All eyes were on him, but he didn't notice. His gaze wouldn't focus anymore. He tried to take a step forward and instead found himself falling. His mind had gone dark before he hit the stage floor.

Chapter 40

Something cool settled on his forehead. Toshi groaned softly as his eyes fluttered open. He stared at Himiko's face as it hovered over him. "Himiko-sama?"

Her face left his field of vision. "He's awake!" When he saw her again, a smile was playing on her lips. "How do you feel, Toshiro-san?"

Before he could answer, he was being propped up and a cup of broth held before his lips.

"Drink it down, boy." The old healer's face crowded out Himiko's as she tried to get him to drink.

A little dazed and confused, he didn't question her orders but did as he'd been bid. His stomach rumbled as the bitter broth filled his insides.

Weakly, he pushed the cup away as the healer tried to get him to drink a third cup. Moving his gaze to the left, he looked again into Himiko's face.

"Where?"

To his astonishment, he saw her blush at the question while turning her eyes away.

"You're in my chambers, Toshiro-san," she said. "Kirin-san and I felt it would be the safest, most protectable area in which to keep you. We've been able to use the ninja incident to expel all of my maids and place loyal guards around us. I'm sure Tsuyu is livid; but, because of the concrete proof of the threat, there's not much he can say."

At the mention of Tsuyu's name, he felt his heart grow cold.

"The kettle. Where is it? Did they take it?"

"No, Toshiro-san, it's right here."

He looked at where Himiko pointed on his right and found the kettle beside him.

"They would have had to take you to get the kettle. Even while unconscious, you wouldn't let go of it." A teasing smile lit up on her lips.

He didn't resist as the healer prompted him to lie back down. "What's wrong with me?"

"You have a fever and are very weak," the old woman said crisply. "Sitting under nightlong storms is not what I usually recommend for young patients with injuries. Fasting is not one of my favorites, either."

He almost laughed out loud as the old woman gave him a look threatening mayhem if he dared to try it again.

"Toshiro-san, if I might be so bold, what happened to you in the courtyard last night?" Himiko asked.

He closed his eyes, trying to gather his unruly thoughts. He wasn't sure just how much to tell her. "Tsuyu's men left the courtyard soon after the storm started. The rain eventually put out the lanterns and left us in darkness. As lightning lit the sky, ninja attacked your father's men.

"I should have died last night," he admitted. "Tsuyu was taking no chances. He sent a score of ninja after me." He hesitated, noticing the frown developing on Himiko's face. "My lord and his people came to my rescue then. They defended me throughout the night. They're the only reason I'm still alive."

Himiko stared at her hands. As he said nothing more, she looked up, not able to contain her curiosity.

"How was that possible?" she asked. In her eyes, he could see how she struggled to believe him.

"They followed the ninja into the castle grounds. I didn't think they could, but they did it. They kept me alive."

"Where are they now?" she asked softly.

"In the trees, in the garden." He stared raptly at her, feeling her doubt. "Himiko-sama, this is not a fever-dream. They were—are—here. But they can't be found during the day, only at night; and then only if they allow it."

He saw her uncertainty intensify. "Why don't you sleep for now,

Toshiro-san. It'll help you regain your strength."

It hurt him a little that she didn't believe, but only a little. He couldn't possibly expect anyone to accept such a fantastical thing.

"Himiko-sama, why did you stare at me so strangely when you entered the courtyard?"

She had been in the process of standing, but sat back down at his question. She wouldn't meet his gaze. "I was just surprised, that's all. Your hair —"

"My hair?"

"Yes," she said. "Overnight it, it has gone from black to white."

He stared at her as she shyly glanced at him to see the effect of her words. He laughed out loud, not able to help himself as he realized the constant rain had washed all the ink out of his hair. It must have been a most startling sight.

He stopped laughing as he saw worried looks pass between Himiko and the old healer.

"I'm sorry, Himiko-sama," he said. "It just hadn't occurred to me the rain had washed the ink from my hair."

"Ink?" She looked puzzled.

"Yes, a trick taught to me by my lord's geisha," he explained. "I would have been too obvious to our enemies if I hadn't dyed it black."

"You mean to say it was like this before last night?" Her confusion grew.

"Yes, and no." He could see he wasn't really helping. "It wasn't like this too long ago. But it was part of the price for being allowed to take the kettle from where it was hidden at an abandoned temple."

Himiko stared at him, her eyes still not showing full understanding. "I suggest you don't tell that to my father when you see him tonight."

"*What?*"

She grinned from ear to ear. "You did it, Toshiro-san," she said proudly. "You got my father's attention. He demanded to know who you were this very morning, which is why Tsuyu's men tried to get rid of you and any evidence of the ninja attack, planning to tell my father it had all been a joke. When you fell on the stage, Tsuyu's men were going to fight to take you, but my father appeared. They were all so surprised, we were able to whisk you away." Her smile was very bright. "Oh, how I wish you could have seen him! How he ordered Tsuyu's men around. It was almost like old times; he seemed himself again."

Turning his face away, he felt his emotions trying to overwhelm him. If nothing happened to interfere, he would meet Lord Asano tonight! Success was finally near.

"Himiko-sama, since I'm awake, couldn't I see your father now? I'd rather not give Tsuyu the time to figure out some way to stop us."

Her eyes darkened. "It's because of Tsuyu that your meeting is scheduled for tonight. The moment he realized you weren't in his power, he took Father away on the excuse of emergencies needing his immediate attention. Father was insistent about meeting you and only went with him when Tsuyu told him he would do so tonight. I am sure he is using the time to find a way to stop it."

"So, he still hasn't given up." He felt his hopes lower a notch.

Himiko's eyes lit up again. "That may be true, but just as he has spies, so do we. We will do our utmost to make sure the meeting is kept."

He smiled at the hard determination on her face. "I'm very indebted to you, Himiko-sama."

She looked away, her cheeks tinged with red. "You owe me nothing. If things were as they should have been, you would never have had a problem gaining your appointment. If anything, I owe you for bringing back to me some of the happiness I'd thought forever lost."

It was his turn to look away. His cheeks felt warm.

"You really should rest," she said. "I'm not sure what my father will be like when you meet with him, so you may need all your strength. Kirin-san has already assured me he'll make sure you don't miss your appointed time."

He sighed, his shoulder tingling, feeling too excited to rest. "I'll try, Himiko-sama."

She gave him a soft, sweet smile and then got up to leave. "Toshiro-san, might I ask a favor of you?"

"Anything."

"When your business with my father is over, would you tell me the full story behind all this?" She faced away from him, giving him the opportunity to gracefully refuse.

"I would be honored to," he said with true sincerity. "Though I'm not sure you'll believe it. At times, I have a hard time believing it myself."

He found his gaze suddenly trapped by her own. "I'll believe it, no matter how unlikely. Thank you for agreeing to tell it to me."

With a smile and a rustle of silk, Himiko left. He stared after her until she was out of sight and then closed his eyes.

* * * * *

"Toshiro-san."

He opened his eyes as he became aware of the soft whisper in his ear. Himiko was kneeling beside him, her body close.

"We have a bath waiting for you in the next room. We've also found some new clothes for you. And O-baa-san has more of her broth for you to drink."

He grimaced at the last but made no comment. Himiko helped him stand and then handed him the kettle.

Feeling a little groggy, he walked slowly as she led him into the next room. A large, steaming tub sat close to one corner, with soap and cleansing water on the side. The old woman was waiting for him there.

After shooing Himiko out, the healer helped Toshi undress so he might bathe. He washed and then entered the bath after he'd rinsed. The old woman crooned over him, checking his shoulder as he soaked in the scalding water. He relaxed in the soothing warmth and fell into a doze before long. The old woman nudged him awake again.

"Come on, young one."

The healer helped him get dressed, making sure to leave his bandaged shoulder exposed. As he was led back into the first room, he could feel a current of excitement building inside him.

The room had been cleared of his futon and blankets, which had been replaced by a large, squat table containing his few possessions. Himiko and Kirin sat around it, bowing to him as he came in.

"Kazete-san, we hope you're feeling more like yourself again?" Kirin asked.

"Yes, I am, thank you. I'm feeling much better."

Himiko served him tea as the old healer set a large bowl of broth before him. He reached for it without much enthusiasm. He drank as much as he could stand and then set it aside. He immediately reached for his tea.

"How long before the meeting?" he asked. He kept his voice low, trying to keep his nervous excitement under control.

"Less than an hour from now," Kirin told him.

"Yes, long enough for you to drink the rest of your broth," O-baa-san said.

He sighed as the healer refilled his bowl.

"Has Tsuyu attempted anything?" He held his breath as he gulped down more of the healer's bitter concoction.

"He's been very quiet since he left my father in his rooms," Himiko informed him. "All of his higher officers seem unusually subdued as well."

"It's a bad sign," Kirin said.

Toshi saw Himiko trade agreeing glances with him.

"What options does he have though?" he asked. "What can he do to stop the meeting?"

Himiko and Kirin traded glances again.

"His best ploy would be to attempt to detain you on the way, if not kill you outright under some trumped-up pretext. He may have one of his better men challenge you to combat for an imagined insult, which would allow him to get rid of you with a minimum of questions." Kirin's tone was matter-of-fact.

"Is there no way around this?" He felt his excitement ebbing away. Even if his shoulder hadn't been injured, he knew he didn't have what it took to go against a truly skilled opponent.

"You won't be going alone, so that should help make it more difficult on them," Kirin said. "Plus, there are a number of ways to get to Asano-sama's rooms. Tsuyu will, of course, try to anticipate which we will use. But there are a few secrets to this castle I'm sure he is not aware of."

Toshi stared at his lap and sighed. "I have no right to ask you and your men to place yourselves in danger on my account. If he's desperate enough, there's bound to be a lot of bloodshed."

Kirin smiled, but there was no humor in it. "We would only be guaranteeing our lord's wishes by making sure you reach your meeting. All of our people are only too aware of who was responsible for the deaths of our comrades at the hands of the assassins. We're only doing as we must."

Toshi bowed, accepting the aid, not able to think of a way of refusing it that wouldn't offend them. "Thank you. Your aid will be most welcomed."

Everyone stiffened at an unexpected knock at the door.

"I fear, Kirin-san, perhaps we have underestimated Tsuyu's gall." Himiko withdrew a sheathed blade from one of her sleeves.

"Would he knock, though?" Toshi asked.

Her eyes grew thoughtful. "I guess we'd best see. Stay here."

Gracefully, Himiko rose to her feet, leaving the blade's sheath on the table. With quick shuffling steps, she hurried to the door, hiding her armed hand from sight. She opened the door just a crack.

He heard her gasp then watched as she stepped back to pull the door wide open. Beyond it stood a well-built man with an unreadable face. His gray-streaked hair was pulled back into an immaculate topknot.

"Father!"

The man's eyes flickered in Himiko's direction. "Daughter. It's been a long time."

He nodded slightly before walking past her into the room. After a moment, Himiko broke her stunned gaze from him long enough to close the door.

Toshi struggled to stand and bow as all others in the room bowed low. Kirin stood away from the table and escorted Asano to the room's place of honor close to the rear wall. "Lord Asano, it's good to see you."

"Yes, my old friend, it has been too long." Both men's faces softened for a moment.

Asano sat down, his hard gaze glued to Toshi's face. He glanced at the others for a moment.

"You will all leave us now," he commanded. "I don't have much time, and I wish to amuse myself as long as possible."

Toshi dared not look at Kirin or Himiko as they and the guards quickly filed out of the room. His heart beat faster as he heard the door pulled close behind him.

"Approach," Asano said.

Bowing deeply, Toshi grabbed the kettle and stepped forward. Stopping an appropriate distance from the man, he sat and bowed until his forehead rested on the mat beneath him.

"What is your name?" Himiko's father demanded.

"Kazete Toshiro, Asano-sama."

"I've heard you've been wanting an audience with me."

Now that the moment was here, Toshi was quivering inside. "Yes, that's true, Asano-sama." He waited for the question that must surely follow. It didn't.

"Over the years, I've had a number of unusual people come to visit me," the lord said casually. "Not a small number of them have had a kettle looking very much like yours."

Toshi's surprise flashed across his face before he could try to conceal it.

"Who sent you, boy?" Asano's voice turned harsh.

He swallowed hard, feeling crushed beneath Asano's steel stare, and forced himself to answer. "I'm here on behalf of Asaka Ietsugu, Asano-sama."

"Asaka Ietsugu is dead." There was no emotion in the lord's tone.

"I know that, sir," he said, "but even so, I'm here on his behalf."

The look of incredulity that passed across Asano's eyes reminded Toshi of his first meeting with Himiko. "Can you prove he sent you here?"

A light tone of mocking disbelief colored Asano's voice.

Toshi's mind went blank. "Uh, yes, lord, I can."

Reaching inside his kimono, he removed the bamboo tube containing the writ. For the first time, it occurred to him to wonder if it had been damaged during his vigil in the rain. Sending a quick prayer to the gods, he crawled forward to lay it close to Asano's feet and then moved back. He tried to keep a sudden wave of nervousness under control as Asano leaned forward to pick up the bamboo cylinder. Stifling a yawn, the lord removed the paper rolled up inside.

Toshi held his breath as Asano read through the writ. He watched the lord's face harden as he read it a second time, all signs of boredom disappearing. His cold gaze rose to meet Toshi's.

He threw the writ to the floor. As it landed, Asano began to laugh. There was something in the sound that sent shivers scurrying down his spine.

"This interview is over," Asano said.

"Sir?"

Asano laughed at the open shock on his face. "What, did Tsuyu truly believe I would fall for this only because he'd somehow obtained Asaka's permit and set up a good show? It seals his guilt, if nothing else. What a fool he has become to think I would fall for it. I haven't lost my wits so far that I'd believe Ietsugu somehow sent a young boy to me years after his death." Asano's harsh laughter filled the room again. "He really outdid himself this time."

Toshi felt his face drain of color. "Lord Asano, you must believe me! I was sent here to complete the mission you gave to Asaka-sama. I know it's hard to believe, but it's the truth! I'm not affiliated with Tsuyu. He has twice tried to have me killed. Please, I beg you, at least examine the kettle. It should prove if I'm telling the truth or not."

He placed his palms down and bowed to the floor in supplication. He ignored the pain his shoulder brought him, still too confused at how all of this was going wrong.

"Excellent, Kazete-san, excellent!" Asano clapped in obvious amusement. "An almost magnificent performance. Tsuyu would be quite proud of your efforts. Nevertheless, this interview is over."

Hot tears pooled on the matted floor as he heard Asano rise to his feet. It couldn't end like this! Not after all they'd gone through. How could Asano just dismiss him, without even giving him a chance? He was negligently damning the others to eternally roam the earth.

Suddenly, Toshi's heart hardened with anger. "You say Lord Asaka was dead long ago, and that is true. But, I have, regardless of that fact, spoken to him."

He sat up and stared at Asano's startled face. "Shinto speaks the truth, spirits are *real.* Tortured souls do remain bound to the earth as they search for atonement or retribution."

He stared hard at the man he had sought for so long.

"I have seen and spoken to those who drowned on the way to do your bidding," he continued hotly. "They tore me from my life so I might help them *serve* you."

He reached up and touched his whitened hair. "I paid the price wanted by the spirit of a priest to retrieve this kettle for you. Of my own choice, I traveled all the way here to bring it to you. I came into Shiroyama alone; but over a night ago, they entered the grounds using the very same means as the assassins Tsuyu had hired to kill me. I have seen with my own eyes the dead can haunt the living."

He carefully removed Asaka's wakizashi from its sheath. "I swear to you, if you do not accept what I have brought and restore the honor due to the Asaka clan, I will commit seppuku right here and now and haunt you with my spirit the rest of your life."

He didn't wait for Asano's reaction, but instead focused on the naked blade before him. He wasn't samurai, but he would come back. He would give the ultimate protest by ending his life and then force his spirit to return to perpetuate it—for eternity, if need be. What Asano was doing was wrong, and he wasn't about to allow all he and the others had gone through to be in vain. He would haunt Asano and those of his line until justice was served!

Laying the blade on the floor before him, he parted his kimono to expose his stomach. He tucked his sleeves beneath his legs to hold him upright if he should falter. Ignoring Asano, he took up the blade. His shoulder flared with pain, and he tried not to flinch as he grabbed the blade with both hands. He turned the wakizashi until its sharp point was aimed at his belly, the residence of his soul.

Closing his eyes, he calmly begged the Great Buddha not to allow him to be taken to his next life. Quickly, he tried composing a short death poem, as he'd heard samurai often did; but nothing he came up with satisfied him. Instead, he pictured in his mind the way he had dreamed Asaka and Miko would have appeared in real life. He let Himiko's young face drift above theirs and was again sorry she and Miko would never meet.

Slowly, he stretched out his arms and tensed, his eyes still closed. With a sharp intake of breath, he pulled them in to plunge the blade into his stomach.

"Hold!"

The order came too late. He couldn't stop himself. Yet, the blade never pierced his skin. He opened his eyes in confusion as two strong arms continued to hold him back.

"Blood will not be spilled from a guest in my house," Asano said, his eyes locking with Toshi's. "If you'll give me a moment, I will look at the gift you have so graciously brought."

Staring in disbelief, Toshi didn't fight as Asano pried the wakizashi out of his taut fingers. His left shoulder spasmed painfully as he tried to relax. He watched intently as Asano placed his wakizashi on the floor several feet away before returning to his previous seat, kettle in hand.

Toshi's whole body shuddered. His face was flushed, his breathing labored. His eyes settled on the wakizashi's glittering blade as he tried to come to grips with the fact he wasn't going to die.

A cracking sound made him look up from the blade to Asano. The castle's lord sat cross-legged with the kettle in his lap and a small eating blade in one hand. He heard the cracking sound again as Asano slipped the knife between the kettle's wooden handle and its metal hinge and broke it away. Horrified at the obviously uncaring destruction of what he'd labored so long to bring, Toshi could do nothing but stare. Was Asano mocking him?

The samurai lord pulled the handle free from the kettle; and, grasping it in both hands, he twisted each end in opposite directions. A cracking, ripping sound echoed through the room as the handle split suddenly in two. Toshi gasped as Asano tipped both ends and a small cylindrical object fell out from the one in his right hand onto his lap. Asano picked it up and studied it carefully.

He was taken aback as the lord bowed deeply in his direction. "My profound apologies, Kazete-san. You have, indeed, brought me that which I have sought for so long."

His heart soared. It was done. Asaka's mission had been completed. He started to smile, until he saw Asano sit on folded legs and draw out his wakizashi. "Lord Asano?"

With one swift stroke, Asano struck the small cylinder and split it long ways. He hacked at it again and again until the cylinder was no longer recognizable. Crestfallen and confused, Toshi looked behind him as the room's sliding doors were violently thrust open.

"Lord Asano! What are you doing here?" Tsuyu strode into the room, six guards following behind him—more stood waiting outside.

"Ah, Tsuyu, how nice of you to come," Asano said pleasantly. "I was wondering how long it would take you to get here."

Tsuyu had been gracing Toshi with a hate-filled stare until something he heard in Asano's voice brought him up short.

"Tsuyu, come here and look at the wonderful gift this young samurai has brought me."

For the first time, Tsuyu noticed the discarded kettle and its broken handle. Toshi saw Tsuyu's face pale even as he stared at the small bits of wood chopped up in front of Asano.

"Ah, I see you recognize it for what it is. It's so pleasant, isn't it, to finally be able to comply with our daimyo's wishes?" Asano's words were sweet, but his face held a murderous grin.

"Are—are you sure it was the real one? This boy could be trying to pull some sort of trick."

"I am absolutely sure, Tsuyu. *Absolutely* sure." Asano's hand drifted toward the hilt of his katana. "You and I have been playing a most fabulous game these last few years. It's time, however, it was brought to an end."

Tsuyu took a step back. "I have a large number of men under my control. You can't say it's over just because of this," he stammered.

Asano's grin widened as he stood. Toshi stared at the newly forceful countenance before him, not understanding what was going on between the two men.

"If you wish to play that game, I'm more than willing. Thunderclap has wanted a taste of Tsuyu blood for some time."

Asano placed his thumb beneath his katana's guard and snapped the blade a quarter of an inch out of its sheath. He took a commanding step forward. All signs of boredom and lethargy were gone. Asano's face was hardened rock with flaming fury showing in his eyes. Tsuyu stood his ground, his face flickering with emotions.

Asano took another step forward, and suddenly Tsuyu took one back.

"This isn't over! My father won't allow it to be over."

Asano took another calculated step forward. "I give you permission to leave. Take your men with you but leave all else. *All* else."

Toshi felt dizzy watching the exchange. All of Tsuyu's power had rested on the fact Asano had not gotten a seal?

Tsuyu backed hesitantly out of the room, never daring to turn his back on Asano. The lord of the castle continued advancing until he'd reached the room's doorway.

"Kirin-san!"

Asano's call echoed down the hall even as Tsuyu and his men sped up their retreat. Within moments, Kirin appeared before him.

"Ah! Kirin-san," Asano said. "Would you please do me the honor of escorting our no longer welcome guests out the front gates?"

"With pleasure, Asano-sama." Kirin bowed, a grin tugging at his lips.

"Please feel free to do so with as many of our men as might wish to say goodbye to them."

"Hai, Asano-sama." Kirin left.

Toshi stared at Asano's back as the latter watched his vassal leave. As soon as Kirin had gone out of sight, Asano began to close the doors into the room.

"Father?" Toshi recognized Himiko's voice, but couldn't see her.

"Himiko-chan."

She gasped in surprise at her father's use of the endearment.

"Would you be so kind as to serve your aging father and his guest a cup of tea?"

"Yes, Father." Shyly, she entered the room as Asano opened the door wide for her. She shuffled toward the table as she sent Toshi a glance filled with hope-entangled misery. With shaking hands, she filled two cups with cooling tea. Asano returned to his place of honor and watched her as she poured.

Still shaken by all that had happened around him, Toshi stared at the transformed man before him and then at Asano's suddenly demure daughter. Himiko took the cups and, while staring at the floor, took one to her father. Leaving him, she still stared at the floor as she placed the other into Toshi's hand. Bowing to them, she then turned to leave.

"Himiko-chan," Asano said.

She stopped, shaking, and turned around.

"I understand you know this young man?"

"Yes, Father." Her uncertainty and long-hidden pain shone clearly in her eyes. She wouldn't look at him.

"Has he told you much of how he came to be here?"

Her eyes rose momentarily in Toshi's direction. "No, not really, Father."

"Ah, well, then, join us," he said amiably. "I was just about to ask Kazete-san to tell me his story."

Her look of uncertainty, now filled with something more, swept again in Toshi's direction. He tried to give her what reassurance he could by flashing a small smile. Nodding to him in return, she sat close to the closed doors, to be out of their way.

"No, here, daughter, next to me."

Out of the corner of his eye, Toshi saw Himiko close her eyes and moan softly. One of her sleeves rose to dab at her eyes even as she hurried to sit by her father. As she did, Asano gave her a wide smile. He then riveted his gaze to Toshi's face.

"So, Kazete-san, would you grace us with the telling of your involvement in these matters?"

"I'll tell you all I know, Asano-sama, though you may not believe all I say." He hoped that, if he cooperated, Asano might deign to explain some things as well.

"Do not concern yourself with that." Asano waved the thought aside. "Just begin at the beginning."

"Hai, Asano-sama." Butterflies stirred in his stomach as he reached for his teacup to wet his suddenly dry throat. Haltingly at first, but then with rising confidence, he told his tale.

Chapter 41

More than three hours later, Toshi was able to wind his tale to an end. Drinking his cold tea, he glanced up at his two listeners, trying to gauge how much they had decided to believe. To his chagrin, he found both their faces unreadable. He sighed, feeling drained. His shoulder throbbed and he was hungry, but there was one thing he just had to know.

"Sir, might I ask a question?"

"Of course."

"I don't mean to seem ignorant, but I don't understand how a seal could hold so much power."

"Ah, yes, I see." Asano stared off in the distance for a moment before speaking again. "The seal you saw belonged to my lord. It was the seal he used for important matters of state. No document would be considered legal unless his mark appeared on it. On his disappearance, no evidence was found to indicate he had not done so willingly. There was nothing to show something had actually happened to him. Many were of the opinion he'd secretly gone to a monastery to watch how we'd react and thereby finally decide who'd be his heir.

"Once I'd taken possession of his house as bade in his orders, however, a paper was found. On it were written suspicions of a plot against Lord Shura, and a riddle. It was then I understood the daimyo was dead. The puzzle had to do with his seal and how he had hidden it for safekeeping."

Toshi shifted uneasily, still not understanding.

"You see, since Lord Shura's death could not be proven, if his seal were found by those who had gotten rid of him they could forge documents with it to give themselves power. At the very least, they could have written new final orders and left them for someone to find. These new orders would have stated Tsuyu's adoption by Shura, giving him and his clan claim to all the lands, including mine."

"Those honorless bastards." Himiko's eyes were blazing.

"Yes," Asano agreed. "A few years ago, Tsuyu arrived and hinted he'd recovered the seal for his father but hadn't seen fit to give it to him just yet. He also implied he'd use it against me unless I cooperated. His people had been at the temple, and he knew too much for me to assume he was bluffing. The Tsuyu family is well known for their internal strife. So, I bided my time, looking for any sign he was lying, knowing my turn would come, though, in so doing, I was forced to alienate those close to me." He sent a look in his daughter's direction. "And you brought my turn to me, Kazete Toshiro."

Toshi stared at the floor, trying to understand all the complexities of what Asano had revealed. He wasn't sure he was cut out to play such games.

"So, you say Asaka and his retinue are here?" Asano asked.

"Yes, Lord. I wouldn't have survived the ninja attack without them."

Asano nodded slowly. "Then it would seem I'm being a very irresponsible host. Let's go at once to meet them."

Toshi scrambled to his feet, wondering if this was just a test to prove he was crazy. He retrieved his wakizashi and returned it to its sheath. He had to work to hide a grin as his mind pictured Asano's and Himiko's expressions once he'd proved his companions were real.

Guards joined them as they exited Himiko's rooms. As they reached the main level, Kirin joined them as well.

"Lord Tsuyu and his men have been escorted to the outskirts of the city," Kirin informed them.

"Hm, excellent." Asano nodded, pleased. "Tsuyu Akira won't give up as easily. But, between the destruction of his ninja lackeys and the expulsion of his son, we've bought ourselves some much-needed time."

They all followed Asano out into a night-filled courtyard.

"Lord Asano, if I might beg your indulgence? I think it might be easier to find Asaka-sama if I went looking for him alone," Toshi said.

"If that is your wish. Do not hurry, however. I have some long-overdue conversations to hold with those dear to me."

Toshi bowed to Asano and the others and, after borrowing a lamp, took his leave. With sure but tired steps, he left the main courtyard and made his way to the place where he had spent his two-day vigil.

The night was quiet, the air holding a slight chill. He rubbed his shoulder, staring at the still puddles of water left from the previous night's storm. Not long after, he entered the isolated courtyard. Stopping to rest for a moment, he sat down on the raised stage, already feeling beads of perspiration gathering on his brow despite the cold in the air. He felt drained and euphoric at the same time. He'd done it! It was finally over. Asaka and the others would now be free.

"Asaka-sama," he called.

He waited expectantly, yet nothing disturbed the night's stillness. A tingle of apprehension worked through him. If they were truly free, did that mean they had already gone?

He stood, saddened by the realization he'd not even gotten a chance to say goodbye. With a sigh, he made his way to the courtyard's entrance, wondering how he would explain this to Lord Asano. The lord would think him mad for sure. Farther in the back of his mind, though, was the question of what he would do now that his ordeal was over.

"Toshiro-san."

It was Asaka. Toshi stopped as a dozen pairs of glowing eyes lined the trees around him. With a quick smile, he dropped to his knees and bowed to the ground.

"Lord."

"Stand and report."

He stood, still unable to get rid of the smile on his face. He stared at each of the dark forms around him before returning his gaze to Asaka.

"Sir, I have met with Lord Asano and presented him with the kettle as you requested." The green-lit eyes behind the demon mask flashed with a new intensity. "Lord Asano wishes to grant you an audience, if you're willing."

"He knows of our presence here?" Asaka asked.

Toshi wasn't sure how to read the samurai's tone. "He asked me to tell him what had brought me here, and how. I told him all I could, and he didn't seem to doubt me. He asked for me to find you and bring you before him. He felt he might be neglecting some of his guests."

The samurai hesitated for only a moment. "Then we should not keep Asano-sama waiting."

His exhaustion momentarily forgotten, he led the group to the main courtyard. Miko joined him.

"How are you, Toshi-kun? We've been very worried about you," she said.

He stared at her white Noh mask and the blue light shining from its eyes. His smile grew wider. "I'm happy, Miko-san, happier than I've ever been, now that you're here," he admitted. "I'd started thinking maybe you had all left before I'd had a chance to see you again."

"Silly boy," she chided, "we would never do that to our appointed savior."

He looked away, feeling his cheeks grow hot; but his smile, if anything, grew wider.

As they neared the lit courtyard, Miko dropped back to stand with Asaka. Leaving the group in the shadows, Toshi approached the castle's lord.

"Asano-sama, Lord Asaka wishes for me to convey to you his willingness for an audience." He felt Asano's gaze fall heavily on him before it shifted to look past him. Himiko hovered near her father, her excited face going from Toshi to the shadowed forms behind him and back again.

Asano leaned forward and spoke softly. "If you would, Kazete-san, ask him to please present himself before me."

Toshi nodded and rushed back to his companions.

Asano's guards clustered about their lord as Asaka stepped forward. He stopped a short distance away and bowed low. As he looked up, gasps ran through those close by as they saw the green glow coming from behind his mask's eye slits.

"It has been a very long time, Asano-sama."

"Much too long, Asaka-san." The samurai lord looked unperturbed by the enigma before him.

"It is my great shame I couldn't come sooner," Asaka replied.

"It's to your greater honor you've been able to come at all."

Asaka lowered his head for a moment but said nothing.

"We have much to discuss, you and I," Asano added. "Much is owed. Many things are left to be taken care of. Would you take a stroll with an aging man?"

"I would be honored," Asaka said.

"Father, no." Himiko clung to her father's side. His guards surged forward, fear reflecting in their eyes.

"This man is my trusted vassal," Asano roared. "He has made every sacrifice a samurai can make for his lord and more. Do not shame me by your actions! There's nothing to fear."

Himiko released her father's arm. His men reluctantly fell back. Walking side-by-side, Asano and Asaka moved past Toshi and the others, who moved to let them through.

"Who's the young lady, Toshi-kun?" Miko whispered. "She seems to be trying to catch your attention."

"Huh?" He drew his gaze away from the direction the two lords had taken. "Oh, that's Lady Himiko, Asano-sama's daughter. She helped me figure out a way to get an audience with her father."

"Do you know her well?" Miko asked.

"I guess so," he replied. "We've kept each other company during most of my stay here."

Silver bells tinkled in the night as Miko nodded her head knowingly. "Have you pillowed with her?"

He choked. "Miko-san! She's the lord's daughter!" He glanced behind him, hoping Himiko hadn't overheard them somehow. The geisha's soft laughter cascaded to his burning ears.

"Oh, Toshi-chan, you are such a delight!"

He glanced back again—Himiko was, indeed, trying to gain his attention. "Miko-san, would you—would you like to meet her?"

Though he had hoped for this often enough, now that the opportunity was there he was no longer sure.

"Oh, yes, I'd love to," the geisha said eagerly.

He left Miko's side and went to join Himiko. As soon as he'd come into the area protected by Asano's samurai, she rushed forward to meet him.

"Kazete-san! It's true, it's all true," she said. "I beg you to forgive me. I thought your recent fever had clouded your mind. Though I had tried not to, I doubted your tale." She wouldn't look him in the eye.

"There's nothing to forgive," he told her. "You believed in me enough to help me and that's what counts. If I'd been in your position, I would have never believed a word of it."

A soft smile crossed her lips before she turned shyly away from him.

"Himiko-sama, I've someone I'd like you to meet," he said. "It's someone who means a great deal to me."

Her wide almond eyes turned to meet his own. "Meet? One of them?"

"Yes." He nodded. "It really would mean a lot to me. I've hoped for some time the two of you might meet."

"The geisha?"

"Yes." He tried to read her slightly paling face.

"You want us to meet?" she asked again.

"I'd like it very much."

Himiko glanced in the skeletons' direction. After a moment, she straightened up, a smile on her face. It was only a little frayed around the edges. "Please introduce us. I'd be honored to meet her."

She took his arm as he led her away from the ring of guards toward his companions. Miko left the shadows and met them partway. She bowed deeply. The two of them quickly did the same.

"Miko-san, I'd like to introduce you to Lady Himiko. Himiko-sama, this is my friend, Akiuji Miko."

"I'm pleased to meet you, Akiuji-san." Himiko's awed and frightened gaze wouldn't leave the geisha's white mask.

"It's my pleasure," Miko said. "I see there's much of your father in you."

She blushed. "Thank you."

"We're grateful you helped Toshi-kun achieve his task. By helping him, you helped all of us."

"I truly did nothing," Himiko countered. "Kazete-san did all the work. I was just grateful for his company, never suspecting how much more he would eventually do. If not for him, my father and I would never have gotten our lives back from those who'd stolen them."

Toshi blushed crimson.

"He does that rather well, don't you think so?" Miko asked mischievously.

A small smile lit Himiko's face. "Yes, I think you're right, Miko-san. He does do it quite well."

With his cheeks now burning even more intently, Toshi stared helplessly from one to the other as they laughed behind raised sleeves.

"This is why practicing the way of the sword is better," Mitsuo confided quietly from behind him.

He glanced at his teacher, nodding in agreement with the stooped samurai.

"Kirin-san." Asano's deep voice startled them all as it cut across the courtyard. Kirin hurried off in the direction of the call, to reappear moments later. He stayed in the courtyard only long enough to pick out a couple of men before disappearing with them into the castle.

Wondering what was going on, Toshi stared after them. In less than two minutes, the three men reappeared. One carried a mat, the other a table. Kirin's arms were loaded with paper, brushes, ink and several other items. The three stepped without explanation across the courtyard and off in the direction Asano and Asaka had gone.

Silence settled as everyone waited to see what might happen next. As the minutes dragged on, a low murmur of whispers could be heard growing on both sides. Silence instantly reigned again, however, when the two guards rushed back into the courtyard.

The two men hurried to the middle of the open yard and set the mat on the ground with the table on top of it. Kirin returned, soon followed by Asaka and Asano, who were still deep in conversation. Toshi couldn't help but eavesdrop as they walked by.

"His clan has always used many dishonorable methods," Asano said. "I am not surprised he hired an assassin to thwart your mission, even if it meant sinking your ship and taking the assassin with it. There was no way you could have known."

Asaka said nothing.

The two men drifted on to the waiting table. They continued to speak, but their voices were too low for him to overhear anymore. After several minutes there, Asaka rejoined his group. Asano stood and called for everyone's attention.

"I wish to warmly welcome all of you to my humble home. Your coming has brought me more joy than you will ever know," he stated. "Your mission is over, your duty is done. What you have so selflessly given goes beyond the bounds of Bushido. A shrine shall be built in your honor where your names shall be praised throughout time."

Asano stood tall, as a man reborn, his gaze carefully memorizing every one of the skeletons before him. "Your clan was wronged during the time of your absence, its existence struck from the records. This I have sworn to rectify. The Asaka clan shall exist once again, all its previous lands and more placed under its control."

Toshi stared at Asaka, his heart soaring at the news. He knew the samurai would have never asked for this, though there was probably nothing he wanted more. He knew he was right when he saw Miko hide her face behind her hands.

Asano withdrew a rolled parchment from his sleeve. He carefully smoothed it open and then handed it to those before him. The parchment was written in a meticulous hand, Asano's signature stamped in red at the bottom. The excitement amongst Asaka's men was almost palpable. It abruptly died, however, as they all recalled no living heir remained to the Asaka clan.

"An heir has been found by means of adoption." Asaka stepped forward to stand at Asano's side. "I have found someone worthy of carrying the family name. All that remains is to obtain his consent."

Asaka had found someone to become his heir. Toshi felt his own excitement growing. Yes, surely during all his years of travel Asaka had found someone worthy long ago. Now that his own mission was over, he needed to make a new life for himself. He could never go back to what he'd been before. Asaka had paid for his freedom. Perhaps the heir would allow him to become one of his servants. The idea appealed to him very much.

"Chizuson-san, would you consent to become my adopted son?"

For a moment, Toshi didn't realize the question had been directed at him. His eyes grew wide as he realized what had just been said. He'd heard of a few rare occasions when a peasant warrior had been raised to the status of samurai, but him? He was just a boy! How could a samurai of Asaka's caliber want a mere mapmaker as the new head of his clan?

Shaking, he dropped to his hands and knees, his heart threatening to burst with emotion. "Sir, I'm not worthy of such an honor!"

He stared hard at the ground as he heard Asaka step toward him. He trembled as the samurai's fleshless hands reached down for him and slowly drew him to his feet.

"You have given us great honor with your efforts on our behalf," Asaka said softly. "Yet, it isn't for your sake I wish for you to become my son, but for the clan and its lord. What I offer you isn't easy, for it means following the ways of Bushido, with all the joys and hardships that go with it. I owe you much more than this, but I am selfish. Though I've already asked so much of you, I would ask this one more thing."

Toshi stared at the samurai's green, glowing eyes, his breathing growing ragged. His gaze went to the others. All their eyes glowed intensely. His eyes came at last to rest on Himiko. She was smiling. It would be a burden, one he wasn't so sure he would be able to live up to. But the rewards could be great.

He faced his lord again. "I would consider it a great honor and privilege to become your son, Asaka-sama." He bowed low.

A roaring cheer rose up from those around him. Asaka and Asano both converged on Toshi and steered him to the small table so he might sign the proper documents before he could think to change his mind. His vision clouded as he realized he would no longer be Chizuson Toshiro, peasant mapmaker and, of late, adventurer. Now he would be Asaka Toshiro, a samurai lord. His doubts, and the new burden he'd taken on, were pushed behind him as everyone gathered around to offer congratulations. There would be time enough to worry about it all later.

"For the few months left before you reach full manhood, Asano-sama will be your guardian," Asaka said. "Learn from him all you will need to know."

"Hai, Asaka-sama." Miko had been right about him all along.

"You will become an exceptional samurai, Toshi-kun. I know you'll make us all proud," Miko said.

He blushed at the strong conviction in her voice. "I'll do my best." He hoped it would be enough.

"I know you will," she said happily.

Toshi became the recipient of a quick hug.

"Find a teacher of good repute," Mitsuo instructed him. "And do not forget to practice daily. Zen, art and swordsmanship are indispensable to a samurai." His stooped form seemed to be standing straighter than before.

"I won't forget, Sensei."

One by one, the rest of Asaka's men presented themselves to him and bowed deeply. He understood they were saying goodbye. His stomach tightened as he realized he would soon be on his own again.

"Miko-san?" he asked.

"Yes, Toshi-kun?"

"Must you…" He shook his head. "When will you go?"

Her eyes shone as she turned to look at him. "The sun will soon be here. We haven't seen it in a long time. After that, we will go."

"A sun-watching party?" Himiko sounded excited. "What a delightful idea! We'll do our best to make your last moments as joyful as possible."

With tears glinting in her eyes, she left them in a flurry of silk, calling for servants as she went. Colorful paper lanterns were brought out, lighting the area brightly enough to make it seem like day. Servants with tables streamed out into the courtyard, their shock barely hidden as they caught glimpses of their unusual guests.

Toshi watched in wonder as Himiko drew each of the skeletal warriors to a table and set them to painting, composing poetry or playing games. She was the perfect hostess, in no way giving the impression she saw them for what they truly were. Realizing this, he became aware he hadn't thought of them in that way for some time himself. They'd gone from frightening captors to uneasy allies to something much more than he would have ever thought possible.

The next few hours passed. Laughter echoed off and on throughout the courtyard. To his amazement, he even saw his adopted father laugh with abandon. It felt strange. Though he had no true way to tell, he was sure Miko was beaming behind her mask.

As dawn approached, all the lanterns were extinguished. Everyone around him was filled with joy, but Toshi's own happiness dampened as each of the lanterns was put out. His friends would be leaving soon.

All of Asaka's men stood as one and gathered in a line in the middle of the courtyard, facing east. Miko hugged Himiko in earnest and thanked her for the lovely evening. Toshi stared at the ground as she then came to bid him farewell.

"Take care, my man-to-be," Miko said. "If I can, I will look in on you from the next plane." She hugged him, and as she did so, she whispered into his ear. "Hurry and find yourself a wife so the clan will grow. I also just happen to know of a young lady who's eligible."

"As you say, Miko-san." He pulled away gently, glad she liked Himiko but embarrassed by her words nevertheless.

She left him then and, much to his chagrin, returned to speak to Himiko. He was thinking strongly of trying to put a stop to whatever mischief the geisha was up to when Asaka stepped before him, blocking his view.

"Toshiro-san."

"Sir?"

"I think you'll like my old home."

He had never heard the samurai sound so at ease, so human.

"There are places of harsh beauty there, and others are infused with the harmony so many of us try to attain for ourselves. When you reclaim it, search these places out for me. Let them bring you joy, just as they did for my brothers and me in our youth. Share it with those who come after us." Asaka's voice was soft and full of feeling, just as it had been in that dream so long ago. "I can never repay you for what you've done, but I'll make sure your way into the next life is made much easier for it."

Toshi swallowed hard.

"I have given you my family name, and it's a burden I'm sure you'll carry well. Yet, I wish to give you something that has no weight tied to it." Slowly, Asaka removed his sheathed katana. Holding it in both hands, he presented it.

"Asaka-sama, I can't! This is—"

"Take it!" The samurai's harsh whisper contained some of the steel Toshi had come to know so well.

"Yes, Father. Thank you." He bowed as low as he could and then gingerly took the sword from Asaka's offering hands.

"Her name is Swift Wind. Take good care of her, and of yourself." Asaka bowed low.

Not quite daring to slip the sword, and all it signified, into his sash, Toshi held on to it tightly as Asaka walked away. He noticed a piece of rolled paper protruding from the sword's guard, but dismissed it as the samurai joined the others.

The sky brightened with pinks and oranges. It lightened all around them as they stood waiting. The sun rose to peek over the wall.

Toshi's eyes never left his companions, his knuckles white as he held onto the sheathed katana. He didn't even look as he heard Himiko move to stand beside him.

As the rays of the sun struck the courtyard, the colors of the kimonos worn by the skeletons began to fade. Parts of their clothing soon became transparent.

Tears welled in Toshi's eyes and rolled unhampered down his face. As he wept in mixed joy and sadness, he saw both Asaka and Miko reach up to remove their masks. As the two masks fell to the ground, they turned away from the sun to look upon Toshi one last time.

He heard Himiko gasp beside him as their faces came into view. Their bones were barely visible, most of their bodies barely outlined. Yet, unlike before, they had a semblance of flesh, one as pale and transparent as the rest of them had become. Miko and Asaka's youthful faces looked at him with joy-filled smiles. The rest of the group turned toward him then and bowed as one before abruptly disappearing. The soft tinkling of bells filled the air.

Toshi looked down at Swift Wind. He removed the note left there for him. His blurred vision fell on the carefully written poem within.

Just as a swift wind can
bring the scents of change, so
can a young wind. Blessed
be all the winds.

The End

About the Author

Born in 1964 in Rio Piedras, Puerto Rico, Gloria bounced around several states during the teenage years, finally ending up in Texas for good. Married for twenty years, she is the proud parent of a very independent daughter. She originally entered the University of Texas in Arlington to obtain an Aerospace degree, but eventually moved over to the University of Texas in Dallas to gain a BA in Interdisciplinary Studies, and is currently working in the finance/accounting field.

Her hobbies at present are reading, writing, watching Japanese animation, collecting music, and translating Japanese comics.

LOOK FOR THESE GREAT TITLES AT:
www. Zumayapublications.com

PARANORMAL FICTION

SCARY CREEK by Thomas Cater ISBN: 1-894869-21-4
SUBTERRANEAN HEARTBEATS by Diana Kemp-Jones
ISBN: 1-59109-070-9
HOUSE OF CAPTURED FANCY by Tom Cater ISBN: 1-894869-36-2

SCIENCE FICTION

EMBRACING THE SKULL by Martine Jardin and Diana Kemp-Jones
ISBN: 1-59109-051-2
DYSTOPIC VISIONS by Diana Kemp-Jones ISBN: 894869-28-1 *SISTERS OF THE WIND* by Diana Kemp-Jones ISBN: 1-59109-055-5

THRILLER

THE MANDYLION by Thomas Cater ISBN: 159109-069-5
TULPA by Ron Landry ISBN: 1-894869-43-5

ROMANCE

UNORTHODOX PROPOSAL by Martine Jardin ISBN: 1-59109-053-9
BLUEPRINT FOR REVENGE by Martine Jardin ISBN: 1-59109-050-4

HISTORICAL FICTION

THE START OF MAGIC by Dr. Bob Rich ISBN: 1-894869-23-0
THE MAIDEN'S SONG by Debra Tash ISBN: ISBN: 1-894869-25-7
THE PINECROFT THOROUGHBREDS by Selwyn A. Grames
ISBN: 1-59109-054-7
THE VANDALIANS by Thomas Cater ISBN: 1-894869-47-8
HIS MAJESTY'S ENVOY by Richard Patton ISBN: 1-894869-38-9
THE RELUCTANT COMMANDER by Richard Patton
ISBN: 1-894869-57-5
THE MOTHER'S SWORD by Dr. Bob Rich ISBN: 1-894869-45-1

MAINSTREAM FICTION

YESTERDAY'S TEARS, TOMORROW'S PEARLS by Martine Jardin
ISBN: 1-59109-167-5
MANIPULATIONS by Shrinivas Sharangpani ISBN: 1-894869-32-X
PARADOX OUTPATIENT by Bernie Schallehn ISBN: 1-894869-16-8

MYSTERY

TRACETRACKS by Larry Rochelle ISBN: 1-894869-14-1 *BEN ZAKKAI'S COFFIN* by Harley L. Sachs ISBN: 1-894869-20-6 *DEATH AND*

DEVOTION by Larry Rochelle ISBN: 1-894869-30-3 *DANCE WITH THE PONY* by Larry Rochelle ISBN: 1-894869-18-4

FANTASY

CRYSTAL DREAMS by Astrid Cooper ISBN: 1-59109-065-2
THE BLOOD CIRCLE by Ellen Anthony ISBN: 1-894869-34-6

EROTICA

SEA ORPHAN by J. Kramer ISBN: 1-59109-062-8
SCIROTICA by Cameron Hale ISBN: 1-59109-063-6
WHY SHOULD GUYS HAVE ALL THE FUN by Cindy X. Novo ISBN: 1-894869-40-0

HORROR

THE CHRONICLES OF A MADMAN by Michael LaRocca ISBN: 1-59109-068-7

GOTHIC

ECHOES OF ANGELS by Caitlyn McKenna ISBN:1-894869-41-9

YOUNG ADULT

FIVE DAYS TILL DAWN ISBN: 1-894869-51-6

NON FICTION — SELF HELP

HOW TO MANAGE ANGER AND ANXIETY by Dr. Bob Rich ISBN: 1-59109-064-4

EDUCATION

PROF RAP by Professor Larry Rochelle ISBN: 1-894869-53-2

SEASONAL CHILDREN AND ADULTS

SANTA OF THE LIGHTHOUSES by Bernie Schallehn and John Galluzzo
BLUEGUM CHRISTMAS: A Miracle at Sassafras Creek by Marlies Bugmann
A TROLL FOR CHRISTMAS and Other Stories by Harley Sachs

SEASONAL ROMANCE

CHRISTMAS PARADISE by Gale Storm
A CHRISTMAS WITH SARAH by Janet Miller

Look for them at:
www.zumayapublications.com
www.booksurge.com
www.fictionwise.com